KT-482-314

The Wilding

MARIA McCANN

faber and faber

First published in 2010
by Faber and Faber Limited
Bloomsbury House
74–77 Great Russell Street
London WC1B 3DA
This paperback edition first published in 2010

Printed in England by CPI Bookmarque, Croydon

All rights reserved
© Maria McCann, 2010

The right of Maria McCann to be identified as author of this work has been asserted in
accordance with Section 77 of the Copyright, Designs and Patents Act 1988

*This book is sold subject to the condition that it shall not, by way of trade
or otherwise, be lent, resold, hired out or otherwise circulated without the
publisher's prior consent in any form of binding or cover other than that in which
it is published and without a similar condition including this condition being
imposed on the subsequent purchaser.*

A CIP record for this book
is available from the British Library

ISBN 978–0–571–25187–2

HEREFORDSHIRE LIBRARIES	
638	
Bertrams	18/11/2010
HIS	£7.99
HC	

4 6 8 10 9 7 5 3

HC

The Wilding

Maria McCann's first novel, *As Meat Loves S*
in 2000 to huge a   r fiction h
various anthol   vi
working in Somerset, apart from one year spent teaching in
France. She combines teaching and writing with other inter-
ests such as voluntary communities and the running of an
allotment.

Praise for *The Wilding*:

'As pleasurable to read as its predecessor, a novel to finish and
start right back at the beginning.' *The Economist*

'The writing is spare and compelling, slashed through with
vivid details of food, clothing, and especially smell . . . McCann
has written a novel that is both satisfying and disquieting: a
well-crafted plot, with twists and turns.' *TLS*

'McCann puts a fierce spotlight on her handful of sharply
delineated characters and creates a gripping narrative . . . It has
been well worth the long wait.' *Daily Express*

'Skilful and atmospheric.' *Sunday Times* Best Summer Reads

'Any readers still worried – even after *Wolf Hall* – that
English historical fiction must involve bodice-ripping fol-de-
rol should succumb to McCann . . . Language and setting both
shine as cider-maker Jonathan is squeezed by universal moral
dilemmas that ripen on this vividly local patch of ground.'
Independent Best Summer Reads

'Expertly researched, abso

740005776388

'A chastening tour de force . . . Like the best novels about the past, McCann's is an angry rebuke to our present difficulties.' *Independent*

'Jonathan makes an unusually endearing narrator, and the yarn he tells is a good-hearted one, enriched by a strong flavour of the times.' *Mail on Sunday*

'*The Wilding* exerts a powerful pull, sustaining mysteries to the end.' *The Lady*

'McCann's new masterpiece has all the same hallmarks of perfect pace, delicate precision and powerful ideas [as *As Meat Loves Salt*] . . . A historical novel of brilliant imaginative depth and power but also true to its time and written with exquisite style, detail and language.' *Lancashire Evening Post*

Praise for *As Meat Loves Salt*:

'A fat, juicy masterpiece. The writing here is flawless. These pages flow like claret.' *The Economist*

'Riveting.' Lionel Shriver

'An electrifying erotic thriller, rich in secrets and surprises.' *Independent*

'Outstanding . . . with all the dirt, stink, rasp and flavour of the time.' Andrew Marr

by the same author

AS MEAT LOVES SALT

For SMH, who is both clever and wise

1672

1

Of Apples in Eden

How well I remember it! There had been a village wedding that day. We had put the couple to bed and were bringing away our gloves and favours and cake; as we approached the house I saw the moon, huge and yellow, hanging over the roof as if to spy on us. Being tired and tipsy, I stumbled in the path and my father said, 'Mind how you go.' We were no sooner inside, and my mother gone to her chamber to take off her good gown, than there came a tapping at the door. Wondering who could want us at that time, and why the person had not spoken to us in the road, I opened it and found a little boy on the step.

'Please, Sir,' he said, 'I'm to give this to Mr Dymond and nobody else.'

I now perceived something white in his hand. 'Don't you mean Mrs Dymond? It's a childbed, is it?'

He shook his head. 'Mr Mathew.'

'I'm his son, you may give it me.' I held out my hand, but the lad put his behind his back.

'I won't steal your letter,' I said, laughing. 'Come inside, before you fall asleep' – for the little fellow was yawning and rubbing his eyes.

'I did fall asleep, Sir, in the garden, Sir.'

'You've come a long way, then?'

'Please, Sir, from Tetton Green.'

A long way for a child in the chill autumn weather. I looked at him with new interest. 'From my uncle – Mr Robin Dymond?'

Now it was his turn to look at me. 'Is he your uncle, Sir?'

As we entered my father was standing at the hearth urging the fire into life. He had never caught the trick of building a fire and the flames had a flimsy, frivolous look. As he took the paper from the boy I seized the poker and raked the wood together until it roared, my father turning away in order to have its light on the letter. From where I stood I could see that it was but a few lines long, yet I had breathed in and out perhaps twenty times before he turned round. I saw his hand move as if to throw the thing into the hearth, and then draw back.

'It's too late for you to return alone,' he told the boy, tucking up the paper into his coat pocket. 'You shall stay the night here and return tomorrow.'

'Sir, I was told not to. No matter how late, I'm to take you back with me. That's what the man said.'

My father hesitated. The lad seemed to think he was being disbelieved, for he repeated, 'He said that, Sir.'

During all this time Father had not looked at me. Now he said, 'Jonathan, go and tell your mother what's happened.'

I said, 'I don't know what's happened.'

'My brother's in a difficulty. I must see him.'

When I heard that *difficulty*, I knew I was not to be told the truth. My father was kindness itself and the word was his way of hedging round anything shameful: a drunkard who had fallen on his scythe and an unmarried girl with child were equally 'in a difficulty'.

'Then take Dunne's horse,' I said. I had already arranged to borrow the animal for my round the following morning; it was only a matter of begging a saddle.

'No, no. It's not so far to Tetton. Pray tell –'

'It's ten miles or more,' my mother said, coming back into the room. 'Who wants to go there?'

'Robin has need of me.' He handed her the letter. My mother is a slow reader who sometimes spells out words under her breath, but on this occasion she was watchful and let nothing slip. 'Take the horse,' she said. 'Jonathan won't mind, not this once.'

'Indeed I won't, Father.'

He shook his head. 'I can walk. But give this lad a bed, I'll go faster without him.'

When Mother saw that he was adamant, she took the boy into the kitchen where she gave him some hot ale. Then Father put on his hat (his coat, he had never taken off), kissed both of us and set out under the inquisitive moon.

Such messages as the boy had brought were usually for my mother. She was trusted by all and yet remained a kind of stranger in the village, having gone there with Father shortly after their wedding. Our home had belonged to Dymonds for generations, but not to our branch of the family; Father would never have inherited if not for the Civil War, which swept away a number of heirs and so handed the Spadboro house to us.

Before that time they lived in Tetton Green with Uncle Robin Dymond. Father had wished to install his younger brother in Spadboro along with us, but Uncle Robin stayed behind in his native village where he was about to make an advantageous match.

My mother, unlike Uncle Robin's wife, was not a wealthy bride, but my parents did well enough. Though soft-spoken, they were active, hardy, contriving folk. In addition, they could both read and write, a great blessing; my father was even something of a scholar in his way, a lover of learning, and he brought me up to read and write likewise. They had married for love (though so, perhaps, had Uncle Robin) and there were never disputes about money or anything else in our house since my parents were agreed on the best way to live: the way of simplicity and honesty.

I have said my mother was not a wealthy bride. What she brought my father was more precious than mere cold coin: with some little help from our maid she did all the things that good wives do – ordered the household, made medicines and preserves, mended and cleaned our linen – and sometimes helped out at births, especially those that were taking too long. This was what brought messengers at all hours of the day and night. As a boy I once asked her what she did on those mysterious occasions. She replied that her first task was to soothe the women, who were always afraid 'because childbed is oft deathbed' – a saying that made a lasting impression on me. Sometimes she stewed up herbs that helped the child to be born, or pressed on the woman's belly to turn a baby coming out the wrong way. She witnessed agonies and wonders.

Those she ministered to must have respected her skill, for she was called upon more frequently as the years went by, until there was scarcely a married woman in the village who had not sent for her. And yet, despite bringing so many through their hour of need, she remained something of an outsider. My father was always that bit cleverer than his neighbours, and both my parents made corn dollies differently at harvest time: small things, to be sure, but small things loom large to country people.

Still, settle down they did, and I with them. All my childhood was passed in Spadboro; I grew up a proper village man, woven in. We had a bed of beans and cabbages and suchlike, a patch of corn, an apple orchard (with the odd pear tree) and a pig. There was plenty to do and I made myself useful, as boys must.

One task I relished above all others, so much indeed that it was not labour to me, but a pastime. This was the making of the cider. From October through to January I would hang around any farm or house where apples were ready. Alas, a child was of no use where the householder had a proper mill, except to help bring fruit to it. I much preferred houses where the crop was broken by hand, where some kind soul might pass me a stave so that I could stand alongside the other workers, fancying myself the best of any as we beat down the apples into murc. That done, I would whimper and whine to be allowed to help stack the murc and straw into a cheese for pressing. During those early years I was much too small for this task, and forever under the men's feet, but they bore it good-humouredly. At last the cheese would be built and someone would hold me up to the press so that I could work the screw, or rather so that the man whose hand rested on the lever with mine could do so, I glowing with pride the while at my supposed strength.

There was always laughter and singing at cider-making time; I cannot recall any occasion when I was shooed away. Instead, the men would take turns at holding me up to the press so that I could try again; and when the first and sweetest must flowed from the cheese I was handed a barley-straw so that I could suck it up and pronounce it good.

My father soon noticed my love for cider-making, a love that did not diminish as I passed through boyhood and began to look and talk more like a man. Any boor can press apples, and some fathers might have felt shamed and tried to break me of such humble pleasures. Mine, however, believing that God implants a particular excellence in each man, and that only sin offends Him, tried to humour rather than thwart this strange propensity of mine. Having given thought to the matter, he set aside money each year (as my mother told me later) for when I was grown. In this way I came to have my press. He made me a gift of it on my twenty-first birthday, and told me that now I was of age, I was to run it for myself.

It was a thrilling, newfangled thing. Father was always full of projects, eager to improve anything that would bear improvement. Unknown to me, he had been months talking with the carpenter, fretting over its design.

'You see?' he said. 'It comes apart. You can pack it up and take it about.'

Every other press I knew was a fixture, wedged tightly under the cider-house roof. This one could move, could travel; it was like no other device. I could scarcely wait for the next cider-making when I would load up, hire Dunne's horse and take myself off to the houses where they had apples but no press.

When I finally set out the following October my father's judgement was proven sound. The screw was strongly made; our neighbours were pleased with the amount of must it forced from the fruit and I was asked to return. The cider-maker was always a welcome sight. Not everyone's apples would be ready – some would need to sweat longer, the late varieties would not even be fallen – but those families whose fruit was ready, who were eager for the new cider and consequently fond of me, would help me load up the press, plying me with food and with news: who was married, who sick, who ruined, who with child, who grown rich, who dead since last I went that way. What with this, and the novelty of unfamiliar faces, I passed the time very pleasantly. But enjoyable though it all was, what I loved most of all was the making itself.

Certain smells seem old as Eden: heaps of apples on the turn, smoke coming off sweet wood, the earth opening up in spring. As long as there have been people, there have been these – so ancient they are, so God-given. I loved the heady stink of fermentation – 'apples and a little rot', as the cottagers said – and the bright brown sweat that dripped from the murc even before the screw was turned, the generous spirit of the apple that made the best cider of all. The villagers said 'Good cider cures anything,' and I agreed.

Once all the apples were milled and pressed the people would sometimes cut me a log by way of thanks, even though we had trees of our own, so that during my first two years we had several of these logs. My father complained that this was greedy and not the true custom, but my mother (who like me loved the scent of apple wood) quietened him and made him give in. All this happened in my first year with the press. I was twenty-six, and preparing for my fifth harvest, when my father was called away from home.

&

When I woke the following morning, it was a moment before I remembered Father was gone to Tetton Green. I opened the chamber shutters: the weather had turned mild and clear, excellent for travelling. His good fortune was mine also, for today I was to set off on my round.

My mother stayed with me as I ate breakfast, then came outside to see me off.

'I'll stay, if you wish,' I told her as I harnessed Dunne's horse. 'Until we know what's the matter with Uncle Robin.'

Smiling, she shook her head. I then asked after the boy, thinking I might question him and thus find out more, but Mother was again ahead of me; there was a glint in her eye as she replied, 'You must get up earlier, son. He's gone already.'

'I'll be back in a few days. The rest can wait.'

'No need.'

'I will, though.'

She kissed me and went to open the gate as I swung myself up behind the horse. The cart rattled out of our yard and onto the road. I waved to her, drew a deep breath of sweet crisp air and just touched Bully (that was the horse) with my whip. He bounded away and I felt myself come alive.

It was five miles or so to Medgeham. The village enjoyed a

kind of local fame, for the girls there were exceedingly pretty, though it must be said they were vain with it. The loveliest came out of three families, all cousins: the Strakers, the Lacks and the Fannings. Mrs Straker, Mrs Lack and Mrs Fanning were sisters and once the cider harvest was in their husbands would hold a feast in the Strakers' barn, and their daughters would dance. Then all the boys of the village would make up to them, and sigh, and hope they might find favour before the next cider-feast. It was high time the older girls found husbands, now, and since the last harvest some of them had done so; but they had married wealthier men from outside the village, leaving childhood sweethearts to sigh in vain.

With these cousins, I knew I stood no chance; but I did hope to marry within the next few years, both for my own sake and that of my mother, that she might have a daughter-in-law about her as she grew older. I could have married earlier, but nobody in the village suited me and my parents were too tender-hearted to arrange anything against my will, believing that I would come round to it in my own time. In this, their kindness perhaps outweighed their wisdom, but I saw no reason to despair. There were still willing girls enough; some, indeed, that would not have stayed for the wedding, but these I shunned, not through any extraordinary virtue – I was young, after all – but because my father was not a man to wink and talk of 'sowing wild oats'. He had trained me up to conduct myself more honestly, and he meant me to keep to it.

I was there for the pressing, then, and nothing else. The Lacks had a press of their own, which they shared with the Strakers and the Fannings and with other villagers besides, but this year they had so many apples that they had sent to me asking the use of mine. I lent a hand at the milling, too, and in return the labourers helped me build up my 'cheese' in the usual way: a layer of barley straw, a layer of murc, more straw, more murc, over and over, the whole held in place by a wooden lift, until the press was piled high and thick. Then the finest must, that made the best cider, oozed forth of its own nature, without pressure. It was a dear sight to the men and women of the house. Charles, the youngest of the Lack boys, was brought forward to taste and pronounced it sweet, and then we began screwing down the press. The trickle swelled to a soft brown stream, and the labourers cheered.

By nightfall on the second day we were winning the battle, and by the end of the third I could wash down the press and begin my preparations for departure.

The cider-feast was held, as usual, in the barn. I had long considered Kate Fanning the handsomest of all the cousins; she was of good behaviour and reputation, but her eyes, as black as if God had touched them in with a sooty finger, had a wanton look that promised well for her husband. Kate did not dance much; she sat most of the evening in talk with a tall, gangly lad, his face mottled with freckles. In person and manner he was unworthy of her, but then he was heir to two farms, as I gathered from an old woman seated close by who never stopped talking of him. As for me, I danced a while with Eliza Fanning, who was nearly as pretty as Kate but much more of a romp. A frolicking hoyden, she bounced me up and down the set until I happened to glance up and see the look on her mother's face. Eliza was destined for greater things, so I excused myself and sat down, out of the way.

It was no sacrifice, if I am honest. Eliza, though a good soul, could never have drawn me while Kate was in the room. What with the wedding I had attended in Spadboro and then the cider-feast, I felt like a man who has kept holiday for a week; but even holidays pall in time and my thoughts were turning more and more towards home. I was now very ready to hear, if Father would tell me, what had befallen Uncle Robin at Tetton Green. The Medgeham people would not want me for the late crop, since for that their own presses would suffice, so the following day I loaded up my cart and drove off, promising to return, should I be wanted, at the same time next year.

&

Dunne, seeing me come along the drove and ever watchful for his beasts, eyed Bully to check I had not lamed him. I did not resent this look, which I knew he could not restrain. It showed a man who took care in all he did and hoped others might do likewise.

He winked. 'Back already? Fallen out with them, have you?'

'I thought Father might need my help.'

'You've heard, then?'

'Heard?'

'There's news in your place.'

'Thank you,' I said, meaning that I did not wish him to tell me any more. 'Will you be fetching Bully back tonight?'

'Aye.'

'Only I'll want him again soon, for Parfitt's.'

'Let me keep him tomorrow. I can spare him after.' He touched his hat and I did the same. As we moved off the horse tried to turn into his familiar field and I had a job to pull him back.

It was not far to our house. I drove Bully into the little yard at the side, watered him and let him go free in the orchard.

When I entered Mother and Father were sitting together by the hearth. Though the house was cold at this time of year, as a rule they kept warm by keeping busy; they only sat like this in the evening, after their labour was done. Yet here they were, even though the fire was unlit, side by side in broad daylight and staring into the ashes.

'Jonathan!' When Mother rose to kiss me, I perceived she was dressed in black. My father, whom I now saw was also in black, started as if he had just realised I was in the room. I gestured towards Mother's clothing. 'Uncle Robin?'

Father said, 'Yes indeed,' but remained sitting. His brittle voice told me that he was near tears; I had never known him weep before.

'Dear Father, he had you to comfort him.'

My father's face worked but no sound came out.

'He was already gone when your father arrived,' my mother said softly.

'I'm sorry,' I repeated, thinking: If only he had taken the horse!

Father nodded. It seemed he did not trust himself to speak.

'Mathew,' Mother said. 'Pray go and lie down.' She was giving him the chance to get away from me, as in another minute he would have sobbed outright. As he left the room she whispered, 'Don't ask about it. He's tormenting himself.'

'Why? He went as soon as he could.'

'So I keep telling him, but all he says is "I could've ridden." He'll come right in time. For now, you must do your best to comfort him – amuse him. You'll do that, won't you, Jon?' I nodded and she hugged me to her. Amusing Father seemed a hopeless task, but I was in no doubt that she meant me to try.

'Harriet sends gloves and a ring for you,' she went on, releasing me.

'No blacks? *You* have blacks.'

'Of the worst quality. Look here!' Mother held up her skirt, spreading out the coarse stuff for me to see. It was shameful; we would have provided better for our maid Alice.

'I can't go to the funeral without blacks,' I said.

'You shan't go at all. He was buried yesterday.'

I blinked. 'What? So soon!'

She lowered her voice. 'He wouldn't keep; he was stinking.'

'In this weather?'

My mother shrugged. 'So Harriet said. She prayed the parson to get him in the ground. The sexton stayed up late on purpose.'

'Disgraceful,' I said. 'He can't have been as bad as *that*.'

'Unless it started before he died. That can happen, you know; but if he was going so fast, why didn't she send to us earlier?'

I was about to reply when someone knocked at the door.

'That's Dunne.' I went with him to fetch Bully, who stepped out smartly on seeing his master. When I came back, my mother had also left the room and so put a stop, for the time being, to my questioning.

&

'He was a handsome boy,' my father said.

We were in the orchard, picking up windfalls. Obedient to my mother, I had not mentioned Uncle Robin, but my father could not stop speaking of him, though never mentioning the stench of corruption that had so offended Aunt Harriet.

'A dead man looks young again, have you heard that, Jonathan?'

He had already said this twice, so I knew what was coming next.

'They shaved him and with his face all smooth you wouldn't have known how old he was. Only the hair – it was the hair gave it away.'

Uncle Robin's hair was one of those legends that are passed on down the generations. As grown men the brothers seldom visited each other – only now, seeing Father's unfeigned grief, did I wonder why – and on the rare occasions when I had seen him, my uncle had been middle-aged and his florid features framed by a wiry, grizzled mop. To my father, however, this Uncle Robin was merely an illusion created by time. Robin's true form was the one he remembered from his youth: a boy whose hair hung in ringlets of spun gold and drew glances wherever he went. In a family made up entirely of blonds, Robin had somehow contrived to stand out.

My father said wistfully, 'The village girls called him Absalom.'

'We've all got that hair,' I said. 'The Dymond hair.'

'Not to be compared with *him*.'

It was natural, I thought, that Uncle Robin should have attracted the richer wife. And yet I could scarcely believe that they were as happy as my parents, especially since Aunt Harriet had a sharp tongue and a temper to match. That, and her pride, went some way to explain why visits had been few and far between: my aunt was not a woman to throw wide her arms, let alone the doors of her house, to her humbler relations.

Father paused as we dragged the basket of windfalls over the grass.

'It's getting heavy,' he said. 'That'll do.'

We hoisted it between us, my father grunting a little, and carried it into the shed. As we put it down he tutted in annoyance.

'Will you fetch my coat, Jonathan? I've left it in the orchard.'

The coat was thrown over a low bough. As I shook it, in case of ants, a crumpled scrap fell out of the pocket. I knew at once what it was, and what I should do, and was not going to do. Checking that nobody could see me from the house, I unfolded it and read:

... a vicious wretch and with your help must make repara-
tion. Say nothing of this to my wife, she is (here some words had been torn away) *in you as the best of men, you will not fail* (again some words missing) *her rightful ...*

That was all. Whatever my uncle had to confess, it seemed he was in fear of being found out by Aunt Harriet. Perhaps this was why he had waited for so long, only to go before his Maker with his reparation unmade and his secret weighing down his soul.

You will not fail. Poor Father, I thought. How those words must cut him now! I felt in the rest of the coat but found nothing; it seemed he had torn and perhaps burnt the letter but missed this one piece. I put it in my own pocket and made my way back to the house.

2

An Interlude

The lane up to Broad Leigh was steep and Bully strained in his harness, clouds of steam huffing from his nostrils. I got down from the cart to ease him and as I did so saw Poll Parfitt in the act of clapping the house window shut.

Within a minute she was in the lane with me.

'Where you been, Jon? We thought you weren't coming.'

'My uncle died. I had to stay home a day or two.'

'Ah. I'm sorry to hear that, truly I am.'

'Are you?'

What a lovely little hypocrite she was. Looking at her, I could almost believe that she cared more about Uncle Robin than I did myself.

'*I'm* not sorry,' I told her.

Poll's face brightened. 'No more am I, then.'

'But I hate to see my father grieving.'

She was again serious.

'Come, Poll, you don't care! Why should you?'

'Ah – you know why,' she pouted.

'You took a vow to cut off your hair when my uncle died, is that it? I won't like you with no hair, Poll.' We trudged up the lane together, Poll walking very straight and dignified now that I was making fun of her.

'We've no Redstreaks this year,' she said. 'All blighted.'

'Shall I go away, then?'

'We've got Stubbards. And a good few Barn Door, this year.'

'Barn Door' was the name they had given their wilding – a bastard tree, sprung up without planting. It stood outside the barn, hence its name, and bore a dark red apple, a bit like Sops-in-Wine.

'Never mind, you'll have your drink all the sooner,' I said, though I didn't care for Stubbards – ugly, bunchy things and not half as good drinking as the Redstreak. Somehow being with Poll made me talk nonsense. I could not help looking at her deep red lips – 'like a scarlet thread', as the Bible says. Add to this a pair of little bright eyes like cornflowers and you have an idea of Poll Parfitt, who at that time was in the habit of dallying with me. During the last cider-making I had kissed and joked along with her, though without giving her any serious thought, and I was glad of her company as I led the horse into her father's yard.

Joshua Parfitt shook my hand, saying, 'We've been looking out for you.' The air was thick with the scent of concocting apples. Despite my dislike of Stubbards I drew a breath at the sight of so many of them spilt in heaps. When I picked one up and squeezed the pips were black; the fruit was more than ready.

'We thought you'd be here a week back,' Parfitt said. 'The murc off these can go straight to the press, I reckon, no need to stand in the mill.'

'No, indeed.' In fact, as I knew, there was no mill on the premises. The family and their servants beat the apples by hand and called it 'milling'.

Poll was hovering behind us, hoping for a chance to catch my eye.

Her father whirled round on her. 'Go away, will you, girl!' he cried. 'Do something useful, tell Martin and the rest of them to get out here.'

As Poll trotted off I noticed that she was holding up her skirts in an affected manner to keep them from trailing in the mud. Her father turned to me half laughing, half in exasperation.

'Her and that gown! Did you ever see the like?'

'It's too long for her,' I said.

'She *won't* turn it up. Missy has to wear it long, like the rector's wife.'

'The hem'll get filthy,' I said. 'She'll trim it then.'

He grunted. 'What she needs is to be wed. She's not bad, just a bit giddy; if she gets a steady man, she'll grow to him.'

Here he gave me a gauging sort of look.

'Well,' I said. I unhitched Bully and led him away before unloading the cart.

As I was setting up the press all the Parfitts, even the toothless old grand-dam, turned out to pulp the apples. They threw basketfuls of fruit into troughs and slogged at it with staves, mallets, anything that came to hand. Martin, the hired man, helped me fit the parts into place and draw back the screw.

A layer of murc went on, bound by straw, then another. Already the first of the must was trickling through. I felt sorry that their Redstreaks had been blighted, but even Stubbards were better than nothing.

Parfitt could not have chosen a worse time to drop his hint about Poll. My head was full of Uncle Robin's letter, which came back to me at all hours of the day. Every so often I would pull it out of my pocket for another look, trying to patch together its meaning. Something about *her rightful.* Aunt Harriet's rightful what?

Poll, whose job it was to bring out the bread and cheese, was not long in noticing. 'What's that, a love letter?'

'No.'

'It is! Let me see.'

Martin winked as she plumped down next to me in the straw. I was pretty sure neither of them could read, so I passed her the scrap of paper and let her pore over it.

'It's from a girl,' she pronounced, watching me like a cat.

I swiped it back out of her hand. 'It's from my uncle that died. Not much of a scholar, are you, Poll?'

Martin laughed and Poll flushed scarlet, not because she could not read but because I had mocked her in front of the hired man. After that she stayed away, and we got on faster. When everything was done and I was ready to leave, she did not come to wave me goodbye.

&

My next stop was at Little Leigh, where I made not much more than a few costrels of cider, and then I pressed for some cottagers in the village of Brimming. None of these households could find bed-space for me so I put up at the inn, a frowzy, mouldy place where I was obliged to go into the stables to make sure Bully was looked after. The ostler did not like me, but I cared more for Simon's good opinion than for his. Then on to West Selsden, where I pressed for another three or four cottages and slept in the rector's barn.

During the time I passed there, I crawled each night to my sleep, tired as I was with labour and softened with the cottagers' drink, yet no sooner did I drop off from the world than I began to dream, and always the same. It seemed I was setting out again, the horse jolting away in front of me. Through the morning mist I saw a man standing by the roadside, and as the cart came up he pulled off his hat and began to gesture towards me. Seeing the bright hair, I was seized with that childish dread that comes only in dreams. The dead man was holding out a paper, seemingly intending that I should take it. I knew that if I once touched it I should never be free of him, so I whipped up the horse and drove past without looking into his face. When at last I dared glance back I saw him crumpled in the road as if I had driven over him, and at this point I always woke, oppressed with guilt and shame. I would lie awake a while, making myself think of the apples pressed and the money I had pocketed, but as soon as I went back to sleep there would be the horse's head again and in the distance a grey figure in the mist.

The pressing at West Selsden brought me to the extreme end of my journey in one direction; in order to reach the others who needed my services I must now double back. I finished up the work, loaded the cart and bedded down for the last time among the rector's sweet hay, where I suffered my worst night so far; in addition to the dream, I had to endure the ghostly calls of owls above, and once a bird swooped down near me so that I woke in a great fright – there was a beggar at Spadboro who had been blinded by an owl. I laid my hat over my face for protection and lay thinking about Uncle Robin, picturing the handsome youth who had courted and won Aunt Harriet. Did he bring his secret, whatever it was, to the marriage altar with him? Or did all that come later?

When I woke the following morning the hat was fallen away but the owls had left me my eyes. The light streaming from the barn windows was shot through with dazzling flecks – 'angels', we called them at home – and as I lay admiring them I was aware that at some point during the night I had come to a decision. My father was gentle and trusting; he had returned home too soon, given up the chase too easily. It was understandable in a man oppressed by a brother's death, but another man, loving Robin less, might serve him better.

I came out from the barn into a fine autumn day and harnessed Bully to the cart. He seemed, like me, eager to be off: I had only to lay the reins on his back and he sprang forward.

'Bully,' I said to him, 'that's the spirit! We're not going home, yet, my lad. There's been a change of plan; we're off to Tetton Green.'

3

Of Mrs Harriet and her Household

'I see no call for this,' my aunt said. 'Does Mathew think I've lost my wits along with my husband?'

We were in the small room at End House, the home she had shared with Uncle Robin. It was a dim, north-facing apartment; creepers at the window filtered the day to a chill green as if the light were struggling through a sheet of river ice.

'My father thinks no such thing,' I said. 'His only wish is that I should call in upon you, pay my respects and –'

'Take over,' she finished. Widowhood had not softened a single line in Aunt Harriet's face: her eyes were as bold and her lips as clamped as ever. She looked as if she could see right through my skin.

'No, indeed,' I said soothingly. 'Father said I was to be bound by your wishes. To be of service to you.'

My aunt hummed and tutted and straightened the folds of her mourning dress, which was of a much richer stuff than the one she had given my mother. Her cap, of a harsh, unbecoming style, pressed her hair tightly to her scalp and thus threw into relief her sharp, beak-like nose. I remembered the owls. 'I thought you'd be pleased at the courtesy,' I hinted.

She was silent, thinking.

'I could press your apples, Aunt – I'm skilled at it.'

My aunt stared at me. 'What for? Binnie is to press them.'

'Then I can spare you his fee.'

Both Uncle Robin and Aunt Harriet were known to be tight-fisted. For the first time, she looked at me with something like approval.

'How long will you take?'

I just managed to bite back the reply that with my new press it would take no time at all and said instead, 'It's of no consequence. I'll stay until the job is done.'

'You can have a bed,' said Aunt Harriet, adding, 'We've a fine crop this year.'

My heart flooded with secret joy. I had cut Binnie, whoever he was, out of a job, but I could perhaps square that with him. Nothing mattered except that I was where I wanted to be.

As a child, I never thought about the name of End House. Now, visiting the place as a man, I saw it was the last in a line of dwellings backing onto Tetton Wood. These houses facing the Guild Hall, as the locals called it, were considered the best in the village and in my opinion Aunt Harriet's, with its broad front of yellow stone and its delicate mullions, was the most handsome of all.

The bedchamber into which she showed me was large, bare and dusty. She frowned as I slid my bag from my shoulder.

'That's all you've brought?'

'Yes, Aunt.'

'Does Mathew expect me to clothe you?'

'I've everything I need.'

'You've no call for a manservant, certainly,' she said, as if I had asked for one. 'Come down when you're ready, won't you?'

I nodded. What else did she think I might do? Aunt Harriet moved away out of the room, her rich dress brushing the floorboards, and I was at last able to look round unobserved.

The windows of my room were set deep into the wall. Neither overlooked the front of the house, but the side window faced the lane where it disappeared into the wood. By opening the casement and leaning out, I could glimpse a corner of the Hall, on the other side of the way. Even for a large village like Tetton Green, it was an imposing building. I believe it was left to the village, for some charitable purpose, by a rich penitent; it had been used at one time by craftsmen who set up stalls within (hence its odd name) and had even served, during the Civil War, as a billet for the King's army. Since then, the family had seized back what they felt was theirs, as sometimes happens, and now nobody lived in it – indeed, nobody went in there save the descendants of the man who had given it away.

I went to the other window and found myself above the back of the house, with a stable door visible to one side, some other outbuilding on the left and a well in the middle of a cobbled yard. Above and beyond, the trees of Tetton Wood flung their tops to and fro; a whitebeam glittered as its leaves spun on the breeze. Perhaps I had so disgraced myself with my paltry baggage that Aunt Harriet preferred to keep me round the back, out of sight of passers-by.

I would not say as yet that I disliked my aunt, but I was not far off it. Whenever I had thought about her at Spadboro (which was not often) I had dimly pictured her as reserved and perhaps a little proud, nothing worse. Now, in her house and in her sole company, I was inclined to draw uncharitable comparisons between her and Mother, who made our home decent, though simple, and who bustled merrily about her work. Aunt Harriet *progressed* along the passages and looked as if she would not deign to peel herself an apple, let alone drag a baby out of a howling woman. Though there must be servants about the place, she had let me carry up and unpack my own bag. My mother would never have been so neglectful, even of an uninvited guest; if need be, she would have carried up the bags herself.

Sighing, I rested my gaze on the furthest trees. From a distance their whipping back and forth in the wind resembled a carefree dance and I wished I could be out there with them. I was already regretting the impulse that had brought me here. Was it likely that I should discover secrets hidden from my aunt, who had shared this house with Robin for so many years? A childish notion! Perhaps I should be content to press the apples and go home. My parents would be surprised to hear where I had been, but nothing worse would come of it.

It was while thinking this that I noticed a coil of smoke rising from the wood. I had not seen it previously because it had been scattered and broken; but now, as the wind died down and the dancing trees were momentarily stilled, a fragile blue trail rose against their mingled green and gold.

'Charcoal-burners,' I said to myself, 'or tinkers,' but thought no more of it because just then a servant came into view in the courtyard below. She let a bucket down into the well, reeled it in again, and bore it off into the house. I was struck by the ease with which she handled this bucket, which was large and appeared full to the brim; though unable to see her face, I judged her to be young and toughened by constant labour.

There must be others who had known my uncle. That servant girl, for instance, and the boy who had come to Spadboro. I had not yet turned over all the stones.

It was time to return to Aunt Harriet. I combed my hair and beat the dust off my garments; then, clearing my throat though there was nothing in it, I descended the stairs.

'Aunt, may I please have some paper to write to my father?'

As soon as the words were out of my mouth I realised this was a mistake. Aunt Harriet had been speaking of her youth and her own father's pride in her cleverness; for the first time since I arrived, her face had grown soft. Now it took on the beaky, suspicious expression that had originally greeted me.

'You're to make a report on me, is that it?'

My intention was in fact to let my parents know where I was. I almost said so, but swallowed the words just in time.

'A report on myself, rather. I was a little unwell when I left home.'

'Then I'm surprised they let you travel.'

'I can be stubborn.' I smiled, saying this, to show that I was a modest man and my stubbornness of a mild and pliable sort. 'And they thought you'd be pleased to see me – you might be lonely without my uncle –'

She snorted with laughter. 'Tell them I'm not lonely enough. I've had to repel a siege here – women coming round sighing and smirking – as if I don't know what they want!'

'What *do* they want?'

'For me to write their children into my will, of course. They think to feast off my carcass.'

I flushed. There was no way for me to clear myself; no matter what I did, it would still look as if I was about the same business. I said, 'There'll be no report on you, Aunt, how can you think so? You shall read the letter before you hand it to the servant.'

I had thought, as any one would, that this would soothe her, but her mouth pinched itself into a cold, judging smile.

'My servants take no letters,' she said, scrutinising my face to see how I received this news. 'A man from the inn comes to the house. I pay him to do so, and' – she seemed almost gloating, as if she had thwarted some design of mine – 'he takes nothing except from my hands.'

'Then you shall give it to him,' I said, with a lightness I did not feel.

'You'll give no letters to servants while you are here,' she added. 'They are forbidden to receive them.'

Say nothing of this to my wife.

I nodded submissively, concealing my excitement. How had Robin contrived to write to my father? And where was the boy who had brought his message? There was no sign of him about the place. Perhaps he had never been in my aunt's employment at all. Perhaps someone else, some household Judas willing to defy her, had passed the letter to him.

'I'll give you paper after dinner,' she said.

I was so taken up with the new possibilities opening before me that I am afraid I thanked her ungraciously.

'In the meantime,' she went on, 'let me show you the crop. You can tell me how long it will take.'

There was indeed a splendid apple harvest already gathered in, though the latest and best-drinking fruits still clung to the trees. I stood and marvelled at the gleaming heaps within the cider-house. My aunt's orchard supplied her with a greater variety than was usual, some kinds so small and hard that, next to their larger brothers and sisters, they hardly seemed apples at all.

'Well,' I said, 'you're blessed in your orchard. But why isn't your cider-making started yet?'

'The screw seized up. Binnie's been trying to loosen it.'

'We can use mine,' I said, delighted at this good fortune.

'How long, then?' she asked. It was the question I had been trying to sidestep since I arrived, but faced with the crop I could no longer avoid it.

'It depends,' I said, 'if you want all these pressed together, or if you want some mixtures – a sweet cider, a bittersweet –'

'Is that better?'

'Much better.' And would take longer, since there would be repeated sortings, loadings and unloadings. I added cunning-ly, 'That's how the big houses have it done.'

My aunt was not too ambitious to pause and consider. 'But would it answer here? Our crop is smaller than theirs.'

'In size, yes,' I admitted. 'But the fruit is as good. Why should you not have as good a cider?'

'Very well,' she said. 'You can start tomorrow.' She spoke grudgingly, as if granting a favour, but I could tell nonetheless that she was pleased with me and perhaps even a little impressed at my knowledge. I was pleased with *myself*: after a number of false casts I had at last found a way to wind in Aunt Harriet. My bait was the very oldest, and still the best: Pride.

My Dear Father and Mother,

  Pray do not worry on my account since I find myself well and strong enough for any amount of work. Aunt Harriet, who greets you cordially, is also well, though sadly grieved by my uncle's death.

  There is an excellent crop of early apples here and my aunt's press has been broken by ignorant handling. I am therefore pressing them for her, the various sorts separately; my stay must be some days before all is done.

  Should any ask after me, tell them I will be with them in good time and none will be neglected.

  Your most loving son
  Jonathan Dymond

'Hardly eloquent,' my aunt grunted, reading this. We were sitting at breakfast, the day after my arrival; I felt vigorous, restored by a good night's sleep during which I did not once see the ghostly figure of Robin Dymond beckoning from the road.

I smiled to myself, being well satisfied with the letter, which had cost me some pain to compose. Seemingly simple, it was a masterpiece (I thought) of cunning: it conveyed everything I needed my parents to know and gave the impression that they had approved my visit, yet there was nothing my aunt could interpret as spying.

A maid brought in rolls warm from the oven. At the scent of them the spit rose in my mouth; I reached for one and ate eagerly.

My aunt stared at me. 'Don't gulp hot bread like that, you'll get a bellyache! Didn't your mother teach you?'

'We don't have anything like these at home.'

'What do you have for breakfast, then?'

'Stale bread, fried up.'

My aunt was pacified.

'You must understand letter-writing very well, Aunt.' I already knew, from her talk at dinner the day before, that her education was among her favourite topics. 'Did my grandfather teach you?'

'My father was a learned man,' she said as if this was news to me. 'My grandfather couldn't keep him at home, but he had him schooled and sent to the university, and found him a place as tutor to Sir John Roseholm when Sir John was a boy. It lasted until the Roseholm family moved to France; my father was unwilling to leave England, so that was the end of that. He then went to tutor the sons of a rich merchant and was most handsomely paid. They wanted him for his blood, but he was also –'

'For his *blood*?'

'My father was the natural son of a gentleman. That's why he couldn't be kept at home,' she explained as if to an idiot.

'My parents never spoke of it,' I said lamely.

'Oh – well –' she dismissed them with a wave; they were not of noble blood. She had at last told me something new, and interesting in its way; I could now trace her pride back to its roots.

'Yes, my father taught me,' she went on, returning to my question. 'He wished for a son to breed up and send to some nobleman's house where he too could have an opening in life, but it wasn't to be, so he taught me instead. He said I had as much mother-wit as any boy.'

'Did he teach you everything?' I asked. 'Latin, Greek?'

'A little. Mostly he gave me learning suited to a woman.'

I wondered whether she ever used this learning; as far as I had been able to see during the short time I had been in the house, she did nothing herself but left it all to the servants. Perhaps she meant music and French rather than the household arts.

My aunt was still engaged in the contemplation of her own glories. 'He called me his little Amazon, said I was born to be a lad, and had I been, I'd have beaten most of them from the field. Whereas my sister –'

She stopped.

I had never heard of this sister before. 'Wasn't she as clever as you, Aunt?'

'She was a foolish, pitiful creature.' Aunt Harriet frowned as if to end the talk, but my curiosity was aroused.

'Was she? What did she do?'

'She died,' my aunt answered, as if that were proof of her sister's folly. My thoughtless question must have distressed her, for she rose from table.

'Forgive me,' I murmured, but too late; without further ado she left the room. I dared not follow and sat, angry with myself, drumming my fingers.

After a while I looked up to see the maid standing awkwardly opposite me, as if unsure how to proceed. Concluding that she was a new servant, as yet unpractised, I gestured to her to take the things away.

I had not, before this, paid the girl much attention – she had been nothing but a curtseying form behind a dish of rolls – but now, as she gathered up plates in the crook of her arm, I was able to study her. She was nothing like our maid at home. Alice was a stout, familiar creature whose solid presence gave promise of comfort. This girl was wiry and so straight in her bearing you might think her entire body was in stays. Her sleeves were rolled up to reveal tight, hard forearms ending in well-shaped but not particularly gentle hands. I had heard a ballad about a youth who dressed as a woman and went into service in order to kill the mistress of the house, and I now glanced nervously at the maid's bodice. My glance dispelled any such wild notions: though thin, she filled out the front of her gown as females are supposed to. This was certainly a girl – the servant,

I guessed, who had shown herself so vigorous as she heaved the bucket from the well.

She was altogether an extraordinary sight. Her expression was bitter in the extreme, but not, I thought, from any immediate displeasure at me or my doings. Rather, her features appeared to be grown that way from constant hardship and disappointment, and yet for all this she was not ugly. The straggles of hair trailing from her cap were amber-coloured; she had the wedge face and lucent eyes of a fox. That is about as far as I go in poetry; if I have still not made myself plain I will say bluntly that she was not beautiful, but she held the eye longer than many women who are, partly because of this striking physical presence but also because there was something terrible about her, as if, like the beast she resembled, she recognised no kinship with ordinary Christians.

'You may clear away,' I said. She obeyed me at once; I was glad to see her so prompt to my command.

The next day I took cartloads of apples to the stone cider mill, and then (having promised Dunne that Bully should not be put to this drudgery) I went with my aunt's permission to her stable and chose a patient old horse to drive it. Once the mill was in action I unloaded my press, piece by piece, and fitted it together next to the old one, a fine construction and well worth the mending, but just now standing dusty. From time to time I left the shed to scrape down the mill and throw in fresh apples. The more I ran about, the happier I was; my spirits were always high when I was making cider, and the work was of a kind that hurried my body but left my mind at liberty to think.

Now that I *did* think, it struck me that I had slid from not liking Aunt Harriet into suspecting her of wrongdoing. Yet the sense of Uncle Robin's letter seemed quite to the contrary: whatever his wickedness might be, he had feared her discovery of it. This was a lesson to me. My feelings about my aunt had clouded my judgement, and I should be more careful in future.

I was crossing the yard as I made this resolve. Happening to glance up, I saw a casement open and the maid's face visible within. She disappeared at once, and the window was pulled to.

This strange young woman: what was she doing in my aunt's house? Why would Aunt Harriet, with her passion for deference and decorum, employ such a creature?

Perhaps, I thought, they shared some secret – but there I was again, suspecting my aunt when Robin's letter gave me no cause, and of what? What *could* I suspect her of, but procuring or hastening his death? Put thus, the very notion was laughable. I again reminded myself: my purpose was to discover the crime Robin had wished to expiate – to ease his ghost, and my father's anguish, by carrying out the instructions he had not time to give.

I went back to the shed and continued to feed the mill, but had not been there long before I looked up to see the maid standing in the doorway. She curtseyed to me but remained, seemingly at her ease.

'Pray make yourself at home.' I spoke coldly, but she seemed not to notice and nodded as if to accept my invitation.

'Where's Binnie, then – sick?' Her voice had a rough edge surprising in so young a woman, like the hoarseness of one that lives outdoors.

'Sir,' I hinted, and was about to add that she had no business to address me, when she repeated, 'Sir. Is he sick, Sir?'

'I've nothing to do with Binnie.'

'Oh. I thought you were his man.'

Surely she could not *mean* to be so impertinent? I studied her face but could detect no conscious insolence. I said, 'Does your mistress have Binnie's man to supper and to sleep in the house?'

She frowned. 'No-ooo. Only he came for the apples last year. Who are you then, Sir, if you're not with Binnie?'

'I'm Mrs Dymond's nephew.'

This made a great impression, I could see: she hung in the door, chewing on her knuckles as if she had heard something incomprehensible. At last she said, 'Whose son are you – her sister's?'

I was not used to being questioned by servants, nor to maids who referred to their mistresses as 'her'. I said, '*Mrs Dymond* is not a blood relation of mine. Haven't you any work to do?'

'So whose son are you?'

I began to think that the girl was 'not right', and that her shining eyes betokened some disorder of the mind. If so, there was nothing to be gained by rebuke, so I said more mildly than before, 'Mr Robin Dymond was my father's brother.'

'You're Mr Mathew's son,' she said slowly.

'Yes. Mr Robin Dymond's nephew.'

'Not blood-relation to the mistress. I see, Sir. I see.'

'Well, thank Heaven for *that*,' I was about to retort, but just then her smile burst out and it was one to make the angels rejoice in heaven. Evidently there was no love lost between her and Aunt Harriet. The girl seemed a simpleton; but if not, I had perhaps stumbled on the very person I was seeking: the Judas.

⁂

'Has Tamar been bothering you?' my aunt asked that evening as we sat by the fire.

'The maid? A little.'

My aunt bent forward to poke at a log. 'She's no jewel, eh?'

'She seems an unskilful servant.'

'And so she is. She came to me when Robin was soiling his

bedding. At my time of greatest need, the laundress went back to her family and then the nurse I'd hired for him did likewise. They needn't show their faces here again.'

'So you did it all yourself,' I murmured, scarcely able to picture this.

'For a while,' she agreed. 'I let it be known in the village that I would pay handsomely provided I got a girl with a willing heart, but none came forward. There was still preserving to do, brewing, work to be had in the fields. Who'd choose to mop up the vomit and flux of a dying man?' She gazed into the embers. 'Then Tamar came wandering through the village, a vagrant, and the vicar sent her to me. She was better off here than taking a whipping. She did it all without complaint, but –' She shrugged.

'But what?'

'Do you know these vagabonds, how they are? They're not Christians. It seemed to me as if she'd got some hold over him, towards the end. *I* wonder did he give her money. He could never resist a young woman.'

I felt a shock run through me. I am not sure how much of this arose from the thought of my uncle, in his disgusting condition, making up to the maid, and how much from his widow's speaking so calmly of it.

'From what you say,' I remarked, 'he was too ill for anything of the sort.'

'Perhaps,' my aunt replied. 'But be she pure as the driven snow, she can't stay here. I want a laundress who can turn out bands and frills.'

'What'll happen to Tamar?' I said. 'You wouldn't wish her to be a vagrant again?'

'What she does is no concern of mine. She might find a place in the village.'

'There are people here wishing to hire a maid?'

'Or something,' my aunt said acidly, her face so bitter that for a moment she resembled the young woman she spoke of. The mad thought came to me that Tamar was Aunt Harriet's illegitimate daughter. Mad, because everyone knew that Aunt Harriet was unable to bear children. She had tried for years, only to bring into the world a succession of little corpses; my own mother had presided at one of these gruesome childbeds, and had come home weeping. So Aunt Harriet had no heir, which was why the mothers of Tetton Green tried to engage her affections to their own offspring. Besides, when I looked at her again her face had cleared. Seen thus, she no more resembled Tamar than an apple does a thistle.

4

Of Wandering

'You'd get on faster if Geoffrey sent some of the men to you,' my aunt said.

'No need to take them from their work,' I replied. 'What's milled can lie there and concoct till the time comes to load it. There's nothing more to do for now.' Standing back, I wiped my hands and admired the dripping press.

She sniffed. 'I smell rot.'

'All to the good, if it doesn't go too far.'

'Then watch it doesn't. I don't want my cider turning to vinegar.'

'That can always happen, Aunt.' I took up my coat and made for the door, only to find Aunt Harriet following along as if she meant to drag me back. 'There's no more to do,' I repeated. 'I'll come back in time, never fear.' And with the coat slung over my shoulder I crossed the yard and left by a little gate that opened onto the lane at the back of the house.

It was my plan to walk a while in the wood and breathe its freshness; I had been indoors, hunched over the press and the vat, for too long. That autumn day was unusually bright and crisp; soon would come rain, and mud, and sitting with steaming legs before the fire, but for now I felt the need to move my limbs. When I was finished with the wood, I intended to go along the road and up to the green, and see these neighbours from whom I had to be stowed away in a back room.

I was not five minutes into the trees before I saw a woman ahead of me, decently clad in a white cap and plain dark gown, and hard put to it to prevent her clothes from tearing on the briars as she pushed her way through, for she was constantly having to untangle them. From time to time she stopped and glanced over her shoulder, but as she never turned right round, she did not see me; had she done so, she must have observed me at once. I judged by her motions that she was young, agile and perplexed: she moved like one that is doing wrong and knows it.

My curiosity was tickled and I decided to follow her some of the way. I guessed, of course, what she was headed for and listened out for the approaching lover, but of him there was no sign; he seemed to be coming by another way. We hurried on quite far into the wood, where the sounds of the village shrank to nothing. More than once she almost fell: I could hear the gasps as she staggered on concealed roots or stones. It dawned on me that I was a fool, and that she might think me worse than a fool: if she found me following she would scream, bringing the man running and placing me in no very enviable position. I had indulged my whim quite long enough, and turned to retrace my steps. But when I did so, the path we had travelled seemed to branch off at once into three. Worse, I had no longer any idea of where the village lay. I paused, wondering if I should wait in hiding and follow her out again – if indeed she chose to come back in the same direction. Just as I realised I had no choice but to continue following, the woman slid sideways off the path, as if down a bank, and vanished.

Cursing, I ran towards the place where I had last seen her. She had passed by an ash tree with a holly bush near it: I was now standing between the two. I stood very still and forced myself to breathe quietly. Birds trilled about me; the trees creaked as the wind stirred their tops; but the woman seemed to have passed into a world where sound was not. She was flesh and blood like myself: no matter how carefully she walked among the twigs and brambles she must needs make a noise, and yet . . .

A cold air seemed to blow on me. I recalled certain tales of my childhood, stories of spirits that lured men into lonely places and there delivered them over to the Black Woodcutter, a ghostly figure who swung his axe three times in the air. The children of the village would chant:

> *Off* went the right arm,
> *Off* went the left –

after which the Black Woodcutter would slice through the victim's neck, throwing the severed head into a tree. My parents laughed at such tales; still, a man from the village claimed to have seen the Black Woodcutter, late one night, prowling near the churchyard.

At that moment I smelt something comforting: smoke. The Black Woodcutter did not light fires, as far as I knew – the only trunks he was interested in were the human kind – and I looked about me for the familiar blue haze. But I could see nothing, and when another whiff came to me a few minutes later I realised from its flavour that this was the scent of an *old* fire, lingering among its ashes. The flames, wherever they had been, had been doused.

I spent a few minutes poking about beside the path. There was no sign of habitation; a steep slope led down from where I stood into a vicious-looking thicket of brambles some thirty feet below. The way was plainly not that way, and I turned back.

Now I had lost the woman there was nothing for it but to guess. I took the middle path and after some ten minutes' walk began to hear noises from the road near the duck pond. Despite the fear I had felt a short while earlier, I was now very satisfied with my own powers, and it was with a cheerful heart that I emerged some way along the road from End House, and was able to see it there among the rest.

'Black Woodcutter, indeed,' said I to myself.

I was still not inclined to go back to my aunt and thought I would carry out the rest of my plan, namely to take a tour of Tetton Green. That it had once been prosperous could be seen by the make of the houses, but the Civil War had thoroughly lanced its swelling coffers: rings, goblets, furs and countless other comforts had disappeared onto wagons and into soldiers' snapsacks. My father had told me about that time; he was already living at Spadboro, where things were much quieter, but Uncle Robin and Aunt Harriet were caught up in the thick of it all. To judge by Aunt Harriet's style of living, however, they had suffered no lasting harm. That was perhaps because Tetton Green was occupied by the King's forces and the Dymonds have always remained loyal to His Majesty.

I was struck by the peculiar appearance of the Guild Hall. The windows were in the new elegant style, good in itself but out of tune with the rest of the building. I remember that I remarked on this to an old man passing by; he told me that they had been smashed during the war and not replaced for some years afterwards. Folk had scarcely enough to feed themselves, let alone replace windows, and as a result rain and wind had been let to play the devil with the interior, though all was now made snug again. I said it was a shame, and Cromwell the Dictator had the sufferings of an entire nation to answer for. He said it was not the rebels that did it. I said it came to the same thing, since the rebels must bear the blame for the war. Then I made the round of the houses, walked down to the duck pond and traced the stream uphill until I arrived back at my aunt's house.

Crossing the yard, I heard a movement inside the shed where my press was. Aunt Harriet had gone against my wishes and put someone to meddle with my work. I walked smartly up and flung open the door, crying, 'Come out of there.'

Tamar was within, laughing and holding a hand to her heart. 'You did give me a fright!' said she.

'What are you doing in here? I said nobody was to touch it.'

'I haven't touched it, Sir. Look, I'm nowhere near.'

I could not deny that she was seated some yards off, on a heap of sacks. Trying not to look as foolish as I felt, I checked the press. All was as it should be, and the vat brimming with liquid gold.

Tamar said, 'I came to ask if you'd give me a dish of murc.'

'Isn't that something you should ask my aunt?'

The girl looked crestfallen.

'Very well,' I said, 'what do you want murc for?'

'To give to someone. The mistress won't notice, will she? It's nothing to her.'

She was asking me because Aunt Harriet was sure to refuse. I hesitated. It was true that my aunt wouldn't miss it, unless of course she had sent the girl to test my honesty. Then I remembered that Tamar was a vagrant, without a friend in the world. It seemed harsh to refuse her something so trifling. Besides, if this girl had secrets to sell, a dish or two of crushed apple given now might repay me a thousandfold later on.

'Who wants it?' I asked.

'An old woman. A bit of that, stewed up, might move her bowels.'

I laughed. 'She'll need plenty of honey to go with it! These are like crab apples. You were going to take it, weren't you?'

'No, Sir. What would I put it in? I haven't a bowl or anything.'

I thought a bowl might be concealed beneath her skirts, but I could hardly ask to see *there*; besides, being suddenly afflicted with a picture of her waddling off, a bowl of murc wedged between her thighs, I struggled in vain against laughter and having started, went on until the tears came in my eyes.

'Are you well, Sir?'

'If you fetch a bowl, I'll give you some,' I said, able to speak at last and waving away her thanks. 'This old woman lives in the village, does she?'

'She'll pray every night for you, Sir, and if – if –'

'What?'

'The logs, Sir, the ones they give you. If you could let us have one.'

'But there are trees all about here!' I exclaimed. 'Why don't you make yourself a woodpile?'

'We've neither axe nor saw.'

'And you haven't a neighbour to borrow from? Or to cut wood for you?'

'Nobody that's willing, Sir.'

'Couldn't Geoffrey lend you his?'

She shook her head. 'He says I won't bring 'em back. We use the smallest pieces of wood, Sir, but they soon burn through.'

I gazed at her. By dint of a few questions I had learnt more than Aunt Harriet had discovered in weeks: that Tamar was not a solitary vagrant but part of a 'we', a household, and that this household had an old woman in it; also that nobody in the village would help them to a fire. No wonder this girl was so hard and spare and fox-like: she led a fox's life. Her words might be humble but her eyes, gazing back at me, were not as respectful as a servant's should be. I was even, for an instant, a little nervous of her.

'I understood from my aunt that you "lived in" here,' I said.

'I do, Sir, for now. But I help out at home when I can.'

'Fetch the bowl, then.'

She did not wait to be told twice and was soon back with a wooden dish which I filled to the brim with pulped apple.

41

'Remember to sweeten it well,' I warned her. 'Otherwise your old woman won't be able to eat it.'

'I'll take care of that, Sir.'

My aunt could be heard calling from the house. Tamar curtseyed and was gone.

5

On the Natural Deceitfulness of Women

Dearest son – my mother had written *– God be praised that
you can render your aunt service at such a time. That is all
to the good. But I would wish you to come away directly she
no longer needs you. Your father is sad and lumpish and
talks often of your return, and we have our own cider to
make.*

*We therefore look for you at the end of this week, no later.
Pray give our regards to your aunt and ask her if we may help
her in any way.*

Your loving Mother.

In fact her letter was not so well expressed or neatly written
as I have set it down here and took me some time to puzzle
out. Of my parents, my father was much the better scholar
and I wondered why he, rather than Mother, had not taken
up the pen. I was pleased, however, at the words Mother had
chosen, for her letter came to me already opened; it was a
kind of triumph that Aunt Harriet, spying into it, had found
nothing but kindness. Love for my mother and father
swelled in my breast, the more tenderly in that I was about to
disappoint them: I would return home only when I had
done what I came here to do, and that would take longer
than a week. Had they really needed me to make the cider, I
would have returned; but I knew Father could do it all by
himself.

Leaving the letter in my chamber, I made my way downstairs. My aunt was standing near a window at the bottom of
the staircase, examining some silks a merchant had sent to

her, and holding them under the light; she looked up on hearing my approach. As she did so, her glance fell on the window, which gave onto the front of the house. I saw her body stiffen. She put down her silks, calling, 'Geoffrey! Geoffrey!'

Curious, I went to the window. All I could see was a beggar-woman, her shoulders bent and her head concealed in a clout, standing outside in the lane. She did not seem to be looking at our house more than any other, but I guessed she had glimpsed my face at the window, for she started to hobble away. The next minute, Geoffrey rushed past me and out of the front door, holding a stick. The beggar moved off, but not before he had fetched her a swingeing blow across the shoulders. I had heard my aunt calling, 'Geoffrey! Geoffrey!' before, but this was the first time I had seen him; he was a big man and as he entered again, panting after the sudden call to arms, I felt sorry for the woman he had driven away.

'She's gone, Mistress.'

'She's forever hanging round,' said my aunt to me. 'In league with robbers, most likely. Any time you see her, Jonathan, tell Geoffrey at once.'

I turned back to the window just in time to see what nobody else saw: Tamar standing outside, staring after the beggar. She must have run around the side of the house. As she turned back towards me her fists were clenched and her face more bitter than I had yet seen it.

'Does Tamar chase her away, too?' I asked when the girl was safely out of sight.

My aunt looked surprised. 'It's Geoffrey's job. Tamar hasn't time to chase after witches.'

'Witches, aunt? Is she really a witch?'

'Who knows?' my aunt responded irritably. 'Whatever she is, she's not welcome here.'

'Where does she live?'

'You know beggars. They drift with the wind. You may go, Geoffrey.'

She settled back to examining her silks.

♗

I was now getting to know something of the servants kept about the house. There were six in all. Besides clearing tables and laundering clothes, Tamar helped in the stillroom when the mistress wished to make cures, perfumes and so on. Geoffrey Barnes, whom I had seen in action against the beggar, seemed to combine the tasks of a steward and an over-gardener. With the help of hirelings from the village he managed the heavy work about my aunt's property and also went with her to market, lest she should meet with annoyance there; he was so trusted by Aunt Harriet that during busy times he was permitted to hire on his own authority. Geoffrey's wife, Rose, did all the cooking and preserving of edibles; between her and Tamar there existed an uneasy truce. Anne James wiped furniture, swept floors and beat hangings; there was also a lady's maid called Hannah Reele who was rarely seen outside my aunt's chamber. Lastly there was a dwarf hunchback who looked after the stable and who was known simply as Paulie, like a child, perhaps on account of his short stature. Paulie had once been married, and had a young son who did not take after his father but was of the usual size. Mostly the dwarf preferred his own company, or that of the horses; it was said he had been melancholy ever since the death of his wife.

It was plain to me, even after a couple of days, that the house could have been run with fewer servants if my aunt had pleased to do more herself. In some ways she scarcely knew her own household, and seemed to consider this ignorance a duty she owed to that famous noble blood of hers.

My intelligencer when it came to the servants and what they did was not Tamar but Rose Barnes, a motherly woman who had warmed to me as soon as I ate my first meal at that house, when my plate had gone back to the scullery clean as a bone and Rose had asked Tamar who had so good an appetite. During the lulls when there was nothing to do but wait for the apples to give up their lifeblood, I could step across the yard to the kitchen and chat to Rose, who was of an inquisitive and talkative disposition. My aunt would have disapproved of my conversing with servants, had she known, but since she rarely if ever came into the kitchen, disliking the heat and the grease though liking the finished dishes, we were safe enough. On the day of the crone's visit I called in to discover what Rose could tell me.

'I see the old beggar was round here this morning,' I said.

Rose, sitting peeling a dish of pears, nodded.

'Is she really a cunning woman, Rose?'

She laughed. 'Not very cunning, from what I hear.'

'You've not been to her, then?'

'Oh, I wouldn't, Master Jonathan! But I know folk who have.'

'Do you, indeed? What does she do?'

The kitchen was stifling; Rose wiped her brow. 'She makes charms. A woman in the village had one to call home her husband but he never came back. I don't think God likes us to meddle with such things.'

'What's in the charms? Herbs?'

'Writing.' Rose pushed aside a heap of peel and started on another pear.

'Marks on paper, you mean – magical signs?'

Rose shook her head. 'Proper writing. I can't do it myself but I know what it looks like.'

'She can *write*?'

Rose shrugged. My curiosity now well and truly inflamed, I watched her tip the peel into a crock.

'My aunt says she doesn't live anywhere. How can people consult her, then?'

Deftly, scarcely looking at them, Rose began to slice the pears. 'She lives in the wood.'

I recalled the twist of smoke I had seen go up from between the trees. It could have been anyone: a charcoal-maker, a woodcutter, a tinker. Then I remembered the respectable-looking woman I had seen stumbling along the path. Perhaps she had been on her way to consult the witch. I wondered if I could find my way back to the place where she had slid off the track and vanished.

'Your aunt wouldn't like you to go there,' Rose said.

I was amused at her guessing my thoughts so easily. 'I'm curious, that's all. I've no use for amulets.'

'Or anything else, eh?' She was looking slyly at me now.

'What do you mean, Rose?'

'Men go there as well as women.'

'Do they? Why?'

'That I couldn't tell you. You must ask a man.'

'Rose,' I asked, 'how is it that you know where the beggar-woman lives, but my aunt doesn't? Hasn't she heard the talk?'

'Your aunt doesn't speak with many people,' Rose returned. 'It was the same when your uncle was alive, always private in everything. You know what they say in the village?'

I shook my head. 'What?'

'"None so deep as a Dymond."'

I laughed. 'They can't have met my father, then! He'll talk to anyone.'

Rose said, 'Yours is an established family, of course, but when Mr Robin married your aunt he had more of a position to keep up.'

She spoke respectfully; yet I could have sworn she was laughing at all of us.

That night at supper my aunt put me to the question.

'You say Mathew received a letter from my dear husband.'

'Yes, Aunt.'

'Who brought it?'

I was at once on my guard. 'A boy.'

'A boy? Doesn't he have a name?'

'I don't recall hearing any.'

'And you didn't see him?'

'Not well. It was dark when he found us. Why do you ask?'

'I ask,' she said grimly, 'because I sent no letter. As I explained to you, my servants are forbidden to carry messages from anyone else.'

'But surely – from Uncle Robin?'

She took a sip of wine and softened her voice a little. 'You forget what I told you, Jonathan. Towards the end of his life your uncle's wits were wandering; he was bedevilled by fears and bugaboos. When a husband grows impotent in his mind, a wife must assume his authority.'

'But my father was glad to have that message,' I said. 'I can't think it did any harm.'

'I would've written to Mathew myself, but the end came on faster than expected,' she replied. She looked around to make sure that Tamar was not present, then, lowering her voice, continued: 'Robin's fingers were so stiff he could scarcely move them. And yet he managed to write, or get someone to write it for him, and have it carried out of this house in defiance of me. It's that girl, I'm sure. She had a hold over him.' It had never occurred to me that Uncle Robin had not written the letter himself. My father had found nothing unusual in the writing – or had he? I could think of no suitable reply.

'The boy who brought it – would you know him again?'

'I don't know, Aunt.'

'We shall see.' She picked up a bell from the table and rang it. Tamar appeared at the door.

'Fetch Paulie's son,' Aunt Harriet barked at her.

Tamar vanished. After a few minutes, during which neither of us ate anything, she was back at the door with a young boy who gaped to see the supper table and all the good things on it.

'Come here, Billy,' my aunt said, beckoning. 'Tamar, you may go to the kitchen.' She waited for Tamar to get far enough off. 'Now, Jonathan. Is this the boy you saw at Spadboro?'

'I don't know, Aunt. May I hear him speak?'

'Say something, child.'

'Mistress . . .' the boy began, only to trail off.

My aunt tutted. 'Say the Lord's Prayer. I suppose you know the Lord's Prayer?'

Awkwardly, as if he had only just learnt it, the boy stammered through the sacred words until at last he came to 'the power and the glory' and faltered again into silence.

'Well, Jonathan?' said my aunt.

'I don't know.'

She gave me a look so sharp that her eyes could have sliced through my bones; but supposing they had done so, she would have found no deceit lurking in my marrow. Even after hearing the boy speak, I did not know if he was the one I had seen at Spadboro. I really could not tell.

❧

A fine big apple log stood at the door of the cider shed.

'There,' I said. 'If my aunt objects, tell her this is the one Geoffrey cut yesterday. I've only given you what would have come to me.'

'Then I thank you, Sir, from the bottom of my heart.'

'I've plenty more,' I said. 'I can spare you this.'

'We won't forget your kindness.' She blushed as she spoke; I thought it made her almost pretty.

'How will you get it to your – old woman?' I asked. She had no cart or barrow to carry the log away; I wondered what my aunt would say if I lent my own cart to a servant girl.

Tamar laughed, the first time I had seen her do so. 'That's no trouble at all, Master Jonathan! I'll take it with me next time I go to her.'

'But it's heavy.'

'No, no!' and she bent and lifted it with ease. 'I've carried more than this many a time.'

We left it propped up outside the shed so that she could fetch it whenever she chose.

'I'll come with you one day,' I said, 'and cut you some wood. We can borrow an axe and saw from Geoffrey.'

'He won't lend them, Sir.'

'He will to me.'

Tamar hugged herself with pleasure and I decided to take my chance.

'Tamar?'

'Sir?'

I lowered my voice to a whisper. 'Did Mr Robin ever ask you to take a letter for him? Or send a letter to anyone?'

Her face, that had been bright and exultant, now grew wary.

'I'll not get you into trouble, Tamar. No matter what you say to me, my aunt won't hear of it, I swear.'

After a little hesitation she said, 'He did, Sir.'

'Do you know who it was for?'

'No. He asked me to give it to a man in the village, and the man was to pass it on again.'

'You were a good servant to my uncle, it seems.'

'He said so, Sir. He gave me this.' She fumbled in the neck of her gown and pulled out a gold ring threaded on a cord. 'I can't wear it on my finger. He said never to let Mrs Harriet see it. You won't tell her, Sir – now you've sworn?'

I could see why my aunt would disapprove. 'A ring? Why?'

'For cleaning him up when he was stinking,' she whispered. 'Mrs Harriet wouldn't, you see.'

'I thought my aunt cared for him until she took you on.'

'She burnt rosemary in the room, Sir, and scattered orris. But she never went near the bed. It wasn't a job for her; she's of noble blood.'

'So you did all that.'

She nodded. 'And laid out his body, Sir.'

'You were with him a long time, then . . . Did you ever think, Tamar, that my uncle had something on his conscience? Something he wanted to put right before he died?'

Tamar's eyes had been veiled, turned towards the ground. Now she lifted her face and looked directly at me. She was nearly as tall as I and for a moment we stared at each other in silence. Something was working behind her fox features, sharpening them to a new intensity.

'Yes, Sir,' she whispered at last. 'He talked of it. He'd done somebody a wrong – he had to make amends. He was frightened of dying, Sir.'

'He told you that?'

'It wasn't like telling me, Sir. He didn't know I was there, not at the end. But he said it over and over. I heard him very clear.'

'Who was the person? The person he had injured?'

Her eyes swivelled away. 'He never said.'

It would do no good to press her just then. Instead I said, 'When did this happen?'

'Just before Mr Mathew came.'

'My father arrived because of a letter. That was the letter you gave to the man in the village, wasn't it?'

'If you say so, Sir. Mrs Harriet was angry, she didn't want Mr Mathew here. You won't tell her it was me that brought him, will you?'

'I'm a man of my word, Tamar. If you remember anything more –'

She stiffened. 'Listen – the Mistress –'

On the breeze came my aunt's voice: 'Tamar! Tamar!' The girl gathered up her skirts and ran into the house.

My dear son,

I write again to call you home since your father misses you greatly. There is another reason why I would wish you to be with us – a matter of some importance. I know that after reading this you will not remain longer than is necessary to render good service to your aunt in her time of need and will soon return to your most loving

Mother

Dearest Mother,

I am in receipt of yours and will return as soon as I may. My aunt has yet a good many apples to be picked and pressed, but I proceed with all haste. I am concerned at your 'other reason'. Pray send one of the village boys to me if something ails you; let me know it, and I will render what assistance I may. I am sure you can find a way of wrapping it up that will leave him none the wiser and I will gladly reimburse him for his trouble.

Your loving son,

Jonathan

As I had informed my mother, there still remained a goodly number of apples to pick and press, but I was not 'proceeding with all haste'; I dawdled and spun out my time as I pondered what Tamar had told me. Aunt seemed to take pleasure in talking, for once, and was in no hurry to send me away; everything was playing into my hand.

I must not go just yet. A few days more and I might win Tamar's trust; I was now convinced that, if she chose, she could point to the injured party. She had been with Uncle Robin through his last hours. If he was indeed raving, surely he had spoken the one name that pressed so cruelly on his conscience? As I worked I left the door of the cider-house open, and I waited.

At last, shortly after breakfast one morning, I heard a scraping sound outside.

'Let me help you, Tamar,' I said, emerging into the sunshine.

'Thank you Sir, but the mistress says I keep you from the cider.'

'Nonsense. Besides, it was I that proposed it; a walk will clear my head. So – where are we taking this most wonderful log?' I asked playfully. 'To the wood, perhaps?'

Her eyes widened.

'You'd be surprised what I know,' I said, laying a finger to my nose. 'Here – catch hold of one end.'

Out of the little gate we went and into the wood. This time there was nobody else about; we had the path to ourselves.

'Won't my aunt miss you?' I enquired as we tramped along.

'She's gone to market,' said Tamar.

The cool, fresh air under the trees soothed my spirit. Tamar set a brisk pace; she walked faster, I think, than any woman I have known before or since, stepping easily on the uneven ground and carrying her end of the log without strain. All this she did in her long, heavy gown while holding herself bolt upright. I wondered if she really did wear stays all over, or perhaps no stays at all. Then I thought of other things: of her cleaning Robin's body in his bed, and laying it out afterwards.

I wondered at my aunt over this business of the laying-out. She should have employed an older woman; it was not usual, perhaps even a little shameful, to give such a job to a young maid. But perhaps Aunt Harriet knew what she did; perhaps Tamar was not a maid in every sense of the word, if my uncle –

I must stop these thoughts, which threatened to taint with lewdness my memory of a man so dear to my father. As soon as I fixed my mind on our progress, however, I realised that we were on the path I had already trodden, the one leading to the place where the woman had slipped away from me. That was it, then: she had been hurrying towards a forbidden meeting, but not with a lover.

'Tamar,' I said.

'Sir?'

'This old woman we're visiting – is she the beggar-woman – the one Geoffrey drove away?'

She answered without turning round, 'Did he?'

Was it my fancy, or was Tamar growing less respectful as we advanced deeper into the wood? It was impossible to read the back of her head. I have lowered myself to oblige a servant, I thought, and this is my reward. My aunt does well to cherish her hereditary rights.

We were approaching the place where the other woman had got away from me. As we reached the holly bush, Tamar slowed and put down her end of the log.

'Now, Sir, I must show you how to proceed.'

She moved off the path onto the grass slope I had observed before and had taken only a few steps when she dropped through the ground, as one might drop through water, and vanished.

The sweat burst out on my skin.

'Tamar!' I called.

Her head popped up out of the grass like a rabbit's. 'Leave the log, Sir, and walk down to me. Take care where you put your feet.'

I made my way down. When I had almost reached her the ground gave way and I fell, crying out, into a sort of dry ditch or ha-ha, a wrinkle in the face of Mother Nature running right across the slope but invisible from the top of it. Tamar and I were again side by side.

'From here, Sir, you just look for that oak' – she indicated a fine tree to our left – 'and walk along towards him, and in no time you're there.'

'There' was such a place as I have never seen before and hope never to see again. It can only be described by the word *hovel*: an opening into the bank, partly shielded by hurdles smeared with clay and hung with scraps of oiled woollen cloth. At the entrance lay a mess of grey ashes, remnant of a past fire, perhaps the very fire I had smelt from the path.

Next to the opening stood a blackthorn bush from whose prickly arms dangled small greyish objects, threaded along with bird bones and nutshells on wisps of sheep's wool. These I took to be the amulets of which Rose had spoken.

'Let me warn her first.' Tamar pushed aside a spider's web and entered the darkness within. Left outside, I felt equally compelled to follow her and to flee; these opposing impulses so warred within me that I was paralysed, unable to move in either direction.

'She wishes to thank you,' said Tamar, reappearing. 'Come this way, Sir.'

Going in, I thought of foxes, of witches, of the Black Woodcutter. The darkness at first blinded me, but as my sight cleared I found myself in a cool, ferny place smelling of clay and damp.

'Through here, Sir,' came Tamar's voice from the shadows.

Moving forwards, I stretched out my hands to protect myself and felt one of them graze against something smooth and hard: stone. I was, I realised, in a cave. The beggar-woman had found herself a shelter against the rain and the wind, one that no farmer or landlord could pull down, and she was snugly earthed. I could smell her now: the stale scent of a female beast in its lair.

'How long has she lived here?' I asked.

'She comes and goes,' was the answer.

'Surely she's too old to be travelling?'

'Is she, Sir?' Tamar said. 'Pray ask her.' At that moment my foot knocked against something soft; I recoiled in distaste as Tamar's laughter rang out: 'Mind yourself, Joan!'

The softness at my feet wheezed and shifted.

'If you stand aside, Sir, you'll see better,' said Tamar, and I realised that I was blocking the light. I moved to the left and two milky dots appeared in the darkness: the beggar's eyes.

At first I could see no more than that, not even that she had a head, but soon I was able to make out an indistinct shape. Swaddled in rags, the crone was sitting on the ground, her back propped against a wall of rock. This place served her, I suppose, for dining room, bedchamber and everything else besides, and when not wandering about begging alms she had nothing to do but sit there. God knows how long she had waited thus, motionless, for Tamar to return. I had not thought Englishwomen capable of it, only savages.

'Thank you for your great kindness, Sir,' she said, and at those words I started, for despite the cracked harshness of her speech, put out of tune by cold winds and wood-smoke, it seemed to me that I had heard it before.

'Mistress, do you know me?'

'How should I, Sir?'

There it was again, that faint familiar note. Tamar began, 'She has a deal of pain in her back, and –'

'Christ preserve us!' The air over my head split into screeching and scrabbling; something scaly clawed at my hair and was gone before I could strike at it. The women roared with laughter.

'It's nothing,' shouted Tamar.

'Nothing?' The thing, whatever it was, some loathsome bat perhaps, was still flapping in the darkness of the cave.

'Only Hob.' She smacked her lips, inviting it to approach. 'He won't hurt you, Master Jonathan.'

Concealed in some fold of the rock, the bird now commenced chuckling to itself in a wicked little goblin voice. One word – *tomorrow* – coming out very plain, the women again began to laugh.

'Tell me, Mistress,' I said, addressing the old woman, 'is it true that you can read and write? I hear you make amulets to cure straying husbands.'

These words put a stop to their laughter. 'No amulets, nothing like that,' said the old one, somewhat unwisely since I had walked past a row of them on my way into the cave.

'Just good fortune, no harm,' Tamar put in. 'You know there's no harm, don't you, Sir?'

I answered nothing to that; I was not displeased to have brought them up so short. Again I addressed the old woman.

'But you can read and write?'

'I can guess at some words.'

'And write them?'

'No.'

'I know someone who says you write like a scholar.'

She cackled. 'Do you hear that, Tamar? Folk will say anything!'

Just then a cloud dissolved and a branch shifted in the wind, so that a sunbeam struck deep into the cave, right to the place where the crone was sitting. Again I started, for (allowing for dirt and neglect) Joan was not so old as I had fancied. I was not talking to a woman of sixty, but one perhaps twenty years younger.

'Can you write your name?'

She shook her head. It occurred to me that Tamar and I should be getting back to End House; now that I could find my way into the cave, I could always return later.

'Well, I wish you joy of the log,' I said. I was about to add, 'and will fetch you more,' but on consideration I did not like her enough to promise that.

'God bless and keep you, Sir,' she whined in the tones of the professional beggar.

'Farewell.' Disgust rising in me, I turned and made my way out of the cave, Tamar shuffling after. It was a relief to emerge into the light and air of the outside world. I yawned and stretched, then looked about me and cried out: 'Tamar! Who's that?'

'Who?'

'Over there,' I said, pointing. As she turned, I plucked an amulet from the thorns outside the cave door.

She strained forward like a dog that scents game. At last she said, 'There's nobody there.'

'A man in a blue cloak.'

Tamar shook her head. 'Gone.'

I could not tell if she was glad of this or not. I remembered what Rose Barnes had said about men visiting the witch, and wondered was it perhaps Tamar they came to see.

❧

At last, in the privacy of my chamber, I was able to unravel the amulet, which was fragile and cost me some pains to penetrate without tearing. Unwrapped, it consisted of a piece of writing in the shape of a diamond, with a scrap of rag stained reddish-brown, a few hairs and what looked like a dried mushroom folded inside it. The paper had been scrolled around them to form a lozenge-like shape and then sealed with some sort of gum. It struck me that the outside of Joan's cave must be well sheltered from rain, for the writing, though faint and purplish – it looked like blackberry juice, or sloe – was still clear. It appeared to be a love charm. The legend, complete with marks, ran thus:

◆

turn
wanderer
turn three
times round three
three times across and
three times back three
◆ *Under His tail & Out by His mouth* ◆
Contrariwise, the Lord of this world
Three hairs on his head
Three nails on his foot
home again
wanderer
turn

◆

When I say 'ran thus' I mean it was something *like* that: ungodly gibberish and not easy to remember, though I would swear to the marks at each corner. The lines were uneven but the lack of a table would account for that. It seemed, then, that Rose had told me the truth: one of the women, at any rate, could handle a pen. I crumpled the spell in my hand and then opened the thing again, poring over it as if it might shed some light on the trackless way where I found myself; but I was as mired in darkness as ever.

*

Not so long ago, I had imagined I had only to wait until Tamar gained courage and spoke out, revealing my uncle's secret. Now that I had spied into this wretched amulet, however, all manner of possibilities had opened to me along with its scribble: Tamar writing a letter under his dictation; Tamar substituting her own letter for his; Tamar taking his letter to Joan, who read it and then produced another more to her own taste. Each seemed equally likely, and equally pointless.

The worst possibility was that Robin had never written at all. He had no crime to confess and nothing to put right; the women themselves had written the letter my father received. Even if I knew this for certain, and I was very far from knowing anything, what might their reasons be?

Had they perhaps done Robin some harm? My first childish thought was of spells, but I am sceptical of witchcraft. Poison, though . . . none could deny the power of poison. Slip it into a baked apple or a dish of broth, and what follows? Flux and vomit. Uncle Robin suffered both, and as a result my aunt stayed away from him, leaving all the nursing to Tamar. He was alone and helpless. My aunt had said his hands were stiff. How easy for Tamar to rub them as if to soothe the pain, and to slide the ring from his wasted finger. But (I now recalled) hadn't my aunt said that Robin was already soiling his bedding before the girl arrived? It was just as likely that my uncle's comfort had been increased by the ministrations of his strange but diligent servant. All I could do was proceed with care, and wait.

☙

'Your mother's written,' my aunt said when she came home.

'Thank you, Aunt.' The seal on this letter was unbroken. To avoid opening it in her presence, I put it in my pocket. She raised an eyebrow but said nothing.

'Did you find what you wanted at the market?' I asked.

'Yes.'

I understood her: two could play at secrecy. Well, I'd be sworn my secrets were as interesting as hers. I bowed to her and withdrew to my chamber.

Son

You must return now. I can say no more. Leave the apples and come away. You can return to them later. Your father and I will be sorely displeased if you again fail to return.

Your loving

Mother

I went downstairs again. Aunt Harriet was standing by a window, looking out onto the road; she seemed to be waiting for something to happen. As I put the letter into her hand, she flashed me a peculiar look. It came to me that what she had been waiting for was just this moment; she knew why my mother had written.

'*Can* you leave the apples?' she asked.

I considered. 'Yes. What's in the press is nearly finished; put someone to make small cider from it and we'll press new in a few days.'

'And what about the murc left in the mill? How long before it goes sour?'

She made no pretence of caring about my mother's distress; she was not even curious as to its cause. I was secretly angry at my mother for calling me away at a time when I had already too much on my mind, but I loved her a great deal and Aunt Harriet not at all.

'I couldn't say,' I replied. 'Have it watched over and if needful send for Binnie. I've already saved you a good part of his fee, dear Aunt.'

Was I pleased to return to Spadboro? To greet my mother and father, certainly, though both seemed distant and distracted. Mother kissed me and helped me off with my coat; Father, looking tired and pale, patted my shoulder and said it was good to see me safely returned home. It was a chilly afternoon; Alice was summoned to light the fire earlier than usual and we sat round it. My parents several times exchanged looks but seemed in no hurry to begin, while the silence thickened round us like ropey cider.

'Well,' I said at length. 'I thought to find one of you dying, or the thatch burnt off. Am I to know why you called me back?'

Again they exchanged looks. At last my father said, 'Your aunt wrote to me. She says you are ensnared by a whore from the village.'

Blunt words indeed, from him. At first I could make no sense of them, and was silent as I tried to fit this intelligence together with what I knew of my aunt and the time I had passed with her. Afterwards, I realised that my silence had done me harm; my parents were waiting to hear a loud clamour of innocence, but I was too puzzled to make it.

'I don't understand,' I said. 'I've never consorted with whores. I have *no* kind of acquaintance in Tetton Green, and my aunt knows that.' A thought came to me. 'Does she mean Tamar?'

Mother shifted uncomfortably in her seat.

'And that's how you call her, by her Christian name?' asked my father.

'Because she's a servant – she lives with my aunt! Is Aunt Harriet saying she keeps a whore in her house?'

My father here gestured towards my mother, who got up and left the room. Watching her go, I felt afraid as I had never before done with either of my parents.

'Now, Jonathan,' my father said. 'What have you done with this girl?'

'Nothing.'

'Harriet says you stole property and gave it her, and that the two of you go walking in the woods and hiding from decent people.'

'Property? I gave her a log – mine to give – and a bowl of murc that she begged for a sick old woman.'

My father looked grim. 'Is it your business to give gifts to your aunt's servants? This girl isn't company for you, child. Your aunt took her off the streets.'

'It wasn't an act of charity. She got herself a good servant – not very polished, perhaps, but –'

'A good servant doesn't angle for men who come to the house.'

'What do you mean, angle? She asked my help, that's all.'

'You defend her as if you were her husband,' my father said quietly.

My cheeks grew hot. 'No, Father, indeed.'

'Then tell me what you were doing in the wood. If you lie to me, Jonathan, and that girl comes here later with a big belly, I swear I'll marry you to her, be she the biggest whore in England. Be honest, however, and I'll stand your friend. Is that understood?'

How had Aunt Harriet known where we were? I had no time to think about that now.

'Well?' my father prompted.

'Believe me,' I stammered, 'my aunt's mistaken. We haven't so much as looked at each other, not in that way.'

'What, then?'

'It was only the once. The old woman I spoke of lives there. Tamar took her the log and I helped carry it.'

'She lives in the wood?' My father was incredulous. 'What in God's name does she want with logs?'

I echoed Tamar's own words. 'She's neither saw nor axe.

She's a wretched old woman, an outcast; had you been there, Father, you'd understand. We came straight back to my aunt's house and all this time nothing took place that my own mother might not have witnessed.'

'So you say; but you didn't tell your aunt where you'd been. That argues a bad conscience.'

'I thought it best. Aunt Harriet has a dislike of her servant.'

'It's your place as her nephew and her guest to respect your aunt's feelings, not to side with a serving-girl against her.'

'I know, Father, but Aunt Harriet can be hard to side with.'

Father was silent a while, apparently weighing this statement against what he knew of his sister-in-law. At last he said, 'You'll see no more of this girl.'

'I've yet to finish the pressing,' I said. 'If Aunt Harriet's apples are not to be wasted.'

Severity did not come easily to my father; nor was he the sort of man who could calmly contemplate the loss of another's property. I saw him torn, and was sorry for it.

'My aunt should've spoken to me,' I complained. 'All this is needless.'

'Harriet has her own way of going about things,' my father murmured, not meeting my eyes. 'She means to do you good.'

I did not like this last speech, which made me think he was keeping a secret from me. At last he met my gaze with something like his old frankness and gentleness.

'It would grieve your mother to find you in a difficulty,' he said.

We were friends again – but nothing, after such treachery, would make me friends with my aunt.

⚘

When my father, after some grumbling about our own apples, finally gave me permission to return, I had regained a measure of self-control and was the picture of filial obedience. I smiled – I was quietly spoken – I promised to behave well all the time I was away; but it was with rage and humiliation gnawing at my heart that I set off for Tetton Green. Whatever Uncle Robin's secret might be, I cordially hoped that in discovering it I might heap misery upon Aunt Harriet.

As I approached End House I smiled maliciously to myself. She would not be expecting my return, and I was curious as to what sort of welcome she would give her dear nephew. I got down from the cart and tied Bully to a post in the lane so as to make the last part of the journey on foot.

To knock at the front door would bring a servant. My intention was to enter at the back and thus beard my aunt without warning. I was in luck: the door leading from the lane into the yard was unlocked. I tiptoed across the cobbles and into the kitchen.

The room was empty. A tart of minced meat and onions stood on the table, waiting to be trimmed: Rose had already cut the pastry lattice but had gone away before fitting it into place. In a dish near the window lay a couple of skinned rabbits swimming in blood.

I crossed the kitchen and walked slowly along the corridor that connected it with the dining room, put my head in there just to be sure I would not miss Aunt Harriet, then went on through all the downstairs part of the house. She was nowhere to be found. I came back into the hallway and mounted the stairs. The treads creaked; my breath came quickly. I reached her chamber and tapped at the door. There was no sound from within. I dared not open the door. If I barged in, and Aunt Harriet was sitting inside, I would have played into her hands; my aunt was nothing if not cunning and would immediately pass off any shock as the natural surprise of a woman who finds her privacy violated. I wanted to see her dismayed with no cause for dismay; I wanted to see her shamed and struggling for words.

Where *was* she? Gone to market? Not gone to visit a friend, for she had none as far as I knew. I stood outside her chamber, feeling a fool.

A door banged at the front of the house. This was not at all what I had planned; instead of catching her, I would be caught. There followed a silence, and it came to me that what I had heard was not someone coming in, but someone going out. I crept to the banister to check if the way was clear. Thus it was that my aunt, newly entered from outside and fiddling with her gloves, glanced up and saw me standing at the top of the stairs.

Her reaction was everything I could have wished: even from where I stood, I could see her face drain of colour.

'*You* . . . !' she cried.

I smiled, but otherwise remained silent and motionless. My aunt made to walk towards me, but after a few steps she sank down with a tiny, suffocated cry, keeling over sideways before sprawling full length on the floor. Alarmed now, I no longer acted the statue but ran down the stairs towards her. When Rose came through the door with my aunt's basket, she found me sitting on the floor and Aunt Harriet lying senseless, her head in my lap.

❧

While Geoffrey carried my aunt up to her chamber, there to deliver her over to the care of Hannah Reele, I went to fetch Bully from his station in the lane. Once he was safely in the stable, Rose took charge of me. She brought me to the kitchen and gave me gingerbread and cider-royal.

'Who'd have thought it?' she mused. 'She's tough as an old hen. Tell me again what happened.'

'There's nothing to tell. She saw me, said "You," and fainted.'

'She's banged herself, all right.' Rose picked up the pastry lattice and arranged it over the pie, deftly pinching the edges together.

'Shall I send Tamar for the doctor?'

'Tamar.'

'What's that look for, Rose?'

'What look?'

'My aunt's been talking to you, has she?' I blazed up. 'It's all false! That is,' for Rose was now narrowing her eyes and I thought perhaps I had overstepped the mark, 'my aunt's mistaken.'

'I don't know what you mean, Master Jonathan. Your aunt doesn't discuss her family business with me.' I felt as if I had been slapped. Rose went on, with a little air of dignity, 'But I do know that Tamar is no longer part of this household.'

I gasped. 'Because of me?'

'Because she's a thief,' Rose countered. 'She took a ring from the master, God rest his soul. My word, you're like snow! Don't *you* go fainting on us, Sir.' She moved the jug towards me. 'Have a drop more cider-royal.'

6

Of Murc and Rot

During most of that day I was kept from my aunt's room. Geoffrey relayed instructions that I was not to venture near and Hannah Reele, coming downstairs after an hour or two, reported that Aunt Harriet was delighted to learn that I was in the house, but was not yet equal to seeing me. Hearing this, I knew I had lost whatever advantage I might have gained by surprise. In the privacy of her chamber, protected by her loyal servant, Aunt Harriet had now ample time to compose her face, her voice and her excuses. I even wondered if her swooning had been feigned.

There was nothing for it but to go back to the cider-making. I went to Paulie and asked if his boy would help me. The lad came forward willingly enough and I took him with me to the cider-house.

Despite my instructions, it appeared that nobody had examined the mill since I had gone away. The murc we had previously ground lay slimy and stinking beneath a cloud of flies.

'Will it serve, Sir?' the boy asked doubtfully.

'No. Fetch a bucket of water.'

Together we rinsed and wiped down the mill with a view to starting the next batch clean.

The press was also in a sad condition, the cheese of apples and straw all dried out and shrunken. I put a few jugfuls of water through it but not even paupers would have drunk what came out. Sighing, I unpacked the cheese with the boy's help and set it aside to be spread on the vegetable beds.

The boy and I then loaded the mill with fresh apples. He seemed eager to stay but I was sick of his childish company and sent him away, telling him I would be wanting his help later on.

Once he was gone I did not bother with the horse but turned the mill myself – turned it until I felt the sweat on my back – stopping only to scrape down the pulped apples. I craved exhaustion; it seemed only right that I should be going in circles since I had discovered precisely nothing, except that my aunt had noble antecedents and her maid was half a vagrant. This princely intelligence had cost the girl her livelihood and would cost me mine if I made my other customers wait much longer.

I hated Aunt Harriet. For the first time in my life I cared nothing for the cider I was making; I would gladly have pissed in it. And yet, with all this, I could not leave without seeing Tamar. No matter what Rose said, I was sure my aunt had dismissed the maid to get her away from me. How would Tamar and Joan live, now? On herbs and mosses and a few pennies from making up amulets?

When I had ground enough apples I brought back Paulie's boy. Barley straw was piled ready and together we heaped up the murc with the straw, layer by layer. Again that sweet, generous juice ran into the vat before my arm was put to the press. This first must should have been carefully reserved to make my aunt a special cider, but instead I left it there, to be lost in the inferior pressings that would follow. I hoped that this cheese, too, would soon run dry and have to be helped along with water; I hoped to see it ooze with a nasty, murky paste squeezing between the stalks. They say good cider cures anything. I felt just then that a drop of the bad sort has also its uses, and would be the very drink for my aunt.

When we had rebuilt the cheese I returned to the house to wash off the sticky sap that clung to me. Hannah Reele was climbing the stairs as I passed below; I nodded to her and she paused, then came down again to tell me that Aunt Harriet was not yet out of bed, but ready to receive me whenever I could leave my labours in the cider-house and pay her a visit.

I thanked her and asked if she knew why my appearance had so affected my aunt, for (I put on a long face) she was not one for faintings and swoonings, and I was anxious lest being widowed had undermined her strength.

'She took you for a ghost,' said Hannah.

This was the last answer I expected. I repeated stupidly, 'A ghost?'

'Yes, Sir. The master's.'

As far as I could tell, Hannah was a girl who spoke little and generally the truth. I said, 'Nobody's ever taken me for Uncle Robin before. Am I so like him?'

'Not very,' Hannah admitted. 'Only your hair.'

My hair does crinkle like Robin's. It seemed Aunt Harriet was inventive, in her way, but not inventive enough. I said, 'How could she see my hair and not my face?'

'She can tell you better herself, Sir, if you ask her.'

'I'll be certain to,' I said. 'Surely she can't think my uncle's ghost would walk? He's in the bosom of Abraham.'

'Amen,' said Hannah with a prompt certitude that I myself was far from feeling. 'But his widow's troubled, Sir. Troubled by dreams.'

Now she had caught my interest. Hannah slept in a small closet off Aunt Harriet's room; she was well placed to know about any sleepwalking, sleeptalking or other signs of guilt. I again strove to appear sad and sympathetic.

'My poor aunt! Does she suffer often?'

She nodded. 'I've seen it before, Sir, in widows.'

I cast out a line to see what I would catch. 'She dreams he's with her, is that it? And then wakes to find she is alone?'

'She didn't say, only that the dreams are about him. I can always tell when she's having one; she whimpers in her sleep.'

The notion of Aunt Harriet *whimpering* was an astonishing one to me. 'Shall I tell the Mistress you'll come to her by-and-by?'

I realised she was waiting to be dismissed. 'Yes, of course. Go to her.'

As I watched Hannah go back up the stairs she seemed to glide as if she too had passed into the realm of dreams. Any moment now I would wake and find myself in my chamber at Spadboro, with my mother knocking on the door and calling me a slugabed.

On the landing Hannah paused and looked back, since I had still not moved. She was now standing directly in front of a great window that shed its wintry light on the stairwell; she was, in fact, just where I had stood when Aunt Harriet spied me from below. The outline of Hannah's head was picked out against the window but her features were lost in shadow, reducing her to a mere silhouette. When I stood in her place, I too would have been silhouetted. All Aunt Harriet would have seen of me was my curls.

⅋

Wind keened in the tops of the trees. In the cave opening, on a dead, ashy patch of ground, lay my apple log with one end blackened and a few small twigs laid around it. It had not burnt, being unseasoned, and the women must have known it would not; but despair will try anything.

'Tamar!' I called.

There was no reply. Despite my good woollen coat, I shivered; I could not stay for her unless I got out of this biting air. If nobody was at home, I could not be said to intrude, so I entered the cave, holding my hands out in front of me so as not to walk face-first into the rock. The interior was as dark as ever but once fairly inside I was out of the wind and surrounded by

71

– I will not call it warmth, but a lesser cold. The keening in the treetops also died away and my ears picked up something else: a faint rustling. I tensed, expecting the raven to fly at me, but the sound, now that I was studying it, suggested a more weighty motion than that of a bird. I thought of Joan, newly awakened and raising herself on her bed of rags.

'It's Master Jonathan,' I called. 'Don't be afraid.'

The sound stopped at once, but there was no reply. Now I was the one afraid, sick in fact, in dread of wild boars, or worse, laid up in there. A robber inside the cave could see me, though I could not see him; it was like walking blindfold among enemies, and as I realised my disadvantage my legs grew clumsy and weak. I began to back out of the cave without turning round, so that if someone came rushing at me out of the darkness we would at least be face to face. My painful breath and shuffling footsteps filled the silence, announcing my whereabouts to the silent, unseen presence within; at any moment I expected a knife to flash through the air and stick quivering in my heart.

All this took less than a minute, but in my sweating panic it seemed much longer. As soon as I emerged into the dull light of the wood, I turned and fled along the dry ditch and withdrew, faint and shaking, behind a tod of ivy.

Even sheltered there, I had to check several times before I was satisfied that nobody leaving the cave could see me. When I was convinced of this I crouched down, breathing deeply to quieten my leaping heart, and listened: no steps, no rustling, no sound of pursuit. I began to feel less frightened and more curious. I stood again, clamped my hands in my armpits and waited.

How long I was there I am not sure. I had just begun to find the cold intolerable when I heard a voice. Half fascinated, half in terror, I moved to the side of the bush and then had to duck as a man in brown passed so close that I could have laid a hand on him. He was perhaps thirty, burly and sallow-skinned; as he scrambled up the slope, his back to me, I saw that his garments were fresh and good, not shabby or stained with grass. This was no vagabond robber but a man from the village, and not the poorest neither.

If he had spoken, he was not alone. I kept very still as his footsteps traced the path overhead. When I could no longer hear him pushing aside the bushes I peeped out again. Tamar, wrapped in what looked like a blanket, was peering out from the cave mouth and seemed to be checking, like me, that the man was gone. She then pulled a hurdle across, to keep off the worst of the wind, before retreating inside.

I was not as surprised as I might have been. Certain ideas had formed in my head, while I waited behind the bush, as to the meaning of those mysterious sounds and the silence that followed as soon as I called out.

So this was what Rose had meant about the village men. My aunt had hinted as much more than once and had openly called Tamar a whore in her letter to my father, but I had paid no attention; I had known better. Humiliation, disgust, a sense of betrayal – all these surged within me, curdling into a bitter and poisonous brew.

I was not wise enough to go away and think. Instead, I pushed aside the ivy bush and stumbled back along the dry ditch, bellowing like a child: 'Tamar! Tamar!'

Silence.

'Don't try to hide, I saw you!'

Like a ghost she glimmered from the depths of the cavern – clad not in a blanket, I saw as she came into the light, but in a gown, or what had once been a gown, a filthy affair in ancient cream-coloured satin. Her hair, no longer gathered in under a cap, fell in knots and tangles over her shoulders; her feet were bare and blue and her eyes as fierce as if she meant to fly at me.

'Hold your noise,' she said.

I did as she ordered, not through obedience but because I was shocked dumb by her insolent manner. When I found my tongue again, I said, 'You forget I'm your mistress's kin.'

Tamar hawked and spat. 'I've no mistress. No mistress, no work, and a mother that far' (she pinched her finger and thumb together) 'from starvation.'

'You've other resources,' I said.

'Is that what *you've* come for?'

'Of course not,' I reproved her. 'I'm here to help.'

She looked disbelievingly at me. 'Yes?'

I took out a coin and put it into her hand. Her fingers closed over it.

'At least be civil,' I said. 'If you want my help you should –'

'Thank you, Sir.' She said it pat, without feeling.

'Now, tell me what happened. Rose says you were dismissed for theft.'

'Rose is right.'

'The ring?'

'*Somebody* told her.'

'You're mistaken,' I said softly. 'I swear on my life. I was called away by my mother, and when I returned I found you were gone.'

She shifted from foot to foot, considering.

'On my life, Tamar.'

'It was gold,' she lamented. 'I could've sold it.'

'Did you show anybody except me?'

She began to shake her head, then halted as if some new idea had presented itself. At last she said sullenly, 'It fell out of my gown once.'

'Was anybody there?'

'The mistress. She never said anything; I didn't think she'd seen.'

We were still standing at the mouth of the cave, the pitiful hurdle between us. Tamar's dirty satin bodice left her neck and breast half-naked; the exposed skin was dappled with mauve and her shoulders hunched with cold.

'Where's your winter gown?' I asked.

'She made me give it back.'

'Then let's go into the cave, for God's sake.'

She scowled and did not move.

'Tamar,' I said patiently, 'if I meant you harm, which I don't, I could do it just as well out here.'

At last she put aside the hurdle. We entered the cave together and sat side by side on the heap of rags where Joan had previously lain. This was one of the better-lit corners, a dusk rather than a darkness, but there was a foul stink of rags, or Tamar, or both.

'Joan's your mother?'

'Mm.'

'Why do you call her Joan?'

'It's what I've always called her.'

Not to call one's mother 'Mother': I reflected that vagabonds had strange ways.

'Where is she now?'

'Gone to ask the parson for help.' She turned contemptuous eyes on me. 'There won't be any.'

'I'm sorry,' I said.

'That there's no charity in the parson?'

'To see you so reduced. Take care, Tamar. You won't help yourself by making God your enemy.'

'He doesn't mind me whoring myself and making amulets, then, as long as I bow down to Dr Green?'

'Well,' I said. 'It's best not to make amulets, or – the other thing.'

'Is it pleasant being so virtuous, Sir? And having food, and fire, and a warm coat?'

'Let's not quarrel,' I said. 'Everything's so strange just now.'

'Is it?' said Tamar, meaning, I think, that for her things were much as they had always been.

'Very. I'm haunted, Tamar. By Uncle Robin.' I related my dream of the cart. The sneer faded from Tamar's face as she listened.

'So, you see? It's him, he's doing it. This means something,' I said.

She said, with a mixture of fear and delight, 'He can see us, then. He's still with us. But Sir, he didn't die under a cart.'

'Well, I know *that*,' I said. 'But these dreams must have a cause. Else, why have they stopped since I came here?'

'Oh, that's easy, Master Jonathan.'

'Easy?'

'The spirit can rest a while. When you do what he wants, he leaves you alone.'

'How am I doing what he wants?' I protested. 'I don't know what it is.'

'But you're trying to find out. You asked me about that letter of his. Your aunt, she's hiding something.'

Servants are at all times prone to think evil of their betters.

'What could she be hiding?' I asked. 'It was my *uncle* who had a secret.'

Tamar began to hum under her breath.

'That's not an answer,' I remarked. The smell of unwashed flesh and stale urine was growing oppressive, so I rose.

'Now,' I asked, 'what shall I bring?'

'Firewood,' she said at once. 'A saw – an axe. Blankets. Something cooked, soft – Joan's teeth are bad –'

'If I can. Anything else?'

She turned towards me with a curious expression. 'Paper. Pen and ink.'

'Can *you* write, Tamar?'

'No.'

'What will you do with it, then?'

'Joan can make a spell – ill-wish our enemies.'

'I hope you don't mean me,' I said, though I cared nothing

for spells. 'Or do you still think I told my aunt about the ring?'

'Not when you're so kind, Sir.' She looked up at me pleadingly. The thought crossed my mind that if I *had* desired this girl, and wished to make her subservient to me, I could scarcely have done better than to betray her.

'Can you get my ring back?'

'No hope of that,' I said. 'My aunt's convinced you stole it.'

'You don't understand, Sir.' Tamar shook her head. 'She's never thought that, never.'

'Why else would she dismiss you?'

'Because the master took it off his hand, and put it on mine.' She smiled. '*That's* what she knows, Sir. That's what she can't forgive.'

⁂

When I got back to End House I went straight to my aunt's room and tapped at the door. Hannah Reele, who answered, glanced at me approvingly and I saw she had been waiting for my visit.

Aunt Harriet was propped on a mound of pillows and quilts, surrounded by drinks and titbits. As I entered she was rubbing an unguent into her hands; Hannah bent over her and wiped it away with a cloth so as to protect the bed from grease-spots.

'You may kiss me, nephew,' Aunt Harriet announced in a clear, firm voice.

I stepped up to her bedside. My aunt's cheek was sweet-smelling; the hair looped about her neck and ears retained its youthful gold. I knew that she used washes and perfumed waters of various sorts. In another woman that would be vanity; in her it was more a desire to get the greatest use out of everything, even her own skin.

'She's told you why I fainted.'

'A curious error, Aunt: I'm not so like him.'

'More like him than anyone else in this house. What were you doing on the stair?'

'I intended to knock at your chamber door,' I lied. 'There was nobody downstairs when I arrived so I let myself in the back way.' Another lie, and a stupid one since I'd had the horse with me. Had I gone to the front door first she would have seen him waiting there, but mercifully her mind was on other things.

'I've rid myself of that girl,' she announced, peering at me in the hawk-like way she had, but thanks to Rose her blow fell short; I only smiled.

'You've found yourself a laundress?'

'Not yet. But she had to go.' She held out her fingers fanwise so that I could admire her ring, which I now saw was of gold, engraved with a pattern of dog-rose. 'She took this from Robin while he was incapable.'

'Shameful,' I responded. 'When did you find her out?'

'The day after you left.' She was a better fencer than I: the answers came back pat, without a pause.

'What ingratitude, and you not over his death yet. He must be constantly in your thoughts.'

'Indeed.'

I recalled what Hannah had told me. 'My mother still dreams of her father, you know.' (This was true.) 'She says he's watching over her from the other world.'

'If Barbara thinks that, I'm surprised she doesn't turn Papist,' Aunt Harriet shot back. '*I* stand by good Protestant doctrine. The dead don't go wandering about our heads at night.'

'Then why do we dream of them, Aunt?'

'Why do we dream of cabbages?' Aunt Harriet sneered.

There was no doubt about it: she was fully recovered and back to her old self.

The cider-apple season is a long one. Even so, I could no longer stay at my aunt's since so many villagers also had early varieties needing to be pressed; I would soon be obliged to return to the neighbourhood of Spadboro and my work there. There was no difficulty in doing this: I could easily finish up my aunt's earlies and return for her lates.

First, however, I had to carry out my promise to Tamar. I knew nobody in the village who could supply me with pens, ink and paper, so I took some from my aunt's private store, leaving her money in return along with a note that said, 'I have not time to explain now, dear Aunt, but you will find this amply repays what I have taken' – as indeed it did.

I had no expenses at End House and consequently had not touched the wages paid to me by Joshua Parfitt and other people. With these in my purse I went to the market the next day – Aunt Harriet, supposedly still weak, was staying at home – and purchased two good thick blankets from a weaver. I then bought a heap of hot pasties, folded them in the blankets and walked from the market directly along the lane and into the wood where Tamar and Joan (who had, as foretold, left the parson empty-handed) lay huddled against the cold. They were more than thankful; they wept. When I saw how they fell on the pasties, tearing at them like starving dogs, I thought the villagers could not be paying much for their wicked pleasures.

Afterwards they huddled together to keep in the warmth, bundling themselves in the blankets like a courting couple so that they resembled one body with two heads.

'We spent months like this once,' said Joan in that curious cracked voice that nagged at my memory. 'Tamar was a tiny mite; she won't remember.'

'Where was that?'

'Somewhere up in Gloucestershire.'

'What, in a cave?'

She smiled at my ignorance. 'Not as good! A cottage burnt out during the war. It was bitter cold – worse than this. When we weren't looking for food we slept the time away, kept our strength in.'

'But you must've eaten.'

'Snails, roots, anything. I'd catch birds with a string. If you sleep you don't eat so much; we just about hung on. Sometimes a labourer'd bring us a cabbage or a bit of pottage, something left over.'

I wondered what he had received in return. Joan's words opened a window through which I glimpsed an unimaginably hard time, the wheeling years of hunger bringing round biting winters and blistering summers that had fused mother and daughter together. And yet, even while I pitied them, I also felt a strange envy of their wandering life. I had always thought of myself as a careful and hard-working son. Now I saw that I had grown up like a puppy, gambolling about in my careless way, while they had faced out hunger and violence; they had known and endured more than I ever could. This it was that made Joan seem so old, when her daughter could not be far into her twenties, if that. I recalled the unease I had felt on first meeting Tamar, the feeling that she was not of the same breed as ordinary folk.

And Tamar – what did she see when she looked at me? Just that, no doubt: a pampered puppy. *Is it pleasant, Sir, being so virtuous?*

The portrait being scarcely flattering, I was glad to turn to the next part of my errand.

'You asked for pen and paper.' These things had so little in common with the life I had just been picturing that I thought perhaps Tamar had begged them in a spirit of mockery – this, in spite of my having seen the amulet.

It was Joan, not her daughter, who answered. 'Yes, indeed Sir, if you please.'

'You say you can't write,' I pointed out – not unreasonably, I thought.

'I can, though. I'm telling you different now, Sir; I trust you now.'

I brought out the paper and pens from under my coat. Joan grew as excited as when I had handed them the warm pasties. It was extraordinary to see an old beggar-woman so delighted with the tools of scholarship.

'What do you want them for?' I asked, passing her the paper. 'Can't you make your amulets from leaves and bones?'

Joan seemed not to hear my question but pressed the paper to her breast, her eyes wide and wet. She was gone away into another world and there was something pitiful in her dumb, gleaming face.

'She's overcome,' said Tamar. 'You'll be glad of your kindness one day, Master Jon.'

'Yes. Well.'

'Now if we had firewood we'd lack for nothing, nothing at all.'

I marvelled at the shamelessness with which she turned thanks inside out. She was not a vagrant for nothing: here was one who could beg an apple peel and end by carrying away the tree.

'There's none to be had,' I said. 'I'll cut you some for next year; but as for seasoned wood, my aunt will never give it.'

'I know that, Sir,' said Tamar.

There was a silence. I thought about that 'next year'. By then they might be gone, or dead.

'Where's your raven?' I asked to turn the subject.

'Out scratting for food. He'll come back when it's dark.'

'Did you teach him to talk?'

'He taught himself.'

Another silence.

'Your aunt has a big woodpile,' Tamar said after a while.

'It's overlooked by the house. No, Tamar, I can't.'

'Of course you can't, Sir,' cried Joan, coming back to herself. 'What're you thinking of, girl? He'd be thrown out by his ears!'

'He has a home to go to,' Tamar said, grinning to show this was an attempt at wit.

Joan also favoured me with an almost toothless smile. 'We have to take care of our Master Jonathan. No, Sir, you just make sure the gate's unbolted when it comes dark. Tamar'll do the rest.'

Panic rose in me. 'What about Geoffrey?'

'Don't worry, Sir,' Tamar said. 'He'll be none the wiser.'

Perhaps not, but I would. My conscience pricked at the very thought of it; I saw myself transformed in the moment of consent from a dutiful nephew to a whore's accomplice preying on his own kin.

'Supposing I did, it could only be for one night,' I warned them, secretly glad that this was the case. 'Tomorrow I leave for home.'

They bowed their heads in acceptance.

'My word, Sir! Listen to the wind!' said Joan. As if on cue, she and Tamar fell silent. Even inside the cave, I could hear how it wailed. Shuddering in the draught that blew in through the hurdle, I knew I would do what they asked.

⁂

'What of the Redstreaks and the rest?' my aunt demanded the next morning. 'You won't forget?'

'Of course not. As soon as all the earlies are pressed I'll come straight back and have a look at them.'

'Very well,' she said, as graciously as if she were paying me.

We liked each other no more than we ever had and I thought

with longing of my parents. I missed their honest faces; I was more than ready to continue in my old round, with good fellowship and laughter, taking a bit of bread and cheese and gossip along with my wage.

I had, as agreed, opened the gate the night before: my final act of friendship towards Tamar and Joan before my departure. Strolling to the well in order to give the press one last sluice down, I glanced at the woodpile. I could perceive no difference in its size or shape, but then I had never observed it with any care until now. The gate was securely fastened. However skilful a thief, Tamar could hardly have bolted it after her; Geoffrey must have found it open. He would be on the watch in future.

There was nothing I could do: the women must lie cold, unless Tamar could wheedle firewood from one of her men.

She could not ply her trade in Joan's presence, surely? But then it came to me that Joan might well have done the same in her youth, and raised her daughter to think nothing of it.

It seemed I had gone about the world deaf and blind up until then; I felt I was learning a great deal, in those days.

7

Of Home, and the Dreams I Had There

Though I knew my mother to be strong in her way, and capable at times of guiding my father with a firm hand, I had never been so aware of the warmth and force of her nature as when she opened the door to me and at once, without a word, folded me in her arms. I felt I had indeed come home. In my mother there was none of my aunt's spiteful pride, none of the sly, fierce, spiky comradeship of the young fox and the old, just the generous love of a mother towards her son.

I held her tighter and longer than was my custom. 'End House is well enough, dear Mother' – I kissed her cheek – 'but I'd rather be here with you.'

'My darling son! We've missed *you*,' cried my mother, still clinging to me. 'Your father's in the orchard, piling up, you must go to him. Oh, and Simon Dunne's been asking after the horse. I promised you'd see him paid.'

'My aunt had such a crop of earlies, we're only just done.' I took her hand and we walked together into the house. 'I hope you didn't think I was dallying there, Mother. The girl's gone.'

'We had a letter from Harriet said as much,' my mother admitted. 'And how did you leave your aunt? You were of help to her, I hope?'

'She sends cordial greetings to you both,' I lied. 'She's not like anybody else in our family, is she?'

Mother shook her head. 'A different breed of person.'

'Is that because of her noble blood?'

'Perhaps. Your father knows her better than I.' My mother smiled as if, though sorry for Aunt Harriet's loss of her husband, she had often felt the need of patience when dealing with that disagreeable lady.

I said, 'I think noble blood must be half vinegar.'

Mother laughed and squeezed my arm. 'You went there of your own free will! Go and find your father while I tell Alice you're here for supper.'

Father was turned away from me, bent over a heap of apples. I thought he looked stooped and burdened, but when he turned, saw me and straightened up, he at once cast off the years and flung out his arms in welcome, his face aglow with the kindly cheerfulness I remembered from childhood. I ran to him and he enfolded me, patting my back as if I were still a little one, though I was now as tall as he – perhaps taller.

'I'm delighted to see you looking well, Father.'

He said nothing; I think he was unable. But his embrace left me in no doubt of my welcome.

'It's a fair crop,' I said, pulling free at last. 'Shall I start at once?'

'That's a right helpful, dutiful offer,' Father said, beaming on me. Though I smiled back, I was not so very happy at this speech, which told me he had lately been considering me neither helpful nor dutiful. He then went on in a more practical vein. 'If between us we pick 'em – you, me, your mother – and then allow time for digestion, you can do a four-day run, come back and help us mill, eh?'

I said of course I could, and showed willing by going with him round the orchard, noting which early trees had a bright ring of cast-off fruit encircling the roots, and which still had apples clinging to their boughs and would need to be finished off by hand.

Smooth going, so far. The awkward part began at supper, which we sat down to an hour later.

There was a little bustle at the start, since my mother had

85

changed plans for the meal in honour of my return. They had cut into a ham and had the very best cider glasses, engraved with apple boughs, put on the table. These glasses, a wedding gift to my parents from Aunt Harriet herself, were grander than anything we usually drank from and were hardly ever brought out, for fear of breaking them. Though hungry, and eager to begin, I could have wished for something simpler. To my troubled conscience, the mingled perfume of food and drink carried a whiff of the fatted calf.

Father said grace and then proposed a toast in cider: 'Here's to this year's. May it be equal in brilliance and beauty.'

My mother laughed as we clinked glasses. 'Are you sure it's the cider you're toasting, and not some fine lady?'

Since he was a devoted husband, as she well knew, we all joined in the laughter, and set to with a will. The ham, cut into little pieces, had been stewed with onions and cream and I know not what besides. It was exceedingly rich, even after the food at my aunt's house; I think my mother meant to show me that home, too, had its comforts.

'Talking of fine ladies –' said Father.

Now I was for it. They were eager for news of Aunt Harriet, of End House and also (since I seemed to have unshackled myself from her) of the mysterious whore who had been sent packing.

'You've pressed a great many apples for your aunt,' my father began. I took my cue and described the varieties I had milled and pressed, the combinations thereof, her mill (which was of a different make from ours) and the loss of good fruit when I was called home and my instructions neglected.

'And with all those servants!' my mother exclaimed, baffled by such profligacy.

I said it was a pity, but my aunt had been taken up with the discovery of the thief and retrieving Uncle Robin's ring, and had forgotten to give the necessary orders.

Father nodded his head. 'Harriet won't be what she was, not now she's widowed,' he said.

I said I had never known her as well as I might but, widow or not, she was an altogether formidable lady. At this my parents exchanged glances.

'Did she seem to like you, Jon?' Mother inquired. I recalled what Aunt Harriet had said about that famous will of hers, and how women wanted her to inscribe their children in it.

'To be honest, Mother, I think not. I can't say I liked her.'

'Your relations were civil, though,' my father urged.

'Yes, of course. I said I'd go back for the late varieties.'

'Then we can ask no more.'

We were already overheated with the rich food. Father mopped his brow. 'It seems the – difficulty – has blown over.'

'Difficulty, Father?'

'He means that girl,' said my plain-speaking mother.

'Well,' I said, 'I've scarcely given her a thought of late. Shall I tell you what I know?'

Mother said, 'If it's fit to be told.'

'He would not repeat anything unfit, I'm sure,' said Father, crediting me with his own delicacy.

'She had a gold ring of Uncle Robin's. Aunt Harriet says she stole it.'

'Of course she did,' said Mother. 'Robin never gave a thing away in his life.'

Father replied, 'He may have done, Barbara. He knew he was dying.'

My mother's expression altered as she looked back at him. Recalling herself, she went on, 'And the girl was brazen enough to wear it?'

'Whether she did or not, Aunt found it out.'

'And took her before the constable?'

I stopped, brought up short. 'I suppose so. I don't know.'

'He'll send her back to her parish,' said Mother.

I wondered what my parents would say if they could know that she was earthed in the wood just behind my aunt's house, warmed and fed by their son; that she claimed she was the only one to care for Robin in his last days; that their son partly believed her, despite having witnessed certain proof that she was a whore, a filthy Maid Marian, just as Aunt Harriet had said; that I was now become her protector in every sense except the carnal one; and that my most recent exploit in the Robin Hood line had been to help her prey on my own family. But why had the constable not whipped her away? Thinking aloud, I said, 'Tetton Green may *be* her parish. Her mother –'

'Mother?' they cried in chorus.

'She begged in the village,' I said with a calmness I did not feel. 'She's gone now.'

I had stumbled badly there. I must keep what I knew separate from what I was supposed to know, even in my own mind, lest one should fly out and smash the other to pieces.

'These beggars are a plague,' Mother remarked. 'After the war, yes, there were bound to be beggars with so many injured and ruined and what not. But not now.'

'They grow wild,' Father suggested. 'They forget what it is to be industrious.'

I said, 'Well, the girl's turned out of doors in this weather. That's surely punishment enough.'

❧

Before bedtime I took Bully over to Simon Dunne's house.

Dunne looked suspiciously at me, as if he thought I was bringing the horse back under cover of darkness to conceal some injury.

'You've never stayed away so long before,' he said.

'It was at my aunt's – that's a new one for me. She'd a huge crop, Simon. She could keep Spadboro in cider.'

'Fine for some folk,' he grunted.

I saw he was annoyed. 'I didn't know it'd take so long,' I said. 'I've a lot of houses still to call at. Did you want Bully while I was away?'

'No.' He shed some of his surliness with this admission. 'I won't be wanting him now, as long as you pay up, only I like to know where you are, and then I know where *I* am.'

We had agreed to settle at the end of the cider season but I felt I had abused his patience a little and therefore paid him what was owing up till then. The money restored Simon to his usual self but lightened my purse, which had already been bled by Tamar and Joan; had I not been provided for at my aunt's house I think I would have ended that season in debt.

'It's only four days now, and then I'm back,' I said. 'Another village, and Tetton Green again. I'll come for him in the morning.'

He nodded. 'Agreed, Cider-Rat.'

This was a name given me from childhood, when I first used to hang about the press. I disliked it, but a nickname is like quicksand: the more you try to struggle free, the tighter it clings.

❧

That night Alice mixed us a posset of wine and cream and eggs that fairly knocked me out, so that I was half asleep as I kissed my parents goodnight and went up to my chamber.

It was soothing to be held (such was the power of the posset, I might even say *rocked*) in the embrace of this old familiar room. In the chill, elegant chamber I had occupied at my aunt's house I had always felt that the very walls did not welcome me and were trying to thrust me out. Here I was at my ease and as I snuggled down between the sheets with their familiar odour of rosemary, I was so glad to have returned, so tired, so comfortable and so warm (Alice having been before me with a pan of embers) that I melted away at once.

During the dark hours I woke to find my mother in the room with a candle. She said I had been crying and shouting in my sleep; I had now done it two or three times and had just started again when she had risen and come to me.

'I hope you have no bad conscience, son,' she said gravely.

I shook my head. It was the cart dream, just as I had dreamed it before I went to Aunt Harriet's: the misty figure, the sinister bright hair, the body lying crumpled in the road.

The next four days passed in much the same way as in previous years. Apples fallen, apples not yet fallen, apples going rotten, folk with mills, folk with no mills beating their fruit with wooden staves, murc standing in the mill, murc going straight into the press, the trickling of sweet must. My days passed in an innocent intoxication of the senses: the scent of crushed apples, the bite of the bitter-sharp cider they brought to me and the burn of the strong cheese they offered me with my bread, if I was lucky. All this I relished – and yet, perhaps, not quite so much as in the past.

Some of those waiting chided me for my lateness: Mr Drew at Tinsden, whose apples were far on in digestion, and Mistress Chinney at Lasden Magna. Hers turned in no time to vinegar, so we had to doctor them with honey and spices; but then they were an inferior kind to start with. Everywhere I went I begged pardon for the delay, and they were so relieved to see me that they mostly granted it at once. I cared little whether they forgave me or not; I had my parents to think of, and my aunt, and Tamar and Joan, and Robin – most of all Robin.

Like a great crow circling overhead, the dream cast a shadow over me. It followed me from my parents' house, hunting me from orchard to orchard, and followed me home again. No matter where I was, or how exhausted when I fell into sleep, it came to me every night – worse, it did not leave me by day. I could never forget it, now. Each time I mounted the cart and clicked my tongue to the horse, I felt a sickly pang. If a mist came over the road (and there was mist aplenty in that season and that country) I sweated with fear lest this should be the journey when that dreadful sight would appear by the road-side, far from any help, and with no chance of waking.

&

'And how's the press, my boy – is the action still smooth?'

'As silk, Father. Everybody says it's a marvel.'

My father was like a child on the subject of my press, forever wishing to hear it praised, but as a rule he was the least child-ish of men so I was very willing to indulge him. His design *was* a marvel, cunningly made so that it came apart easily and yet, when screwed together, exerted as much pressure as a fixed device.

He had an excellent understanding of what was necessary and convenient, and was so observant that he could draw something onto a sheet of paper straight out of his head, with-out having it set before him. He would have made an ingen-ious artificer, had he ever been apprenticed. Instead he had been trained up as a secretary (his own father having noticed his quickness in reading and writing) and before I was born had actually been employed as such. Since inheriting our home in Spadboro he had laid down his quill and would read only what interested him: works on farming, on philosophy, and sometimes sermons and poetry in place of the begging letters, flatteries and threats which were, he said, mostly his portion before. He was independent, now, and his time mostly taken up with improving his house and land. Though liked, he was considered an oddity by our neighbours, because he had more wit than the rest of them put together; as soon as I was old enough to distinguish wisdom from folly, I saw this and honoured him accordingly.

'I reckon your press has earned a rest,' he said, twinkling. 'We'll use the old one.'

I helped him load a cart with apples for our mill. It was my second day at home after finishing the last few pressings and I was feeling the lack of sleep, the nightmare having dogged me all round the villages and right back into my bed again. I told myself there was no help for it; I could hardly return to my aunt's house before her late apples were ripe, and besides, I perceived that Father had been hanging on, braving the risk of his crop turning to vinegar, for the pleasure of the two of us making our cider together. I must therefore stay where I was and defy the apparition.

We pushed apples into the mill, my father pressing them down.

'Ready, Jon?'

'Aye, Father!'

I turned the handle with a will.

'Sure and steady,' he said. 'Remember me holding you up so you could reach?'

'I can't have been much help.'

'You are now.'

Where I was concerned my father was easy to please. All I had to do was labour alongside him; such simple companionship could win his mind, for a short while, even from his brother's death. I reflected that it was a thousand pities that I must set off again for Tetton Green just when our own late apples would start to come to ripeness. It seemed to me that my father needed more sons, and my mother needed daughters to talk with in the kitchen and at the fireside. There was a sad dearth of children in our family: though my father and Robin had been two out of six, the other four died in infancy, while Aunt Harriet had no children at all.

'If only Robin could be here,' my father said, chiming with my own thoughts. I glanced at him; the familiar haggard look was once more stealing over his face.

'Did he enjoy cider-making, Father? I never thought of him in that way.'

'I mean, I wish he were still with us.'

I nearly said, 'Perhaps he is,' but held back. My father claimed not to believe in ghosts, but he had failed to carry out Robin's last wishes and had not forgiven himself. To tell him of my dreams could only give him pain.

This seemed a good time, however, to ask about the cart. Had the idea come a few minutes earlier I would not have spoken, for fear of spoiling his mood; since, however, he was already grown melancholy, it could do no harm. I dropped the handle so that the mill grew quiet.

'Father, was Uncle Robin ever hurt by a cart or a coach?'

'Hurt?' Father exclaimed.

'Didn't you say once that he was?' As I spoke, I wondered too late if he, too, was plagued by the dream and I caught my breath. His face, however, showed nothing but puzzlement as he shook his head.

'Not as far as I know. Somebody else must've told you that.'

'I was sure it was you. Oh well, I dreamed it, then!' I laughed and again began to mill, turning the handle faster and faster while the apples hopped about inside.

&

Tamar and I were lying bundled together in the blanket. She said, 'Won't you look?' and began sliding up and out of it so that I could see she was naked, her red-gold hair tumbling down over her shoulders and front. She parted the locks of hair like curtains and showed off her breasts to me: hard, unripe little things, the teats long and very red. She was thin and curved, like those figures carved on the fronts of churches, with a pale sheen on her skin, and rough, reddish patches under the arms and between the legs. She sat astride the bundle, with me still wrapped within, and rocked back and forth on her patch of tawny fur. I struggled against the blanket, trying to push her off, but she held onto me with her legs, jiggling and laughing at my attempts to free myself.

I woke with a soiled nightgown.

8

On the Desirability of Marrying Off Young Persons

I peered at the direction: my name did indeed appear there, along with instructions that the package be left with 'Mr Simon, that keeps the horse Bully'.

'From my aunt?' I asked.

Dunne grinned. 'A word of advice, Cider-Rat. Don't be a fool, and don't take me for one.'

'I never have, Simon.'

Just the same, I hurried home without telling him my thoughts and managed to get upstairs unseen by my parents. My hope was that the package might contain a letter from Tamar. Ever since that dream I had found myself thinking of her, wondering if her nakedness had anything in common with my night visions, lost in this fancy until with a shock I recalled the real Tamar: she of the bluish feet, who skulked in a cave and stank like a polecat, she who had not even a comb for her hair. Yet I had seen a man come away from her, wretched as she was. Surely he must desire brutish pleasures! And drive a harsh bargain, too, so that she feared and dreaded him even as she hoped he would return.

I had begun to mull over the idea of a rescue.

One way was to bring her back with me and throw her on my parents' charity. I did not think this would succeed. My mother was generous to the honest poor, but Tamar did not come under that heading. Besides, even if Mother should embrace her, which was far from my expectation, what of Joan? She could not be left behind, which meant I would be saddling my parents with two beggars to feed and sustain. It was impossible; they had not the means.

In my chamber I put a chair against the door and unpicked the outer wrapping. The package was a fair weight. What could they have sent me? Some magical thing, perhaps – a pig's heart studded with nails, some foul charm that I would have to smuggle out of the house before my parents saw it. By the time I got it open I was shaking. There was nothing inside but a good many sheets of Aunt Harriet's paper, covered in an uneven hand and disfigured with splotches and scratchings from the pen. I unfolded the first sheet and read on, as follows:

Master Jonathan,

You will be surprised, Sir, to receive this. Not an amulet, you see, but a letter. You did not believe I could write one, perhaps, but then I never had paper from you before so now I will try my hand, see what I can do. I trust you can read this, I lose all my trouble else. It is hard going with the paper on my knee and the draught moving it about, but I have all the time in the world and I persevere.

My daughter wishes me to say why she had the ring from Mr Robin and why she should get it back. She must be patient, I have other things to tell first. I am so frail now in my body that they must be told or else they will be lost with me and then the rest cannot stand by itself. Be patient, Sir, if you are patient you will see how it goes.

I came into this world in 1623, not far from the place you know of where I am now so reduced. I was not born a beggar. My father was an educated man, respected by all that knew him.

My mother was his second wife. When they met he was a widower with one child, a daughter, and my mother a quiet, homely sort of person, with a good dowry but not in her first youth and not much given to reading or conversation. However, in time they made a good match of it and I believe

96

they were happy. I was born within a year of the wedding; his first daughter was at that time four years old.

When I was about three a little boy was born to my parents, and then a girl when I was five. Both these babes died. My mother had no more children and when I was eight she died of a swelling in the womb, so my father was now a widower twice over. He loved both of us children tenderly and chose not to marry again so as to protect our inheritance.

Two years passed, during which I mourned my mother. At the end of them I was only ten and still a child but my sister (for so I called my half-sister) was now fourteen and greatly admired by a local man. What is more, she claimed to return his affection.

Father was against it from the start. His first wife had set aside money in her will so that my sister might have a dowry that would attract men of substance and reputation. This man had not the land or the wealth that must join with my sister's fortune. It was whispered that he was in love with that fortune, and not with my sister, and Father refused to let her throw herself away.

Oh, she was in a rage! She wept and screamed that our father had married whom he wanted, twice over, and she should be allowed to do the same. He told her he was a grown man, and rational, whereas she was a lovesick girl. She threatened to kill herself. I begged her not to, it was a terrible sin, and she called me a little cringing fool for my pains. We went on like this for days, my sister calming down and then breaking out again, until Father was driven to slap her face good and hard. Then she shut herself up in her chamber. Food was brought to the door but she refused to come out and take it.

My sister had always bullied and belittled me; I was not displeased to see her nose put out of joint. Hearing her sob behind her chamber door, I walked away and out into the garden where I sat listening to the tinkle of a fountain, thinking how pig-headed she was and wondering when she would come to her senses.

You see how violently my sister set her heart on this man, and how little I entered into her feelings. She was half a woman, while I was still a child incapable of understanding what ailed her. More than this, we had always been different. My sister took after her mother. This lady had been very beautiful (though my sister was not exactly that) and clever, and also pampered and indulged from a child, so that she could not bear to be crossed, and so it was with my sister. As for me, I took after my own mother, and my nickname was Miss Mouse. I was not so forward as my sister in courage or understanding, and (as she often reminded me) I had an inferior dowry. I desired nothing so much as to please everybody – I would have pleased even my sister, had she consented to be pleased. I never pictured myself accepting or rejecting a bridegroom, but always as being submissive to another's choice.

The battle in our house continued for weeks. Hunger soon obliged my sister to begin eating again but neither she nor our father would give way. Perhaps my sister would have buckled under in time, but in December Father fell ill. She was frightened then, and tried to make up, but he wanted her to promise she would not marry the man after he died, and she refused, sticking it out to the end, so that she and Father were never reconciled. We buried him three years after my mother. His two wives were laid in the same grave and he went in with both of them.

Father had threatened to write a will that would leave her penniless should she marry the man, but we found he had not carried out his threat. Instead, he had appointed an uncle as our guardian. Uncle Toby took much the same tack as Father had done: he was all for my sister marrying into wealth. He spoke to her most unkindly, saying that her wicked disobedience had killed Father. She wept so piteously at this that even I was sorry for her.

Something changed, however, and within a few months Uncle Toby announced that my sister (who had just turned fifteen) might marry whom she would, provided she would wait until she was twenty-one so that nobody could say he had slacked his duty. I will not say my sister rejoiced, since I saw her crying, but she was a step closer to liberty. As for me, I could not understand why our uncle had set aside his brother's dying wish. My belief now is that he received money from my sister's lover in return for consenting to the match. Perhaps Uncle Toby hoped to have his bread buttered on both sides, as they say, for it was six years off and should my sister change her mind, he could keep the gift and perhaps get another such from another man. But this is all fancy and supposition.

From fifteen to twenty-one is a dreary long time, to be sure. Offers were made, some of them most advantageous, but my sister was adamant in refusing every other man as long as her sweetheart continued to court her. I sometimes hoped one of the disappointed suitors would turn a tender eye on me, but none ever did. They could not excuse the smallness of my dowry or the plainness of my features. I was not so very plain, neither, except when I was standing next to her, but that was most of the time.

My sister was married in the February of 1639. Apart from Toby we had an Uncle Jeremiah, an Aunt Susan and an Aunt Elizabeth, all on Father's side, all of whom declined to attend or help in any way since they said my sister's wilfulness had put Father in his grave. It made a shabby, shameful business of the wedding, but my sister said she did not care: she was as lawfully wed as any of them. Our only visitors were her bridegroom's brother and a sister-in-law who turned out to be respectable people, civil to my sister and gentle towards me. They treated us better than our own kin had done and I was sorry to see them go.

My sister's husband now ruled our household. I will own that at first I disliked him, partly because it seemed insolence, even after six years, to step so easily into Father's shoes, and partly because I was jealous. Though a tyrant, my sister had always been one of the pillars of my young life, more often than not my sole companion. Now she was forever with him, doting and whispering, and for hours I wandered about the house alone.

Our new master was a handsome young man, big and strong in body but lazy, fond of the table, good-natured as long as his wishes were met. I say now that he was handsome but I could not see it then. I found his face too red, his breath too meaty. He tried to coax me into friendship and would pull me onto his knee. I would blush and wriggle away, leaving him laughing. Then my sister (who barely acknowledged me at other times) would be angry at both of us, and he would call her his jealous little wild-cat, and kiss and embrace her until they made it up.

He was not one for bickering. If the food was not well sauced he would shout and swear – eating was a great thing to him – but give him a good table and a good cellar and he was always in humour. I had expected him, as a fortune-hunter, to gather up my sister's goods – all her coin, jewels, and bills – in a sack and run off with them, yet he was still with us, seemingly content to carry out his side of the bargain. He behaved kindly to me, unlike my sister, who showed only too clearly that she found me an encumbrance.

A year after the wedding I was persuaded my father had been mistaken about him; two years after that I spoke as trustingly with my brother-in-law as I had once talked with Father himself.

I was now nearly nineteen, but still babyish and shy, with no notion of putting myself forward. Most of the time I stayed at home, practising my music and embroidering in wool. I would have liked to go into the kitchen and talk to the cook, but that was forbidden, and we made few visits to local families. When I did meet with young men, their manners repelled me. They were often loud and boisterous and I preferred the easy-going company of my brother-in-law. Had my mother lived she would have taken thought for me, plotting likely matches among her acquaintance, but my sister was too wrapped up in her own concerns to bother about getting me a husband.

Now, however, my sister decided it was time to bring me to market. My brother-in-law said, 'Certainly,' but took no trouble over it, and this angered her.

'She's not pretty,' she said. 'All she has is freshness, and it's fading already.'

She said this as we were finishing up our dinner. It was a cruel and wicked speech but I did not notice that then. I thought only that I was ugly. My lip quivered and I bit it to keep it under control.

My brother-in-law whistled as if to say she was too harsh.

'I wish to help her,' my sister cried. 'You should do as much.'

'As much as what? Have you settled on a man?'

She had not, and he knew it. She turned the question on me. 'Miss Mouse? Have you someone in mind? Or shall I hawk you round the market cross in a basket, like stinking fish?'

I could not bear it. I went to my room, where I cried a good half-hour.

The best excuse I can make for my sister is that she was then with child. She had already lost a boy, stillborn, and the *dragging pains in her back were coming on again. She spent much of each day lying down with her feet higher than her head, drinking concoctions to strengthen the womb. (They did her no good: that child was also lost, like the one before it.)*

And at this very time, when a woman most craves peace and protection, my sister had another cause for fear.

I am not sure when I first realised that my brother-in-law no longer loved his wife. Ah! you will say, your father was right, he was a fortune-hunter, but (if you will forgive me, Sir) you are mistaken. We heard tales of these men, coming down from London to the country places, dazzling silly wenches, flinging their dowries about in a fine show and then running away from the ruin they had made. Nothing in our house smacked of that. Leaving aside his eating and drinking, my brother-in-law was not extravagant. He cared nothing for finery, horses, gaming; you could even call him close-fisted. It was as I have said, he did not love my sister and that was all. I mean it was ALL, the coupling without which nothing else holds; but I would have taken my Bible oath he loved her when they were first wed. You are thinking, perhaps, that a Bible oath can mean little to a woman like me. It was a heavy matter to the girl I was then – and I would have sworn.

Since my brother-in-law would go a long way to avoid a quarrel, and would always make one up if he could, I perceived the falling off in his feelings before my sister did. She was so sure of him, it took a thousand little things before she understood. I watched to see what she would do. She said nothing to him, but paid out double to the rest of us, the servants and me; I was treated worse than they were, on account of being a useless mouth. To me she was a demon, but never in her husband's presence; he only ever saw her impatient.

One day I spied on her from the window. She was standing in the orchard below, her hand on her belly and a look of sadness on her face. I pitied her then. Her first confinement (that

*was the boy) had brought forth a dead eight-months' child –
a horrible sight, and the midwife had let her see it. What is
more, it tore her body in coming out and her maid whispered
to me that the flesh had not knitted afterwards. She was
always tired and fretful after that. Now she was again pale
and misshapen, fearing that there would be nothing at the
end of all her suffering but a bedful of blood.*

*My pity endured until she came into the house and met
with me on the stairs. She at once turned on me and began
lashing me with her tongue, and I will not conceal that I
hated her.*

*Though I have not written of it so far, all this time the war
was raging round us. I say 'round us' because it had never
penetrated into our village; we had not yet found ourselves in
the path of either army. The biggest landlord in our part of
the world, Sir Ashley Sellis . . .*

This name caught at my memory. My aunt lived not far from
one Sir Gilbert Sellis, a gentleman with extensive holdings in
land, whom I took to be the son of this Sir Ashley. So Joan had
been raised near Tetton Green, as indeed her way of speaking
suggested. I mused upon the possibility of finding her people
and prevailing upon them to take back both Joan and Tamar,
unless, of course, they had also been beggared by the war.

*. . . had taken out no commission and raised no troops. He
was known as a lukewarm sort of man, not caring whether
the country was ruled by King or Parliament and asking only
to be left in peace. Since I never saw him in the flesh, I always
picture him as looking like my brother-in-law; their souls
were cut from the same cloth.*

*Though safe in our house and with land of our own, we
felt ripples from the war. There was the loss of trade. The
price of corn rose. My sister complained that the packman*

*was not come and there was no salt to be had in the market,
my brother-in-law that we had not as good a cellar as for-
merly. We heard from the pulpit each week of the hideous
crimes of the rebel soldiers, whom our Vicar never failed to
compare to the rebel angels, and we gave thanks that they
were not yet come in our way. We had reason to be thankful,
since our neighbour . . .*

'Jonathan! Jon!'

I jumped, scrambled the letter back into the package and
shoved it into a bag, out of sight.

'Yes, Mother?'

She opened the chamber door. 'What are you doing in here?
Your father wants you in the orchard.'

❧

He was piling up apples into a barrow. To me, still bound up in
Joan's tale, it seemed that none of my surroundings was quite
solid and real: not Father, not the trees, not even myself.

'You said you'd come directly you'd been to Simon Dunne's,'
he said, contenting himself with this mild rebuke though I had
kept him waiting half an hour.

I apologised.

'And is he better?'

'Ah –' I had to remind myself. 'Yes. Simon says he'll be ready.'

In the excitement over Joan's letter I had forgotten my reason for visiting Dunne in the first place: Bully had strained a
fetlock but was now coming on well.

'Your mother and I think of buying a horse.'

I started. 'Won't that be very dear, Father?'

'We've saved enough. We're not as young as we used to be;
it'd be a help to us.'

'Then that's the best reason,' I said. 'For myself, I'm happy to go on hiring Bully; but if you purchase a beast I'll put my cider money towards it.'

'Oh, that's too much,' said Father.

'Not enough,' I said firmly.

There was a pause before he said, 'Jon.'

'Yes?'

'If we're to buy a horse, there are other things to balance out. To settle.' Father turned away from me to pick up some windfalls and I saw he was about to broach a 'difficulty'.

'Yes?' I repeated as he straightened to dump them in the barrow.

'This business with the girl at your aunt's.' Seeing my expression, he held up his hands. 'We won't talk of it – only, the thing is, Jon – I'm old but I do understand these things, you're a man like other men –'

I waited.

'Your mother wonders if you've thought any more about Ann Huxtable.'

'No,' I said, not helping him. I made no pretence now of moving apples but stood arms folded.

'She's an excellent young woman.'

I made a face.

'Aye, young men set great store by beauty,' my father said gently, 'but virtue wears better. Ann's a good girl, strong and cheerful, and she'll have a farm of her own.'

'My mother was beautiful when you married her – at least, so you always say.'

'It was her goodness I loved.' My father looked abashed, and I thought he had probably not liked her any worse for being a beauty.

'I *couldn't* have Ann Huxtable,' I said. 'Find me a woman I can take to, that's all I ask.'

'But you, son. Is there nobody you like?'

'Nobody,' I said. 'If I were you I'd buy the horse.'

At supper it was my mother's turn. Forced to admit defeat in the matter of Ann Huxtable, she sought at least to move things forward and she wanted my blessing on the search.

'It is not good that a man should be alone,' she quoted against me.

'Or unhappily wed,' I retorted. 'A man can marry in his fifties; there's no hurry.'

'But children, Jon! Your support in old age.'

'They can come later. Father didn't marry this young.'

'He had to earn his living first.'

'My wish was to be married earlier,' Father agreed. 'Most young men are eager for a wife.' He was studying me, as was Mother, and I realised I was under suspicion.

'I haven't a mistress,' I said. 'That's what you think, isn't it?'

Both of them immediately denied this and Mother returned to the attack.

'If you don't like the village girls we can look elsewhere. What about Poll Parfitt?'

'*Poll?*'

'You often spoke of her last year,' she insisted, as I silently vowed never again to mention a woman's name in Mother's hearing. 'Parfitt would be glad to make the match, I know.'

'You've talked with him!'

My mother smiled and winked. I could not remember when I had felt so angry with her.

Father said, 'We both thought you liked Poll.'

'Not to marry.' I stared down at my plate, marvelling at how fast we had sunk to this stupidity. I blamed it on the lack of children in the Dymond family: my parents evidently feared my dawdling might cause us to die out altogether.

'If you think of anyone else,' I said, getting up from the table, 'pray have the goodness to ask me before you hawk me through the village like stinking fish.'

My mother cried, 'We've never done that!' and I realised I was quoting from Joan's letter.

'No. I'm sorry, Mother. But please don't talk to Parfitt, it won't come to anything.'

'Will you help me this afternoon?' Father asked, seeing me about to leave. He seemed anxious to soothe me, but I was in no mood to be soothed.

'I feel a bit queasy,' I said. 'I'll lie down first, if I may.'

They could have nothing to say to that, and they let me go.

I lay on my bed riffling the papers until I got to the place where I had left off:

> . . . *We had reason to be thankful, since our neighbour told us his cousin, who lived over the other side of Brimming, had been away from home when the New Model passed through. The cousin was known to be loyal to His Majesty, and he returned with his wife and children to find their house occupied, soldiers throwing furniture on the fire and eating up every last grain of the stores. Our neighbour said the wife's hair turned grey overnight. That was nothing, as I later found out: that was but quartering.*
>
> *Have patience, Sir, you will understand me in time. I think perhaps you understand me a little already. I would give much to be able to see you now, reading my words. But perhaps, being a witch, I can consult my familiars – tell me, is there not a spider busy somewhere in the room?*

Despite myself, I glanced up at a nearby web but it appeared to be empty.

This ink you brought me must be the Elixir of Youth: I can even jest with you, like a young woman, though there is little to laugh at here. In truth, Sir, it has cost me a deal of trouble – a great deal, I would say – to write so much, yet it is nothing compared with face to face. Face to face, I could not have uttered a word.

My sister's second child was born dead and the mother came down with a fever. Though the doctor was with her constantly, after two days there was no change except that she grew weaker.

We all believed my sister was being called before God. The servants crept about; her husband paced up and down, schooling himself to take a loving farewell of her. He could not grieve as a husband should, yet he wished her to die at peace, assured of his constancy. I saw nothing wrong in that; I loved her no better. My one wish was, that after her death he might turn his eyes on me.

There, I have written it. Pray do not stop reading, Sir. Consider that every crime set down here has been paid for many times over.

At the time I had no foreknowledge of what was to come. In mind and understanding I was still very young, if that may stand as some excuse. As long as I could remember, my sister had been cruel to me, and now she was good as dead; had she been the kindest sister ever born, I could do no more for her. Love might have held me back, but I felt none (in this I was far less shamefaced than her husband) and the most sacred duty was nothing against my feelings for him. We went together into my chamber. Afterwards he put his head on my bosom and cried. I was glad that he could do that at last, but he was not crying for her. He said he had ruined me, and I swore I would never give him away. And he promised that after her death he would make me his wife.

I laid down the letter, strangely moved. The shrivelled creature in the cave had once been a lonely young woman on
whose breast a man had sobbed out his heart. Until I pictured
them lying there – the man crying, her arms around him –
nothing in Joan's history had touched me. I now began to
guess how Tamar had come into the world and I read on:

Such things never happen once.

*We gave ourselves up to sin, and God visited on us an ingen-
ious punishment formed out of a blessing. Had we been what
we ought, the blessing would have been pure and unmixed: my
sister came out of her fever and was pronounced cured.*

*We were now in a pitiable condition. By indulging our
lusts we had increased them, so that we could not keep away
from one another, and each day my sister grew stronger. As
soon as the doctor would permit, she left her bed and sat
about the house, taking in with her hawk's eyes everything
that passed. How he bore it I know not; for myself, I was in
terror twenty times a day. My sufferings did not end when the
sun went down, for now she bedded with him again while I
lay lonely every night. The more I strove to conceal my feelings, the more I revealed. If he and I were in a room together,
my flesh seemed to dissolve away with longing; I could not
help looking at him, even though she might be sitting there,
watching us both.*

*'What shall we do, what shall we do?' I would ask if, by
some blessed chance, we found ourselves alone. He would
shake his head, as if to say he did not know. I thought he
could not be as frightened of her as I was: he was a man, and
God has given man dominion over woman. But then my sister had the marriage vows on her side, and a devilish temper.
She said nothing, but I knew her: it was not her way to put
questions unless she already knew the answers, and she was
biding her time.*

Nor was this the end of our sorrows, for while we were thus
perplexed the quartermaster of the King's troops came seeking
billets for his men. My brother-in-law bought the man off
with his wife's money, as I believe he once bought off Uncle
Toby. Few could have driven such a bargain. As far as I know,
he bribed twice in his life and to great effect on both occasions
– he had a feeling for what to offer and when. What he pur-
chased was a signed document to the effect that nobody
should be billeted with us. This was indeed a comfort – I
think none of us could have borne soldiers in the house, we
must all have run mad – but he had paid the quartermaster
an ungodly sum to secure it. Thus lust led in no time to
deceit, and shame, and bribery, and waste, and with all this
we still could not escape the soldiers entirely. A number of
them were to be lodged in the Guild Hall, and any goods that
could be removed were taken out in anticipation. Here I end
my tale for the time being, Sir, since my stiff old fingers can
write no more. In time you shall read the rest.

I had halted before she did, when I saw the words *Guild
Hall.* The only one for miles around Tetton was in Tetton
Green itself, which was by far the largest and most prosperous
village. It seemed that Joan did not come 'from near there' but
from the place itself, and certainly she spoke like its inhabitants – which would explain why, after the theft of the ring, she
and Tamar had not been whipped on their way. They were
Tetton Green's very own filth. Every human society throws off
such, just as every human body voids its urine, faeces, sweat
and so on.

But this made no sense at all considered alongside the rest.
Here was a young woman steeped in sin, certainly, but of
respectable birth and breeding, a woman who could read and
write, who could play music, whose sister had been rich
enough to attract a handsome (if corrupt) husband and main-

tain him in comfort. Her people kept servants; they employed a doctor instead of making do with the wise woman.

Do not mistake me. I was not such a fool as not to know that sin – yes, even a man lying with his wife's sister – infects the most solid citizens along with beggars and thieves. Were not those hypocrites, the Parliamentarians, riddled through and through with the first and most devilish of all sins, Pride? And where Pride is, you may be sure other sins will follow. But – and this was my difficulty – families finding such sin in their midst punish severely, as is right, but also under cover, to protect their other children. Else, blasted by shame and scandal, how would these more innocent ones find husbands and wives?

Papists are said to banish their soiled daughters to convents. Our Protestant gentry send them away, if there be a lying-in to get over, and then bring them back as from a cousinly visit. Or, if matters are not so far advanced, they shut them up in the house like bitches on heat, and then marry them off as fast as may be.

All this I knew, but I had yet to hear of an established, respected family in which the erring woman had been launched on a life of beggary. Perhaps, in the heat of the moment, her half-sister would gladly have scratched out her eyes and thrown her on the street, but – living in a wood! Catching birds with a string! And then the whining for money, and the rest. Joan's kin must surely be dead; how else could they face down the spectacle of their own flesh and blood mired in such disgrace?

Unless the entire history were lies. I had allowed myself to be moved by this woman's words, when by her own admission she and her daughter were thieves and worse than thieves. Pity is one thing; but in weighing a man's opinions, we should weigh along with the words the character of the speaker. A writer is always an unknown quantity, never more so than when the writer is a woman. It is a deceitful sex.

Still, I would have given much to find out these people of whom Joan had written. My mother was busy seeking a bride for my consideration; a fine thing, if through ignorance I married into that tribe of outcasts, and we found ourselves kissing-cousins to Tamar and Joan!

I now had to turn my mind away from all this, in order to finish off my work at home and elsewhere. I could go no further with Joan's letter, nor with Robin and my nightmares, until I could get back to Tetton Green, and *that* I could not do until my aunt's late crop was ready to be pressed in January. Until I had reason to return there, my aunt, I was sure, would not afford me board and lodging.

All this time, I was dogged by the cart dream. It never changed in form, its events unravelling in the same dreary order each night, and I was now able to get through it without the sweating terror it had first occasioned. From constant repetition I had at last reached that stage of dreaming in which the dreamer is aware that the dream will end. Even as the pale figure stretched his arm towards me and I whipped the horse forward, I knew that I should wake up and find myself at home. This, I suspect, is why my mother no longer came into my room to ask why I was making such a noise: familiarity had taken off much of the fear.

But not all of it. I still dreaded long drives during misty weather; I had a suspicion that if I kept away too long, Robin would break from my dreams and find another way to come after me.

❧

It was now nearly Christmas and my parents' plans to marry me off , or purchase a horse, or both, were abandoned so that my mother and Alice could get beforehand with the festive eating and drinking. During this season our plain-living household considered it a sign of right thinking, a rebuff to the sour, spiteful Puritan ways, to celebrate with traditional plenty, with goose and pork and the well-loved cakes and puddings that filled the kitchen with tantalising perfumes. All day I heard my mother shouting directions as she ran to rescue a burning pastry case or a curdling sauce and even Alice, calm and experienced as she was, had a tight-lipped way with her. Nor was my father idle during this time, though without doubt the women had the worst of it.

As a boy I was envious of friends whose houses, at Christmas, were filled with kin. Not that I was an especially loving child, or addicted to company; no, what I coveted was the great variety of dishes on a table where so many sat down together. My aunt's Christmas would of course be full of pomp and splendour; I wondered if she would dine alone during the entire Twelve Days, and what Rose would find to serve her. I even toyed with the notion of asking my parents to invite her to our home, supposedly in a spirit of goodwill but in reality so that I could accompany her home afterwards – 'I cannot let you travel with just a servant, Aunt' – and so arrive early at Tetton Green. Since, however, her presence would have ruined the feast for all of us, I soon gave up this fancy. Nor do I think my father would have permitted it.

9

Concerning That Broad Highway, The Road to Hell

Sir, we are suspected for the blankets you brought us, also the paper & pens. Of your goodness pray bear witness these were your gift. Tamar has been taken up by the constable.

J

That was all. I crumpled the thing and put it in my pocket, Dunne observing me closely.

'Who brought this, Simon?'

'One of the village lads. What is it, then?'

'Oh, nothing.' I frowned to warn him off but he chose not to be warned.

'Don't say "nothing", not to your old friend Simon.'

'It isn't my business to tell.'

'Course it is, your name's on it.' He added importantly, 'Mine, too.'

I was tempted to smile at this. His name was the only thing Simon could read; whoever brought the letter must have told him who it was meant for.

He said, 'I could get into trouble.'

I had been about to bid him a good day but those words fixed me. I turned the letter over: the seal was broken now, of course, and I had not checked it before reading. I held it under Simon's nose.

'Did you open this?'

I regretted the words at once but it was too late to call them back. Simon flushed a dark red.

'I've the right, if I'm to be mixed up with your . . .' He could not find a word, or perhaps held back the one that came to him. 'I'm a plain man. I don't like dishonest dealings.'

What *I* didn't like was his manner; I would have told him so, but in the nick of time I remembered I would need the horse and must therefore humble myself. 'Forgive me, Simon. I never asked this person to write to you.'

'Then tell her to stop. If she was up to any good, she'd send to your father's house.'

'What makes you think it's a woman?'

He gave an infuriating smirk.

'This letter concerns some blankets I gave to a beggar,' I said. 'She writes to say she stands accused of stealing them.'

'Beggars writing letters,' he murmured, flushing again. 'D'you take me for a fool?'

Really, the sooner my parents bought a horse of their own, the better.

'No fool, Simon. She's a gentlewoman, ruined by the wars. I'll tell her not to write to you again.'

Simon snorted.

'But I'll need Bully,' I finished hopefully. 'Can I come for him in an hour?'

''Tisn't convenient just now, it'll cost a penny extra. Mind you tell her, though. Next one I get goes in the fire.'

And off he trotted, mightily pleased with himself, his virtue and his bargain.

Having got through this awkward brush with Simon I must now think how to reconcile my parents to my journey, for I was sure they would not like my leaving home at Christmas and certainly not for such a reason. Rack my brains as I might, however, I could find no lie that would serve, and so was forced to fall back on the truth, or something like it.

Simon had called on me just after breakfast, a period of the day when my father was often in a good mood. I therefore

went to him without further loss of time, and found him looking over his accounts. I both liked and disliked the room where
he carried out this task, which is to say I relished the quiet of it,
and the ancient paper-leather smell of the books, and the fen-
nel, blooming outside the window, which brightened its panes
in summer. What I disliked was the air of neglected duty
which for me pervaded its walls like a creeping damp. My
father had not found me a willing pupil and I still considered
book-keeping a tedious business; I inclined to the view that
only the man who wastes his money need track it so patiently.

Not so my father, who loved figures and ciphers and greeted
me, as I entered, with a smile of happiness.

'What do you think, Jon? We needn't wait to buy the horse!'

'I'm glad to hear that,' I replied, and indeed after my talk
with Simon Dunne I was become as keen as Father himself.
'Didn't you say as much last night?'

'Yes; but I find we can afford it even if you marry. Your
mother's managed, I've managed –'

'Now, Father,' I said, 'beware Pride.'

My father said, laughing, 'I hope I do. So, Jon, what did you
want?'

'I have to go away. I've been sent for – friends in distress.'

His laughter stopped at once. 'It's that girl! Isn't it?'

'I've done no wrong, Father. But I performed an act of charity which has turned sour.'

'Turned sour? How –'

'I'm not in trouble. Before I came here last time, before the
girl was dismissed,' (here I bent the truth a little) 'I took pity on
her and on her mother and I made them some gifts.'

'That was wrong of you. I said so at the time.'

'Not the log, Father. Nothing to do with Aunt Harriet. And
not what you may imagine, not rings, trinkets, nothing of that
sort. I gave them blankets to keep off the cold, out of my own
money, I mean. And then the old woman begged pen and

paper –' I faltered here, recalling that I had taken those from End House, so it was not quite true that they had nothing to do with Aunt Harriet; but then I had left money in payment.

'I asked you to be honest with me, Jon.' Oh, the sadness of my father's face! 'Why did you never tell me of this?'

'I feared you would misinterpret.'

Up until now I had remained standing. Father silently waved his arm towards a chair, inviting me to sit by him.

'Very well,' he said as I did so. 'How could this act of charity, as you call it, turn sour?'

'They stand accused of stealing the goods I gave them. The daughter is taken before the constable and her mother writes pleading with me to go and bear witness.'

My father's eyes seemed to have gone inward. At last he said slowly, 'We've had many a vagabond here in Spadboro, yet I never knew you give one a blanket. Your charity was tainted, and so God does not prosper it.'

For an instant I was reminded of Joan's 'ingenious punishment' formed of a blessing. However, this was something quite otherwise. I had done good; it was another man's suspicion and cruelty that had caused the harm.

'A constable has torn the blankets from two paupers,' I said. 'Is that God's justice?'

'How did the woman write to you? I saw no letter here.'

I cringed. 'Through Simon Dunne.'

'Why to him?' asked my father at once.

'Not on my instructions! Her daughter and I spoke of Simon, and of my hiring the horse. I suppose she feared to write here, and remembered Simon's name.'

My father said no more but held out his hand. I watched him read, his face exchanging one perplexity for another. I thought he must at least see that nothing in it cast me as the girl's lover; it seemed he did grasp that, for when he next spoke it was more gently.

'This agrees, up to a point, with what you say. But consider, child, how could a beggar write even such a short letter as this? She's bought it of a forger, and his payment is the pen and paper; this is but a ruse, and as soon as you get there she'll want something else. You're too honest to deal with such people.'

I blushed at his undeserved faith in me. 'She can write, Father.'

Father pounced. 'You've seen her do it?'

I hung my head as it came home to me that I had not; I did not even know Joan's surname. But then, her secrecy might argue that her kin were not dead after all. Perhaps they could be found and prevailed upon; perhaps, after all, it was not too late. I strove not to betray my excitement.

'No beggar wrote this,' my father repeated, looking sadly at me. 'They'll wind you in. There'll be more to do for them, and more and more.'

At least he hadn't forbidden me to go. I took a deep breath.

'I'm not such a fool as you think, Father. I'll be away two days. As a Christian I can do no less.'

'Your mother won't like it,' said Father, and I knew he had given way. I took his hand and kissed it, and started away in tears – not for Tamar or Joan, but for his goodness.

&

The lock-up resembled an animal pen with a roof to it. It was intended to cool off drunkards overnight; the constable informed me that Tamar had been there, on bread and water, for three days. Unlocking the door, he waved his hand as if to say I might enter but for himself he preferred the air outside.

It was dark within, with a reek of urine and the peculiar chill that comes off stone in winter. When my eyes cleared I perceived Tamar slumped on the earthen floor, her back propped against the wall. She was wearing her old satin gown, her feet drawn up under it in a hopeless attempt to keep warm, her head sunk on her breast. She paid no heed as I entered, taking me, I suppose, for the constable.

'Tamar.'

She looked up like one stupefied.

'Sir?'

This one little word brought on a fit of coughing. The lock-up was colder than the cave, and she had no blankets and no one to huddle against. I shuddered at the sight of her bare arms and neck.

'How can you live?' I exclaimed.

Tamar smiled bitterly and began to cough again. When she had caught her breath she said in a voice like a creaking hinge, 'If you brought a coat they'd take it off me.'

I cursed myself for not having brought one anyway. Squatting down next to her, I said, 'I've given evidence. You can leave.'

She did not move.

'Come on.' I rose and held out my hand to her. 'Tamar, you can go. Get up.'

She grasped my hand and tried to pull herself upright but fell back grimacing.

'What is it?'

'My feet, Sir – I can't feel them to stand on.'

'Try again. You don't want to stay here, do you?'

At this she stood, though with much wincing and with tears in her eyes. From the doorway, the constable looked on unmoved. I said, 'This is a barbarous way to treat a prisoner – freezing her to death!'

His lips twisted into an insolent smile. 'She knows how to earn a blanket, *Sir.*'

'The blankets,' I said, remembering, 'are my property. Fetch them here.'

He was unwilling to do so. He was obliged, however, to give

them up, so they were brought, wet and dirty like everything in that place, and we took them with us.

With help Tamar was able to step up into the cart and seat herself next to me. I put one of the blankets round her shoulders and arranged the other over her feet. I could well believe she was unable to feel them; they were so cold to my touch, and so discoloured, that I wondered how they would ever return to warm, flexible flesh. Her hands were little better, purplish and covered with bloody scratches.

The wretchedness of the lock-up, the brutality of the constable and the pitiable condition in which I had discovered her persuaded me against taking Tamar straight back to the cave as I had originally intended. Shivering in the bitter air (which made me wonder anew: how could she bear it?) I clicked to Bully and drove him out onto the road.

It was some time before Tamar understood what was happening. When she did her eyes grew wide.

'Where are we going, Master Jonathan?'

'Away from Tetton Green. We're going to get you some clothes.'

My father had said the women would draw me in and there would be more and more to do for them. You were wrong, I answered him in my heart, she asks for nothing.

'Away – yes,' she murmured.

In a nearby village where I pressed cider for the cottagers, there was a dealer in worn clothes, and it was for her house we were headed. Tamar travelled mostly in silence. From time to time tears slid down her face. She wiped them away listlessly, making ugly smears on her skin.

When we reached the place she was too weary to climb down off the cart, so the clothes-seller came out into the road to judge her size.

'There's nothing to her, she's like a drink of water,' the

woman said, eyeing me. I understood her: respectably clad and well fed, I cut a strange figure with my scrawny, bedraggled companion.

'She's been ill and unable to eat,' said I.

'Or comb her hair, by the look of it.' That was all the comment she allowed herself before taking me into the little shop at the front of the house, where she began to lift down women's garments from shelves and racks.

'I want warm things. Everything as warm as possible.'

''Tis cruel weather.' She pulled out a pair of stays. 'Will she be wanting these?'

I had been thinking more of shawls and cloaks, but I nodded. The woman's faint answering smile seemed a mask. I wondered what she made of me: a charitable person clothing the destitute, a young blood on a mad freak? I had brought all my cider money with me and I paid for a shift, stays, a dress, a cloak, a pair of gloves, some heeled shoes (perhaps too fine for Tamar, but very good quality) a shawl and woollen stockings. When I saw my five years' savings in my hand I understood that I had never intended to go straight back to the wood; when I had set out, I had brought my money for precisely this purpose.

I came out with the clothes in a bundle. Tamar did not look at it.

'How are you now?' I asked, throwing it onto the cart beside her.

'Cold.'

It was dusk when I drove into the yard of the Blue Ball, lifted down the bundle and told the ostler to feed and water Bully. I led Tamar, staggering with weariness, into the inn where the landlady weighed us with the mistrustful eye of experience.

'She's been hurt,' I said. 'Do you have a chamber where she can change her garments?'

The landlady folded her arms. 'I don't know, as yet. How'd she get into that state?'

'Set on by ruffians,' I said, astonished at my own artfulness. 'I found her lying in a ditch.'

'Found her, Sir?' She was growing more and more perplexed. 'Then you're nothing to her, it seems?'

'You mistake, I was looking for her. We –'

'My ring,' croaked Tamar in her broken voice. 'My gold ring.' The corners of her lips drew down, her mouth became a square hole and she began to wail. It was impossible to doubt this grief, which heaved and choked its way out of her until my own throat hurt at the sound of it.

The landlady now appeared to relent a little in sympathy to a wife who had lost her wedding ring. I was sure the ring in question was Robin's, taken by my aunt, and Tamar howling for the warmth and food it could have purchased, but I hastened to press our advantage, saying indignantly, 'I wish I had them here. I'd soon teach them to knock a woman on the head and rob her.'

'It's a scandal,' the landlady said.

'*Two days* I've been searching – it's a miracle she's still alive –' ''Tis, Sir.'

'Then have you a room and hot water?' I urged.

'We have; but who's to pay?' the woman asked. 'Are you her husband?'

I hesitated. What should she be – cousin, sister?

'Husband,' Tamar replied in her hoarse whisper.

'Never mind your ring, my love,' said I. 'You shall have another.'

We were given mulled cider to drink while the chamber was being prepared. Tamar could hardly wait for the cider-shoe to heat up; when it was ready she drank greedily, pushing so close to the inn fire that her skirt, scorching from the embers, released a foul dungeon smell into the room. The men clustered round the hearth made noises of disgust. They would have driven her off, but could not do the same to me, being all too old, so that in the end they, not us, were forced to move away.

'Why did you say that?' I hissed when nobody could overhear. 'I can't stay with you.'

She had been quietly crying, on and off, ever since I took her from the lock-up. Now the tears started again.

'It isn't decent, Tamar.'

She mumbled something in her hoarse, choked voice. Through the sobs I at last made out, 'Frightened.'

'Frightened? *You?*'

She nodded.

'But I've rescued you, what can you be frightened of?'

She wiped her nose on her hand. 'Dying – on my own. I thought I would. I never felt so bad before.'

'Not now, though?'

'Yes, I feel bad now. I do.'

Her head dropped forward; fresh tears fell into the folds of her evil-smelling dress. I put my head in my hands. If my father should ever hear of this night's work . . . !

With luck he would not. I straightened and prodded the bundle with my foot.

'You'll feel better with these on.'

'God bless you, Master Jon.'

'That's all the thanks I require,' I said grimly, remembering the constable's jibe about earning a blanket. 'And I'm your husband now. Call me Jon.'

The landlady came over to us.

'The chamber's ready, Sir.'

I showed her my purse. 'Is there a woman who can go up with my wife – help her?'

'There's Sarah.'

'Be so kind as to send her here.'

Sarah arrived. She was only a little thing, fourteen or so, with a creamy freckled skin and reddish hair not unlike Tamar's own.

'Now Sarah, my wife's been attacked and left lying in the dirt and cold. You see her condition?'

The maid nodded, her young face full of pity.

'She's very weak, and sickly; she needs warm water and towels, to cleanse herself. You must help her undress, and wash, and put her into a well-warmed bed. And take food up to her room.'

Sarah nodded. 'And you, Sir, will you be eating with –'

'No. She must sleep and get back her strength. Pray lay out these clothes for her.'

Sarah picked up the bundle and stood doubtfully studying Tamar. 'And the dress she has on, Sir?' she said at last.

'Use it for rags, burn it, whatever you please.'

She nodded. In truth the cream-coloured dress was not so far gone as rags; for all I know, a skilful laundress might have done much with it, but I was determined Tamar should never wear it again.

I ordered salt pork and ate with relish; there was nothing else to pass the time. After a while the maid came down for Tamar's food. I could not catch the landlady's whispered questions. I did, however, hear the words 'lousy' and 'piss-sodden' from the maid, at which point I could not help glancing round. Both mistress and maid were staring at me as if they no longer put any faith in the robbers of my invention. If they did not take me for a prankster who had brought a street whore under their roof, they must think me a monstrously cruel husband.

I felt myself insulted. Here was I, performing an act of Christian charity while everything conspired to present me as an unchristian, even devilish, man. Yet I no longer cared as much as I might have done, say, a week earlier. For one thing, I was muzzy with cold and travelling and pork and cider; for another (I see now) my sense of right and wrong had coarsened. Mistress and maid whispering together vexed me, to be sure, but I felt I could live without their good opinion; I had begun to discount the judgement of ordinary honest folk.

I watched the maid take a covered dish upstairs to my 'wife'. The puzzle now exercising my mind was how I should conduct myself once inside the chamber. Tamar's exhaustion was plain; given food and warmth she must surely fall asleep, and then I could go quietly into the room and dispose myself to sleep also. 'My heart is pure, and God sees the heart,' said I to myself. That was my comfort. If the constable, landlady, maid, old-clothes-seller and even my mother and father had gathered round in a circle and cried out against me, it would be my comfort still.

As soon as I entered, I heard a faint snoring from the bed. The bed curtains were drawn, so that I was able to keep my candle lit without waking her. Even so, I slipped on something and almost fell, so that it was with difficulty that I suppressed a cry. Steadying myself, I saw that the object I had trodden on was a dish, wiped clean of gravy: the relics of Tamar's supper. I wondered why she had left it thus on the boards, when she could have used a table or a window sill, and concluded it was the habit of the cave.

To my relief, the chamber smelt no worse than any other innkeeper's room: in shedding her whore's livery, Tamar had also parted company with its fearful stench.

I cast about for a place to sleep and settled on a scarred old chair. There I spent the first half of the night, my coat thrown over me, until I woke with a relentless cramp which drove me out of it and forced me to stretch myself out next to the bed.

Somewhere a bell chimed seven, and then a quarter past. I must have slept again, for next thing it was chiming eight and birds were bickering in the eaves. I opened my eyes upon a strange scene. Instead of my bed, I seemed to be lying on a hard floor; the window was in the wrong place and the shutters had grown great cracks in the night, with grey light leaking through. I must be in some village, pressing; but I had no memory of coming there the night before. Only when I turned my head and saw the bed curtains drawn did I recall where I was, and with whom.

Supposing that after a night's rest Tamar would be eager to return to Tetton Green, I sat up and listened for her snore. Her breathing being much quicker and lighter, I thought she was coming out of sleep, so I spoke softly through the curtain, saying I was about to rise and would leave her the room to dress in.

Downstairs, I breakfasted on a bowl of hot, salt broth. The landlord, now serving in his wife's stead, asked if I had passed a pleasant night. I answered that I had (that was polite enough, I think, when every bone in my body ached) and intended to make a start as soon as my wife was dressed. I asked him to keep a portion of the same broth for her as it seemed a good, hearty food to take in preparation for a journey.

After that I listened to the church chime the half-hour, the three-quarters and the hour, yet Tamar did not appear.

I went back up to the chamber and knocked. There was no reply. On entering I found the bed curtains still drawn and the snoring begun again.

'Tamar, get up,' I urged her from the other side of the curtain. 'Tamar, you must wake.'

There was no response. At last I moved aside a curtain and peeped in.

She was lying on her back, one hand flung up beside her cheek. The marks of injury and harsh weather were plainly visible, but I had never seen her look so clean – I would say innocent, but *that* of course she was not – or so young. Her dreams seemed happy ones, her pointed features no longer sly but childish. It came to me that had she been well fed and comfortably lodged all her life, she might now look very different. Perhaps Mother Nature had intended for Tamar soft and delicate features, a fine complexion and a woman's gentle form instead of her tough, bony, servant's shape.

To chase away the sadness occasioned by this thought, I tried again – 'Tamar! Tamar, wake up, wake' – and pulled at her arm, but to no avail. She stopped snoring, but was otherwise like a dead woman. I was obliged to go downstairs again and fidget about.

The landlord asked me did I want my horse. I told him I had changed plans, since it seemed my wife must have a long sleep to recover from yesterday's ordeal. He hastened to assure me that it was common: 'Folk that've had a mishap are always tired next day. It's the fright.'

I thought he probably said this to gain another night's fee, but since I was in any case unable to rouse Tamar, there was nothing to be done and I thanked him for his advice.

At noon I went up to her again. I was becoming worried: what of my parents, what of Joan? By dint of calling and prodding I induced her to open her eyes, but she at once rolled over, shutting me out of her sight. All this while she was wearing a good linen shift that I had paid for.

'Aren't you ever getting up?' I demanded.

She murmured, 'I'm hungry.'

'You can't have any more food brought up here. If you want to eat, you must get dressed.'

She burrowed deeper into the pillow and I realised I had blundered. In Tamar two cravings were in conflict, food and sleep. Her being in a soft, warm bed gave the advantage to sleep; hunger could only prevail if I brought her a steaming, savoury dish that tickled her nostrils. I duly went downstairs and asked for chops and eggs, then carried them up to her myself.

This time she turned toward me, her eyes widening in greed.

'Sit up, then,' I said, reasoning that once the food was in digestion and the spirits coursing about her body, she would remain awake. I had drawn the bed curtain and she looked beyond me, all over the room, her gaze wandering to the walls and ceiling and window and then back to her plate of chops.

'I've never been in such a bed,' she said, heaving herself up from the bedclothes. 'Or an inn, neither. You're not eating with me, Master Jon?'

I shook my head. Some remembrance flickered in my mind – nakedness – but Tamar's breasts were concealed by the shift.

'I've never had *anything*,' she said, strangely I thought; I could not tell whether she was talking to me or herself.

'You can have this very good breakfast,' I said, and moved the dish to her lap.

Tamar fell on the chops: every last scrap of meat, fat and gristle went down her throat. She continued sucking the bones for some time afterwards, laying them at last on the plate with an expression of regret, before turning her attention to the eggs.

She did not know how to eat these. I watched her pick at them with her fingers, trying (I thought) to be mannerly.

'It's an egg,' I said after a while. 'Haven't you had eggs before?'

She was indignant. 'The wood's full of 'em. But this thing's *flat*.'

'Why, how do you eat yours?'

'Out of the shell.' She prodded a yolk, sending it spurting over the bedcover.

'Mind,' I said. 'Sop it up, like this,' and I dabbed at the mess with a bit of bread.

'Oh – it's gone on my neck!' she cried, vexed; whether at spoiling her unaccustomed cleanliness, or at losing a scrap of food, I could not tell. 'I can't see. If you don't mind, Sir, could you do it for me – please?'

Conscious of a certain charm in the situation, one that I chose not to examine too closely, I wiped the soft traces from her throat.

'If you ate that bread, now,' said Tamar.

'What?'

'You'd be my sweetheart.'

'What nonsense! Is that what your mother tells the village girls?'

She only smiled.

'Let us try the truth of it,' I said, and bit into the bread.

In that trivial outward action I passed inwardly from one life to another. Tamar, divining the change in me almost before I knew of it myself, said, 'The spell's working, Master Jon. The spirits are rising.'

Her hand caressed me so deftly that I had not time to think before I was roused. *Roused*: it is a curious word, as if something asleep in the flesh wakes and rages. One is roused to anger and roused to lust; I was somewhere between the two. I was ready to curse her insolence, yet said nothing. I could have pulled away and left the room, yet I did not move.

With her other hand Tamar pushed the plate to the far side of the bed and turned to me with a wanton smile. 'Come in with me, Husband? It's your rightful place.'

'Take your shift off,' I said, my voice abrupt as the Flesh itself. I remember that I disliked hearing it; I suppose that Conscience, though hamstrung, was still feebly grappling with Appetite.

'I will; but only if you come and keep me warm.' She knelt

up in the bed and pulled off the shift, revealing herself much as I had seen her in my dream: thin, with the same creamy skin and the tufts of reddish hair. Her poor scarred feet were hidden beneath the covers. I touched her between the legs and felt something soft, slippery and yielding there. Tamar wriggled so that my fingers slid into her honey pot and my stomach turned over.

'Ah! Look at you,' she whispered, busy at my breeches. Freed from the cloth, my prick leaped obediently into her hand. There was not time to do more than climb onto the bed and lie on her. Tamar locked her legs round me and arched her back. Her body opened to me like a flower, and Conscience quit the field.

10

After Fire, Ashes

I squirm with shame at the memory of that day – at my lust, certainly, but more at my stupidity. When a man arrives at an inn with a half-naked woman and presents her as his wife; when her clothing comes out of his pocket; when they share a room and eat together, and all this is paid for by him – would you not say that the end is predestined? And yet (great virtuous booby that I then was) I did not think so!

Nor can I plead virginity (though I *was* virgin), since I had not the excuse of the innocence that often accompanies it. I knew that my parents, seeing me lodged with Tamar, would have been horrified, and I understood why. I knew how nature is performed, and how, as the fumes of lust rise and heat the brain, Reason is smoked out and Madness takes her place. Knowing all this, I still imagined myself virtuous and clear-headed enough to stay by Tamar's bedside, untempted. It was sheer pride, and it has been scourged right out of me since then.

I stayed with her the next night, fancying myself her lord and master when in truth I was her pupil and servant. All that I pass over in mortification. One other thing is worthy of mention: I was worn out by lust, yet Tamar told me that all through the hours of sleep I kept waking, crying out in fear of Uncle Robin. 'He came after you, and beat you,' she said. I had no recollection of it, and I never afterwards dreamed of him striking me. But then, my conscience that night was more than usually troubled.

It may appear that in recounting this affair, I blacken Tamar in order to clear myself. Let me repeat that I acted in full knowledge, compelled by stupidity and lust; I cannot be cleared of this, nor do I want to be. I am resolved that everything of importance should be told – not to injure her, for I hold her no worse than myself, but to shine a light into dark corners. Some pure-minded folk in this world, who had rather leave such nooks unlit, may cry out in disgust: what good to go peering into them? I can only answer as follows: a man who walks in darkness, from dislike of the cobwebs, may catch a spider in his mouth unawares.

&

The day after my nightmares I took Tamar back to Tetton Green. Knowing what I knew, I found it curious to see her sitting on the cart, transformed from shivering drab to warmly clad country girl. Nobody so much as glanced at us, now: our outward show was respectable and corrupt, like the times. Even Tamar's voice was healed, and as we passed through the villages she would call out to food-sellers by the road, asking how much for their wares, and then purchasing (with my money) pies and pastries for her mother. I did not like her manners, nor her making so free with my purse. I may add here that she had ordered up dishes of food again and again as we lay in the inn, until I thought she would never leave off eating; I let her go on, all the while observing privately that it is as they say – put a beggar on horseback and he rides to Hell.

As we approached Tetton, I remembered that I had said nothing to Father of staying away two nights or more. When I had set off, it had been without thought of where I should sleep; there had been no call for thinking, since at that time of year, with the roads empty, I was sure of a bedchamber wherever I went. I must now season him a dish of lies to account for my two days at the inn: not the truth, but something very like it. Thus I went on from lust and waste to fear and deceit, all in the grand old way.

We reached Tetton Green just as dusk began to fall. Lights were burning in Aunt Harriet's house and I whipped Bully quickly past; since I was not paying a visit, I could hardly put the horse and cart into her yard. Nor could I drive them into the wood or leave them, in the growing darkness, in the lane. I therefore dropped off Tamar and her bundle (all that she was not wearing on her back, plus the blankets) at one end of the path leading to the cave. I then drove the cart to the inn in Tetton Green, to be called for later, before following Tamar on foot.

She was at home, if I may call it that, before I could overtake her. As I approached the cave I heard her muttering impatiently, 'He's *with* me, I tell you.'

'I've been fretted with worry,' came the older woman's whine.

'Here are the blankets, look. Move your legs.'

'What about the constable?'

'Never mind him. Move your legs.'

I entered in time to see Tamar bend and tuck the blankets round her mother's prostrate form. There was something new: a lamp in a corner of the wall.

'Has your mother been lying without any covering?' I exclaimed.

'She's two dresses on,' said Tamar.

'But in this weather – at her age –'

'We've slept in less.' She pulled out a pasty from under her cloak and handed it to Joan. 'It's not the lock-up.'

I did not feel very friendly towards her just then, nor was I inclined to be easy on myself. Between us we had forgotten that Joan, too, must lie alone without even those wretched blankets. This was bad enough in me, but how much worse in her daughter! At the same time, I was forced to agree that the cave was snugger than Tamar's cell had been, perhaps from Joan's constant presence, or the heat thrown off by the lamp, or merely some softening in the weather. While pondering this I became aware of a rustling sound and realised the old woman was lying on straw.

'Where did you get that?'

'Near here,' said Tamar. 'You thought I'd left her naked, eh?'

I guessed that 'near here' meant my aunt's stable, and wondered how she had got into it. Did she perhaps have some arrangement with Paulie? She might; he was not likely to receive comfort from any other woman. At that point, a hank of straw floated down from the cave ceiling, causing both women to exclaim in amusement.

'Hob's a naughty thief,' said Joan. 'Stealing our bed to line his own. See, he's made himself a little house up there.'

She pointed. I was just able to make out the creature's head turning from side to side, and the gleam of its cruel beak.

'Don't you want to know about the lamp?' Tamar asked.

I was curt. 'No.'

She flashed me a warning look before turning to her mother. 'I got out this morning. Master Jon fetched clothes for me.'

Joan eyed the plain, serviceable garments. 'Beautiful,' she said. Was she mocking Tamar? I could not tell. 'You're a true friend, Sir. Oh, and I've something for *you*. Tamar, fetch my paper.'

'The rest of your history?' I asked.

'Not all, not yet.'

'It's a memorable one, indeed,' I said, trying to remember: she had been seduced by her sister's husband, and then the sister had recovered, and war was come to the village. It was a history, certainly; yet just at that moment my own life interested me more.

'*Robbing!*'

I jumped at the dry little voice of the raven. The women, on the contrary, seemed to have lost all power of motion and stared at me, unblinking.

At last Joan said, 'He babbles night and day, now, what with the lamp.'

'*Don't come here.*'

'He wants you to go,' said Tamar maliciously. She thrust a single folded sheet of paper into my hand.

'Is this all?'

'You'll find it plenty,' said Joan.

'Has Tamar read it?'

'She can't read.'

'And wouldn't want to,' said her daughter, 'it's for fools' – and she laughed in my face.

I perceived that this scorn of reading was put on in order to mock me, and I was not a little angry. Only yesterday she had pulled me down to her in bed at the inn. True, she had shown the way throughout, as befitted a woman of her kind; but even so, I had anticipated having to comfort her, if not to swear love, then at least to extend protection. I had always under-stood that when a man lay with a woman outside marriage there was a price to pay, that sooner or later the woman was overcome with shame and then began the sighing and the pleading (which in the man's case went before the act rather than afterwards) and that even harlots feigned these regrets, going through the motions while clamouring for gifts. Yet Tamar gave no indication of throwing herself on my mercy; rather, she seemed possessed by growing scorn for me. Even now she was saying, 'I've more pasties here, Mother, and a piece of boiled beef,' laying them down on Joan's blankets without a word of thanks to me, who had purchased these good things.

'I'll be gone,' I said.

Joan peered up at me. 'You'll not stay a little, Sir?'

'I must hasten home. It's almost – time.' I had nearly said 'Christmas', but that would be cruelty. 'And', (I wanted to be thanked) 'the tale ends well, since you have your blankets.'

'You're all goodness,' Tamar said shortly. Then she bent down as if I were not there and began to make room for herself next to Joan. The last I saw of them was the two women huddling together, Tamar pulling the blankets over both.

Fortunately there was a moon that night, or I should have been lost. I came out of the wood and hurried towards the inn, brought away the cart and started at once for home. In my coat was Joan's paper; from time to time, hearing it rustle as my body swayed to the motion of the cart, I had a strong impulse to fling it away. What were these women to me? I had been drawn in, as Father had foretold, and had performed an act of stupid lust – but here I stopped; I could not call it an act, precisely; it had resembled a state or condition lasting an entire day. So much the worse. When it passed, like the fit of madness it was, nothing remained but deceit, extravagance and shame.

The extravagance had very real consequences, one of them being the loss of the best part of my earnings. I had nothing in hand for my father's accounts or (I realised with horror) for Simon Dunne. I should now break off from these beggarly leeches; I should shake the dust of their dwelling from off my feet, as the Bible says, wipe them out of my recollection and pray that when I came back to my aunt's house I would find them drifted away like the vagabonds they were.

In this fashion I berated myself as I was first starting out, miserably heated and distressed. When I say 'heated' I mean just that: in the physical turmoil brought on by my agitation I was obliged to leave my coat unbuttoned; my cheeks burned in the night air. As I drove on, however, my body cooled, and then my brains, and I at last began to think.

I had been enticed into lewdness. Very well: many young men did the same or worse. I could at least say for myself that it was over. Nor had my conduct been always and entirely shameful. Nobody hearing of my exploits at the inn would now believe it, but I had honestly pitied both women – had wished to stand their champion and friend. No maiden had been debauched, no innocent ensnared – unless, I realised with fresh humiliation, that innocent was myself. No wife could now bestow on me the delighted surprise that should bless the bride-bed. The first time could come only once, and I had thrown mine away upon Tamar. I fancied I saw my father look sadly at me and shake his head.

But Tamar – I had done nothing to offend her. Why, then, had she treated me with such contempt? Mist lying across the road like a veil, illuminated and thickened by the moon, seemed the very image of my perplexity. I pulled my coat more tightly about me and drove on, my head above the mist-layer as the cartwheels cut through it.

Solitude is the mother of thought. Without that drive back to Spadboro I might never have understood, at least in part, the events of the previous two days. Even now, I would scarcely offer my interpretation in a court of law; I will only say it accounted for much of what I had witnessed, and it ran thus. Tamar had acted out of neither love nor lust. She disliked being in my debt for so much as the clothes and the inn might come to, and had settled in the only coin she had. Having done so, she need thank no more. This, then, was the key to her insolence: she did not like my angling for gratitude, and would give no more, because it was demanding over and above the settled price; in effect I was demanding to be paid twice, in lewdness and in honest respect. Be he the King of England, a man cannot have both.

Yet why such marked contempt? As a rule, a man feels little respect for a woman whose virtue he has conquered, whereas a woman becomes attached to her conqueror – yet here was a notable exception. I was obliged to turn these notions inside out, as it were, and spy into them through Tamar's eyes. Thus examined, it appeared that she had my measure now: I was like the men who came to the cave. At the beginning, I had given without taking; this had pleased her, but also troubled her notions of the world and its workings. Since our adventure at the inn, I presented no such puzzle. I could be laid in the same box as all the other men, and was the more contemptible in that I had foolishly paid over more than was necessary. Tamar's trading was of the simplest kind: she gave pleasure in exchange for money or goods. Male protection, of the kind that obtains in the marriage contract or, in a lesser way, when a whore finds herself a bully, was not one of the goods she sought; she had never known it. Men and women were to her a perpetual market, in whose dealings she and I were now quits.

Here I recalled the gold ring she had clung to and still hoped to retrieve. Was that merely because of the comforts it would have purchased, or because it was freely given? To know, I would have to pry into the relations between her and my uncle. I was not sure I had the stomach for that, even if I could have done so to any purpose.

I was now crossing a damp place where the mist, which had dissolved as the cart came uphill, began to set round it again. My heart beat furiously when a woman with a white clout round her head loomed up close by me; I shouted at her, demanding what in the Devil's name she meant by wandering there so late at night. After that I whipped Bully on until we were high up on the dry ground near Spadboro. From there he knew the road, and how close we were to home, and consequently needed no whipping.

&

I refuse to dwell on the pleasures of the Twelve Days. Let it suffice that my mother and Alice had wrought marvels of baking and roasting; that my late return and the suspicion attaching to it – which my father chose not to broach, for fear of spoiling the holiday – nevertheless cast a shadow over our merriment; that on Christmas Day itself a man came to say his wife was in mortal agony with a breech-birth, so that Mother was obliged to leave the table and go to her aid, and came back a day later with tear-swollen eyes, having saved neither mother nor child. In short, that our festival, so lovingly prepared for, mostly came to nothing.

The patient disappointment of my parents touched me as deeply as if I were the tender father and they my little ones. This was the first time, I think, that I ever experienced that particular grief, which was doubled by knowing my own part in it.

I could not think of recent events without shame, and with Tamar and Joan to point the comparison I was more than ever struck by the honest and open respectability of the home in which God had placed me. More: I was ready to don sackcloth and ashes, and to become as prompt, obedient and humble a son as anyone could wish for, even to abide by their wishes in the matter of marriage (excepting only Ann Huxtable). I would give them no more pain. I would marry and bring forth children. All the labour of my breeding would then be crowned with success and my mother and father could rest content. So I thought, and I began immediately to put aside my own wishes and fit myself to theirs.

This was not altogether well judged. The fact (I may say it plainly, without vanity) was that I had always been a good son, leaving aside my reluctance to wed and my recent overlong stays at End House. The first effect of my resolve, therefore, was a show of fanatical virtue that (as my father later told me) rendered them both uneasy, suspecting as they did that only a severe singeing in the fires of wickedness could have brought it on.

I was not virtuous to the point of madness, however. I had settled in advance that I would permit myself a measure of deceit in everything relating to my stay at the inn. As yet my father had asked nothing about my time away from home. He was the last man to let such things go; I therefore kept my lies ready and polished up, for at some point I was sure to need them.

So I passed the holiday time, in waiting, and most uncomfortable it made me. On New Year's Eve we stood at the front door, wrapped up against the frost, and watched the burning bushes being taken over the fields. We had done this as long as I could remember, from the time when I had to be hoisted on Father's shoulders before I could see the lights. At last, far away but high and clear, came the cry of '*Auld Ciderrrrrr . . . !*' We went back to our blazing fire, smiling at one another, but somehow the thing had fallen flat. It was the same at Twelfth Night: a lad with toast and cider was hoisted into our oldest tree, the guns were fired off and everyone drank deeply before the Wassailers passed to the next orchard. It had been my joy to drink as deep as any and to bawl out each verse of the songs. As it was, I felt as if someone else, not me, were singing, and when the men trudged away under the trees and their farewells faded down the lane I felt a Puritan's relief that all was done with for another year. I wondered much at myself, and could only think that my secret wrongdoing had bled these honest, neighbourly customs of the pleasure they had once given me.

On the seventh of January (having scrupulously waited until the end of the feast) Father called on me to account for the time spent away from home. I told him that I had gone at once before the constable, given evidence, seen the girl released and set off home (thus despatching all that part of the business in a single sentence). Becoming ill on the journey, however, I had pulled in to the side of the road where, overpowered by weariness, I had fallen asleep at the reins. (Note that I did not say I fell from the cart: I had given due thought even to bruises.) I had a vague remembrance of shouting, and of a dark man bending over me, before waking in the house of some excellent Christian people, the very type of the Good Samaritan. It seemed that the dark man I remembered on the road was not of their persuasion, for they had found him in the act of picking my pocket. He had been seized on, however, and deprived of his spoils. My rescuers then looked after me until I was ready to continue my journey.

This farrago seemed to me impregnable until my father looked hard at me and asked, 'Why didn't you tell us before?'

I said it would have been a pity to frighten my mother and spoil the festival, particularly when the affair was past and no harm done.

'So you think, I daresay!' Father said. 'But young men exposed to viciousness may receive great harm without knowing it. In your place, son, I should shun that road.'

His face showed plainly that he guessed something close to the truth, and I felt I had disappointed him all over again.

⁂

I had yet to decide what to do with that other history, Joan's. I was at first disinclined to read it; I had turned my back on these tricksy people.

Had I been as honest, or as strong, as I believed myself, I would have thrown the paper away, or given it into my father's keeping so that one day I might return it to her unread. Instead, like the weak, divided creature I was, I put it under my mattress, too far in to be detected by Alice's busy hands. After that, it was the old story. A few days after Twelfth Night the itch started up: I grew curious and I must needs be reading. Excuses are never lacking in these cases. I told myself it was wrong, and cruel, to take away something that had given an old woman so much labour if I would not read it as promised, and thus talked myself by degrees into what I wanted to do.

My parents must not catch me at my studies, but I soon found a way: the orchards in Brimming had late cider-apples that I usually pressed about this time. I would take Joan's writing with me, reading it while I was there. I could easily burn it before I returned home, and then it would be as if the thing had never existed.

The day after that I was in Brimming. Their apples were not of the best, but my labours went smoothly enough. I was permitted to sleep in the barn of one of the wealthier inhabitants, one whose own press was in use but who would help out his neighbours if asked.

'You'll not sleep with it next to you,' the wife said, handing me a lantern.

I was grateful for the allowance and swore I would not. Faithful to this promise, when I retired to rest I hung the lantern on a nail and stood beside it in order to open Joan's letter. It was as I had thought, a single sheet folded over and sealed. Weariness, cold and the faint light made it hard to decipher her cramped writing, but I was determined. I wiped my tired eyes and read on.

You will remember, Sir, how I left off: I was in a wretched condition, infatuated with my brother-in-law, and the soldiers on their way to us. I come shortly to a most terrible part of my tale, and I warn you, you must have a strong stomach to read it, but first you must learn how we were discovered, for we were, as wickedness always comes out, or so they say.

My sister, as I told you, went on living with us day by day, watchful and patient as a spider. I cannot say how many times she netted us without our knowing it, and let us go again; but she hauled in her web at last, and was mistress of all.

Do you wonder at my hard-heartedness, Master Jon?
Surely you must. Yet I was full of remorse, and not only
through fear of my sister. Pray remember that our father, who
in our youth had guided and taught us, was a God-fearing
man. I knew full well that I had taken what was not mine,
and was a trespasser in my sister's bed. I had but one excuse,
a bad one, for beginning, namely that I had thought my sister
as good as dead, and I had another (a worse) for continuing,
which was that I could not leave off. My heart seemed pierced
by a cord, and the end of the cord in my brother-in-law's
hand, so that he could pull me along with him wherever he
chose. With all this, I was yet sorry for what I had done, and
often cried myself to sleep for very hopelessness, and came to
breakfast with eyes as sore as if they had been poxed, and still
my sister said nothing.

I have not cried for my sin these many years, and never
will again. My heart is like hers now, a stone.

In a few weeks my sister was restored to health. No sooner
could she walk about than she developed a trick of losing
handkerchiefs and gloves. She would send one servant to seek
through the house, another to search the outbuildings and a
third, the orchard, while she herself prowled about scattering
more trifles, that she might cry out upon their loss later. Thus
was I thrown into a constant terror, afraid not only to
exchange loving words or touches with him, but also to speak
of the most innocent matters, or even to be observed close by
where he was. I was brought near screaming at this but hid it,
telling myself the work was as disagreeable for her as for us,
and full as wearying, and that the servants must in time be
sent about their duties, and her gathering of intelligence
cease.

We had one sweet day when my sister was laid low with a
painful vomit. My brother-in-law at once played her at her
own game. He sent our manservant for the physician, for (he

said) nobody else could be trusted with such an important task, bidding him wait if Doctor Tanner was not there. At the same time he set my sister's maid to remain by her side, and ordered all the rest of them to their duties. Then he and I went to my chamber. It astonishes me that we ran the risk, but we were desperate and not a little mad. In any event, it was our last time together. The next day my sister, having questioned the servants, rose from her bed in a savage humour.

Things having reached this pass, the arrival of the King's troops was at first a blessed distraction. That is, it was to us; the poorer villagers obliged to provide billets were soon singing to another tune, but my brother-in-law had his paper signed by the quartermaster and none could gainsay it. And when I heard about their antics, such as smashing all the crockery in a widow's house and throwing her harp into the pond, I concluded that my brother-in-law had shown great foresight in this, if not in other matters.

Now, however, I had troubles of my own to be thinking of, since a few days after the arrival of the men I began to fear that I was with child. My woman's bleeding was not come and one morning I was sick in my chamber upon rising. As soon as I understood what this might be, I fainted dead away from terror. Luckily I was resting on my bed at the time, but I came to in such a trembling that going down to breakfast I stumbled and almost fell on the stairs.

My sister was sitting at table. I said I was sickly and could not eat; she took one look at me and her eyes seemed to blaze up. And: 'You must try this, you must have that,' says she, and she had the maid bring fried meat, and eggs in butter, and I could not touch a thing; though I tasted some broth I could not swallow it. My brother-in-law, who was ignorant of her meaning, said I was bilious and should not be forced, but my sister had the whip-hand now and she had blood-sausage brought, and grilled tripe, until my brother-in-law (still at a

144

loss) sat astonished at the tyranny and waste, and I broke down crying.

'Now,' she says, 'now we see your wickedness, you little whore!'

At this my brother-in-law leaped up. 'What?' said he, 'For shame, your own sister,' and she turned on him, screaming 'I see you defend her, will you own her bastard too?' and my brother-in-law dropped back into his chair as if his legs had failed him. Then we all fell silent, I snivelling like the fool I was and the husband and wife glaring hatred at each other, and I thought it was as though Satan had put his fist through the world and rent it.

From that time she was wild to be rid of me, Master Jon, and I will tell you what she did. But I must first tell you something else. You have perhaps wondered why, while unveiling offences, I should veil the offenders. The answer is, had I given you names at first, you would not have read the rest – and now you know that, you can surely guess my secret. This gentlewoman who behaved so inhumanly to her own flesh and blood – this weak man who could not hold off from his wife's sister – are no strangers to you. They are your near kin: your uncle, Robin Dymond, and his wife, Harriet.

I cried out and threw the paper to the ground. Guessed her secret? We were not accustomed to such foul and disgusting secrets in our family – and here I shook, actually shook, for it came to me that 'we' and 'family' no longer meant what they had. If this dreadful tale were the truth, Joan was my aunt's sister, and Tamar – God have mercy on us, had I only known it at the inn! – was my bastard cousin, my father's brother's child.

And then, how could this happen? How could one sister cast out the other under the eyes of – I was about to say, her hus-band, should I not rather say, her sister's seducer? – and the cast-off sister vanish from the sight of decent people while Robin Dymond continued in comfort and respect? She had lost her name and her honour, to be sure; she would never be able to marry – but were all her kin, and all her neighbours, so lacking in charity towards this lost lamb that none would help her to a crust of bread? She should have been brought before the minister, counselled, made to repent, punished and reclaimed, before she vanished down the broad road that leads to destruction.

What of my own father? This account, if true, made him Joan's brother-in-law. But then I pictured his kindly, honest face, and I knew he would never share in anything so wicked.

I snatched up the paper again and turned it over. There was no more writing. With trembling hands I thrust it into my shirt. That there *had* been a sister I knew from my aunt's own lips; Aunt Harriet had called her a fool. I could think no more, only that I must go home with all speed and talk with Father. I put out the lantern and lay down in the straw, waiting for the cart dream to come and crown my misery. Would I had never read that scrap of letter from my father's pocket, never gone to End House, never set eyes on the maid there, never gone into the wood and most especially not to the inn, because in doing so I had put my fist through the world, and rent it.

꒰ꃔ꒱

Thanks to my clever trick of reading Joan's letter while at Brimming, I found I could not go home just yet. I was a prisoner until the apples were pressed, and passed the next two days hopping from one foot to the other, eating without tasting, conversing without hearing, drinking without getting drunk. I even tried to dismantle the cheese before it was dry, causing an outcry among the people: 'We've not waited all year for you to squander our apples,' they said, so fiercely that I had to pretend I was mistaken and in short, to back down.

'You're looking sickly, Cider-Rat,' said one of the more peaceable men. 'You're wanting to get home, I reckon.'

I said that was it and set myself to wait their miserly pleasure. Only when the last few wretched drops had been squeezed out, and the cheese was ready to scatter over the fields, was I permitted to leave. The villagers were constrained in their farewells. I did not even return them; I was onto the cart and gone before the words died on their lips.

None So Deep as a Dymond

'Lord, Jon, what is it?' My father half rose from his beloved account books as I came stumbling into the room. 'Has your mother seen you, child? You're green.'

'I've heard something very bad, Father.'

'Bad? What?'

'About Aunt Harriet – Uncle Robin.'

The warmth faded from Father's face. He seated himself and indicated that I should do likewise.

'Now, son,' he said, pressing his fingers into a steeple, 'start at the beginning. First tell me who spoke to you.'

'He's of no consequence – a drunken fool from Brimming. It's *what* he said.'

'Yes?'

'That my Aunt Harriet had a sister –'

Father nodded, his eyes never leaving mine.

I stammered, 'And this sister was – was –' Why didn't he help me? Why didn't he take over, telling me it was true, or lies, instead of watching and waiting? 'Was ruined,' I finally brought out.

'Ruined?'

'By my uncle – Uncle Robin.' I brought out the words in a rush, expecting Father to cry out in rage at the insult to Robin's name.

'Did he say any more?'

'There was a child.'

Was it my fancy, or did his eyes flicker there, as if I had hit him a blow in the face?

'A child,' he repeated.

'A daughter.' I wondered should I tell him that this daughter was even now – no, God, no, that might lead to further revelations. I flinched from the idea of *those* as from the flames of Hell.

'And did your drunkard say anything else?'

I shook my head.

'Yes, surely. Surely he did.'

I took a deep shuddering breath. 'He said this sister and her child were cast out. Aunt Harriet – and Robin – left them to perish.'

'So my brother and his wife behaved with pitiless cruelty while your mother and I stood by and let them? Is that the story?'

'Yes.' I put out my hand to him, touching him on the arm. 'Don't mistake me, Father, I know *you'd* never be cruel, nor Mother. But my aunt had a sister. She said as much herself.'

'If you weren't told, you can be sure we had our reasons.'

I waited for more, but nothing came. At last I said, 'Then what this man said is right?'

He regarded me a moment, then said abruptly, 'Your aunt's half-sister was debauched.' The ground seemed sinking away beneath me as he went on, 'Harriet's father married twice. Don't think I ...' He paused, picking his words. 'Don't think I know it all. The younger creature, Joan, continued to live with Harriet after she and Robin were married. She was a strange girl: meek and downcast in appearance, but spiteful.'

I recalled Joan's mention of the kindly in-laws who had talked with her: my own mother and father. Trivial matters that had seemed tedious in the reading now loomed like Fate. 'How was she spiteful?' I asked faintly. 'What did she do?'

'Oh, not much, at first. But your aunt warned us of her nature, and in time we witnessed it for ourselves. The thing was, she envied Harriet – envied her sister's superiority, and also her being married. As I've told you, Robin was an exceedingly handsome fellow. Women pined for him.'

'Why would he marry Aunt Harriet, then? For property?'

A melancholy smile gleamed on Father's face. 'I won't say he hated the property, but he married for love. Harriet was an excellent match for him, you know: she was a beauty then, and, as far as a woman may be, a wit.'

I was willing to take that much on trust, but as Father himself had said, he did not know everything. Joan had written that Robin went to her as Harriet lay dying. A corpse is not beautiful or witty, and grief makes any comfort precious. By the time Harriet recovered it was too late; the lovers were infatuated with one another. None of this could be revealed without revealing who had told me of it, and that would lead on to the lewd act I had committed, so I held my tongue.

'Joan was nothing by the side of Harriet,' my father continued. 'You wouldn't look at her; such a mousy little thing!'

'Somebody must've looked at her, if she was debauched. If you please, Father, I should like to know what happened. Truth is best, after all.'

'Dear boy!' my father exclaimed. 'You don't know what it is, yet!'

'Then tell me. Let me judge.'

'Very well,' said Father, with an air of taking up the gauntlet. 'Joan was not cast out, as you put it. She left the protection of her home and went along with the soldiers.'

'Went along with them?'

'As a camp follower, a whore, a drab. You understand those words, I daresay.'

I stared at him. 'I understand.'

'But you don't believe me,' he said, almost triumphantly.

That something of the kind must be Joan's fate, once she left home, was only too plain; yet I had never pictured her embracing it of her own free will. 'She could've married one of them,' I suggested. 'Wives also follow –'

Father shook his head. 'She wasn't among the wives. She was one of the other sort, and she departed with the rest of that crew.'

'How do you know?'

'Because I went after her as soon as I heard from Harriet. I thought the girl might be reclaimed.' He shook his head. 'The men had broken camp so I hired a horse and overtook them. I spoke with officers, with the men, with the wives. Joan wasn't married, that was plain as day. She'd already parted company with the army, or didn't want to be found.'

'So you –'

'We never saw her again.'

There was a silence. I felt as if someone had gripped my head and swivelled it right around on my shoulders, like an owl's.

I said at last, 'I *cannot conceive* why a woman should degrade herself so horribly.'

'Who knows?' he replied. 'Perhaps the cravings of a diseased appetite, perhaps to bring disgrace on Harriet.'

'And did she have a child?'

He shrugged. 'As I said, we never saw her. She lived such a life . . . who can tell?'

⊗

I stayed at home after that. My excuse, a good one, was that having neglected our earlier crop, I would make it up to my parents by pressing our 'lates' before other people's. The truth was that I shrank, as if burnt, from contact with anyone outside our house. I needed time to reflect.

My father's revelations had shocked me, not least the fact that he had kept quiet until now. I understood his reasons, of course: since Father himself was blameless, why should he polish up and display such a shame attaching to his family? Then I recalled that it would be remembered only too well by some of the neighbours, regularly brought out and polished up by *them*; it was a measure of how well my parents were liked at Spadboro, or perhaps of the distance between there and Tetton Green, that my first inkling of all this had come from Joan. And yet I was a man, and had been for some years; surely Father might have told me before! And I remembered that when Rose, the cook at End House, told me of the saying, 'None so deep as a Dymond', I had laughed, and said they could not know my father.

I shall not conceal that from the very first, a feeling of selfish relief was mingled with that of shock. Whether Joan had run away with a single soldier or had been the common property of all, the outcome was the same: there was every chance that Tamar was some trooper's child, and consequently not blood kin to me.

Which brought me back to Joan. What – *what* – should I think of her? What a figure she cut, now I had spoken with Father! Yet I could not deny that in places her account chimed with his, or might be made to do so. While reading her words I had been convinced of their truthfulness, the more so because she took no pains to hide her hatred of Aunt Harriet or her unlawful passion for Robin – or, for that matter, her fear and dislike of the soldiers, though that might be a lie framed to cover up the truth of her dealings with them.

In one way she was only too easy to understand. Uncle Robin had no legitimate offspring; now he was dead, she wished to present Tamar, honestly or dishonestly, as his child. Had she heard somehow of Robin's illness and returned to Tetton Green, or was she already settled nearby? Whichever it was, dug in behind End House the mother and daughter were well placed to receive silly women and lustful men, to pick up village gossip and to spy, under guise of begging, on Aunt Harriet. It was just as the laundress departed, leaving my aunt desperate, that Tamar had fallen foul of the authorities. Was this by accident, I wondered, or by design? At any rate, my aunt had seized on this seemingly helpless creature and from that point onwards the enemy were within the gates. Here it came to me that Robin's illness might not have been chance, that Joan might indeed have powers I had failed to reckon with, but I soon rejected this notion since in that case she would surely have killed off Aunt Harriet many years ago.

She must have rejoiced when Tamar told her of my arrival. She had seen in me an innocent, had begun to shape her tale for Master Jonathan's ear, and had so far succeeded that I had felt pity for the outcasts and tried to sweeten their lot. But Aunt Harriet had not taken to me, which meant my powers were fatally limited. Had I been the most passionate advocate ever fee'd, it would be of no use.

I did not say so to his face, but my father's story also had its flaws. I never doubted that he had gone in pursuit, striving to snatch the wandering sheep from the jaws of the wolf. He would have done that, I knew, without a moment's delay. But it troubled me that so much of his account came from Aunt Harriet. Father had not been present at Joan's running-off. It might even be that the reason he failed to find her was that she had never been with the soldiers at all, in which case . . . what? Had Harriet swept her from the house with a broom? And meanwhile, what of Robin?

Had Joan been with child by him, or had she only thought as much? There was no proof either way, and there could be no further comparison of accounts, let alone judgement, until I could read more of hers. How I was to obtain more, after my quarrel with Simon Dunne, I did not know. I supposed I must return to Tetton Green, but I had a horror of seeing Tamar. Not for the first time, I was going round in a circle: until I learned what Joan had to say of her departure, I had no hope of knowing whether I had used my own cousin as a whore, yet while I remained in ignorance of this I could hardly bear to go back to Joan. I fancied she must be waiting for me. She would expect her tale to fetch me running, and if not for events at the inn I would be hurrying there even now.

My greatest perplexity came from my musings upon Tamar, and these I found impossible to leave off. Not so long ago I had thought to understand her: she had seemed a hard, blank thing, like the walls of the cave she inhabited. Now she was again become as shadowy as its deepest, darkest reaches. If she shared, as she surely must, in her mother's ambitions, pretendings, delusions – I knew not what to call them – what had she told Robin during the time she was nursing him? Had she received the ring as his daughter, or for some other reason which my mind shrank from contemplating?

I wondered, too, if after all these years my father would still wish to rescue Joan from her degradation. Chasing after her had been an act of charity bordering on foolhardiness, but it had at least the virtue of promptitude. He might have carried Joan home, soiled and unmarriageable but forcibly prevented from sinking any further. Now there was no knowing how deep she had sunk, and it was a very different matter to take on a woman hardened in degradation, with a daughter far advanced along the same road.

If I did reveal to him who lay in the woods behind End House, I should have to reveal all my dealings with them, and I could not think how to do it.

At last I resolved as follows. There was no need to tell my father as yet: Joan's tale had been so many years in the making, that the few days since I had read it were as nothing.

I therefore stayed at home, as I have said, and pressed the apples. Our principal late variety was the same as Aunt

Harriet's: the Redstreak, king of cider-apples. From it we got a drink so brilliant and fragrant that some folk preferred it to Rhenish. I had always held that our house must be specially blessed to have such fine cider in our hogsheads and I worked with a will to replenish them.

What does Solomon say? 'Comfort me with apples.' Everything about them is kind and comforting: the mild eating apple, the sharp or bitter fruit that crushes to a miraculous sweetness, the homely apples, like tried and trusted friends, that serve all purposes. Comforting too is the steady rhythm of milling, the scent of the murc, and the first tricklings of the must which Mother Nature, without need of hops or yeast, turns to the purest crystal. The drink's virtue lies in its noble simplicity, and I wished everything in life could be as clear as the task I was about.

But cider, too, goes amiss, and my thoughts turned another way: to apples that are naturally bad-fleshed and inferior, to must that grows slimy, or ropey, or sours to a vinegar only fit for sauces, to drink that men are obliged to doctor with honey in order to save anything at all. And I wondered if Joan was naturally bad-fleshed, or if living with Harriet had rotted her, and whether she could have been corrected and doctored with love, and if anything could sweeten Harriet and bring her back from vinegar, and whether Robin were really as weak and washy as I thought him; for that was not like our family.

&

The horse went before me with a strange jerking movement of the head, his mane floating on the air, and I realised it was lighter than any horse's mane ever seen, and this was because it was of spun gold. I was about to reach out and touch it when I perceived a swirling in the mist ahead, a darkness forming, as yet suspended but clotting and thickening even as I observed it.

I at once tried to pull the horse around, but the strength was gone from my arms. The beast drew steadily towards the place, forward and forward, the shape now elongating, becoming upright, a figure, a hat. The hat moved and (oh, horror) a pale glow broke upon the mist.

No, no, I must not see, I *would* not. I laid on the whip and put my other hand over my face, ready to drive blind rather than look; I breathed deeply and screamed so loud as to fill the air, deafening myself, and thus, blind, deaf and screaming, rattled past. At last my voice cracked and I could scream no more. I opened my eyes and looked behind.

Grey and level the road stretched away into the mist. There was nothing on it, no standing wraith, no crumpled figure.

He was vanished.

As I made to lay the whip aside, something touched my arm: the paper, clutched in a hand so white and wasted that I could see the bones in it. With dread, I raised my eyes to my companion. His skin had the gleam that one sees on rotting fish, and as for his face – looking into the pits of the eyes, I moaned with the terror of a child.

'Stay,' he said. 'Stay –'

My mother was in the room, shaking me. It was over.

So: the dream had played me a trick. I had learnt to tolerate it, but it did not wish to be tolerated. I feared it most devoutly now. I shuddered at the memory of the face, and the soft, insinuating voice of the dead.

Thus plagued, it could not be long before I was again planning to call at End House. My father and mother looked unhappy when I said as much.

'Next year, Jon, I think you might leave Aunt Harriet,' Mother said. 'She's not been kind to you.'

'Shouldn't I help my aunt?' I replied.

'She doesn't need your help. She thinks you're fawning.' This was unusual, for Mother. As a rule, there being so few Dymonds, she tended to cherish even the most distant and unpromising relatives, but she had evidently had enough of Aunt Harriet.

My father nodded his agreement. 'She never asked for you,' he reminded me. 'Carry through everything you promised, but don't go there next season.'

That would start in October, too far in the future for me to worry about now. I said I would be glad not to go, provided I could finish up my work this time. I made my usual arrangement with Simon Dunne (he held out for his extra penny), loaded up the cart and was on my way.

The weather was cold, but clear; had it been misty, I might have been tempted to stay at home. I passed through lanes whitened by frost where a thin snow had fallen, unnoticed, during the night. I thought of God creating the world, and of its beauty, which in His kindness and wisdom He fitted to the tastes and appetites of mankind. Even frost and ice, I thought, are fashioned in such a way that they please the eye and thus, to some degree, repay the sufferings of winter. But then my hands grew cold and clumsy and I remembered the women in the cave, and wondered what they were reduced to, and whether they had fire and food. Perhaps they spent most of their time sleeping to keep their strength in, as Joan had said.

Perhaps they had moved on.

My aunt was not at home when I arrived and Rose Barnes opened the door. She said my aunt was gone to meet with some of the villagers.

'Will she be long?'

'I wouldn't know, Sir,' Rose said, bringing me to a chair by the fire. 'Would you like some refreshment?'

Numb and hungry, I eagerly accepted and she fetched me some cold meat pie. With that, and the wine, and the warmth, I was soon asleep.

A door banged.

'Quite apart from that other business,' a man said. I blinked and started, finding myself in a strange room. Then I knew where I was: End House, sitting with my back to the door, and with a pain in my buttocks from staying too long in one position.

'You see the need,' said a voice I recognised as Aunt Harriet's.

'Indeed, Madam, I see it only too clearly, and as far as *that* goes, you may count me your faithful servant.'

'We are all God's servants.'

There followed a pause during which neither spoke. I wondered if they were praying. I waited a moment and then stood up from the chair.

'Good day to you –'

My aunt shrieked. The prayer-book she was holding flew into the air and narrowly missed the fire.

'– Aunt,' I finished, guessing at once what had happened and fearing I would be blamed for it.

'You *will* enter the house uninvited,' my aunt said sourly. This was her welcome to me. Still, I was forced to admire her powers of self-command: she was recovered already. I picked up the prayer-book, dusted off some ash and gave it back to her. I then bowed to the man, whom I now recognised as Dr Green, the parson Tamar had accused of having no charity in him.

'Rose let me in, Aunt. I'm sorry I took you by surprise.'

'What is it, then? A message from Mathew?'

'Why, no,' I said. 'The Redstreaks. You asked would I come back for them.'

She glanced towards Dr Green.

'We'll talk later,' said that gentleman, inclining his head. They strolled out again through the front door and I realised they had withdrawn here for some private business which I had interrupted. I heard my aunt say, in some agitation, 'Did we speak of . . . ?'

'Not a word,' said the pastor.

12

Lovers of the Gentleman

It was with foreboding that later that day I once more made my way to the cave. The going was easier now, the trees bare and brown except here and there where ivy shrouded one of them, strangling what was nobler than itself. The weather had changed and a rough wind was at my back, surging in wave after wave over the sobbing trees before sinking at last, only to rise again a moment later.

I edged down the slope and dropped into the ditch. The hurdle was still in place. This time I was more cautious than on a previous occasion: I stood at the entrance and called as loudly as I could, and was at last answered by something like the mewl of a cat, which when repeated proved to be, 'Within.'

Joan, trussed in the blankets and half buried in straw, lay bunched behind an angle in the rock. I flinched at the sound of her raw, tearing cough.

'Don't worry, it's only Master Jonathan.'

'Sir.' She could not summon breath for more. I had to wait for her to stop gasping before asking her, 'You're alone here? Where's Tamar?'

'Out.'

'Where?'

She shrugged so weakly it was more like watching her shoulders collapse. 'Ten of the morning – heard the bells.'

That meant Tamar had been away about five hours – *where* she was, I supposed I should never know. Joan's head drooped forward onto her chest as if she was fainting. Her lantern was unlit but I had brought one with me and I now proceeded, with difficulty, to light it.

'How are you living now? Does Tamar get food for you?'

At the word 'food' she flung up her chin and looked straight at me. The sunken skin around her eyes glistened in the beam thrown by the lantern: the rheum of old age, or the traces of weeping? There was plenty to weep about. The deathly cold of the cavern, even during these few minutes, had penetrated to my bones, imparting a chill numbness that made me think Joan could not be long for this world.

I took from my bag some wine and cordial, and a pie from our larder, all given me by Mother as comforts for the journey. Seeing the wine, Joan snatched feebly at it. I made her drink the cordial first and eat some of the pie.

'She finds for herself,' she said through a mouthful of food. Her voice was stronger already; the poor man's crust of bread works greater wonders than the glutton's banquet.

'But she shares with you?'

'Yes, Sir. She does.'

Observing that her teeth were unequal to the pastry, I stopped bothering her awhile. I noticed that she left nothing for Tamar: seemingly the bargain did not hold both ways, or perhaps she suspected the younger woman of keeping things back for herself. When she was almost finished I said, 'I've been with my father. Robin's brother, Mathew.'

'I remember Mr Mathew.'

'He remembers you.'

She stopped chewing at once, her eyes wide and frightened. 'You told him about me? He's coming – coming here?'

'No, no. We talked only of the past.' I was sure she would ask, *And what did Mathew say?* but she remained silent. I handed her the wine again and she took a long, choking pull at it.

'He says you left home when the army left,' I began.

Joan drank some more.

'That you left with the men.' She laid down the bottle and

161

stared at me. 'Come, Joan,' I said. 'Did you think I wouldn't ask him?'

'He says that?' she murmured.

'Yes, he does,' I said, stung. 'My father is the most truthful of men.'

She was taken by another attack of the cough, collapsing afterwards into the straw and moaning, 'I won't see another winter.' Her fingers as she wiped her mouth were a bundle of stained old bones.

I waited a moment, then repeated, 'You left with the men.'

'As soon that as anything else.'

'What, as soon as with Robin?'

'I couldn't. She made sure.'

I let her drink some more, then took the bottle from her. The church clock struck four; outside it would be growing dusk.

'Do you mean my aunt? Made sure of what?'

'That I couldn't return.'

'From where?'

She shifted in the straw. 'It's bad in this cold. Can't write.'

'You needn't, now. You can tell me.' I offered her the wine again, but she looked at me with suspicion and did not take it. I repeated, 'You can tell me.'

She shook her head.

'Come, have some more wine.'

'Yes, and then you'll say it was the drink talking,' she muttered.

'What? What was that?'

She mumbled something more, some insolence, under her breath, but I let it go. One so powerless, so broken down by poverty and vice, must naturally envy me my happy life, and she could do me no harm. I was content, for the moment, to swallow down any insult provided she would talk about her time with the army.

'Don't be angry,' I wheedled. 'I've come to hear the truth from your lips. You want that, don't you?'

I could see it in her, protest as she might. She wished to torment me a little beforehand, that was all. I went on patiently, 'You wrote of how you were with child, and your sister found out.'

'No.'

'Yes – you wrote that.'

'We all *thought* I was with child. But it wasn't long enough to know.'

'You weren't, then?'

'I wasn't sure.'

This wrong-footed me. I had thought to hear crude fudgings that I might set aside, should I wish to. I tried again.

'But you'd been sweethearts for some weeks. What about the sickness?'

'I had a bilious constitution.'

'But in time, you know,' I hinted.

'Oh, Sir!' Her eyes were more than glistening now; a tear was visible on her dirty, wrinkled cheek. I was almost ashamed of myself, and would have stopped but for the fact that she herself had commenced this tale and drawn me into it. Then she seemed to come to a decision; she wiped her face and cleared her throat. 'We had soldiers lodged at the Guild Hall,' she began.

Here we were at last. I said, 'You wrote of them.'

'Women stayed within doors if they could, out of their way. It was a hideous time for me, cooped up in End House.'

'You had Robin's protection, didn't you?'

'Aye; but she had the upper hand.'

'I never thought Uncle Robin was afraid of his wife.'

Joan said with a flash of malice, '*You're* afraid of her. Tamar –' The cough here racked her, forcing her to break off. When it had died down she went on, 'Outside the house there were the soldiers, inside Harriet and Robin at each other's throats. He was too soft; he should've given her a good beating.'

'Perhaps conscience restrained him,' I put in. 'He was in the wrong, after all.'

'Yes; but *why* was he?'

I stared at her, thunderstruck. 'Because he was a faithless husband.'

'That's not my meaning. He and I should've married, so why did we only meet when he was already bound to *her*? I'll tell you something, Master Jon.' She craned towards me so that I was aware of her foul breath. 'The Devil is the Prince of this world. Open your eyes: the proof is all around you. She's one of His own, and that's why she prospers.'

I felt a revulsion towards Joan, poor and helpless as she was. I said, 'It's God who prospers people.'

'God! He's not bothered with the likes of me. The Dark Gentleman gathers in all the rotten fruits God lets slip and He makes something of them.'

'He'll make cinders in Hell of you. Why d'you call him a gentleman?' I waved my hand to indicate the cave. 'Is this how he keeps his promises?'

'You don't know what I asked, and whether I kept my side of the bargain.' I didn't like the way she looked at me as she said this. 'I'm not afraid of Hell, Sir.'

'Then you should be – you should be. But go back to the soldiers.'

'From Him to them, eh?' she said as if I had made an excellent joke. 'Well, one evening I was hiding in my chamber and I heard them shouting. I don't know what'd happened; something stirred them up. A band of them came out onto the green and down by the stream, all fighting drunk. They had muskets stored in the Hall, everybody knew that, and I heard shutters snapping to, double-quick, in case something should come crashing through the windows. I closed my shutters like the rest, but I peeped from behind them. A few of the soldiers started banging on drums, bawling that they were for King and Country and that fighting men must be fed. I can hear them now.'

'What did they do, attack?'

She shook her head. 'They wanted mutton. I don't know who had sheep to spare – we were short of everything – but mutton they got. I tell you, Sir, the Devil's the Prince of this World. They roasted it, too, right there in the Hall. They opened the windows, else they would all have choked, but the ceiling was black with fat and soot. I'm told the place stank months after.'

That was war, I thought: men sinking into beasts, ruining a fine building for the sake of a few mouthfuls of leathery, unhung mutton.

'And then, Sir, they sent word that they must have a woman to dress their meat.'

I whistled. 'I hope the villagers sent a man cook.'

'You're very green, Sir,' she said shortly. 'So was I, at first. The men of the village came out into the lane, to talk without their wives. I heard them settling on who they should send.'

'Not their own womenfolk, I'll be bound.'

'Oh, no! There was a woman, married but she'd been whipped behind the cart more than once; it was when I heard her name that I understood. Their plan was for the soldiers to go to her one at a time, her husband to stand guard. They – the soldiers – were gone back into the Hall by then, and someone went to them to make the offer, but it wouldn't do. They wanted the woman sent in to them, and nobody with her. The villagers dursn't do that, though, not even to a whore, if her man didn't consent.'

I was feeling sick.

'So they were at a loss. Then the soldiers started firing through the Hall windows. They said it was to let the smoke out, but really it was to frighten folk.'

I recalled the altered casements I had seen during my walks.

'And then my door opened –'

'No,' I said. 'No –'

'My sister came into my room, and she dragged me downstairs and out into the street and handed me over.'

'No.'

'She handed me over.'

We sat looking at one another in the faint light of the lantern. I was speechless; I had thought nothing could shock me more than her revelations about herself and Robin, and now I saw I had but dipped a toe in the river. Joan went on, 'I'd no one to defend me, no husband, no brother. She told them I was able to dress any amount of flesh – those were her very words. I hear them in my dreams, Sir.'

Surely this was itself a dream – this cave, this cracked voice out of the darkness, this terrible tale that went on and on. I tried to marshal my scattered wits.

'What of Robin? He wouldn't stand by and permit that, surely?'

'I screamed for him but he never came. I thought they were in it together, to palm off his child on the soldiers – I cursed him to Hell. A long time after, I found it out: how he went to the stable, thinking the horses might be frightened, and when he came back I was gone, and he never knew. He found out too late, you see.'

I trembled. If I rose now and left the wood, in a very few minutes I would be standing before the Hall doors, perhaps as Harriet had stood and watched them close behind her sister. At that thought I could scarcely breathe. My mouth filled with spit and I felt I must get out of the cave. Outside, in the icy air, I leaned against a tree and vomited. There was nothing in my belly, only a little sour froth, but the heaving took some time to subside. Afterwards I felt emptied out, not only my guts but everything inside me, as if I were hollow.

How pitilessly had the soldiers dealt with the girl brought to them! And yet there were things in this story that shocked me more. Let me be clear. I was not, am not, disposed to forgive or gloss over the men's wrongdoing. I say only that what turned me inside out like a glove was the notion that one sister should deliver up another – no matter what the provocation. I wept a little, not even sure I was weeping for Joan. Perhaps it was for the world.

After a while I went back into the cave and sat down.

Joan said drily, 'You don't like my tale, Master Jon.'

We were silent a minute or two, until my thoughts began running on the consequences of what had happened. I asked her, 'When were you released? Did someone from the village rescue you?'

'Who?'

'Anybody! How could people go up and down past the Guild Hall, knowing you were inside – seeing in through the windows?'

She said quietly, 'There's a room without windows. They took me there.'

'God have mercy.'

'They shoved me outdoors the next morning. I could've crawled on the ground, I was so broken, but I came out walking upright. There's pride in everything – in everything. So I held myself up, and as I was descending the steps I saw our neighbour, who had always been kind to me, coming along the lane. I can't tell you how my heart yearned to her; I greeted her and as soon as she saw me, she turned away. I went through the village, and it was the same everywhere – nobody would even look at me, much less embrace me or even take my hand. The wives twitched their clothes away as if I were poisoned.'

'But all that happened against your will,' said I.

'Folk had to believe otherwise, Sir, or what were they to think of their own good selves?'

'And you didn't go to Robin?'

'I didn't know, then, how my sister had tricked him; I thought he'd betrayed me. I went to the field where the camp-followers were, and I passed with them out of the village.'

'And now you're back –' Something here occurred to me, something that, caught up in the story, I had not thought of until now. 'Joan. Has anyone from Tetton recognised you?'

She shrugged. 'One time, Master Jon, I was driven away from End House and you were at the window. What did you see? Nobody. A beggar with her head bound up.'

'Perhaps; but I didn't know you then. What about the women who visit here?'

'The lovers of the Gentleman? They –'

'Lovers of – Good God!' I exclaimed.

'*They* don't call themselves that, Sir; not at first. They don't wish to be seen, you understand; we sit in the dark.' She gave a wheezing laugh. 'Besides, the young don't see the old. If you live to my age, you'll find that out.'

'Very well,' I said. 'But stop this talk of the Gentleman, d'you hear me? You'll bring down trouble on yourself.' Joan looked sulky at this. 'I have to get my bread, Sir.'

How pitiful and disgusting that a woman gently raised should be forced to 'get her bread' thus. There must be monies and goods remaining that had once been Joan's and I had a good idea who had profited from them. I said, 'When will you reveal yourself to Harriet?'

'*Never!*' Joan squealed.

I was not expecting this reply. I said, 'But you must, if you wish to get back what's yours. How else can it be done?'

'You'll tell her nothing about us, Sir! She'd hunt us out.'

'Then how can your money and property be restored? That *is* what you've come back for, is it not?'

'Tamar spoke with Robin about it.'

I sighed and said gently, 'Yes. But your best chance now is for Harriet to acknowledge you.'

'She never will.' Joan's face looked so stubborn and vengeful as she said this that she could have been one of the Rebel Angels; and indeed, she was fighting under the colours of the Gentleman. 'She's had her chance; they've all had their chance. I was the salvation of this village!'

'Shh – blasphemy –'

'Denied, handed over to the soldiers, like your Christ!' Her eyes glittered. 'The people here devoured me, body and blood . . . and they've denied me for nigh on thirty years.'

⚜

Walking back to Aunt Harriet's house in the thickening dusk, I moved like a sleepwalker, twice tripping on dead wood but luckily catching hold of a branch each time. I was, however, very far from asleep. The inside of my head buzzed like a hive, while somehow my feet placed themselves one in front of the other and carried me along the path.

Once I had an aunt by marriage, cold, wealthy and commanding. Now another had been foisted on me – sister to the first, shadow to her substance – and along with her, a daughter, whore to half the village and also to a certain young fool from Spadboro. Our family was certainly more numerous, these days, and to my mind, at least, it was grown a perplexing torment. My father could be said to share the same blood as Robin, which meant Robin's blood ran in my veins; and if Robin were Tamar's father, then Tamar and I . . .

But there I was caught again. Either she *was* Robin's, and my bastard cousin, or the child of a soldier and nothing to the Dymonds. From Joan's account, there seemed no way of telling; my doubts could never be resolved. Damn Joan, couldn't she tell by looking at the girl? Women are said to know these things by nature. A great deal hung upon it, for if Tamar were indeed Robin's child, and Harriet's niece (or should that be stepdaughter?) then provision must be made for her. Modest provision, I mean, not to be compared with the rights of a legitimate heir. A difference must be maintained. Still, we are taught to exercise compassion, to sinners as to the godly. Even bastard children must be clothed and fed.

Getting no further with Tamar, I began to puzzle over Aunt Harriet, and here I found myself oppressed by the most chilling thoughts. I could picture her, fury that she was, so enraged that she scarcely knew what she did, dragging Joan into the lane, frantic to shame and punish her – and afterwards, trembling, sick at the betrayal the village men had witnessed and that Robin must surely discover. I saw her overwhelmed by guilt and fear, knowing her evil could never be blotted from God's book – in short, utterly undone.

Lord knows, this picture was horrible enough. Yet I was soon visited by another so shocking as to seem the prompting of the Gentleman himself, namely that Harriet had acted not in frenzy but in cold cunning. If her sister were with child, how better to make her miscarry? If not with child, surely she would be afterwards; and what surname could she give the babe except perhaps 'Legion'? It was as Joan had said: there was nothing for her to do but vanish. Harriet had visited on her a destruction so terrible that, like the cities of the plain, nothing remained to show where she had been.

Even these vile imaginings were not without a grain of comfort. Since Tamar was come into the world a sport, a wilding, I would wish her to be the child of the abduction, bitter though that tale was – a thousand times more bitter than my father's. It was infernal selfishness in me, but so it was. Tamar must not be Robin's child; else, what should I think of my good self?

꙰

170

'Where *have* you been?' cried my aunt, barging towards me as I made to go upstairs. 'There's a hogshead gone bad.'

I was taken aback. The must had been as clear and sweet as any I had pressed, and I had taken care in preparing the barrels.

'It's vinegar,' said Aunt Harriet. 'You can't have burnt enough sulphur. And when I want to talk with you, the boy tells me you've gone out walking. In this weather!'

'I'm sorry, Aunt.'

'What use is sorry? We've never had vinegar before.'

'Then you've been fortunate,' I assured her with feeling. 'I could boil it with raisins and honey – that might help. Or you could use it as it is.'

'What, a hogshead?' she retorted. 'I could supply all England with vinegar!'

Ah, I thought to myself, you could do that without the cider.

Speaking to Aunt Harriet was now become an ordeal, and not only because she was so disagreeable. Knowing what I did, I could scarcely endure to look on her waxy skin, her pale blue eyes, her fading but still golden hair. Before, these had spoken to me of a life lived in comfort and plenty; now, they seemed the attributes of a carved and gilded tomb figure, a chill, heartless creature. They say the Gentleman appears to women in the guise of a handsome, mannerly lover. *His* hair is not gold, but the colour of night; his eyes sparkle and burn; his nakedness seems made of fire. Yet when he performs nature on a woman, all she feels inside her body is a deathly cold. My aunt had something of that same dismal quality; I could see why Joan called her one of his chosen.

Despite this aversion, which was so strong as to cause me distress whenever I was in company with her, I could not leave End House while my work remained to be done. By 'work' I do not mean the pressing (though there was all that to do) but my true work that had taken me there, the discovery of Robin's guilt and the making of his reparation.

'I'll have a look,' I said. 'See if it can be saved.' My aunt did not deign to thank me but nodded and went on her way.

In my chamber I washed my hands and face and lay down to think. I had done so much thinking in the last day or so that my brains might wear out, at this rate, before I was thirty.

The addled hogshead could be seen as a blessing in disguise in that it gave me more labour. My aunt had not so many late apples as early ones, which meant that in the ordinary course of things my time at End House would shortly run out. I was up to that, and had already resolved to delay the cider-making in every conceivable fashion, a cheat made easier in two ways: firstly, I was assisted not by Binnie, in whose interest it was to finish up and move on, but by Paulie's boy. Secondly, not being paid, I had no conscience about spreading my labour thinly. I would therefore divide up the apples into as many combinations as my aunt would stand for, taking much longer than the task required, all under cover of making drink fit for a queen.

The question now weighing on me was: how was I to move forward? What should I do next?

I thought I knew enough already to piece together Robin's crime. Putting together impressions I had gleaned from my father, from Joan, from Tamar and from Rose Barnes, I understood him to be a man inclined to the sins of the flesh, a handsome, sensual, weak-willed fellow, but capable at the same time of kindness and a lazy, slack-twisted kind of love. Cruelty had no part in him, any more than it had in my father. Feeling himself near death, he had at last found the courage to write a new will and to protect Joan and her child in a way he had never yet dared. But the will was lost, or he had not had time to write it, and now Robin could not lie at peace in his grave.

What did he know about Harriet's part in the affair? I pictured her greeting as he returned to the room; she would be pale and self-possessed and ask after the horses. The next morning she would discover that Joan was not in her chamber, and then would come tears, and the discovery that her sister was gone off with the soldiers. She would no doubt tell him the girl had been desperate, because ruined – she would not fail to twist the blade – and that they must cover it up. Robin could scarcely imagine what had taken place in his absence; if the villagers had any sense they would hold their tongues. Still, he was my father's brother, and most likely shrewd in his way. In time, when it was too late, he might make a guess that came somewhere near the truth.

When it was too late . . . how, after that night, did he go on living with Harriet and with himself? The mystery of other people, their souls opaque and infolded as cabbage leaves, here so overwhelmed me that I felt all the hopelessness of my task, but I pulled myself together. It was of no consequence how he lived with her. That was past.

What I already knew fitted with what he had written to my father: *her rights.* Joan's rights? Or Tamar's? What might they be, in his eyes? Some part of his inheritance? Something he bequeathed them in his will, a will lost or destroyed before my father could reach Robin and take it into his safe keeping? But how could the dying man imagine that Joan and her child would ever come back to claim what was theirs?

Perhaps he already knew them to be near. Perhaps he was among those who, looking on a wizened beggar woman, were able to see not only what she was, but also who she had been. Had Tamar revealed herself to him before his death? Had he known her by some trick of the face or voice? Why did he –

Why did he die?

If Joan and Tamar knew that he had altered his will, then they stood to benefit by his dying. How easy for a tender nurse to slip something into his cordials! On the other hand, if he had had no time to alter his will, or no knowledge of who it

173

was who nursed him, only one person would benefit from his speedy departure: that figure in marble, Aunt Harriet.

This was like sinking into nightmare. I sat up, as if to shake off my thoughts, and as I did so I recalled something: Joan's dragging herself up from the bed when she first thought she might be with child. Only now did it occur to me that this was most likely her old chamber, and that since coming to End House I might have been sleeping in the bed where she passed her 'one sweet day' with Robin. I looked round me: nothing but dim, chill corners, cobwebs and dust, and I shivered in the thickening darkness. Their fire, if it burned here, had left no blush on the sheets, no fragrance in the air. Stones outlive people; they have no passions to wear them out.

13

The Kind of Man I Was

That evening, as I sat at supper with my aunt, I thought I would lose nothing by trying her with the story of the 'drunken fool' at Brimming. If it offended her, she could always bid me hold my tongue.

I had noticed that Aunt Harriet, like her sister, had a fondness for wine. I do not mean that she ever took too much – she was too careful for that – but she preferred to pay more for wine rather than confine herself to beer and cider. I therefore made a point of taking wine with her at supper, and drank off a toast to her health and happiness.

Aunt Harriet, who never missed a thing, said, 'It seems your tastes have changed,' which was the very opening I wanted.

'Cider's still to my taste,' I said, 'but I wish to take less of it.'

My aunt said quite amiably, 'You're scarcely a drunkard, Jonathan.'

'No, but when I was at Brimming . . . still, when a man vomits up slander, it's more than drink talking. It's the wickedness of his heart.'

Shaking my head, I continued to eat. At the same time I was willing her, with every fibre of my being, to ask who the man was, and what he had said. She did not. Smiling through my disappointment, I went on with the meal.

'Who was this?' she asked at last, as if she had only just understood my words. 'Vomiting? Slander? Not you, surely?'

'Oh, no, Aunt! A drunken sot at Brimming. Very quarrelsome and insulting.'

'I'm surprised they stood for it. They're a rough lot out there – the women worse than the men.'

She was hovering round the bait.

'Oh, it wasn't them he insulted, it was us – our family. You know how it is; nothing shuts the mouth of a drunkard. Tell me, Aunt, shall I boil the sour cider in the morning? You'll have to tell me how you want it, so I don't make it too sweet.'

'We haven't much honey,' said my aunt, 'so you're in no danger there.'

We continued eating. I felt like a hunter who sees the prey pass by his trap, come back, sniff it, move away again.

'This man at Brimming. What did he say?'

I made a great show of confusion. 'I'm not sure I remember.'

'Oh, stop that nonsense. What do you think I am, some mincing girl?'

Bang! The trap closed with my aunt inside it.

'I'm afraid you'll be angry with me,' I pleaded.

Her face was grim. 'I give you my word I won't.'

'Very well,' I said, soft and treacherous as the Gentleman himself, 'only remember what you promised, Aunt, because it *is* hateful. The fellow was far gone in drink. He followed me about, slobbering on me and ranting of some evil he said was done here.'

She waited.

'He had the face to say that my Uncle Robin bedded your sister, and he – he fathered a bastard child.'

'My sister was a trollop,' said Aunt Harriet, so calmly that I felt an acute desire to needle her.

'My dear Aunt, what are you saying . . . ?'

'A bitch in heat,' my aunt replied still in that maddeningly blank manner. 'Did your *intelligencer*' – she seemed to sneer at this word – 'tell you about this precious jewel of ours?'

'He said she –'

'She came of a weak and stupid mother – a degenerate – and showed all the signs of going the same way. My late husband was generous to a fault; he bore with her, tried to keep her folly within bounds until we could find her a husband. But then she must make a set at him, too. I put a stop to it at once, to protect Robin.'

'The act of a loving wife and sister.'

She glared at me. 'I'm not one for dressing up wickedness in fine language; I let her know my mind. She didn't like that, so she abandoned our protection and ran after the soldiers. A woman of good family, to become a camp follower through stubbornness and pride! Did you ever hear the like!'

'Never,' I agreed. 'What I *heard*, Aunt,' and here I looked her straight in the face, 'was that someone in the house dragged your sister outside to the village men, saying she was able to dress any amount of flesh, and she was delivered over to the soldiery for rape.'

My aunt remained silent and motionless. I had anticipated exclamations, denials, justifications, but not this. I knew, as clearly if she had told me, that she was trying to work out who my teacher was, what else I might have learnt, and whether I had a witness up my sleeve: in short, where this game was leading.

'He must think me a gull,' I said, as if to comfort her. 'How could anyone believe such savagery took place here, at End House?'

'Envious folk will believe anything bad,' my aunt murmured. Though her voice was soft, the pupils of her eyes had shrunk up like a cat's. 'What's this fellow's name?'

'Oh . . . John, James, something like that. I don't know his surname. He wasn't one of the farm men,' I added, helpfully giving the most useless detail I could think of. My aunt flashed me a look of pure hatred.

'Did he say how he came to know about my sister?'

'He heard about her, I suppose.'

She shocked me by bursting out laughing. 'Is that all he did? She must've lain with half the county since then.'

'Aunt,' I said. 'I've been thinking. If your sister's children were discovered – if such children existed – could you find it in your heart to make provision for them?'

'If, if,' my aunt said. 'Why should I?'

'My father, then, if *he* made them a gift. It might reclaim them, and put an end to rumour.'

'It'd do neither. Besides, nobody knows where my sister is. Did this man say where she could be found?' She looked hard at me.

'No.' I was returning her gaze, assuming an air of the utmost innocence, when to my horror her cheeks bloomed a sweet, delicate pink – as near as Aunt Harriet's waxen skin could get to a boiling flush. Had I not known what it stood for, I might have found it charming, but as it was I felt sick. I had given myself away. She had guessed that my drunkard was a fiction, and that my informant was Joan. At length she said, in a biting voice, 'What a double-dyed fool you'd be, to go after my sister.'

'I'd never go after her, Aunt. You yourself told me, when I first came here, that she was dead.'

Plainly she had forgotten that, and she was confounded. Seeing her blink with panic, I could not help but exult. But it was only an instant before she replied, 'You do right to correct me. I confess, for many years now I've thought of her as dead; but she may live. Has Mathew ever talked about her?'

'A little.'

'And what does he say?'

'That she's an agent of corruption,' I admitted.

'There you are. Mathew's known for his fair-mindedness. Take heed of what he tells you.'

'He *is* fair,' I said, 'when he's told the whole story. Tell him only half of it and he makes mistakes like other men.'

'Then tell him this nonsense you picked up in Brimming. See what he says then.'

'I will,' I said. 'I'll go tomorrow, and I'm very grateful for your advice, dear Aunt.'

*

I had lost my head a little, perhaps because of the unaccustomed wine-drinking, and was not sure what I had achieved apart from letting slip that I knew too much – which was very foolish of me. But I had not revealed Joan's whereabouts, or that her child had been a daughter, or who her daughter might be. As for the story of the rape, I could not say whether Aunt Harriet had condemned or cleared herself. My belief hovered between her and Joan, sure of neither, and I longed to get back to Spadboro and again consult my father.

However, I slept well that night, with no repetition of the cart dream, and I concluded that as far as Robin was concerned I had done no great harm.

❧

The following day I performed a daring experiment. I smoked out a new hogshead with sulphur, poured off the sour cider from the old one into pots and kettles, had it boiled in my aunt's kitchen (and oh, what a time that took), added honey and spices and sealed it all up again. I cannot say I took as much pleasure in it as in making fresh cider. I have, in general, a disgust of doing a thing twice when once should be enough; besides, the heat and steam of the kitchen were enough to turn the mice drunk.

When all that was done I put Paulie's boy back into slavery, and made him help as I milled another batch of apples and set up a new cheese. After that I wiped off my hands before going up to my chamber – Joan's chamber – for my coat.

What with all my delaying tactics I had still not finished up the last of the crop. This was certainly not a time to be going back to Spadboro, making yet another encumbrance in a time full of business, but I had told my aunt that I would and pride would not permit me to back down. First, however, I must make sure Joan was not still lying alone. Were I to go away while Tamar was missing, I might well come back to discover her mother dead.

I hurried along the path, fretting at what I might be about to find. Soon, panting as urgently as a lover, I was standing at the hurdle.

'Joan!' I called. As I did so I heard a tussling sound behind an ivy bush. 'Is that you, Tamar?' The sound came again, and the bush swayed as if something was caught up in it. Picking up a stone, I flung it as hard as I could into the foliage to see what would break cover: there was nowhere to flee to except the next bush, some five feet away. I expected to see a fox shoot away over the grass, or a scolding bird heave itself into the air, but the leaves closed over my stone without giving up the secret. My heart began to beat more rapidly.

'Who's there?'

Thinking it was some wicked boys come to tease the old woman, I threw again. The ivy tod shook violently, there was a cracking sound and two men broke from the bush. Thickset, respectably clad and of middling age, they had not the look of thieves. I wished I had not flung that last stone.

'And who might you be, young master?' said one of them, eyeing me in no friendly manner. I knew him, now: I had seen him worshipping in Tetton church.

'Jonathan Dymond. You'll know my aunt, Mrs Harriet Dymond.' At this the second man nudged his companion, and nodded; the first one now came forward, holding out his hand, though I hesitated to take it. 'And you, Sir? Who are you?'

He said, 'We're on parish business. Come to visit your friends, have you?'

'I gave you my name. What's yours?'

'Never you mind,' said the second man. 'This is a lonely place; I'd watch myself, if I were you.'

'Is that your business – threatening people?'

'Warning them is what *I* call it.'

As one, they turned and made for the path. I stood listening until the sounds they made faded away along the ditch. When

I turned back to the cave, Tamar was standing just inside the entrance, leaning against the cave wall. She beckoned me with a finger and I went inside.

'I heard you,' she said. 'I don't like coming out when they're there.'

'You know my voice, surely,' I said, stumbling along as my eyes adjusted to the dark.

'Yes; but every time I talk to someone they write it down on a paper.'

'Who employs them?'

'Dr Green. He suspects us for witches.' Her voice grew mocking. 'I think you're safe, though, Mrs Harriet's nephew.'

I wondered whether Aunt Harriet had anything to do with the men's visit, and if so, how she could have acted so quickly, or known where to look. I said, 'What does Dr Green want with your visitors?'

'Someone who'll give evidence against us.'

'Have they found anyone?'

'Ann Whinwood. Joan made her an amulet against child-lessness, and now she's with child she can't keep her mouth shut. The parson heard about it and made her bring him here, and my stupid mother won't rest till we're hanged.'

I could now make out Joan lying on the ground nearby.

'This is how she talks about me,' the old woman put in. 'Me, that raised her.'

'You'll have us on the gallows,' Tamar hissed. 'Coming out with your nonsense about the Gentleman. If you'd just shut your mouth, you old bitch, and let me talk!'

Joan's straw rustled furiously.

'It's not like it used to be,' I said, trying to comfort them both. 'They can only go so far, and they know it. His Majesty's no friend to witch-hunts, and nor, I think, is Sir Gilbert Sellis.'

'I've not seen the King or Sir Gilbert round this cave. One day,' she muttered to her mother, 'you'll start your nonsense and they'll take you away. And then I'll turn evidence, by Christ I will.'

'*Robbing*', rasped Hob.

'You wouldn't do that to me,' Joan whined.

'What, not to 'scape the rope! And get rid of that bird, he'll hang you if I don't. If I catch hold of him I'll wring his neck.'

'Who's the robber?' I asked.

They stopped bickering. Joan stared at me.

'Robber?'

'He said "*Robbing*".'

Tamar burst out laughing.

'Not robbing, Sir,' Joan said nervously. 'I thought you knew.'

'Knew what?'

Joan looked down, away from me.

Tamar said, 'Robin. It's Robin. She taught Hob to say his name.'

'He was kind to me,' Joan muttered.

'Kind?' Tamar laughed. 'Did you ever in your life see such a pitiful thing as she is?'

Joan said, 'He did what he could. You don't know, Sir.'

'Here,' Tamar said. 'I'll light the lantern – we've oil, for once – and you can tell him the whole sorry tale. Lord knows *I've* heard it enough.'

Joan's reply to this was an indignant huffing. Anxious lest Tamar should provoke her too far, I said courteously, 'If it please you, Joan, I should very much like to hear.'

'Then for *you*, Sir,' she said, with a sniff in the direction of her daughter, 'I'll tell it.'

❧

It seems that Joan had indeed left Tetton Green in the train of common camp-followers, where her refined manner attracted at once the scorn and envy of a she-bully, a virago who for half a day made her life still more wretched. Fortunately for Joan, that same refinement also brought her to the notice of an officer, who took her aside and asked if she was willing to do honest work. She gladly consented, though without any idea of what was meant by working, and he led her to a wagon full of wounded. These were the men without wives to nurse them, and Joan's task was to supply the lack.

I now understood how my father, searching among the camp-followers, had failed to find her and had gone away. Thus did Joan lose her truest friend and her one chance of rescue, having come so close that I could not bear, even after all these years, to let her know how nearly she had missed it.

She kept at the work for several weeks. The wagon was a covered one, and despite its noisome stink she seldom went out into the fresh air. She had no wish to; she ate her ration, and slept, alongside her patients. It was one of the most extraordinary times of her life, she told me: she saw men in such a plight as to melt the heart of the Gentleman himself, with bodies burnt or gutted, or cradling an inflamed and rotting stump where once was an arm or leg, and yet she handled them without pity, having none to spare. She could look into the face of a young boy sweating with agony and say to herself: You're a man like the rest! Had you been in the Guild Hall, you'd have done like the rest! This lack of tenderness made her a good nurse; when more experienced attendants fainted away, Joan remained unmoved. She cared little if she went on like this forever, lying under canvas among the sick and dying, since she had nowhere else to go. Soon, however, unmistakable signs informed her that she was indeed with child. She stayed on as long as she could before the other nurses observed her condition. 'I was driven away, Sir,' she said. 'Obliged to strike out elsewhere.'

Hearing that her old enemy, the virago, had been quietly despatched one night, Joan went back among the camp-followers, seeking out the desperately poor women who could school her in her new life, and a bitter lesson they gave her. Unless she would take herself a protector, they said, her only way was labour: washing pots or filthy linen, or digging the fields. If she wished for outdoor relief, she must return to where she had been living before. So back came Joan to Tetton Green, not without a whipping or two along the way, hating the place but forced to throw herself on its mercy. She was ready to eat any amount of humble pie, provided a parish loaf came with it.

'I had to, Sir,' she told me. 'My teeth were falling out, what with being starved and the little one on the way.' She was picked up a couple of villages away by a farmer with a cart, and wept with thankfulness, 'for my feet were blistered so bad, like walking on embers.'

On the outskirts of Tetton, however, she began to feel dread at the coming encounter with the villagers. As she sat wondering if she should go back after all, she observed a man walking in the fields by the side of the road. It was Robin, out alone and, I would have thought, with enough on his mind to furnish contemplation for twenty such walks. She sat trembling but he did not see her. After a while she looked back and saw him in the distance, growing smaller and smaller as the cart sped on.

She said, 'Oh, Master Jon, if only I'd talked with him before that day! If only I'd known!'

I thought of my nightmare, and my horror of talking with the ghost. On arrival at the village Joan made her way to the parsonage, where the parson refused to help her on the grounds that she was a notoriously lewd woman.

'Was that Dr Green?' I asked.

'Aye. I came out from his house and it was the same as last time, people spitting as I passed them. And then I saw Robin coming back from the fields . . .' Her mouth quivering, she went on, 'I began to rail . . . I didn't see why *he* should bear a good character. People were following us along. But he just took my arm – he did it in front of all of them, Sir, I never forget that – and said, "Have faith in me," and he walked with me round the back of the house. They didn't dare follow – they thought he was taking me to Harriet, but he couldn't do that, you know.'

'Where did you go, then?'

'He brought me here.'

In the cave Robin explained to her why he had not come to her aid that terrible night. He fetched food and blankets and spoke to her tenderly. Seeing him weep, Joan wept too and was still weeping days later; I fancy she had hopes he might lay down the law to Harriet, and finally bring her sister home. But she had yet to drain the cup of bitterness: Robin was a man who liked his comforts and feared his wife.

'Did he stay in the cave with you?'

'No. No.' She drifted off here, lost in some private contemplation. On coming out of it, she turned her eyes on me in a faintly surprised way as if meeting me for the first time.

I persisted. 'Or take you back to End House? It was where you belonged.'

'*She* would never have allowed that.'

'But if he wanted to provide for you –'

'He couldn't do it, Sir. My sister spied into all the accounts.'

'Wasn't he master of his own goods?' Tamar cried out in exasperation. 'And yours!'

She was voicing my own thoughts: it appeared that Robin had hardly shouldered his burden with a will. Joan's eyes were wide with indignation.

'He wasn't free! You know yourself, Sir, if the village takes against someone, if the vicar condemns them . . . my daughter doesn't understand these things.'

'Whose fault is that?' Tamar demanded.

'He gave me money,' Joan pleaded. 'I went away for the child to be born. After that I was in lots of places . . . where there was field work, I did it. For a while I took up with a strolling man and travelled about with him, until he died.'

'But whenever I came back here . . .' Tamar began.

'But whenever I came back here, I found a way to let Robin know. He'd always bring us something . . . he kept me out of the House of Correction, many a time.'

'And out of your own house, all the time!' Tamar's arms were folded as if she thought her hands might otherwise fly out and slap her mother. 'When I went to nurse him, oh, my eyes were opened! He had goods like I never saw and half of it was *hers*.'

I studied her. 'Didn't he know you?'

'When I first went in to him he seemed to think something. But he hadn't seen me for years, and I'd grown, and Mrs Harriet put a cap on me that covered up my hair. I waited a few days before I told him. Then he asked me to take my cap off and had a look at me like that, and asked me some questions about Joan. And the next day he gave me the ring.'

'Did he ever say he'd provide for you?'

She shrugged. 'I didn't believe him.'

'You thought he'd leave everything to Harriet?'

'He didn't *love* her,' Joan whimpered. 'I was his true love.'

Tamar turned to me, her fierce voice obliterating Joan's whimper. 'I had to go outside whenever he came – even in the snow, once, and I was only a little thing.' She spat. 'I'm glad he's dead.'

Disgust filled me. How far I had come from those innocent days in Spadboro when I had no conversations that might not have been heard by anybody! There seemed no innocence left in me at all; even so, I could not bear to hear any more of Robin's visits to the woman he had ruined. I said, 'I'm going to Spadboro this afternoon but I'll be back soon. What'll you do about the parson's men?'

Tamar said bitterly, 'Nothing we can do.'

'I can't move much, Sir,' said Joan. 'My legs are so bad, now, I can't get along the paths.'

'I've buried her charms and things,' said Tamar. 'If she'd just keep her mouth shut, all would be well, but she *will* try to frighten the men and then we get on to the Gentleman. I tell them it's the ramblings of a silly old woman but they shake their heads; I don't think they have any grandams at home. I'll bring you on your way, Sir.'

I rose and made my way out of the cave. Tamar walked with me, scrambling up the ha-ha in my wake. When we were out of earshot of the cave, she said, 'I've something to tell you, Jon.'

'What?' I said, distrusting that *Jon.*

'I'm with child.' Just like that she said it, without any shame or backwardness; I was the one who felt dizzy and sat down in the mud of the path.

Tamar bent over me, saying, 'Put your head between your knees.'

'I'm not fainting,' I said huffily, though I had been near it. I was no libertine, to be sure: here was the oldest news in the world, and of all the men who have heard it since the world began, I doubt that many have received it in such a craven spirit. I took a deep breath to steady myself. 'Why tell *me* this news, more than anyone else?'

'Why do you think? I can't read, but I can count.'

I considered this in silence. From what I knew of her, the child might be anyone's. Fortunately I was still sitting on the path, which meant I could avoid Tamar's eyes. Looking down, I saw that she was wearing the heeled shoes I had bought her the day we went to the inn.

'You know I can't marry you,' I said at last.

For some reason my honesty enraged her. 'I never thought you would, you cowardly whelp!'

'What do you want, then?'

187

'Money, of course. A midwife.'

'I don't know. I'd have to tell my father.'

'Have you no wage of your own?' Her voice grew shrill. 'Are you any kind of a man at all?'

I had become entangled with a whore, and must now suffer her railing; that was the kind of man I was. 'You'll have to give me time,' I said. It was a feeble answer, but the most dignified I could muster.

&

During this period of my life I more than once envied the Papists, who could confess to a priest and feel the weight of wrongdoing fall away, leaving the spirit pure and free. Do not misunderstand me: I am a good Protestant. I know well that no mortal creature may bind or loose sin, that the comfort given thereby is false and the entire thing a shameful cheat; I say only that to the hard-pressed man, even false comfort seems precious.

I had no comfort at all. As I drove to Spadboro later that day, Joan's papers, light as they were, weighed on me as much as the King's death warrant can ever have weighed on Oliver Cromwell. So wretched was I that on entering Spadboro, I could even find it in me to envy the simple horse. *He* was visibly cheered by the thought of home, and picked up his pace, while I was full of dread.

In such straits a Papist goes straight to the confessional. In whom, then, does a Protestant confide? In Almighty God, you will say; but I needed more than prayer and repentance. When a woman is with child there are practical matters to settle, requiring practical aid. With those, only one man could help me: the very man, above all others, whom I most hated to disappoint.

14

Man to Man

My mother was in the front garden, picking kale; I saw her wave a handful of dark leaves as I guided Bully through the gate. She came to the yard and stood by me as I unharnessed him, all the time asking me questions without waiting for the answers: How was Aunt Harriet? Had I felt so very cold driving back from Tetton Green? Was that the end of her apples, now? Had she parted civilly with me? Had I lost weight? Surely I had, and so on. I was glad that she was content to forgo answers as I could scarcely give her any, being now so tense that my throat had begun to swell as if holding back tears.

'My dear mother,' I said, crushing the kale as I seized her hands, 'I must speak with Father. He'll tell you my news, I'm sure.'

The gladness died out of her face. 'Aye,' she said bitterly, 'that's how it is with mothers and sons. First we're everything to them, then we're nothing.' She pulled away from me and began walking back to her kale patch.

'Ah, Mother, how can you think so?' I called after her, unsure whether to follow. She did not stop but replied over her shoulder, 'You'll find him in the office.'

My heart right up in my mouth, sitting on my tongue, you might say, I knocked at the office door.

'Yes?' came Father's voice.

I entered and found him poring over some sort of plan.

'This is a pleasant surprise,' said he. 'Well, not altogether a surprise – but altogether pleasant.' He rose to kiss me. 'Here' (he indicated the plan) 'are some notions I had about the garden. New seed beds, new fruit trees – and damsons.'

'Excellent,' I whispered. He gave me a sharp look, at that, and motioned me into the chair opposite his, his bright eyes blurring as my own filled with tears. It was not how I had intended to begin.

He said gravely, 'You have something to tell me, I perceive.'

I could no longer meet his eyes. My throat now so swollen as to make speech impossible, I let myself drop forward until I slid off the chair onto my knees, holding up my hands in helpless appeal.

'Up! Up!' Father said sharply. 'Be a man.'

I winced to hear him thus echoing Tamar. He seized my shoulders and pulled me upright before pushing me back into the chair where I sat confounded, hanging my head.

'So, the birds have come home to roost,' he said, at which I burst out into loud sobs. He said again, 'Be a man,' but as I continued blubbering he went to a cupboard and fetched out a bottle and cup. When he uncorked the bottle I scented brandy-wine, a drink I detested, and shook my head. His response was to pour a cupful and thrust it towards me. As the sickly, perfumed stuff burnt its way down my gullet, I gagged, but as soon as that passed I felt myself growing calmer. The knot in my throat began to slacken so that I could speak – hoarsely, but without the spasms that had racked me at first.

'Thank you, Father.'

He waved away my thanks, and waited.

'I need your help, only it's all so – oh, God!'

Father said quietly, 'First tell me why you're crying.'

'I'm in a difficulty,' I answered, thinking that on hearing his favourite expression, he might smile. He did not.

'At Christmas, when I was late,' I went on, 'and I told you I'd been robbed –'

'I know,' he cut in. 'You looked it, you stank of it, you couldn't have deceived a child. Has she poxed you, is that why you're in such a state?'

I quailed beneath his stare. 'It's not as if –'

'*Has she poxed you?*' Father leapt up and shook me by the shoulders. 'It's of the greatest consequence, answer me yes or no!'

'No. I don't think so.'

He let go of me and flung himself back into his chair.

'I didn't mean – but –' Seeing his right hand lift as if to strike, I hurried on, 'I meant no harm. She was in desperate –'

'Harriet's servant,' my father said, terrifying me by the speed with which he grasped the story away from me. 'Tamsin?'

'Tamar. I went to give evidence, and –'

'Didn't I tell you she'd wind you in? Those were my very words.'

'I didn't go for any bad reason, Father, and she, she did nothing to tempt me to it, not then. If you'd only seen her! She could've been lying on ice; her skin was blue. I bought her some clothes, and took her to an inn. That was – the time. Now –' My throat was closing again. 'Now –'

'Now she's with child,' Father said.

I nodded. After that I could not speak for a while, my sobbing so overwhelmed me. Father exclaimed, 'Young men . . . ! Nature takes her course, and you're dumbfounded, you never meant *that*! How could you be such a fool, Jonathan – you, who've helped me take the boar to the sow!'

'Father –'

'And what makes you think it's yours? Surely she wasn't a maid when you lay with her. Couldn't you tell?'

'I was a maid myself,' I said, hot with humiliation. 'But I believe she was not.'

'Of course not,' he said, relenting a little. 'Jon. We've always talked like father and son; let's now understand each other like men. Your young woman is a drab. To buy clothes for a drab and lodge her at an inn is to pay handsomely.'

'But if she's with child?'

'Handsomely,' he repeated. 'You owe her nothing more. Be sure *she* thought what'd come of it, even if you didn't.'

I said, 'It's not so simple when you know all. Tamar is related to us, Father. Her mother is Joan Seaton.'

'*Joan Seaton?*' My father's man-of-the-world manner crumbled in an instant. His jaw dropped and his face filled with blood so that I was afraid he would have an apoplexy. 'And this is her daughter? Have you any idea – no –' He broke off and covered his burning cheeks with his hands.

'I know, she might be my cousin,' I hastened to help him. 'Uncle Robin's daughter.'

A minute passed during which my father remained masked, breathing noisily against the palms of his hands. When he did lower them, it was to refill the cup with brandy-wine and take a long draught. We looked at one another.

'She could be anyone's,' he said, pushing the empty cup away from him. 'You see what comes of secrets! Why did you never tell me this before?'

'How should I know she was connected with us?' I protested. If it came to secrets, I could equally have reproached him. 'Tamar told me her old mother dwelt in the wood, and that I shouldn't say anything to Aunt Harriet. I saw no harm.'

'You and a servant from your aunt's house, no harm? Keeping company with outcasts, no harm?'

'I know, but when I saw how they were living – so wretched, Father, and Aunt Harriet so wealthy. They were accused of stealing some gifts I made them; you know that part. The old woman wrote me an account of her life – I was reading it at Brimming. I have it all here, everything she wrote, and right at the end she puts that she's Aunt Harriet's sister.'

'Good Christ,' my father murmured. 'Does this woman know who *you* are?'

'Yes. I told her I was Mr Mathew's son.'

'Good Christ.'

'And there's something else.'

My father looked up with a curious expression, almost pleading. Had he been a wicked man, rather than one of upright life, I would have said he was sick with apprehension.

He said, 'If it's another secret, Jon, then think and don't be hasty. Best is to have none; next best is not to let them out.'

'It's not my secret, Father – nothing to do with me.' The expression of dread at once cleared from his face. 'You told me Joan ran away with the soldiers.'

'That's right.'

'She says she was Robin's mistress before that.'

'Never,' Father said at once. 'A wicked lie.'

'She says Harriet knew.'

'Well.' My father rubbed his hand over his head as if to clear his thoughts.

'Father, you remember the soldiers billeted at Tetton Green? They held the village in terror.'

'I remember a great deal of that sort,' said my father. 'I pray we never see war again.'

'One night they came onto the green, drunk and armed, shouting that they wanted a woman.'

Father inclined his head judicially. 'Are you saying that's how Joan took up with them? What a tender innocent she must've been! Not even Marian Drew' – this was a woman notorious in the village – 'would go out to a pack of drunken soldiers.'

'She didn't want to go. Harriet handed her over.'

'What *are* you saying, child?'

'She was handed over to them. For use.'

'Sheer nonsense,' Father said angrily. 'Only think. Granted that Harriet would do that to her own sister – which I *don't* grant you – how could it happen with Robin in the house?'

'He wasn't there; he'd gone to the stable. She was taken to a room in the Guild Hall and kept there until they put her out of the door . . . scarcely able to walk,' I added, my voice tailing off as his face hardened.

'*That* sounds like Joan, all right: a corrupt, lascivious fancy. And what of the neighbours, pray? Didn't they see what was going on? Did they just let her be dragged inside?'

'The soldiers were firing off muskets in the dark; most of the neighbours fled indoors. Only a handful of men were left. They needed someone with neither husband nor family to defend her.'

'She's shaped her tale well,' Father said. 'So she wrote all this and gave it you?'

'This isn't in the writing. She told me, and Father, I believe her.'

'But don't you see it's impossible, child? What would Harriet say to Robin when he returned?'

'I don't know,' I answered. 'But she's always been believed, hasn't she? And Joan never. Nothing can be done about that, now. My question is, can nothing be done to provide for Joan?'

He shrugged. 'The house is Harriet's. First from her father and then over again from Robin.'

'The father must've bequeathed *something* to Joan. He wouldn't leave her penniless while her sister had everything. Whatever that was, money or goods, Harriet has it now. And I've been thinking. If Robin did like Joan, he might have left her something in his will.'

'He might, though I can't see him liking such a creeping, disagreeable thing as she was, but d'you think Harriet would stand for it?' He snorted. 'If she ever found such a will, it's gone into the fire long ago.'

'No,' I said at once. 'Harriet never found it.'

'Then trust me, it'll never be found. But how can you know she didn't?'

'She would've seen Tamar's name in it,' I said. 'She'd have thrown her out of the house.'

He smiled at my simplicity. 'Robin couldn't write Tamar into a will. Joan, yes, perhaps; but he didn't know of Tamar's existence.'

'He did know of her, Father! He and Joan were known to one another long after she left Tetton Green.'

My father pursed his lips.

'And if he put Tamar in a will he'd have to name her, and her name can only be Seaton. So I don't think Harriet can have seen any will like that, or she'd never have let Tamar into her house.'

'But did Harriet *know* her as Tamar Seaton?' Father asked. 'What name did she go under?'

I had not thought about this and could not remember if I had ever heard Tamar's surname. 'I don't know,' I admitted, crestfallen. My father looked long and hard at me. When he spoke again it was to say quietly, 'You do realise you're Harriet's heir?'

'How can you think so? She loathes me!'

'Too strong, child. Young folk imagine everything is to do with them. Your aunt's always been prickly, but who else would she leave to? Besides, your mother and I have helped her, in our way, over the years. Now' – he dropped his voice for effect in a way that reminded me of Joan herself – '*if* this woman's Joan Seaton – which she may not be – she's a thieving whore. Why cut yourself out of an inheritance for her?'

'This is my inheritance,' I said, gesturing at the walls around us. 'You come from Tetton Green and it's natural you should think of it, but I belong in Spadboro.'

'Yes,' Father said impatiently, 'but you can live here and still inherit.'

'And I want to sleep well at nights.'

'Sleep?' Father's eyes narrowed. 'Why shouldn't you? Has

this woman threatened you with something – some hocus-pocus?'

'Nothing like that. The thing is, Father, there *must* be a will.' I thought my father would contradict me, but he waited to hear me out. 'You remember my dream about Uncle Robin – the one with the cart and the paper?'

Father nodded.

'I'm still having it, only worse. Don't you see, Father? The paper is the will.'

'You never said this before,' he pointed out. 'First you decide there's a will, then you say it's in your dream; but when you first had the dream you never thought of any will.'

'I didn't understand at first.'

'You don't now. It's your fancy, nothing else.'

'Forgive my asking, Father, but are you sure you've never had this dream?'

'Quite,' said my father with the simplicity of truth.

'And yet you're his brother, and he wrote to you.'

He half smiled. 'Are you asking me to account for your dreams?'

'But do you believe me?'

'I believe you to be in earnest,' he said, not unkindly. 'You said you'd brought the woman's writing.'

I nodded.

'Show me, then. I'll read it and point out the lies.'

'Father.' I reached out and touched his arm. 'Uncle Robin wanted to see you on his deathbed. Suppose this were the business, wouldn't you do everything possible to carry out his wishes?'

'I'll read the writing,' he repeated. 'Let that content you for now. What did you tell the daughter?'

'That I won't marry her.'

'There you showed some sense, for once. But she won't let go so easily, I'll be bound.'

'She doesn't want marriage, only money for food and childbed.'

He groaned. 'Jon, Jon! A bitch of this sort'll couple with any-body. Most likely she doesn't know who the father is, but she's cunning; she looks round for an honest fool. My life on it, she was with child before you boarded her.'

'No, she –'

'Did you importune her? Or she *you*?'

'Well –'

My father smiled knowingly and said no more. I will not conceal that his shrewdness gave me a pang; a young fellow naturally takes pleasure in believing himself desirable and desired. Father poured himself more drink, sipping in a leisurely fashion now, as if to say we had passed the crisis. I had never seen him drink in this room before, and certainly noth-ing so strong as brandy-wine, but if he kept it there he must have taken it from time to time, and he did not appear at all intoxicated. My news was of a sobering sort, no doubt. At last he said, in a voice like the tolling of a bell, 'Give. Her. Nothing.' At the *nothing* I was ready to argue again, but he went on, 'Put your hand in your purse just once and it's all up with you; you're marked as the guilty man. Besides, the babe won't come for months yet – may never come at all.'

'But they're shivering even as we speak,' I said. 'Our own flesh and blood.'

'We don't know they're our flesh and blood. First let me read. And Jon, pray remember: whatever they say to you, this child isn't yours.'

He was sure to be right. Why, then, as I nodded my head, did I feel so wretched?

'What'll you tell Mother?'

'Precisely what you've told me.'

'If you please, then, I'll speak with her first.'

'Very well.' He placed his hand on my shoulder, turned and

began rolling up his diagrams of seedbeds and trees. 'So, where are these papers?'

I took them from my bag and laid them on the table, then went, sick at heart, to break my news to Mother.

15

Attempts at Reasoning

At the kitchen door I paused, listening to the talk within. Mother and Alice were in there together washing something, probably the kale, in a bowl. Alice was grumbling that she wished she could sleep out the time between Christmas and Easter, for there was nothing worth eating between.

My mother gently rebuked her: if God had so ordered things, it was not for us to wish them different. We should rather be grateful for our daily bread.

But in some countries (said Alice) there was warmth, and sweet fruit to harvest, all year round. Everyone in the village was talking of Jim Partlett, who had run off to sea and was now returned. He had served with black fellows, who said that in their country there was fruit even in March. It was a pity God had not seen fit to give England such early fruit.

At this my mother remarked that Jim Partlett was dishonest, as was shown by his running away; but even if what he said was true, it was not for us to know better than God. She added that He had placed autumn conveniently before winter, and not the other way round, so that we might store up provisions; she poured scorn on Alice's blackamoors, who had probably lied (such being their nature), for it was not possible that any nation enjoyed God's favour more than England. It therefore stood to reason that we enjoyed the kindest weather and the best suited for crops.

'For kale, certainly,' said Alice, who could be saucy on occasion. From being with us so long, she was grown almost into a member of the family and (I thought, now that I had attained to manhood) too easy in her ways; though a good loyal servant, and devoted to my mother, she was inclined to get above her station. Just then, however, I could have wished this petticoat theology to continue all day, and all night too, since there was no sadness in it. The sadness was about to enter with me, the poisoner of their innocent world.

'Mother, I must speak with you, if you please,' I said, stepping up to them. (Alice dropped me a curtsey; I nodded, but no more, by way of hinting at the proper distance between us.)

'I'm listening,' said my mother, who had not forgiven me for brushing her off earlier.

'It's important,' I hinted, glancing at the door.

Mother put down her knife and pushed her heap of kale towards Alice. 'You know what to do?'

Alice harrumphed. 'Aye; but it'll be late.'

We went to my chamber. Mother kept glancing at me as we climbed the stairs, but I would not say more until the door was closed behind us. She sat on the bed, her face stony, as I told her as much of my stupidity as was fitting for her to hear, and also of my discoveries since. Though her expression grew steadily sadder, and at times she touched her bosom as if I had struck her there, she did not interrupt me until I came to reveal that Tamar was the daughter of Joan Seaton, when she stifled a cry.

'Are you sure she's the daughter of that – creature?'

'As sure as I can be,' I said humbly. 'Have I done wrong to tell you? Perhaps you'd rather have heard from Father.'

'I'd rather not hear from anybody – oh –' Her sigh here cut me, there was such disappointment in it. 'I thought better of you, Jon! And Joan Seaton's girl! You couldn't have chosen worse.'

'I didn't choose, exactly – I mean –'

'Oh, for shame!' Mother exploded. '*The woman tempted me and I did eat.* Is that how we brought you up? To have no will of your own?'

At this I felt myself disgraced almost beyond redemption. Unable to bear her look, I rose and went to the window just in time to see Simon Dunne, with a face like thunder, leading away Bully, whom in my perplexity I had forgotten to return.

Mother went and opened the chamber door, pausing to say, 'Well, your father must deal for you now. I don't know what he'll do, I'm sure. We hoped to see you married this year.' With that she walked out of the room, leaving me the lowest worm in Creation.

&

Come now, and let us reason together, saith The LORD:
though your sins be as scarlet, they shall be as white as snow;
though they be red like crimson, they shall be as wool.

I felt, rather than saw, the glances of my father and mother as this text was given out. I would not return their looks; instead, I studied the head of the fellow seated in front of me, through whose thinning hair showed streaks of naked scalp, pink as a newborn mouse. The preacher began to urge us to repentance, for each and every one of us was a sinner. Had I known this was to be today's sermon, I would have feigned sick and stayed at home.

It was now a day since I had made my revelations and if anything, the atmosphere in our house had worsened. My mother was grown less angry, my father more so, but neither was in good humour with me.

Mother was on the watch, hoping to detect in me a fuller penitence; to her way of thinking I was too inclined to blame the woman. Granted, she was a whore (Mother had said to me only that morning) but this was no excuse, since I must have known her for one from the start. I could not argue the natural tenderness of a lover, since I was unwilling to marry what I had been willing enough to lie with. I could answer nothing to any of this except that she was right.

My father, on the other hand, was less concerned that I should adopt a humble demeanour, but spoke of 'a dog returning to his vomit' and insisted I should sever all connection with the Seaton women, leaving them to take their chance. Whenever he said this, I fancied I saw Tamar writhing in childbed, deprived even of water to drink and with no companion but that useless old trot. At this, my conscience whispered that there must surely be some other way. Father said there was none. Though agreed that I had done wrong, we could not agree about how I should go right.

Let us reason together. The gentleness of these words had long endeared the prophet Isaiah to me. There was something delightful in the notion of a loving conversation with the Lord; perhaps it would be a little like those childhood talks I had enjoyed with my earthly father, a man ever ready to persuade rather than beat.

Now, however, I was unable to 'reason together' even with him, and the words, once so comforting, struck fear into me. How, reason? Reason in what way? How could a blind, sin-crazed creature bandy ideas with the All-Knowing? What arrogance, to imagine that Isaiah had meant anything of the sort. I had nothing to teach God. My part was surely to be silent and listen while God reasoned His way into my soul, but what if I was stubborn and opposed to His arguments, as I was to those of my father?

'Help,' I prayed. I had not meant to beg for mercy (I wanted to do right before asking God to interest Himself in my misfortunes) but to open myself to the Divine Reasoning, so that I might see my way. This had been my intention, but my prayer, crushed out of me by the sheer weight of misery, was a childish cry of fear. I closed my eyes and continued in the same vein: 'Dear Lord, only help. You best know how. Help them, help me,

Christ our Lord, have mercy; Christ Jesus, have mercy.'

I waited, inside the darkness of my skull, for some sense that God was listening, but there was none. Opening my eyes, I again noticed the head of the man sitting before me. God cared as much for him as for me – perhaps more. Why would my prayers induce God to alter His intentions? Only pride and folly suggested they might.

It was not a new idea to me that devout prayer is a submission to God. I knew it well; the parson (at that moment rejoicing over the lost sheep found again) was the same man who had catechised me in youth, correcting my selfish, childish efforts to pray: not *I want* but *Thy will be done.* Yet as soon as I began to suffer, a suffering brought upon me by my own wickedness, I grew as corrupt as any Papist. I would be praying to the Virgin and saints next, demanding that for the price of a candle they would tinker with God's Eternal Will.

What it came down to was that I wanted the Lord to abandon his plans and set up anew. As I grasped this, something happened to me that has never happened before or since: I had a fleeting experience of faithlessness. The notion of God going about His business, without reference to my likes or dislikes, suddenly removed Him far away, and I saw that I should have to get through life as well as I could without His meddling in my affairs, which in some respects came to the same thing as His not being there at all. As I have said, my mind had grasped this long before, without difficulty. I was familiar with the notion that while God cares for each sparrow, each wandering sheep, it is our souls, not our bodies, He cares for. He wishes us to reach our safe haven, our eternal bliss, but He does not undertake to smooth any man's road thither. It is for us to climb the rocks and ford the rivers. I cannot say why it was then, sitting in church listening to a sermon on repentance, that I began not to understand but to *feel* this great distance between me and God – but thus it happened. It was the difference between knowing that fire burns and taking a white-hot poker in my hand.

Around me the parishioners obediently fell in with the responses while I sat motionless in the pew. I had no more to plead. My conscience must direct me now, and what I most needed was a sheet of paper, to set things down, so that I could think.

Tamar – child
Robin. Left to J in will?
Aunt H

There. I stared at the scribbles as if expecting wisdom to spring from them fully formed, but I was not an inch further forward. I groaned, sprawled full-length on the bed and buried my face in the covers.

Someone tapped at my chamber door. I thrust the paper beneath the bolster and called, 'Come in.'

Father entered, clutching what I took to be Joan's writings, done up in a bundle. The bundle had a forlorn, rumpled look. I thought how easily it might be tossed into the fire, and how much trust Joan reposed in it – how to her, this pitiful production was nothing less than the Great Amulet, charged with the power of turning Fortune's Wheel. At that moment there seemed little to choose between her and me.

I moved along the bed so that Father could sit next to me, but he remained standing.

'Have you read it all?' I asked.

'Fearful. Fearful.'

My heart leapt. 'So you believe her?'

He slowly inclined his head, as if a nod would be too emphatic. 'In part.'

'And you do see that Tamar's kin to us?'

'She may be.'

'Joan certainly is.'

'By marriage,' he corrected me. I perceived that just beneath the surface of his calm and cautious manner, something within him was softening, collapsing. As if to prove it, he sat down suddenly on the bed next to me.

I said, 'I could ask her to write down the rest.'

My father turned to gaze into my eyes. 'Jonathan. Do you know what you're about? Let loose snakes like these' – he shook the papers – 'and they'll sting every one of us. For a start, they put all the women, Joan, Harriet and Tamar, under suspicion for Robin's death. Have you thought of that?'

'I have,' I admitted.

'As for what Joan told you about Harriet handing her over . . .' He spread his hands to signify helplessness. 'It's a beggar's word against a gentlewoman's.'

'I know that, too. But how can it hurt *us*?'

My father's face assumed an expression of weary patience. 'The best that can happen to you, if you go on like this,' he said, 'is that Tamar Seaton inherits some small thing that might've been yours. More likely, your aunt cuts you off without a shilling – a needless loss – and sends this scandal to our own door.'

'But she can't, Father. We've done nothing wrong.'

'Are you a suckling babe, that you think misfortune never lights upon the innocent?'

'No,' I muttered.

'Then don't talk like one. Now, are you sure there's nothing I don't know about – no more little Dymonds tucked away in the woods?'

Though blushing, I was able to look him in the eyes as I said, 'I give you my solemn word.'

'In that case, I have a proposition and I suggest you think it over before deciding. If you stay away from this girl, I'll provide for her and her child.'

'Father!' I made to embrace him but he shook his head.

'I said to think it over! You must stay right away from her, mind – and whatever I give them comes out of the savings for your wedding. If', he added drily, 'that blessed event should ever take place.'

'Agreed,' I said at once, while my father tutted to find me still so impetuous. 'Only, if you pay something, shouldn't Aunt Harriet pay more? What about her?'

'Nothing about her.'

'But –'

'Nothing, Jon! You can never prove what's written here. There are no witnesses.'

I jumped up. 'The men, the men in the village! *They* saw –'

He shook his head.

I sat down hardly knowing what to say. In some respects my father's offer was more than I had dared hope. He had even come round, in some degree, to my view of things. Yet his proposal, while dealing mercifully with Tamar, left justice entirely to one side. I did not think the Dream would let me go free for mere charity. Sitting there perplexed, I recalled something that I had not yet tried.

I said, 'You've kept a secret from me all this time.' I was struck by the sudden pallor that spread through my father's cheeks, giving him the look of a man recently bled by the surgeon, but he said only, 'What secret?'

'When Uncle Robin died. You received a letter but you never told me what he wrote.'

He heaved a deep sigh, signifying defeat. 'Very well,' he said. 'He did acknowledge Tamar, at the end. He wrote a will to that effect, but the letter didn't say where the will was kept. I was to go to him and hear it from his lips.'

The colour was already beating back into his face but his

eyes were still watchful, suspicious even; though the room was chilly, I noticed a faint shine of perspiration at his temples.

'It's what I guessed,' I said to comfort him. 'Did he know who his nurse was? Tamar said he did, and that's why he gave her the ring.'

'He may have.'

'Please, Father, be frank with me. He'd seen Joan since she left Tetton, hadn't he? Tamar remembers him going into the cave with her mother, when she was still a child. Tamar was sent outside,' I added, in case my meaning should not be clear.

'God grant him forgiveness,' my father said wretchedly. 'Few men have his temptations, Jon. It's a wonder he didn't go wrong more often.' I tried to seem touched by compassion for Uncle Robin's thorny path in life as Father went on. 'Yes, he knew Tamar. He wrote that he was in mortal terror.'

'Of her?'

Father shook his head. 'He may have feared her a little, but his terror was of God's judgement. What a thing to have on your conscience!'

For a moment I was boggled: this was my father speaking, the same man who was set upon my abandoning Tamar. But then, he did not believe the child was mine.

I said, 'So the will was a matter of conscience?'

'Of right, of justice, of dying at peace with God. But then I let him down.'

'No, Father! You went at once.'

'I should've taken the horse. You said so, at the time. But his mind seemed clear – as if he was strong –' His voice caught and again I marvelled at the depth of my father's love for his handsome, selfish brother. He got control over himself, however, and added, 'Harriet said he was wandering, at the end. Perhaps he tore up the will and never knew it.'

'She didn't nurse him, to know,' I said. 'He wanted justice and we have to respect his wishes.'

207

Father said sharply, 'Indeed? And how would you set about it – whip your aunt through the village?'

'First we must find the will. That's what the dreams are about: Robin's telling me it isn't destroyed.'

'You and your dreams! Robin had the girl with him, by his bedside. Why wouldn't he give the will to her?'

I thought. 'There might be reasons. She can't read, for one. He needed someone like you to witness it, someone respected who couldn't be pushed aside by my aunt.'

Father surprised me by an abrupt nod. 'I grant you. Or he mightn't want Tamar to know she stood to gain. There's such a thing as poison, after all.'

'If you think that, so would Harriet. She'd point the finger at Tamar before you could say "witchcraft" and blame her for the sickness, everything. No, it had to be given to somebody else, if only to protect her. That's why he kept it ready for *you*.'

'Where, then? Where?' Father rocked softly back and forth, as absorbed in the riddle as I had ever been, then stopped short and put his hand on my arm. 'Jon. You must promise me something.'

'I do. I have.'

'Not that. If we find a will' – here he paused, as if to consider all the possibilities – 'or if you find one when I'm not with you, you must let me read it first.'

I was so delighted at that 'we', which declared us fellow conspirators against Aunt Harriet, that I gladly swore to this condition. My father perhaps wanted to feel himself alone, if only for a moment, with the brother he had lost; he wished to keep faith with him at last. And it seemed that my uncle knew of my promise and approved it, for that night I sank down through the layers of sleep and dissolved in its black waters, dreamless as the dead.

The following morning the windows were blank with frost. In the office Father explained to me his plans for the kitchen garden, both of us wearing gloves and caps indoors and our breath steaming over the paper. I approved his scheme for rearranging the vegetable beds and for training Scarlet Lady beans against the side of the cider-house. We then went out to mark up plots with pegs and string but with the ground so hard there was little we could do. Though I knew how fast Nature's wheel turns, the summer crops seemed distant as America. We had seen days better suited to working outside, and had let them go; I thought perhaps Father wanted me out of the house, so we could talk without being overheard by my mother, but he did not once broach the subject of Robin or his will.

We went into the cider-house. Father took a cup and tapped the last of the early hogsheads.

'Not bad,' I said, admiring the golden transparency of the drink.

He tasted it. 'Aye. It's kept well for earlies.'

'I'll marry, Father,' I said suddenly. I had had enough of murky doings and secrecy. 'I'll marry once everything's cleared up.'

'And if it's never cleared up – if we never find anything?'

'Then I suppose my dreams will continue.'

Would any woman want a man so tortured by the nightmare? And who did *I* want? Poll? To go from Tamar to Poll was an extraordinary thought, to be sure. Father refilled the cup and held it out to me.

'*I* dreamed something last night,' he said.

It was as if the shed was lit up with torches, or as if the Final Trump had sounded. I held my breath.

'I opened this hogshead, this one here,' Father went on. 'It was sealed with seven seals, like in the Bible.'

I thought this horrible, and said so.

'They were like twists of paper. I tasted the drink and it was sour and red. Blood-red. Yet here's the cider, nothing wrong with it.'

Disappointment filled me.

'You see, son –'

'My dream's not of that kind,' I said, handing back the cup.

⚘

The next day I must return to Aunt Harriet, if the remainder of her crop were not to rot. Mother brushed down clothes for me, sealed me a jug full of mulled cider (though this would be cold long before I came to drink it) and wrapped me up some bread and cheese and pie to eat on the road.

'And when you're finished there, I hope you'll come home and we can go on again, the way we used to,' she said.

We were in my chamber, Mother turning out old garments that were now too small for me to wear. Some had lain folded in the press for years, waiting to see light again, but there was no younger brother growing out at heels and elbows who could have used them. She held up a dark-blue jacket.

'Alice can have this for her nephew. Remember it?'

I had some hazy recollection of crowds and booths. 'Did I wear it to the fair?'

'We bought the cloth there. I cut it big, to grow into.' Laughing, she held it against my shoulders. It might have fitted when I was about twelve or thirteen years old.

She wanted to touch me, to make up with me. I wanted it, too; I wanted everything the way it used to be, but life had come between now and then. Mother threw the jacket onto the bed, where it fanned out as if showing itself off.

'Your father's going to Tetton with you,' she said. I could think of nothing to say; I could think of nothing to think. She added, 'To be of help.'

'With what?'

'Whatever's needful.'

She looked as shy as a young girl. She knows, I thought. About Tamar, my dreams, everything.

I said, 'Well, that's good, I suppose. If Aunt Harriet will lodge him.'

'If she won't, he has money for the inn.'

It seemed everything was decided. I was going back to Tetton Green with 'Mr Mathew' by my side.

'He needn't watch over me, you know. I've promised not to see her and I won't.'

'You may have to,' she said, surprising me. 'Better for you if he's there. He won't let them off with a thing.'

❧

The day of our departure was savagely cold. My father's cheeks were mottled red and blue; I had wrapped a cloth around my mouth and nose in order to breathe more easily, for the air gouged at my nostrils. Father drove until his fingers grew numb, then I took over until mine were as bad; he took up the reins again while I scrubbed my hands together and clapped them in my armpits for warmth.

Despite this cursed weather he was in a good mood, mild as milk. I had made up my mind that I was glad of his company, though I found it hard to know what he intended to do apart from taking the reins every so often. I kept turning over what my mother had said: *he won't let them off.* Until recent events had brought out my father's tougher side, I had always thought of him as too gentle for his own good. How much of him remained hidden from my knowledge? He had married late, at thirty; he had been a full-grown man, in a world that did not include me, until a moment's pleasure brought me squealing into that world. Like any child, I found it strange that for most of my father's life I had been faceless, voiceless, not even thought of.

The roads were hard with frost and Bully's hoofs clattered alarmingly at times, but he kept his footing. As our wheels crunched through frozen puddles, I began to ponder the nature of accidents – all manner of accidents, from an over-turned coach to the deaths of my brothers and sisters. Was there a purpose in these things? Why, out of all the children born to my parents, was I the sole one let to live, while the rest, equally innocent and deserving, lay in the churchyard? Was it God's will that I should grow to manhood, in order to put right a wrong?

The cold was growing on me. I closed my eyes and huddled up tighter, allowing myself to drowse off as Father urged Bully along the lanes.

16

The Wilding

'Careful, Father. You have to drop down here, look.' I slid into the ditch and called up to him. 'Once you're down it's solid enough.'

My father slithered after me. 'I know this place,' he said, looking around. 'We used to play here as boys.'

'Did you go into the cave?'

'Sometimes. But this here –' He indicated the ditch. 'We'd walk towards it blindfolded until the ground gave way. Robin was best. Even if you pushed him, he never cried out.'

'Did all the village lads come here?'

'A good few.'

We picked our way over cracked and soiled ice, trampled into the mud by other feet than ours. The sky was already growing dark and the black opening to the cave, when we turned and came up against it, seemed to float in the air, a devouring mouth without a face. I was suddenly loath for him to enter, and said, 'It'll be dark within.'

'I've a tinderbox.' As I made to move forward he plucked me back by the sleeve. 'Wait, son. What if somebody should be inside?'

'Robbers, you mean?'

He coughed delicately. 'No. Well, what can we do? Call.'

I went forward to the hurdle and called, 'Tamar!'

She appeared almost at once, bundled round with what looked like every garment she possessed. Her face, though dirty and bone-sharp, had a sort of shine to the skin; I had seen this shine before on the faces of women who were with child.

'This is Tamar Seaton,' I said.

'Welcome, Master Jon. And Mr Mathew.' Tamar stood nervously, twisting her hands together.

I said, 'So you know my father?'

She addressed him, not me. 'Am I wrong? Beg pardon, Sir.'

'I am indeed Mathew Dymond,' he said, weighing her up. 'Have you seen me before, young woman?'

'At the funeral, Sir. And you look like Mr Robin.'

We stood awkwardly at the entrance to the cave. Someone had cut down the thorn bush where Joan used to hang her amulets. I blew on my fingers to show we were suffering from the cold and Tamar wordlessly indicated that we should follow her inside.

'Is Joan here?' I asked as we entered the familiar stale-smelling darkness.

'She can't move from the place now.'

'Have Dr Green's men been back?'

'Jon,' my father cut in, 'this no longer concerns you.'

Walking behind him, I was unable to see Tamar, but his words must have brought her up short since my father stumbled a little before moving forward again.

We came to the straw-strewn chamber where Joan passed her days. 'Pray sit here,' came Tamar's voice, and I guessed she had guided Father to the flattish piece of rock where I usually sat. I heard him take out the tinder-box.

'Allow me one moment,' he said. I was curious to know where Joan was, and why she remained silent, but not wanting to annoy my father again I contented myself with groping my way to a corner where I could rest my back against the wall.

A spark shot up from the tinder, then another. Then a light caught and grew, bringing streaks of moisture out on the walls, so that what had seemed a boundless darkness shrank around us as Father lit a candle and held it out in the unclean air. At last I was able to make out Joan, lying nearly under my feet.

Perhaps Father was watching me, for almost at the same instant he brought the candle down where its beams fell directly upon her.

She was nothing but a death's head; the fat around her eyes was all shrunk away so that her eyeballs protruded. I thought I could have run my finger round the rims of her eye-sockets, right down behind those eyes, and the fancy sickened me. Deep shadows round the jaws showed where her cheeks were sunken in from lack of teeth.

My father studied her in silence.

'Is she asleep?' I whispered.

He motioned me to silence and continued to gaze. I glanced over his shoulder at Tamar whose own face, away from the candle, showed only as a dim triangle.

'Yes,' Father said suddenly, and I understood: at first he had been unable to reconcile the relic before him with the girl he had known.

He turned to Tamar. 'Be so good as to wake her.'

She came forward, bent over her mother and began softly shaking her by the arm. A wet chink appeared in the bulging eyes, but the sleeper had not yet seen us. When she did there was a spasm of her entire body.

'Tamar!' she gasped.

'Hush,' her daughter said. 'They're friends.'

Joan gave no sign of hearing the last word. She flinched from my father, twisting round in an attempt to hide her face.

'She's still half asleep,' Tamar explained. She hissed to her mother, 'Lie still, will you!'

The old woman subsided into the straw.

'I've never seen her like this,' I said.

'She's failing for lack of food.' Tamar looked up at my father. 'And warmth.'

At this, Father produced some bread, butter, cordial and

cold meat which he had brought with him from Spadboro. Tamar eyed them longingly but made no move to eat; instead, she explained how Dr Green had frightened away those who came seeking amulets. These days they stayed at home, and with them their precious offerings: pennies, loaves, pieces of meat. Nothing, now, in the frozen wood but birds and rabbits, which Joan was grown too frail to catch.

'Can she still sleep out the winter?' I asked.

'If she does,' said Tamar, 'she'll sleep for good.'

'Have you nothing at all to eat?' my father said. Tamar rose, fetched a cloth and showed him its contents: a mess of boiled pease, twisted up in the clout without dish or spoon. I wondered if Tamar had stolen it. They had evidently been trying to make it last; there were blots of mould upon it and a musty smell sufficient to disgust anyone not rendered bestial by hunger. My father looked very grave. Silently Tamar put away the cloth and again bent over her mother.

'Come, wake up. Wake up.'

Joan muttered and curled into herself.

'I can't stay forever,' my father said.

This hint put new strength into Tamar. She shook Joan without stopping until the older woman was forced to open her eyes.

'Joan!' my father said loudly, as soon as she did so. 'I'm Mathew Dymond. Robin's brother.'

Joan turned her face to him.

'And this is my son. You know Jon, don't you? Jon?'

'Know him?' she murmured.

'Good,' said Father, as if he had desired precisely this answer. 'And now, Jon, I want you to go outside and leave us alone.'

'But Father –'

'You too, young woman. Jon, make sure she stays away from here.'

With a sigh, I rose. Tamar followed me out through the cave entrance and into the ha-ha.

'Sent out again,' she remarked as soon as we were out of earshot.

'How dare you!' I snapped. 'My father is an honourable man.'

'I only meant, out into the cold again.' She was laughing at me. 'Or do you think Joan's of an age for sweethearts?'

'Were she the most beautiful woman on earth, she'd be safe with him.'

Tamar walked up and down along the ha-ha, smirking to herself as if she knew better, then turned and pointed back towards the cave. 'See that tree, there? The apple?'

'I can tell an apple tree,' I said coldly.

'You should put your hand on it, for luck.'

Being an enemy to superstition, I stayed where I was and merely asked why that tree above all others.

'It's Joan's wilding. She told me it sprang up when she was with child.'

There was something touching in this sorry little tale. Joan must once have looked forward to a home where her man would plant an apple tree for each child, as others did; she had wanted to be like other women.

'Will you be sad to leave it?' I asked.

'*She* will.'

'But not you?'

'I'd be sadder if it was in fruit.'

There, in a few words, lay the difference between Joan, who had fallen upon hard times, and Tamar, who was born into them. Not even her own tree was dear to her.

She said, 'When will you tell Mr Mathew I'm with child?'

'I already have.'

'What did he say?' she demanded with the first real curiosity I had seen in her since we had arrived.

'I'm not supposed to talk about it,' I said, embarrassed now and even a little irritated with Father, for sending me out with her and thus making it hard to keep to my word.

'He won't know,' she said impatiently. 'All right then, tell me this: what's he want with my mother?'

'To ask her things, I suppose. You're to be looked after, Tamar – have money for the lying-in, and all that; but it's in return for my breaking off with you.'

Her tawny eyes widened in surprise. 'Breaking off? What is there to break off?'

At this I felt a pang. I could not, and would not have liked to, marry her, but to be dismissed so easily! 'You're carrying my child,' I said. 'I take it we'll never be quite strangers to one another.'

Tamar put her head on one side. 'You're not to see me. What's that but strangers?'

'Unless I agree, Father won't maintain you and my son.' I softened my voice and touched her on the arm. 'But I shall often think of you, Tamar – often.'

She ignored the last part of my speech and said as if to the trees, 'Men always think it's a son.'

'Boy or girl,' I returned, 'the child will be cared for. My father does everything fair and square, and that's how I would wish it to be.' If I could have learnt my lesson, I would have kept quiet on the subject of my thoughts and feelings, since they were evidently less than nothing as far as Tamar was concerned.

'What about Joan?' she enquired. 'Is she to be . . .?'

'He won't leave her to starve.'

She looked pleased. 'She'll maybe get through the winter, then.'

'You could at least thank me, Tamar,' I said, mulishly determined to exact some expression of gratitude, of regret, anything that would show I was more to her than the men of the village.

'I thought your father was paying?'

'Not all. I'm giving enough to put back my wedding.'

'You're marrying?' Her frank grin had no jealousy in it. 'Who?'

'Never you mind.'

Tamar began to giggle. 'Jonathan Dymond, married! Well, at least you'll know what to do with her. Such a job as I had, getting it in!'

'And now you can't get me out,' I said. 'So laugh at that.'

She stopped laughing and walked away along the ditch as if to hide a hurt. At once I regretted my spiteful words, but before I could go after her my father came out of the cave.

'She's too exhausted,' he said. 'I can't make myself understood. You must give her some cordial, then some bread and butter and meat.'

'I'll do it directly,' Tamar promised.

'What I wished her to understand is that you must move from here. Wait until you hear from me; I'll deal for you.'

She made an awkward curtsey. 'God bless you, Mr Mathew. Will it be soon?'

'As soon as I can arrange. Say your goodbyes, the two of you.'

I put out my hand. 'Farewell, Tamar. Forgive me.'

'Farewell,' Tamar said, her voice flat, arms by her sides. She had not looked me in the face since she walked away. After my jibe about 'getting me out' she must have thought my apology a kind of feigned virtue for my father's benefit. I cannot blame her; but had she known how much courage it took, and how little my father would approve of his son asking a whore's pardon, she would have judged me more kindly.

'Come,' I urged, 'I wish you well. Let's part friends.'

Since Father was watching, she put a limp hand into mine and said 'Thank you, Sir,' still without turning her eyes on me. I felt such disappointment that for an instant her figure blurred as my own eyes welled up, but I had had enough of weeping and I mastered that.

'Young woman, you won't be seeing my son again,' said Father. 'Is there anything you wish to say to him in my presence?'

'No, Sir.'

'Are you sure?'

'Quite sure, Sir.'

'Then let us go, Jon, we have business to attend to.' He touched my arm to recall me to myself and I went after him, leaving her there. After a few steps, I could not resist looking round. Tamar had disappeared into the cave.

My father has the trick of setting things right and people at their ease with his quiet, unassuming air. So when my aunt stared as we were shown into the room, and did not get up, he took no notice but simply went forward and kissed her, saying he hoped he found her well. As for me, I am easily thrown by such rudeness as hers (I mean I am moved to anger, and cannot always conceal it), so I hung back, letting him smooth the way.

At Father's greeting Aunt Harriet could not but return his good wishes and ask us to sit, but she continued to stare at us in a perplexed manner, until my father asked, 'Is it possible you weren't expecting us, Harriet?'

My aunt's face cleared a little. '*Jon* I certainly expected. My apples are waiting for him.' Here she gave me an exasperated look, but went on immediately to say, 'And of course it's a pleasure to see you, brother-in-law.'

'And for me to see you,' Father said, so smoothly that I was quite struck by his talents as a liar. 'Forgive Jon for wandering off; he'll stay now until the work is finished, won't you, Jon?'

'Yes,' I murmured.

'There. I'm aware, Harriet, that a woman in your position

has a great many affairs to attend to, so I won't keep you longer than need be. I've come here with Jon in order to make a request.'

My aunt rang the bell beside the fire. Rose entered, looking flushed and nervous, as if she had been listening at the door and thought herself detected.

'Cake and wine,' my aunt murmured.

Unlike my father, I was in a position to know that Aunt Harriet invariably offered these to people with whom she hoped to conduct business, and that she must therefore anticipate some profit in granting his request. Rose, with whom I had enjoyed so much gossip in the past, now scuttled away without daring to acknowledge me by more than a curtsey. No sooner had she closed the door than my aunt proved me a prophet by asking, 'Are you talking about a loan, Mathew?'

'Oh, nothing like that! I was wondering, in fact, if you could have a word with Dr Green.'

My aunt drew herself up so tightly that her chair creaked. 'If you seek to interest him in some concern of yours, Mathew, I can only advise you –'

'You mistake me. I've no personal interest in the matter. The thing is –'

Rose entered and served us with our refreshments. When she had gone, and we had praised my aunt's hospitality, my father began again.

'I don't know if you're aware of this, Harriet, but there's a vagrant living in the wood behind your house.'

'There are always vagrants in there,' said my aunt. 'Behind the house, you say? Are we in danger?'

'Oh, no! This is a poor old trot, destitute, derelict. She fancies herself a wise woman – you know the sort of thing. Now, I hear Dr Green has taken men to inspect this so-called witch, and I wondered if you could persuade him to let her be.'

'Persuade him?' Aunt Harriet frowned. 'Surely you don't imagine I instruct Dr Green in his duties?'

'I mean only that you're well respected in the parish. The creature is incapable; she doesn't know what she's saying. I'm sure Dr Green is sincere in his –'

'You seem very well informed, Mathew. Who told you all this – Jon?'

Father inclined his head and my aunt went on, 'You never mentioned this woman to me, Jon. When you went home, I thought you intended to ask about my sister Joan.'

Her hawk's eyes looked right through me.

'Answer, Jon,' my father said mildly.

'I did ask, Aunt, and my father gave me back your own words, almost.' The *almost* was to square my conscience.

Aunt Harriet nodded her head. 'So let us be clear now. This idiot woman in the wood is the mother of my thieving servant, is she not?'

I was sweating. 'I did meet her through keeping company with your servant, yes. That was folly, Aunt, I know it now, and I'll never see them again.'

'He's made a clean breast of it,' Father put in, rescuing me. 'The thing is, through the girl he met this pitiful old creature. Harriet, I would've thought Dr Green would know better. Had she magical powers, she would scarcely be starving in a wood.'

'You forget,' said my aunt, 'that in their fancy witches go gorgeously attired. Satan deludes his servants with false shows of wealth.'

'All wealth is a false show,' Father remarked, perhaps none too tactfully in that house. 'Christ's teachings make that plain.'

'The Bible also tells us, *Thou shalt not suffer a witch to live.* Dr Green is within his rights to remove her.'

From that moment I think we both saw we should get nowhere, but Father battled on.

'I would never argue with scripture, Harriet. My point is, this is no witch.'

'You've met with her, then?'

'Once.'

I wondered: was this another deliberate lie of Father's? Possibly at that moment he considered Old Joan and Young Joan as two different people.

My aunt said, 'Dr Green has spoken with her on several occasions; he always proceeds with care. My dear Mathew, surely you don't think this is the first time he's dealt with such women?'

'You yourself seem very well informed, Harriet,' Father said, with a touch of sarcasm.

'It's my duty to help root out evil from the parish.'

I shuddered at the sight of her, so respectable and righteous and . . . what was the word? I could only think of 'malevolent', and that is scarcely a word one cares to use within one's own family.

'Harriet,' my father said, and his voice sounded like pleading, 'this woman is close to death. Might you not –'

'As for the young one,' Aunt glanced at me, 'pray consider what you are defending. Because of her, men are infecting their innocent wives! What pastor would permit that, if he could once put a stop to it?'

At this I felt a rush of indignation and I opened my mouth to say that Tamar was not poxed. My aunt was watching me with a tiny cold smile, no more than just a curl of the lip, as if to say, 'Come, will you put your head in this noose?'

There was a pause. Then my father very quietly said, 'And does she drag these virtuous husbands to the woods?'

'That they go to her only proves the force of the temptation.'

To me it was plain as day that Aunt Harriet knew who it was that lay in the cave, and I was almost leaping with impatience until I could communicate this to my father. There was an air

223

of suppressed triumph about my aunt that he could not have failed to notice, but I did not think he had worked it all out as I had. The link between past and present was – I saw now – Dr Green. He had known Joan as a young woman, and later when she returned as a vagrant. He had spoken to her face to face, most recently when he had refused charity to her and Tamar. He had visited the 'witch'. At some point he must have recognised her, and told my aunt of his discovery. When that had been, what they had said on that occasion, I would never know, but it had happened recently; I would take my Bible oath that when I first went to Aunt Harriet's house, she regarded Joan as no more than an old beggar who persisted in peering through windows.

As I sat studying Aunt Harriet's pursed, triumphant face, I no longer had the slightest trouble believing that she had made a sacrifice of her erring sister. It struck me that my aunt, who had featured for so long as a dim, ageing figure in the background to my young life, was nothing less than a Cromwell in petticoats. That is perhaps a comical expression, but there is nothing comical about such people. Aunt Harriet would have signed the death warrant of the King of England, had he got in her way.

∂

Before supper, Father helped me lay out everything in readiness for the morning; after that time it was too dark to do much, even with lanterns. The three of us were to eat together, after which Aunt Harriet could hardly refuse to lodge Father overnight. She suggested that he share my bed, saying that in this way we would be more likely both to wake early, he to travel back to Spadboro and I to begin my work on the cider. This seemed a poor, thin reason in a house where there were servants to wake us, and I believe her real object, grudging as she was, was to avoid dirtying any more of her fine linen.

Father said this arrangement would suit us very well, and that we would retire, with her permission, shortly after supper.

That meal passed off peacefully enough; the fire was burnt out of our conversation, leaving us polite and dull. My aunt asked after 'Barbara' and brought Rose out of the kitchen to supply the recipe for a conserve said to be a particular favourite of the Bishop of Bath and Wells; how Rose had come by this, or what connection she might have with the Bishop I am sure I cannot say.

We said goodnight and left my aunt sitting at table. Vexed by a persistent flea, she had taken off her cap, and as I looked back from the doorway on leaving I saw her hair glisten in the dull beams of the candles. Seen in that soft light, and from a distance, she appeared a frail and lonely woman, presiding over emptiness where children should have been.

As we climbed the stairs to my chamber I was wondering why Robin had produced no legitimate issue. If Tamar was indeed his child, the weakness must lie in my aunt. Yet what strength she had, in other ways: strength to bear the evenings alone and in silence, on and on until her death and in plain view of that approaching end. I have never felt myself so alone as she appeared to me at that moment. Though I am of the stronger sex, I am not sure I could have borne it.

We undressed by candlelight and got into what I now thought of as Joan's bed. It was a good size for two people and had the additional advantage that we were able to confer together in whispers. Father told me that although he had already settled upon helping the women in the wood, while talking with my aunt he had come to a further decision, namely that he should return with all haste and fetch them away to a better place before Dr Green could terrify Joan into a confession.

'But Father, what if they catch you?'

'Then I have discovered my sister-in-law living in destitution and wish to take her to my home. I have the right – she hasn't been arrested.'

'Will you take her to Spadboro?'

'If I'm forced to.'

'And if not? Where will you go?'

'*You* should know nothing.'

He was right. Should Dr Green question me, I could answer him in all innocence. On the other hand, it also meant I could never again find out Tamar, unless Father relented. But then, I had only to remember her face as she said, 'What is there to break off?' to realise how little she wished to be found.

'Very well,' I said.

'Good lad. Now: when I'm gone, no hints, no smirks, nothing of that sort. Obey your aunt.'

'I promise.'

He blew out the candle and began settling himself for sleep. After a while I heard him snore. Sleep came less easily to me but when it came it was black nothingness, empty of both joy and fear.

The following morning Father left while it was still dark; I waved him off and when the light permitted, went back to my aunt's cider. I will spare you the details: let me say only that the familiar labour I had loved so long brought me no comfort and I was in no mood to prolong it. But it went slowly enough by itself, since I had all the apples to gather and sort without the help of little Billy, who was gone on some errand in the village, and by the time the second cheese was in place it was nearly dark outside.

Already a day had passed since Father had gone with me to the cave. I stood in the doorway looking out at the sky – clear and starry, the women would feel the cold in their bones – and wishing I could sleep in the stable rather than go back inside End House.

Father had done well to warn me against triumphing over Aunt Harriet. I was sorely tempted, for his departure was the signal for mocks and gibes. As Rose put some stewed fruit on the table my aunt remarked that the charms of the young woman in the wood seemed to have swayed my father, and that it was curious how all the men of the Dymond family shared this tendency to be drawn by crude and impudent attractions.

'You must allow *one* exception,' I said. My aunt's eye lit up; she was so used to slavish flattery from those around her that I believe she expected it even from me. Her look changed, however, when I added, 'Nobody ever considered my mother either crude or impudent.'

My aunt said only, 'You'll finish tomorrow – eh?' but it was too late; I had seen the insult go home. However, this was not the way to keep my promise to Father, so I said more humbly, 'I'll do my best, Aunt. Where was Billy this morning?'

'He's gone to Dr Green's house, with the constable,' my aunt said, 'telling them about some thefts that took place here. Firewood and straw.'

I felt myself grow pale, but she could hardly have perceived that in the dim room, and my voice was firm as I asked, 'Has the thief been detected?'

'Thieves. We hope to have them in our hands soon.' Her smile was cruel, as if the thought gave her delight. It crossed my mind that my aunt had a streak of madness, so sinister did she appear at that moment, but when she added, 'And once they are sentenced we'll be rid of them,' I realised it was no more than her habitual selfishness.

'It's those women, is it? Will they be whipped away?'

'That's for the authorities to decide. They've certainly earned themselves a whipping.'

I winced at the thought of Joan's bony shoulders. 'Even the old one?'

'She's not too frail to traffic with Satan,' my aunt returned with a little air of putting me right. 'As for the other, Mathew and I were right to keep you from her. She'd have devoured you up.'

I could restrain myself no longer.

'Aunt,' I said. 'Do you think Uncle Robin ever looks down from Heaven and sees our doings?'

From swelling with complacency my aunt's features shrunk up small, like a snake's, but she made no reply. Indeed, she said nothing more until we rose from table.

⚜

Undressing that night, I felt wretched. I had brought Joan and Tamar to my father's care, and that was a great thing to have achieved; but I had achieved it at the price of never seeing them again, had burdened Tamar with a fatherless child, and had failed to carry out Robin's wishes. I had but one day to discover the will – for it was plain I would never again be lodged at End House – with no inkling of where to find it; while my aunt, if she understood my game, stood poised to block me at every turn.

I gave myself up to grim fancies. My father's attempt at rescue would come too late. Dr Green, zealous on behalf of his wealthiest parishioner, would see the women jailed – if not for witchcraft, for whoring; if not for that, for theft. With none to speak for them, and my aunt clamouring on the other side, they would find neither justice nor mercy.

Despite knowing it was fruitless, I got up in my nightgown and once more went over the room, since it had once been Joan's, searching every inch, tapping every drawer in the press for hidden compartments and pushing my hands as far under the mattress as I could reach. Not so much as a scrap of paper.

The search was absurd. Had Robin hidden anything here for Joan to find he would surely have let her know. Besides, why should he not have given it to her? She could read. Then I thought, perhaps she *was* once in possession of such a document, had hidden it here and been dragged away by Harriet before she could retrieve it. She might not choose to tell me that. I was a Dymond, after all; I might wish to protect my inheritance by finding the papers and destroying them.

Here I had a new idea. Perhaps, if Robin did write a will intended to protect Joan from her sister, he did so after the scenes in the Guild Hall, after she had left Tetton Green, and so he had never been able to put it into her hand or instruct her where to find it. Meanwhile, if Harriet suspected the existence of such a document, she and her servants would have searched everywhere: house, offices, stables. Yet here I stood poking under a mattress, as if I alone could light on the thing. I moved away, ashamed of my stupidity.

Very well: suppose he made a will and it was destroyed by Harriet. He could have written another, towards the end of his life, and bidden Tamar take it to her mother. On the other hand, as long as Joan and Tamar lived in hope they had an interest in keeping him alive. Robin, so selfishly careful of himself, would never have forgotten that.

No matter how it had been, I could see where my father came in and why he had been summoned. Both Harriet and Joan could read, but my father was the sole person who could read *and* whom Robin held in absolute trust.

And yet ... all this was pure supposition. There was no proof that such a will had ever been written; should I go to a notary, I knew exactly what the man would ask: What makes you so convinced of the existence of this paper? All I could answer was that I was plagued by a dream, and that a dead man required me to make amends.

Why had he picked out *me* for this hopeless quest? I had never been an intimate of his. I could have raged about the room like a baited bear, such was my pent-up frustration; but there was nothing for it but to get tamely into bed. Once there, I grew calmer, and bodily fatigue had its usual effect. Aunt Harriet's linen bolster was perfumed with lavender, and polished (perhaps by Tamar) with the iron: I yielded to its persuasions, and slept.

The horse started up in answer to some mysterious prompting and the cart rolled away. I was at once plunged in the trance of nightmare, my limbs dissolving in fear so that I was powerless to jump down. We entered a narrow sunken lane, hedged in on either side and swallowed up in mist. From time to time I glimpsed branching ways, their dark openings gliding past as if borne upon a stream. Then came a fingerpost for Tetton Green, seemingly lit up from within, and the horse flowed in that direction without any guidance on my part. I could hear myself groaning: my soul seemed suspended, sapped of will by the clammy veils that shrouded us. We descended into a tunnel, swimming through darkness towards the meeting awaiting me somewhere along the way.

At last the tunnel opened out. The mist slid down the sides of the cart and rippled round the wheels. My voice had dried in my throat, else I would have cried out in fear, for this pale sea of mist always came just before, and now I could already see, far off on the road, the dim spot that I dreaded. At first it seemed no more than a thicker patch of vapour, obscure and indistinct as what surrounded it, but as the cart drew nearer I saw parts of it break away and sink to form the hands.

Suddenly my tongue was freed.

'No, Robin!' I screamed. 'Go away – leave me!'

We were almost up with him now, the cart still fixed in its hideous gliding motion. I knew what I must do and looked round frenziedly for the whip, but there was none.

I was sitting up in bed, holding the covers away from me. Shaking, I lowered them and peered into the darkness, unsure whether I was awake or asleep. My neck and chest were awash with sweat; when I felt this, I knew for sure that I was awake, and in a room as cold as the dank lane of my nightmare. The dream was not finished! Why had I woken up before the end? The thought of sleeping again, with Robin lying in wait for me, filled me with dread, but now the air began to chill me in earnest, so that I was forced to lie back and cover myself with a quilt.

I had done all I could for him. Why should he continue to persecute me with these monstrous dreams? I pictured them continuing the rest of my days, breeding inside my head where nobody could pluck them out. Hideous! And what of my promise to my parents, that I would marry? Would any wife welcome a husband incapable of lying quiet in his bed?

I am perhaps diseased in the mind, I said to myself; or if this continues, I may become so. It was not the first time that I had been visited by this fear, but the first time I had permitted it to assume a distinct shape. I decided that on my return to Spadboro, I would seek the aid of our pastor, a kindlier man than Dr Green, and try if he could release me from Uncle Robin. At this moment, as I was arranging myself again in the bed and wondering if I should remain awake all night, I heard a sudden sharp *clink* at the back of the house. In a few seconds the *clink* was repeated, more loudly this time, and I understood that this noise had awakened me from my dream.

I lay in darkness, straining to pick up another sound, and thought I distinguished a sort of shuffling. Slowly, for fear of creaking floorboards, I pulled aside the bed curtains, padded over to the window and coaxed open the casement, then the shutter. As I did so, a delicate ray of light, a will o' the wisp, glided over the stonework and vanished. Icy air poured over the sill onto my bare feet and legs, but I stayed as I was, though shivering. At last, not far off, I spied a twinkle among the leafless branches, as if a star had become entangled in them, but this was a wandering star, and moved uncertainly on its way again. Somebody was taking a lantern along the path – and soon, as the wind shifted, I was able to catch a faint murmur, which at times resolved itself into men's voices before dissolving again into the sigh of the swaying trees.

Silently closing the window, I felt my way back to the bed. The thing had run its course, then: the women were to be arrested. My first impulse, dismissed as soon as considered, had been to run out and attempt to intervene, but that was quite useless. Even were I equal to driving away the men, which was certainly not the case, they need only come back later, since Joan was too feeble to escape. I was sorry for her and sorrier still for that virago, Tamar, who with better luck might have been just such a sweet, romping, harmless thing as Poll Parfitt. I did not think the men would show Tamar much kindness, but she could at least plead her belly –

I clapped my hands to my mouth. She would surely think it worth her while to proclaim that the father of her child was Master Jonathan Dymond. Then what? I was entangled in this business whether I liked it or not, and my first impulse had been the right one. I must get out into the wood, if only to see and hear the proceedings, and perhaps get some idea of where the women were to be taken so that I could tell Father.

As well as I could, I dragged my clothes over my nightshirt in the darkness. Finding a muffler in the press, I wrapped it round my face, for secrecy as much as warmth, and in a very few minutes I was outside in the yard, easing back the bolt. Another minute, and I was in the pathway at the back of the house, and then I was stumbling through the wood.

It is a terrible business, making your way through a dark and deserted spot at dead of night. How much worse, then, when the spot is *not* deserted – when under cover of darkness strangers are concealed, and perhaps nearer than you would like.

The January night was hard as steel, the moon no thicker than a fingernail. I dared not carry a lantern, and struggled along by the help of the stars, which (thank God) were many and glittering. By daylight the way was not so very long (though it seemed many miles further in that tangled blackness), and by stretching out my foot each time, to feel for mud, I was able to keep on the path, though not without a few nasty switches across the face and, once, a thorn bush nearly in the eye. I could hear the men more plainly now: one had a loud, full voice, suggesting a powerful, brutish type, the other spoke more softly, yet I thought he must be in charge of the affair, to judge by the length of time he was suffered to speak uninterrupted. This second, then, was most likely a gentleman, perhaps Dr Green himself. They seemed to be carrying a dark lantern; the open side of this sometimes flashed towards me, causing me to duck, and it was with sweating caution that I inched nearer to them.

Alas, I was not cautious enough. Night and lack of sleep caused me to misjudge the place: the ground yawned beneath me and with a scream fit to wake the dead, I fell into the ha-ha.

They were on me at once, crashing through the bushes and shining their light full in my eyes. I was dazzled, unable to see them, and quite unable to speak.

One of them reached forward and plucked the muffler from my face.

'Well – !' a voice said and they burst into laughter.

'Pray do me no harm,' I said, when I could get my breath. 'I came from the house just there – Mrs Harriet Dymond's.'

'We know,' said the rougher of the two voices. The dark lantern was now turned about so that I could get a look at them, and I found myself gazing at my father, and next to him, Simon Dunne.

'You promised to stay away,' Father said.

'I only came because I saw the lantern.'

'Saw it, how?'

'From my window. And you can be heard from there.'

They exchanged glances and Dunne said, 'They'll have heard *him* at Spadboro, then!'

'We can't stop now,' said Father. 'Did you see the horses, Jon? Back of the house?'

I must have narrowly missed walking into them in the dark.

'You've two horses, Simon?'

'We've one of our own, now,' said Father. 'I thought it best.'

It was awkward work carrying Joan from the cave along the track. My father and Dunne had brought a blanket and from this they made a kind of sling in which to scoop her up. At the ha-ha they paused. Dunne climbed onto the upper path while Father hoisted Joan, supported by me, onto his shoulders. With a deal of frightened muttering from Joan, and of puffing from Simon Dunne, she was lifted to the top. I then went ahead with the dark lantern while Tamar, carrying a pitiful bundle of clothes and chattels, brought up the rear.

I wanted to ask my father how he had talked Simon round

to such an adventure, where he would take the women, and what care would be procured for them. Instead I fixed my mind upon being a trustworthy pilot, holding back brambles so that they might not spring into the eyes of those following me, and warning them of roots or slippery places. Even with the lantern, I strained to distinguish what lay before us. Shadows dissolved and regrouped; gleams of light fled upwards from puddles on the ground, picking out a tree here or there and then losing themselves in the depths of the wood. Somewhere over to my right was End House. I hoped Aunt Harriet was not peering from behind one of the windows, or worse, lying in wait for us, along with Dr Green and his men, in the obscurity of the lane.

We at last gained the cart. While Dunne talked softly to Bully and his yokefellow, turning them round with as little noise as might be, Father and I laid Joan, still in her blanket, on the ground.

'She's light as a bird,' my father remarked.

Hearing this, Tamar swore.

'Watch your tongue,' Father said curtly.

'Beg pardon, Sir. We've left Hob behind.'

'Left what?'

'Joan's raven. He's dear to her.'

'You can't take him where you're going. Stand aside, will you?'

The cart came round and Joan was lifted onto it.

'She'll fret without him,' Tamar insisted as her mother was wrapped round with the blanket. 'She'll pine.'

There was a pause. I sensed that my father was torn, wanting but fearing to allow this small thing.

I said, 'I'll fetch him.'

'No, you won't,' Father said. 'We're going now.'

'Give me the lantern, stop outside the village and I'll catch you up.'

'Is the bird in a cage?' Father asked Tamar.

'He's made himself a nest up in the rock.'

'Then how can you fetch it away?' he demanded of me.

'Your father knows best,' Simon said. 'Come, Mistress, you're to go with us.'

Tamar scrambled into the cart.

'Won't you wait?' I pleaded. The cart creaked softly as Father and Simon climbed into it. Simon clicked his tongue to the horses and they took the strain.

'Move, then,' Father said, not to them but to me. 'We'll stay at the village end until you come.'

I plunged back into the wood. Though it was a familiar way, and with the advantage of a lantern, it was as if an icy wind blew through me. I feared everything and everybody: my aunt, Dr Green, his followers, any wild thing that might be lurking nearby. I even feared Hob, and thought again of the man who was blinded by a bird. Suppose the creature flew at me in the dark, all beak and claws?

Dropping into the ha-ha I nearly extinguished the lantern, and only by the greatest luck kept it lit. I entered the cave, going through the length and depth of it, examining the angles and making sudden springs and turns to be sure nobody was there (though had I found a lurking robber, what could I have done? I was unarmed). When it proved empty, my fear began to subside. The cave, a hell-mouth a few minutes previously, now appeared to me what it was: a shelter.

I paused, weighing up the problem of Hob. His nest was high on a stone ledge marked out, when I shone the lantern along the wall, by streaks of droppings below it. Let him once fly out into the cave and farewell all chance of taking him. My only course was to climb up and seize him before he was awake.

I was not so much daunted by the climb itself. The rock was rough and ribbed; any boy worthy of the name could have scaled it. My fear was of my cold, stiff fingers, and of the trouble of carrying the lantern with me. More, I was not sure how I should lay hold of the bird without losing my grasp on the cave wall. But I had not time to waste in pondering any of this, but must put my powers to the test at once, so up I went.

My lantern must have risen over his nest like the sun upon the wider world. He winked with surprise and rose on his legs, but before he could spread his wings I set down the light and grasped him round the neck. It is no simple matter to keep hold of a full-grown raven; he flapped and screeched so that I nearly let go. When at last I had thrust him, head down, into my open pocket – which luckily was a large, deep one – and fastened down the flap, I felt him turn a somersault inside his prison as I made my way down the rock. Once on the ground, I hurried along the path, vigilant in feeling for branches on the side where Hob lay, lest a chance blow to my coat should kill him.

All was darkness around my aunt's house. For aught I could tell, she might be watching from a window. I was especially nervous of Geoffrey Barnes, and would not have been surprised to find him lying in wait, but evidently he was tucked up in bed with Rose. I left the path beside the house for the open road, hurrying along it towards the wood, and after a short time perceived the cart, pulled in by the side of the road.

As I approached I observed that Father and Joan were speaking together; it seemed that a little food had restored her power of conversation. Then Tamar, hearing my footsteps, turned towards me and the others at once fell silent.

'It's Jon,' I called softly. Still nobody spoke a word until I was almost upon them, when Tamar, seeing me, asked, 'Where's Hob?'

'Here.' I mounted the cart and sat next to her. 'How will you keep him?'

She showed me a piece of cloth. 'I'll wrap him up, until we're within doors.'

'It'll only die,' said Simon. 'You should've left it where it was.'

Tamar felt in my pocket.

'Be careful,' I said, remembering that ferocious beak.

'He knows me.' She seized hold of him and at once wrapped him round. Were I Hob, I don't know that I would find much comfort in being swaddled; I thought Simon was most likely right, and the creature would die, but I had handed him over alive and Tamar must look to him now.

'Back you go,' said Father, leaning across and kissing me. 'And not a word to your aunt.'

'No need to tell me that.'

'Not a look, then. Not a smile. I'll return for you as soon as I can.'

It came to me that this hurried farewell on the road, with Tamar fussing over a raven and all of us shivering and hoarse with cold, was my last meeting with the mother of my child. I did believe the child was mine. Nothing Father said, no matter how reasonable, could persuade me otherwise.

'Tamar,' I said. She was stowing the bundled bird inside her cloak, and looked up as if expecting to hear some question. I had a little ring, a keepsake from a boyhood friend; I groped for her hand and pushed the ring into it. Tamar said nothing, but stretched out her arms as if to embrace me.

'Jon, get down this minute,' my father rapped out. 'Get onto the road.'

I was shamed by tears that would come no matter how I strove to prevent them. The lantern showed me Tamar, looking at me more softly than I ever recall her doing before that moment.

It ended as my father pushed between us. He relieved me of the lantern, hung it on the side of the cart for safety and took me by the shoulders, saying, 'Be a man and *get down*.'

Feeling more boy than man, I climbed down and waved as the cart pulled away. Only my father waved back. Dunne was busy with the horses. Tamar sat motionless, seemingly study-ing me, until her pale face dissolved in the darkness.

As I turned to go back to Aunt Harriet's house I realised that I had made Tamar the same gift as Robin had: a ring. It seemed I could never carve for myself, but must forever be following and aping someone older. I felt very small and wretched as I let myself in by the back gate, locking it behind me.

17

Concerning Corruption in Cider

Next morning I was awakened by a banging on the chamber door.

'Come in,' I called.

Little Billy stood before me. The lad was not an indoor servant: what was he doing here, when he should be with Paulie? Perhaps I was still half asleep.

'Please, Mr Jonathan, the mistress says you're to come down to breakfast.'

'With all my heart; but what time is it?'

'Never heard the church bells, Sir, but Mrs Harriet says you're late.'

It was coming back to me now. I wondered where the Seaton women had woken up this morning: surely not in a feather bed. With the unwieldy fingers of the hasty man I bungled my way into my clothes, my buttons and ties quarrelling with me and my shoes refusing to go on, while the boy stood watching me struggle.

'Tell my aunt I'll be with her directly,' I said. When he was gone I stepped to the window and opened the shutter. Nothing but the familiar outlines of the winter wood, and a bitter edge in the air as if snow was coming.

Downstairs Aunt Harriet was still seated at the table, very splendid in a gown of black velvet but with no food set before her. I greeted her, sat down to my place, and asked if she wished to speak with me.

My aunt came straight to the point. 'Those creatures had visitors last night.'

I pretended to laugh. 'What, in this weather?'

'Drunken men will do anything.'

If ever a woman could testify to that, I thought, she was the one. 'Did you see anybody, Aunt?'

'I? No. Rose heard men behind the house.'

'Robbers, perhaps,' I suggested maliciously.

Her fingers pleating a linen napkin, she appeared to study me. I put my hand to my right cheek, where was some itching and soreness, and found a deep scratch, scabbed over. At once my face burned like a furnace. The heat came in waves, worse and worse, until it seemed it would never go down. I could not think of a single thing to say; my guilt was marked twice over, in the scratch and in this painful blush.

'Robbers,' my aunt echoed. She regarded me with what looked like amusement for a moment and then her gaze went inwards as if she was thinking. My face began to cool, since her eye no longer pierced mine, but I would rather have been any-where than sitting opposite her at that table.

Rose entered and I asked her for bread and broth. This brought my aunt's attention back to me.

'So, *you* didn't hear anything?'

'I slept too well.'

'And yet you're late out of bed.'

To this I had no answer.

'You'll sleep better at home,' she went on with relish. 'Is Mathew coming for you today?'

'I expect him, yes.'

She pounced. 'Oh? What about the bad cider?'

'You mean the one we boiled up?'

'No. There's one gone ropey.'

'Ropey!' I exclaimed. My aunt's house seemed to breed sick-ly cider.

'I got Binnie to look at it; he says you've squandered my fruit.'

'Binnie's never had a ropey hogshead, I suppose.'

'Not here.'

Next year, I thought, he would have the work again, and was welcome to it.

Rose entered with my broth, laid it down and hurried out. Since my aunt plainly regarded me as a poor workman, I thought she would let me off the spoilt cider and hand it over to Binnie, but she went on, 'You'd better sample it – see if you can put it right.'

'Father likes to travel early,' I said lamely.

'Oh, you can take a look,' said my aunt. 'Go after breakfast. Goodness, Rose, what is it?' she cried as the servant appeared yet again. 'You do nothing but hover!'

'I beg pardon, Mistress, but Dr Green is back.'

Just for the tiniest part of an instant, I saw my aunt freeze. Rose had blundered: she should not have said 'back', or not in front of me. Aunt Harriet recovered directly, saying as if in surprise, 'Dr Green? At this hour?'

'Yes, Mistress. He says it's urgent.'

Aunt Harriet flung down the napkin and left the room. I watched the linen unpleat itself as if it, too, felt the relief of being out of her hands.

&

I had hoped my father might come for me as soon as he had delivered the women to wherever they were bound. But perhaps he, or Simon, had chosen to rest the horses first. I had nothing to occupy myself and no one to visit, so I thought it could do no harm to look at the spoilt cider. Having armed myself with a tankard from the kitchen, I went off to the cider shed.

Paulie's boy peered out from the window of his father's lodging as I passed. I guessed he would come out to join me and I was right: after a moment he appeared, wrapped up against the cold, and asked if he could come and press apples.

'Oh, that's over with, Billy. All finished.'

The boy skipped listlessly about me in the yard until I took pity on him. 'Very well,' I said. 'Come and see the ropey cider.' He brightened at once and trotted along like a lamb towards the cider shed.

'So, my aunt employs you within doors now?' I asked him by way of conversation.

He shook his head.

'No? Then how was it she sent you to my chamber?'

'I don't know,' the child said. 'She called me to come inside and wake you up.'

'Where were the other servants?'

'Don't know, Sir.'

Something had been going on while I lay asleep, that was plain: something that upset the running of the household. I wondered about Dr Green's urgent business with my aunt. Had he and his men planned an arrest for this morning? If so, my father and Simon had arrived in the nick of time.

When I pulled open the door to the cider shed, the hogshead stood against a wall, its top lifted off.

'What fool did this?' I demanded of the boy.

'Don't know, Sir.'

'Open to every infection . . . ! Was it Binnie?'

The lad shook his head but I was not convinced, suspecting as I did that Binnie had set out to destroy my credit. He could have spared himself the labour, since I had none for him to destroy.

The boy watched solemnly as I mounted onto a wooden stool, bent over the hogshead and scooped up some of the cider with my tankard. As I broke the surface an unwholesome smell escaped from the drink, and as I let the contents of the tankard drop back again I perceived the ropes of slime, just as my aunt had described them.

Paulie's boy wrinkled his nose.

'Want some?' I held out the tankard.

'Ugh! No!'

'Best thing in the world for worms, toothache, deafness, baldness, Billyness –' I pushed it towards him, and the child ran out of the shed, laughing.

Left alone, I wondered if I could be bothered to go through with the cure, which meant straining out every single rope of slime. I would have to tap the hogshead and drain it through cloth, burn sulphur for purification and start again. Even that was far from being a sure thing.

It occurred to me that Binnie might have taken the top off in order to throw in a rat or suchlike and thus foul the cider. He might even have taken it for a cure; there are fools who fancy cider is improved by every kind of nastiness, when all it needs is good, pure apple-must, a sound barrel, and time. Spying a rake in the corner of the shed, I removed my coat and shirt, shuddering at the coldness of the air, took up the rake and mounted the stool again. The implement reached to the bottom of the hogshead without meeting any obstruction, but in order to make certain, I stirred the cider vigorously and put my arm in up to the oxter, with my face nearly in the icy brew, straining to feel if anything brushed against my fingers.

'Mind the stool,' I said over my shoulder, hearing the door open. The next minute there was an almighty shove at my buttocks, the stool dropped away beneath my feet and I was being upended into the cider.

I was doubly at a disadvantage, from leaning over and from having one arm far down inside. With my free hand I endeavoured to lay hold of whoever was pushing me, but to no avail, and as I let go of the side of the barrel I could no longer brace myself and was forced deeper in. I kicked out furiously with my feet, and struck against the body of whoever was trying to drown me, only to propel myself still further into the liquid, so

244

that my face was under the surface. When I screamed, all that came out of my mouth was bubbles, and now whoever was behind me grabbed my ankles and made to pull them upwards. I curled myself like a shrimp to keep my feet down, but with my nose and mouth full of cider it was not long before I lost the battle. I felt myself turned head over heels, and the hands let go of me. I was inside the hogshead, borne down by my own weight, scrabbling violently but unable to lift myself out.

My brain and body were now those of a dying animal, feebly repeating its useless motions. I was gone – lost in terror and despair – when I received a violent shock all along one side; there was a rending sound and I was again aware of someone pulling me by the ankles.

When I came to I was lying on the floor of the shed with Paulie bending over me, and so cold that my entire body shook as if I were having a fit. The stink of cider was well-nigh overpowering: I looked around and saw the hogshead that had nearly been my coffin a few feet away from me.

'How are you, Master Jon? Can you speak?'

I choked up vile, sour cider out of my nose and mouth. Paulie pulled me so that I was sitting upright. 'That's right, get it out,' he urged as my shoulders heaved.

I now perceived Geoffrey Barnes leaning against the wall of the shed and looking capable, in every sense, of shouldering me into the drink. Seeing my coughs and heavings begin to subside, Paulie asked what had happened. Weak and gasping for breath, I was forced to lie down again on the ground before I could speak, but my wits were neither drunk or drowned.

'I fell in,' I said craftily.

'Give thanks to God the lad found you,' Paulie said. 'I'll tell your aunt.'

Before I could stop him, he left the shed. I was surprised that

Barnes let him take the message, since he himself was often employed as an indoor servant, while Paulie was not. It struck me that if Barnes were indeed the would-be assassin, he had procured himself some time in which to finish me off. He did nothing, however, except pick up my coat and throw it over me, saying I should be put to bed and a poultice applied to keep off the cold. Frightened as I was, and closely as I watched, I could perceive no malice in him, and my fear began to go down.

Paulie returned saying my aunt was in her chamber, but would be with us directly, and then we waited for what seemed an hour. I know it cannot have been half so long, but I was feeble and sick and craved warmth.

'Did you tell her yourself?' Barnes demanded at last.

'I told Hannah,' Paulie replied. 'The mistress was in her chamber.'

'And Hannah went up to her straight away?'

'She did.'

Barnes tapped his feet. At that moment I heard someone approaching the shed from outside, and Aunt Harriet burst in upon us.

I stared at her, trying to puzzle out what was odd about her appearance. Her hair was arranged in its usual style and there was nothing peculiar about her dark-blue gown. Was it that, being taller than my aunt, I was unaccustomed to seeing her face from below? The perspective did not become her: she seemed all jowls as she stood over me, not even troubling to bend down as Paulie had done.

Her first question was: 'Has nobody the sense to cover that hogshead?' She must surely lack a woman's heart, I thought. Her breast enfolds some mechanical device; a clock perhaps, whose ticks serve for a heartbeat.

I said, 'I'm nearly drowned, Aunt.'

'You seem alive enough to me.'

I could find nothing to say to that.

She turned on Paulie. 'How did you find him?'

The dwarf spread his hands helplessly. 'If it please you, Mistress, the boy came running to us, said he heard a noise, a splashing like.'

'Perhaps I might take him inside,' Barnes suggested, seeing me still shivering.

'Perhaps you'll wait until you're bid,' retorted my aunt. Barnes seemed not to resent her temper – he had had years in which to accustom himself to it – but by way of a hint, he bent down and tucked the coat more closely around my body.

'Very well then,' she flared at him. 'If you think best!'

He put his hands under my armpits and asked could I walk. Once he had helped me up, I could walk well enough; we cut a ludicrous figure, for there was not much he could do for me. There was no need to carry me, or even lead me by the hand. Then it came to me that perhaps he knew more than he said, and was staying by me as a form of protection. This did not make me feel any happier.

At my chamber door I told him I could manage very well if Rose would bring me up some towels and something hot to drink, but still he lingered.

'Master Jon,' he said at last. 'May I speak?'

I nodded.

'Sir, have you really no recollection of what happened?'

I thought quickly. 'Why? Is there something I should know?'

'What I mean, Sir, is why would you bend forward so far as to fall in? You know the danger.' As indeed I did; the impossibility of getting out of a hogshead, once in, had been drummed into me from childhood onwards.

'I must've had some reason,' I said.

'If I may suggest something, Sir, I think Rose should stay with you.'

'What for?'

'You've been chilled to the bone and a fever might take hold. You should, Sir. You should have someone with you.'

His eyes seemed simultaneously to warn and to deny. What would I not have given for the ability to read his mind!

'What about my aunt's dinner?' I said.

'I'll send up my wife as soon as it's well in hand. Until then, she can bring you something hot to eat, and a poultice; and I'll send the boy too.'

'That's well thought on,' I said, and passed into my chamber, where the familiar bed-scent of night and my body was quite overpowered by the odour of bad cider. The very first thing I did was to bolt the door: I had no intention of permitting another ambush. My saturated clothes, clinging to me like a shroud, had me swearing before I could peel them off. I could not wait for Rose or the towels; I took a sheet from the press and rubbed my skin until I was dry enough to put on my nightgown and get into bed. There, I curled up tight and pulled the blankets high round my neck, but I continued to shiver.

There came a tap at the door.

'Who's there?'

'Rose.'

I let her in. The tray she carried bore two bowls: one full of the broth I had eaten earlier, and another containing bandages and mustard paste.

'My word, Master Jon!' she said, setting down the tray. 'You're white as snow!'

'And as cold. Could you fill me a warming pan?'

'Aye. When you've had this.'

I gulped down the hot, salty liquid not for hunger but to get its heat inside me. I think I would have knowingly drunk poison, were it only hot enough. The boy arrived while I was finishing it up and settled in a chair near the bed.

Rose hurried downstairs and returned with the warming

pan. She took the empty broth bowl from me and passed the pan down the bed, first one side, then the other, while I rolled about to keep from being burnt.

'You'll be right in no time,' she said, laying down the warming pan and turning to her poultice. 'Here, unbutton.' She smeared mustard over my neck and chest, clapping the cloth on top. 'The dinner's going to be late. Do you think you could stay on your back, Master Jon, to keep this in place? I haven't time to bind it.'

I said I could undertake that, provided she returned within the hour.

'And now,' said Rose, 'rest here, and keep the lad with you, and I'll be back as soon as I can. Do you hear, Billy?' she addressed the boy, who nodded. 'Stay with Master Jon until I come for you' – which made me think that Barnes and his wife understood each other.

When she was gone I bade the boy bolt the door.

Though the genial warmth of the poultice now began to penetrate my breast, my feet and legs continued like dead meat. I wondered why I was so very cold. It was not the first time I had been severely chilled; once, when I was fourteen, a boy braved me to swim the river in November. I came out a single lump of ice, but once I was done hopping up and down, and had been rubbed dry, I did very well. This was different. My body had taken mortal fright and could not recover itself. It came to me, too late, that I should not have eaten the broth; but who could fear Rose?

Her husband was another matter. Barnes was physically equal to the act of tipping me over and I had seen him deal roughly with Joan. Yet he hardly seemed to dislike me, and somehow I could not see him drowning a man by stealth.

Could Paulie have pushed me? He was constantly in and out of the stables and sheds. But he was undersized and not strong; besides, I could think of no reason why he should wish me harm. Should he be the man, however, Barnes was also guilty, for Barnes must be covering up for him.

What of Dr Green? I now recalled that he had been at the house unusually early and I was not supposed to know about it. Had he come with his men to tell my aunt that their birds were flown? Was I suspected of aiding and abetting the fugitives – and had one of his witch-hunters, finding me leaning into the hogshead, decided to pay me out for my interference?

I shivered more and more, and put my head beneath the sheets in an attempt to warm up. As I did so I had a sudden vision of my aunt staring down at me. Something had been strange about her. What?

And then I knew. At breakfast she had worn black, but when she came to see me lying on the floor she was dressed in dark blue – a very dark blue, to be sure, but still not black.

'Billy,' I said. 'Can you do something for me? I want you to wait here. I won't be long.'

The boy nodded. Forgetting the poultice, which now felt like part of me, I stood up, then cursed as I felt it slither away, smearing mustard down my body, before coming to rest on my left foot. I rolled the thing up and dumped it on the window sill, where it oozed a yellow stain onto the wall. I dabbed myself dry with the nightgown, creating another stain to match it.

'Just wait here and I'll be back soon, there's a good boy.'

He watched with big childish eyes as I pulled on my few dry garments over my nightshirt. In her hurry Rose had not thought to take away the wet ones and they lay in a stinking bundle to one side of the bed. That made my task easier, and I blessed her for the oversight.

Rose would be busy about the meal; I crept down the back stairs, hoping I would not run into Geoffrey or Hannah. In the event I gained the wash-house door without being seen. Once there, I stopped and listened but could hear nothing within. I entered and pulled the door shut behind me.

The soiled linen was stored in a hamper in the far corner. Before I even reached the hamper I was aware of a telltale odour. Going up to it, I threw it open and began groping among the linen until my hand touched something wet. I snatched it up like a trout tickled out of a stream: my catch was a richly embroidered shift trimmed with French lace. It could belong to nobody but my aunt, and the front part of it was fairly soaked in sour cider. Since my own wet clothes were still upstairs, the wetness could not have rubbed off from them. I fled back to my chamber, let the boy go and bolted the door again. I would let nobody near me but my father himself.

That was as cheerless a time as I can recall. I examined the ruined mustard plaster on the sill, wondering whether by applying the remains of it to my feet I might drive away the deathly cold that had taken possession of them, and decided it would be of little use. All I could do was get into bed, cover myself up and wait.

My would-be murderer was Aunt Harriet. She might be of the weaker sex but she was tall and well nourished, and had the advantage of surprise. The woman who could find it in herself to betray her own sister could, with equal vindictiveness, dispose of a meddling nephew.

Ideas brewed and bubbled in my head. She had opened the hogshead expressly to tempt me to look inside it. She had not opened the hogshead, but had seized her chance. She would prevent my father from reaching me. She was even now telling him that I was not here. She had written to him to keep him away. She had accused me to Dr Green. She was prowling outside my chamber and would pounce the instant I opened the door.

Another thought came to me. Who had placed the shift into the basket? In the normal course of things Hannah Reele fetched down soiled linen to the wash house, taking such items

251

as could not be washed to her own room where she would dab and brush at them to get off the dust. But this was not dust: this was a soaking in rotten drink. Hannah could not fail to notice it, and if she heard the servants talk of my accident, surely she must interpret? What she might do after that, I had not the faintest notion.

As I lay there, teeth chattering, I felt shame at my own cowardice. I say I felt it, but I struggled to suppress the feeling and after a while I was able to dismiss it out of hand. The Jonathan Dymond who had arrived at End House a few weeks back would not have countenanced skulking in bed. He would have preferred to race downstairs, accusing Aunt Harriet and fighting off her servants if need be; he was greatly concerned with acting the man. I had performed some manly acts of folly since then, and made some discoveries, and I cared less to act the man than to act with wisdom. Hot-headed youths cannot distinguish between the two; but that is their misfortune.

18

On the Disagreeableness of Home Truths

To me, imprisoned in the chamber, it seemed that my father would never come. In the event he arrived not long after Rose brought me my portion of the midday meal, which after much banging and calling she had been forced to leave outside the room. At the sound of Father's familiar voice I came to the door and flung myself on him in welcome. As I did so, I perceived a warning in his eyes: Aunt Harriet stood to one side, watching us.

'What's this?' he said, pointing at the stain on my nightgown as I stepped back. It was entirely like him that he made no motion to examine his own clothing, as many men would have done, to see if it had taken harm.

'Mustard,' put in Aunt Harriet before I could speak. 'To keep him warm after his soaking.'

I said, 'I'm well enough to go home now,' and I felt it. The very sight of Father worked on me like a cordial.

'I hear you fell in a hogshead. How came you to do that?'

'You must ask Aunt Harriet.' I turned to her. 'Why, Aunt, you've changed your gown! Surely you had on another this morning?'

She shook her head impatiently, but just for an instant her eye met mine and we understood each other. She knew I had helped away her witches. She could prove nothing against me, but she knew. That was why I had ended up in a hogshead of cider; I could prove nothing against her, but *I* knew.

Father now asked her with apparent innocence what was become of those troublesome neighbours of hers.

'It seems they had friends who brought them away.' She

spoke with cold disdain, though I knew she would gladly have spitted and roasted the women, and me alongside them.

'They may return,' Father suggested.

'I doubt it. Dr Green tells me the place is deserted, and there are cart-tracks all round this house.'

'They had a cart!'

'Aye. The question is who paid for it.'

Her eye again caught mine. It seemed she had no suspicion of 'Mathew', thinking him too steady, or too stupid, for such midnight goings-on.

Father nodded. 'They could scarcely afford it themselves. If I may, Harriet, I would stay and talk with Jon while he dresses.'

Since she could not watch me pull off my nightgown, this meant she had to leave us alone. With a sour smile she withdrew. Father thanked her, and as soon as he had closed the door, laid a finger across his lips to silence me. He then took out a piece of paper and a pencil and wrote, '*I have much to tell you, and doubtless you me, but SAY NOTHING, we are certainly overheard.*' This he folded up and put back in his pocket when I had read it.

'I'm glad to see you, Father,' I said, singing to his tune. 'Is Mother in good health?'

'She is, God be praised. She and Alice are cooking supper for you.'

'I look forward to that.'

'You may not get the chance to eat it. When your mother sees that nightgown, we may have to leave home.'

I dressed and threw the rest of my possessions higgledy-piggledy into my bag. When all that was done, I pulled back the bed sheets, took the mustard plaster from the window sill, and rubbed it into my aunt's linen, concealing the mess with the covers.

'Jon!' my father cried before he could restrain himself. I laid a finger on my lips and his eyes bulged.

'Where's the cart, Father?'

'Next to the cider shed. Have you taken down the press?'

I could not recall owing to the shock of my near-drowning. Was there a cheese still up? I did not know.

'We can do it together,' Father said. 'Only let's hurry.'

In the shed, the smell of ropey cider brought me almost to fainting: I felt myself back in the hogshead, cramped and suffocating. Sweat burst out on my face, so that Father asked if I was truly fit to travel. I said I would be well enough when we got into the air.

Billy stood gawping as we loaded the press onto the cart.

'Are you leaving, Sir?'

'Yes. It'll be Mr Binnie next year.' I pressed a farthing into his hand and went to the kitchen to say goodbye to Rose, who hugged me and said she was glad to see me still alive after the morning's mishap. I studied her blank, kindly face and saw that I would learn nothing from her.

Coming out of the kitchen into the yard, I said to Father, 'For the love of God, let's go now.'

'Have you said goodbye to your aunt?'

'To what purpose?'

'You promised not to give needless offence.'

'Needless offence . . . !' I began, and stopped. I might never have another chance to speak with Aunt Harriet.

'You do right to remind me,' I said. 'I'll be back directly.'

I knocked at my aunt's chamber door and then, without waiting for a reply, flung it open. In the centre of the room stood a little table; seated at it was not Aunt Harriet but Hannah Reele, who jumped up in surprise. She was holding some dark cloth and as she rose she clutched it to her body, away from me. I could not see if it was the black velvet. The curtain before Aunt Harriet's closet was drawn.

'Is my aunt in there? I must speak with her in private.'

'Sir, it's not —'

'Never mind that. Leave us.'

'Sir.' She drew herself up with a little self-important air. 'With respect, I shall enquire first of my mistress.'

'Oh, she won't want you to hear this. Will you, Aunt?' I called over to the closet.

Hannah walked towards the bell-pull. I made no attempt to stop her and she was about to seize it when my aunt's voice came from behind the curtain.

'Let him be, child.' The cloth flew to one side and my aunt came out holding a cloth and a bottle of Hungary water. 'Is it so urgent that I cannot have a moment to refresh myself? Hannah, you may go about your business. Have no fear for me.'

Hannah curtseyed. She seemed to have plenty of fear for herself since she shrank away as, holding tightly to her black bundle, she passed me in the doorway. I slammed the door after her.

'I've come to say goodbye, Aunt Harriet. And to ask you something.'

My aunt's lip curled. 'I thought we should come to this. You said you'd save me Binnie's fee. What have you spent your money on, I wonder? A cart?'

The eyes she turned on me were so very unforgiving that I shivered despite myself.

'You mistake me. *My* question is this: how do you sleep, Aunt? How do you pray?'

'Oh, a sermon! Pray excuse my sitting.' She put down her cloth and bottle on the little table, seated herself in the chair recently occupied by Hannah, and commenced dabbing her neck and temples with scent.

'In a perspiration, Aunt? On such a cold day?' I seated myself opposite her and swept the bottle off the table, shattering it.

As the odour of Hungary water filled the room, Aunt Harriet's cheeks flushed the faint pink that signalled one of her rages. I went on, 'What need of perfumed waters? Except to drive away the stink of cider,' and fixed her with my eyes. If it cost me my life, I thought, I would not be the first to look away. 'You're a great one for godliness and justice, aren't you Aunt? *Thou shalt not suffer a witch to live.* If you'd hang a beggar for a few scrawls and amulets, what'd you do to a woman who tries to commit murder? If indeed you *are* a woman. I never met one as pitiless as you.'

I had talked too long. My aunt's colour was going down; she was regaining her self-command. I had been a fool to send Hannah out of the room. She was even now hiding the dress and shift and I would never see them again.

My aunt said calmly, 'This comes of shock. Had you bothered to ask, you'd know that I've been here with Hannah since breakfast.'

'Will she swear to that?'

'Of course.'

'Then she's damned along with you. I found your shift in the laundry basket, soaked through with cider. Did it go for a swim by itself?'

Aunt Harriet shrugged. 'My linen's always in the basket. If somebody did push you, I'd say he went into the laundry looking for something to dry himself, and happened on one of my shifts.'

'You'll need a better story on Judgement Day.'

'About what?' my aunt retorted. 'Murder? You're the first carrion that ever sat arguing – and a pretty picture you make!'

'You meant to kill me for helping Tamar and Joan. And I did, Aunt. *I* got them away from you.'

I was all exultation, until I recalled that I had broken my promise to Father. I had not meant to, but her assurance goaded me out of my self-command.

My aunt said, 'Helping, is it? I know that kind of helping. You helped Tamar to my property, and she helped you to a juicy little thing.'

'And I brought Joan paper.'

She snorted in disbelief. '*Paper?*'

I leaned in closer. 'Let me explain. Only forget the dirty old beggar, only *read* her account of her life – written in good English, in a good hand – and suddenly it's most convincing! What a report she gives of her last night in this house! It deserves to be more widely known, and if I have my way it shall be. Only' – I put on a face of mock sadness – 'you don't come out of it well, Aunt.'

At this point Aunt Harriet lowered her eyes and I inwardly triumphed, for I had won the staring contest. At last she said, 'Your witness comes out of *nothing* well.'

'You'll never get them back. They're –'

She bridled. 'Do you imagine I'd want –'

'– protected, free to tell their tale. Don't you wish you could stop them?' I gloated.

'We've laws in this country to punish slander.'

I leapt up. My aunt, seeing me, did likewise but I had the bit between my teeth now: 'What about fraud? Isn't there punishment for that? My father – whom even *you* admit to be honest – received a letter from Uncle Robin saying Tamar was his child and he'd left her an inheritance. Father would swear to that in court. So, *what happened to that will?*'

Her face pink again, my aunt backed away. 'What do you want me to say? I never saw any will.'

'He wrote one.' I closed the gap between us; my aunt moved away again, broken glass crunching beneath her shoes.

'Do you think he'd show it to *me*, you simpleton?' She slapped her hand down on the table top. 'Have you any wits at all? Clearly not, since you were set to inherit my estate and you're intent on throwing it away!'

'I have a house and land from my own parents,' I said stead-fastly, 'and in the absence of a legitimate heir Robin's natural child should inherit Robin's estate.' Speaking thus, I swelled with the conviction that I was both noble and generous: a delightful feeling, while it lasted.

The most curious expression came onto my aunt's face. At the same instant she stopped dead, so that I was also obliged to halt in my pursuit.

'You've done your utmost now,' she observed. 'Insulted me, threatened me. Will you hear me say *my* piece?'

She took a step in my direction.

'You can't deny what you've done,' I said, backing away from her since she seemed about to walk through me. Slowly we cir-cled the table.

'You think Robin's natural child should inherit? Then I ask you: *which* natural child?'

That caught me off guard. 'He had others?'

'My sister was with child when she left the village.'

'Yes, with Tamar.'

Aunt Harriet shook her head. 'Oh, no,' she said, quiet and deadly. 'Tamar isn't old enough. Surely you know your sweet-heart's age?'

The most painful disappointment seized me. To think that all my efforts on Tamar's behalf might come to nothing! I said, 'I never heard this from Joan. That child's most likely dead.'

'It's living.'

'Then his estate must be divided between them. But why should I believe you?'

My aunt said nothing but her lips widened in a monstrous smile.

'What?' I asked. 'What?'

'Go ask your precious Mathew Dymond,' said my aunt. 'He was the one – not me – that decided the child should never know. Oh, it might suspect, perhaps, with neither sisters nor brothers. Its stepmother is barren; the nearest she can get to a babe of her own is to deliver other people's.'

I sat down as if punched in the belly while my aunt stood over me and exulted.

'Here's a riddle!' she exclaimed with diabolical jollity. 'Riddle-me-ree, which would you be: the son of your supposed uncle, with a sister you're already bonded to in *love*' – the meaning she put into these last words turned me quite sick – 'or a little keepsake from your mother's army days, men swarming all over her like maggots on a dead dog? Really, there's no knowing *who* spawned you!'

Her mouth worked on, showering me with spittle, but I could no longer hear the words that distorted her lips. I felt like one sitting within a bubble or a crystal bowl, looking out upon the world: I was not connected with it. My body felt curiously light, as if at any moment I might take off and fly about the room, and there was a palpitation in my throat, or was it my heart?

After a while I said, my voice seeming to come from far away, 'I'm not my father's son?'

'You're somebody's,' my aunt replied.

Swaying like a drunken man, I got up from the table. 'I'm Robin's. He comes to me –'

'Oh,' my aunt cried contemptuously, 'you flatter yourself!'

'He's not at rest – you, you should suffer such dreams!'

'Perhaps I wish it,' said my aunt with that dreadful smile of hers. I became aware of an added chill in the air, a dankness. I have said elsewhere that I am an enemy to superstition, and so I am, but I was afraid to remain any longer. Though I tried to walk slowly, I am afraid that by the time I reached the stairs I was going at a run.

As I emerged through the yard door my eyes watered: it had turned bright outside, the sky an icy cloudless blue. My father – I cannot help calling him that – stood by the shed door.

'You took your time,' he said, looking enquiringly into my face.

'Home truths,' I replied, hugging my arms to my body. The chill of that room seemed to have got into my bones; my aunt's *Perhaps I wish it* whispered in my head, insidious as a curse.

'You're whiter than you were.'

'I've had words with Aunt Harriet. I can't tell you now,' I cried as he put his hand on my shoulder. 'Let's be gone – gone!'

We mounted the cart and turned out of the yard. Rose waved to me from the kitchen window but nobody else from the household bade us farewell. I looked back, until trees hid it from view, at the house where I had been conceived. Despite Aunt Harriet's hateful words about maggots and dead dogs, words that turned me sick each time I recalled them, I knew I was Robin's. It was as if my flesh had always known it; and besides, I had the Dymond hair.

I tried not to think about my aunt's festering mind, or about Tamar, and of course I could think of nothing else; those things, and the deception I had grown up in, were an agony to me.

Father broke in on my silence. 'Your mother didn't want you to come here,' he said when we were some little way along the lane. 'She'll be glad to have you home.'

'Aye.'

'She's killing the fatted calf – leastways, opening the potted ham.'

'Aye.'

'And there's something else, something I couldn't tell you in the house: when you went back for Hob last night, Joan gave me another paper.'

'Did she?' I answered listlessly. For once I was not interested in Joan's scribblings.

Father slowed the horse and turned towards me. 'Let's have a look at you, child. Dear Christ, you're green! We're going back to Harriet's.'

'I'd sooner die,' I said, and meant it.

He stared. 'Strong words! And you left that mess in her bed – why? What's all this between the two of you?'

'Nothing.'

My father now began to look grim. 'Either you tell me or back we go.' He raised the reins to make good his threat.

'It's nothing,' I burst out. 'Only that my aunt tried to drown me in the hogshead.'

'Are you mad?' my father exclaimed.

'*She* pushed me in.' I told him of the dress, and the shift I had found dripping with cider. He listened in silence, his expression graver by the minute, and finally said, 'Why didn't you tell me this before we left the house?'

'Because it can't be proved. She'd only laugh in your face as she did in mine, and –' I couldn't bear that, I thought.

'She admits it?'

'Not in words, but she did it. She knows I helped them away.'

'We're going back this minute,' Father said, and again made to turn the horse around.

I laid a hand on his arm. 'Wait. There's more.'

'More than attempted murder?' he cried in exasperation. 'Well, suppose you go on!'

I could not think how to start. We sat staring at one another, our breath misting on the air, until I said, 'It's a long story. Let's continue this way until you've heard it.'

Father clicked his tongue and the cart rolled forward. He was bracing himself; though he tried to hide it, I knew him too well not to perceive the effort. I said, 'I don't know what names to give the people.'

'You don't know their names?'

'No. Nor my own.'

Father's eyes flinched as if from a blow. I had seen that look of his before, when I accused him of keeping secrets from me. The innocent horse trotted on between the shafts as if no such thing as bastardy or incest existed in the world.

At last I said, 'Why did you move to Spadboro?'

'It was a better house.'

'It was to raise me away from Tetton Green.'

My father let out all his breath in a sigh. For an instant I wished that I had not said anything, that I had let things lie and been as kind to him as he had been to me. However, it was done now and (I told myself) he had always been in possession of the truth, so that his kindness was from a position of strength, whereas I had been kept in chains of ignorance that I must break.

He gave himself a curious little slap on the thigh, as some comfort a dog by patting it, before saying quietly, 'If that's what your aunt told you, it's false. We moved to Spadboro before you were thought of.'

'It's no use, Father. She's told me who I am.'

His face darkened. 'You mistook her.'

'No. I'm the child of Robin and Joan.'

'Harriet said that?'

I nodded.

'Then may Satan and all his crew roast her by turns.' My father cut the horse with his whip. 'You should've given her the lie!'

'I couldn't – can't,' I cried.

'Can't? Have you thought about your mother?'

'What of her?'

'She talks of nothing but your return.'

We passed under boughs that tapped against our hats and powdered our shoulders with rime. There had been a frozen mist here, and the trees were spun into feathers. Their fragile brilliance made me wonder why, into the spotlessness of Creation, God had seen fit to introduce soiling, twisting, rampaging Man.

'I do think of Mother,' I protested. By this time I was close to tears and my voice betrayed it; Father must have heard but he turned his face away. 'What am I to do?' I wailed. 'It's not my fault!'

'Isn't it?' he replied. 'Every day we hoped to see you at home. No doubt you thought yourself a clever fellow, you and your letters! This is the fruit of that cleverness, and I hope you like the taste.'

We sat thus wretched for some time, I weeping and Father refusing to pity me, until we were thrown together by the horse's passing over some uneven ground, which obliged Father to place one arm around my shoulders. I seized hold of his hand, saying, 'You'd forgive me if you knew how I long to be your son.'

He at last permitted me to look him in the face, so that I saw that his anger had mostly gone off.

I said, 'I've brought all this on myself – and on you and Mother. I know that.'

Father kept his arm round my shoulders as the cart jolted forward.

'Well,' he said. 'God's over Satan, now and forever.'

'So they say.'

'And so it is. The wickedness at End House brought forth the love your mother – Barbara, I mean – has borne you all these years. Look at it in that light.'

I wiped my face. 'But – forgive me – first tell me how I came to live with you. Why wasn't I told anything?'

'We naturally wished to shield you,' Father said. 'Joan found her way to us in Spadboro. Whatever Harriet says, we were already living there. You recall Joan's writing of the in-laws who paid her a wedding visit?'

I nodded as understanding broke in upon me.

'There you are, then. We were living at Spadboro when Harriet married, and Joan came to us there. May God forgive me, I almost shut the door in her face.'

'Because you hated her.'

He shook his head. 'Her case being so desperate, I wouldn't have turned her away for that. But she was big with child . . . your mother had just lost a babe of her own.'

I pictured my poor mother looking sadly on Joan's swollen belly.

'We took her in. Barbara was still resting in bed, her breasts bound up. Joan's pains began that very afternoon; everything came upon us at once. Barbara rose from her bed and delivered the child.' His voice grew soft. 'I never met her equal.'

'Did Joan tell you I was Robin's?'

He laughed at my simplicity. 'We could see for ourselves.'

'But did she?'

'She wanted it known, yes.'

'Why, when she didn't care enough to keep me?'

'She knew Barbara's childless condition; she hoped we would take you in.'

I flinched. To be thus handed over seemed a crueller stain even than bastardy, as if my baby features had been marred by a hopeless ugliness not even maternal love could warm to.

My father went on, 'We'd already lost three little ones.'

'Lucky that I lay to hand, then,' I said coldly.

'No, no! You must understand: we loved you like our own. Barbara unbound her breast and put you to it and her milk began to flow.' He patted my arm. 'We took that as a sign.'

'Had I known all this . . . or had it not happened . . .' I gestured for lack of words. How many things might not have come about!

'We meant well,' Father said. 'Are we to blame?'

'What I blame you for is keeping me in ignorance of my sister.'

'I knew nothing of her until Robin's letter. How should I?' He urged the horse through a ford and up the slippery bank on the opposite side.

'I beg your pardon, Father,' I said when we were again on level ground. 'It's certain, then? She *is* my sister?'

He cleared his throat. 'Robin acknowledged her.'

'But she's with child by me!' I cried out, as if exclaiming could alter the case.

'By someone. You must keep away from her and now you know all, Jon, I'm sure you will. Before was ignorance and folly; in future lies repentance, and a fresh start.'

These words, intended to comfort me, had the opposite effect. Not that I wished to marry Tamar; but it was beginning to come home to me how much I was my father's son – the son of Robin, who had never shown me any special love and for whom, as a boy, I had felt scant affection. A man all body and no soul, excited by food and drink, by a woman's walk, by the smell of her flesh; a man who was weak and went after his pleasures in unlawful places. He had left Joan to her fate and had even fathered a second bastard on her . . . This thought brought on a still more terrible one: had there perhaps been more? Now I pictured my mother, *my mother*, walking away from the ditch where she had abandoned an infant. Its forlorn wail persisted far into the night but no rescue came. Towards morning it grew weaker. Dawn showed it stretched out stiff. Who could say what Joan might or might not have done?

Thus I went on, my fancy multiplying horrors, until I saw Joan grown old and battered, too feeble to do more than beg, while Robin lived on in comfort until, falling sick, he grew fearful for his soul. And now I was to cast off Tamar likewise. I came of a divided family and there was no doubt which side of that family I most resembled. I sat in silence, my head bowed.

After a while my father observed, 'You don't ask me what became of Joan.'

'I think I know.'

'As soon as she was recovered from her lying-in, she ran away.' He sighed. 'Utter folly! I had for some time been writing to Robin and was hopeful he might settle a proper maintenance on her. Perhaps she was afraid Harriet would follow her to Spadboro.'

With an effort I banished my horrible imaginings and said, 'I always understood she went back to Tetton. She said so, I'm sure.'

'Then she lied to you, or to me – or her memory's going.'

'Or she went when she was carrying Tamar.'

He shrugged. 'The one thing we do know is that from time to time she returned to that cave. Now, about the document she gave me –'

'I suppose I must read it.'

'It's not for you.'

I blinked. 'What?'

'Nor for me or Barbara.'

'Stop . . . !' I pulled at his arm, causing the horse to look round in puzzlement. 'Please, stop driving for a minute.'

'I can drive and talk,' said Father. 'Joan told me it was given her by Robin, so last night, while you were at End House, I opened the packet. I'll own that I was expecting some crude forgery.'

'But . . . ?'

'It looks real, and he appears to have signed it.'

'Are you saying it's the *will*?' I breathed. 'She's had it all this time?'

'You know the proverb about counting chickens before they're hatched. I don't know what it is. It's all in lawyer's Latin.'

'I never thought Robin was so old-fashioned,' I said, surprised.

'He wasn't. If it *is* a will, then my belief is he didn't want Joan or Tamar to read it. It was meant for a lawyer.'

'They might not even realise it was a will.'

'Quite.'

Not wanting to build up my hopes and then have them crash in ruins, I said, 'It's probably a recipe for hog's pudding written by the learned and accomplished Aunt Harriet.'

'I doubt it, Jon,' said my father. 'It has all our names in it, and Joan's, and Tamar's. I can read that much.'

19

Of Diverse Sorts of Inheritances

By the time we reached Spadboro I had promised my father to repeat nothing of what I had discovered concerning my parentage. He said it would distress, to no good purpose, a woman who loved me as tenderly as ever mother loved child, a woman who had hoped to shield me from such knowledge. The sight of her flinging open her chamber window, bending perilously out from the sill in order to wave, would have persuaded a stricter conscience than mine; I raised my hat to her, and the next minute she was running across the yard to greet us, her breath smoking like a dragon's in the bitter air.

Most willingly did I embrace her as my mother. Joan Seaton might have borne me in her womb, but Barbara Dymond had poured out her generous maternal heart on me, and taken no end of pain in breeding me up.

Dinner was late in the day, since it had been held back for my arrival, and in no time she and Alice were laying out the potted ham and other good things, my mother saying she was sure her boy would be hungry after coming so far in such cold weather.

My father remarked that he hoped there might be enough for a mere husband. She laughed, saying he knew her well enough not to fret himself about that, before turning again to me.

'Where's your soiled linen? On the cart?'

I now recalled that, having changed into dry clothes, I had left my sodden ones at End House. My mother pretended to scold me, but was unable to keep from smiling. 'Oh, well, it's nothing,' she said. 'I'll write to Harriet to send them on.'

Father glanced at me. 'Jon and Harriet have fallen out.'

'Oh?' She looked up from the table. 'Why?'

'She dislikes my way with cider,' I said.

'There's nothing wrong with your cider-making.' Unsatisfied with my answer, she continued to bustle about the table, not looking at me, and then said, 'So you won't be going back?'

'Nor speaking to her, nor having anything to do with her. She's a bad, cruel woman.'

Mother was holding her favourite dish, a large piece of Delft decorated with birds. She laid it carefully down on the table to show she was about to deliver herself of something important. 'Nobody ever thought Harriet too kind,' she said. 'But be very sure of yourself, son, before you cut her.'

I understood. Harriet had much to bestow: who knew what hopes my parents – all of them – had secretly cherished for me over the years? I said, 'You mean I should hold to her at any price?'

She looked me in the eye. 'No.'

Father came to stand by her and put his arm round her shoulders.

'I'm blessed in my parents,' I said. How naked and defenceless would I have been, but for their love: the Seaton boy, unschooled, unfed, driven from any shelter I might find; the Seaton boy, whose mother lived off men. Instead of which I had grown up free and happy, thanks to the people standing before me. If they had deceived me, it was done in kindness.

I could not call them guardians. Mathew and Barbara had been the two pillars between which I sheltered, all my young life. My natural mother, no matter how pitiful her tale, could never come near them.

As for Tamar, my father was right. The best gift I could make her was to stay away. My selfish yearnings could do nothing for her; his purse, much.

Mother was sniffing the air. 'What's this?' she said, moving out of my father's embrace. 'Hungary water?'

I told her it was on me, not him.

A good sluicing with Hungary water would have improved the smell of Master Blackett's house: an odour of creeping mould, though disguised just then with the scent of his last dinner. We were brought through by his clerk to a room crowded with papers and volumes, where Blackett greeted us and invited us to sit.

'Now, to our business,' he said. A packet which I supposed to be Joan's lay on the table, ready to his hand; taking it up, he paused and looked at me over the tops of his spectacles. I had already noticed he had a habit of doing this; I wondered why, if he wore the things to any purpose, he must needs keep peering over them.

'I find myself in an awkward position,' he said, turning to Father. 'Had you taken this' – he drew his finger softly along the top of the packet – 'and destroyed it in ignorance, the law would have nothing to say to you. As matters stand . . .'

'Robin's life was irregular, we know,' said Father. 'Pray proceed.'

Still the man hesitated. 'As his brother you perhaps anticipate some legacy? A very natural, fraternal hope,' he added, as if to retract a slander.

'All I hope for is the satisfaction of having carried out his wishes.'

The lawyer looked as if he had heard *that* tale before. 'And this young man . . . ?'

'Is of my mind,' Father assured him. 'I take it this is a true and proper will, then, and unfavourable to us?'

'It appears to be correctly drawn up.' He unfolded the packet. Inside was the document Father had told me about; I could just make out, in the shadow of Blackett's elbow and upside down on the page, the signature. I stared at it. It appeared fresh from Robin's hand, as if he might enter the room at any moment; yet his urgent body, that had made mine, was now dissolved, invisible save in these black marks that would themselves dissolve as the ink faded.

'Your brother's lawyer was Master Ousby of Tetton Green. At the time of his client's death, Master Ousby should have informed your sister-in-law of the will.' Again he peeked over those spectacles, and there was a flicker of amusement. 'This he failed to do.'

'Then she knows nothing of it?' I asked. Strange to think that, for once, Aunt Harriet had spoken the truth!

Blackett inclined his head. 'Unless, of course, she heard from her husband, as is customary?'

Father said, 'I doubt it. Pray read the will.'

'Strictly speaking, the widow ought to be present.'

'Can't she hear it later? And you must only show her a copy; if this falls into the hands of my sister-in-law, you needn't hope to see it again.'

'Strong language,' the lawyer observed.

'No stronger than is called for. I'll be frank with you, Master Blackett: my brother had dependants not recognised by his wife. She's allowed them to fall into destitution; I hope this may lift them up again, and place them out of her power.'

'May I ask what you mean by "dependants not recognised"?'

'Tamar Seaton, his natural daughter, and her mother. Mrs Dymond has behaved with the utmost cruelty towards them.'

'She's not obliged to provide for such people,' said Blackett.

'But if provision is made in her husband's will –'

'Indeed. *If* provision is made. Pray bear with me a little and indulge my curiosity. You say Mrs Dymond was aware of this irregular union. Why, then, should your brother keep her in ignorance of his arrangements?'

'If you knew my sister-in-law, Master Blackett, you would never ask such a question.'

The lawyer permitted himself a smile. 'Then let me ask another. How did *you* happen to come across it?'

Now I saw where he was leading. It seemed we did benefit from the will, for Blackett clearly suspected us of being its authors.

'Joan Seaton gave it me,' Father said. 'I told you this before.'

'She gave it to Mrs Dymond's brother-in-law? She must repose great trust in you.'

I hung my head, for Joan had never 'reposed great trust' in me. Thinking myself at the very heart of the game, I had been utterly out of it. In taking her son under his protection and raising him as his own, Mathew Dymond had done one thing for Joan Seaton that she never forgot; to her mind, nobody, not even that son, could come near him. Seen in this light, her writings had been a way of sounding me, of preparing me, as it were, for the much more important document that was to come. In time, finding me honest, she might have yielded up the packet, but with Mathew such caution was needless. Meeting him again, she had not hesitated; no sooner had I gone into the wood than she had placed her precious secret in his hands.

Father said now to Blackett, 'I've helped her in the past.'

'And how did Mistress Seaton obtain possession of the will?'

'Tamar Seaton was taken on as a servant at End House and nursed my brother in his last illness. I can only assume she used a false name since my sister-in-law had no idea who she was, but Robin knew her. He ordered her to open a box in the sickroom and take out the document she would find at the bottom.'

'Did he say it was his will?'

'No. He told Tamar the women must keep hold of it and wait until Mr Mathew called upon them. I believe he meant to instruct me accordingly, but died before he could do so.'

Blackett said, 'You will forgive my question. Could the woman have forged it, or had it forged?'

'She hasn't the means or the friends,' said Father.

'Wouldn't Master Ousby have a copy?' I asked. 'Why didn't he come forward when Uncle Robin died?'

'At the time of your uncle's death, Ousby himself was gravely ill.'

Father said, 'But when he recovered?'

'You mistake me. He died of his sickness. His clerk had neither money nor learning enough to take his place, and his affairs fell into disorder.'

'She has the devil's own luck,' Father exclaimed. 'Are all his papers lost?'

'His widow had the sense to keep hold of them. With your consent, I will send my clerk to search.' He looked straight at Father. 'Are you content for me to do so, and to seek out any witnesses?'

'By all means, Master Blackett, only let him say as little as possible. This will could melt away like morning dew.'

'You may rely on me to know my business,' Blackett reassured him. 'Since you are both legatees, I feel justified in reading its contents to you, but I must warn you that if no copy survives among Ousby's records, well!' He shrugged as if to say: you may as well stop now.

Promising to bear this in mind, we begged him to proceed. He ran through at speed, pausing to explain clauses and turns of phrase as he felt it necessary, and skipping over a long list of bequests to past servants and friends in the village, before I made my appearance in Blackett's homely translation as 'my nephew Jonathan Dymond, a lad after my own heart, in whose handsome looks his father lives again'. I flushed at these words, which to my thinking trumpeted my paternity to the world, and I flushed worse when it came to me that Robin had divined my secret likeness to himself – a likeness of more than body – before I understood it myself: *a lad after my own heart.* I almost hated him for it, dead though he was: the Dymond I wished to be cut from was not Robin but Mathew. Blackett, seemingly unaware of my distress, went on to announce that Robin had bequeathed me twenty pounds and a miniature of himself as a young man. For Mother's sake, I strove to conceal my humiliation and appear pleased. My parents had precisely the same remembrance as was left to them in the previous will.

'Mrs Harriet Dymond has a life interest in the estate,' the lawyer went on, running his finger down the page.

My father whistled. 'Only that!'

'After her death the entire estate passes to Mistress Joan Seaton and her daughter, Tamar Seaton. Until they enter into their inheritance, the Seatons are bequeathed an allowance of forty pounds per annum. If I may say so, Mr Dymond, that leaves them very snug indeed.'

Father sat stunned. I heard Joan's cracked voice saying, 'He always loved me best.'

'The deceased names Tamar Seaton as his natural daughter,' Blackett said. 'And that's your understanding also?'

'Yes,' I replied. 'But Joan Seaton may never inherit. She's younger than her – than Mrs Dymond – but sickly.'

'They can't fee a lawyer,' Father added, 'and Mrs Dymond is sure to contest this.'

'It's possible,' Blackett said drily. 'She has no children – the widow, I mean?'

'None.'

'All to the good. He's made fair provision for her. Are you acquainted with anyone by the name of Abel Canning?'

Father shook his head. 'Is he a legatee?'

'He witnessed the will. So, Master Jonathan, how do you like your twenty pounds?'

'It's more than I expected.'

He scrutinised me over the tops of those spectacles, his dark eyes putting me in mind of Hob. 'That is indeed the royal road to satisfaction. The will shall be copied, Mr Dymond, never fear.'

As we walked back through the village, I said to Father, 'Shall *we* fee him, since Joan and Tamar can't? I could do it out of what Robin left me.'

He looked doubtful. 'Let's first see what comes out of Ousby's papers. I don't want Blackett to think this will is forged.'

'Why would we forge it?' I protested. 'We've no interest; the estate goes to Joan and Tamar.'

Father sighed with exasperation. 'A woman protected by your family, who claims she's carrying your child – no interest?'

'That, perhaps, but –'

'The lawyers know nothing of your . . .' – he hesitated – '. . . kinship. You might be planning to marry Tamar, might you not?'

'Why would I marry my uncle's bastard?'

'Stranger things have happened,' Father said. 'Even when the wench was penniless.'

'Am I always to be –'

'Jon! Listen to me. Forgery's a serious matter.'

We stopped and stood facing each other. He was breathing fast, though our walk had been leisurely, and he kept his grip on me, as if afraid I would run off and do myself some hurt. I was not accustomed to consider my father as old, but in that instant I glimpsed the old man he would become.

'You never spoke of this before,' I said.

'I never saw it before but I do now. If there's no copy we can't go on.' Seeing me about to protest, he held up his other hand. 'We must drop it entirely.'

'What of Robin's wishes?' I accused him. 'You said your only desire was to fulfil –' but here I broke off, seeing his eyes spark with resentment. He was so rarely angry, and I so unaccustomed to him in this mood, that I quailed even before he spoke.

'Take care – take care!' He flung my arm away from him. 'I've loved my brother all my life – loved him before *you* were so much as thought of! D'you fancy I'd give up if I once saw a way forward?'

'No,' I mumbled.

'No! Then let's say no more. In any case' – he was already half way back to his more amiable self – 'there may yet be a copy.'

My life now began to settle down into its accustomed round – if I may say that, when my duties remained the same but everything within me was changed. My days of innocence were past; I felt I had grown old overnight.

Days came and went, cold and rainy, cold and clear. Father wished me to be constantly by his side. Though we did only what we had always done, I felt he was reminding me that I belonged with him and Mother. On mild days, when we could get a spade into the ground, we turned over the earth so that the next frost would break it, or dug out corners of the garden that were lying fallow. If the earth was too cold or sodden for work, we mended walls and gates.

During this time a man called Samuel Beast came to help with the heaviest jobs. Despite suffering much mockery on account of their surname, the Beasts were both numerous and industrious, and consequently of some account in the village. Our Samuel Beast suffered like the rest; one day he said to me that it must be a fine thing to be called Dymond, and I wondered whether he would still say that if he knew all. Hearing our talk, Father interrupted and said he wanted to consult me as to the desirability of damsons: he still hankered after these, being partial to damson cheese, but my mother had come out fighting against them since she considered the fruits all stone and not worth the trouble they gave. Though I knew he had asked me mostly to turn the talk away from names, I was glad to give him my advice, which was that he should set them, and that Mother would come round in time.

Everything in our house, nay, our village, was dear to me, even the disputed rights of a couple of damson trees. I would look up from my labours and see the blue smoke rising from our chimney, our neighbours' houses close by and the clumps of trees dotted about the hills. Familiarity does not always breed contempt: it seemed to me that all goodness, all of Nature's beauty, all kindliness, all neighbourly help, were here. This place had been my Eden; as a child I had pictured the Angel waving his fiery sword from the boughs of our 'Old Man', the twisted ancient Redstreak at the top of the orchard. Since then, I had tasted the fruit of a more fatal Tree, yet my love for Spadboro – its well-trodden pathways, the shape its roofs cut into the sky, its fields bare or scattered with blossoms – was grown all the more tender for knowing myself to be a wilding there.

When our fingers were numb and our bellies empty the three of us would repair to the house. A copper shoe in the fire bubbled with scalding cider, so that drinking was a pleasure laced with pain. Samuel Beast was happy to join us in that and in a hunk of bread and cheese before we went out again, flushed and rubbing our hands, to heave up ragwort or split logs. I gave my entire strength to the labour, ate well, and slept soundly at night, and my parents praised me; yet all this time I was straining my ears, like a dog, for some word of Tamar.

Father had not waited for the will before providing for the two women – that much I knew, and would have expected of him – and was kind enough to tell me something of how they were living: he had lodged them at a distance from both Tetton Green and Spadboro, under a respectable roof and in a village where he hoped they might continue unknown. His intention was that, as far as possible, Joan should recover her health, and that in their refuge Tamar's child should be born.

Where might that refuge be? I lay awake at night, considering. Money is much, to be sure, but not everything: there is also reputation. How, then, had he persuaded decent people to take on such disreputable women? Had they been received into some almshouse, under the watchful eyes of attendants bent upon their reform?

At first I hoped he or Mother might let something slip, but when I considered what secrets they had guarded for over twenty years, I saw the folly of such hopes. More and more often, as I stood among the garden plots, surrounded by well-loved sights, a creeping sourness would infect my soul. I attempted to get clear again, to keep my thoughts wholesome, but the sourness spread regardless. It seemed there was no purpose for me in this world, that my existence, for all its hard-won wisdoms, its industry, its patched-up respectability, was bare as the winter earth. There was only this difference: that in a little time the earth would teem with new life.

'You talked of marrying,' Father said one night at supper. I saw him glance at Mother and my stomach gave a twist.

At the time, I had spoken honestly. The trouble was that whenever I pictured my wedding day (and *that* I did only if someone else spoke of it, as now), what I saw at the ceremony was the smiling faces of my parents. The bride, who should have been all to me, was nothing but a gown walking by my side.

Mother reached out and laid her hand on my arm. 'You've waited long enough. A good wife is a comfort and support to a man; you won't regret it.'

On my plate lay a portion of salt pork and winter cabbage. I hacked at the pork with my knife.

'And you'll have children,' Father added.

I stared at him. Did he mean that any young man naturally produces offspring, or that all the fruitfulness of our family was bred into me, son of the only Dymond who had proven abilities in that line of work?

'There's plenty of time,' I said.

'Less than you think.'

Mother said, '*It is not good that a man should be alone.*'

'I'm not alone while you live.'

'You talk like a child,' Father said. 'You must marry; that's how things go in this world.'

I pushed away the pork and cabbage. 'You love me, you wish me to have what others have . . .'

'But?'

'I can't see myself – I mean, there's no woman –'

'*No* woman?' Father said sternly. 'Search your heart, Jon, and your conscience.'

His words silenced me. I heard the clock and wondered if they also heard it, and were drawing a moral instance from it.

'What's the difference?' I said at last. 'Call it what you like; I don't want to marry.'

'Jon . . . son . . . your happiness is of the greatest consequence to me. You know that. I might even consent to your marriage with *her*, if –'

Mother gasped, 'Mathew!'

'He doesn't mean it,' I said coldly.

'If you could marry. The thing is, you can't.'

'I know that. So why shut her away from me?'

'Because I know how it is between men and women – with or without a wedding.' He held up a hand to check my protest. 'You think me cruel, I daresay. A young man sets his heart on a woman, he's all cut up with love . . .' He shook his head. 'It doesn't last. You'll marry and forget her.'

Never, I thought, though I kept silent. That said it just as well, perhaps.

Mother said, 'Has your father ever been harsh with you?'

'Not knowingly.' I turned back to Father. 'Wouldn't any brother want to see his sister?'

'You're not any brother and sister,' he replied.

My hand flew to my mouth. I had broken my promise by mentioning it before Mother. Father had likewise let his tongue run away with him; he would perceive it directly, and what then?

Mother at once took my hand in hers, saying, 'Pray don't distress yourself.' I knew then that my father had gone back on what we agreed and, for some reason of his own, had already enlightened her. I squeezed her hand, murmuring, 'Mother.' If it was only one word, it was the right one; but I was less inclined to be submissive towards *him.*

'Well, Father,' I said, 'would you have given up Robin like this?'

He said, 'You try my patience,' but I saw I had played a winning card: his eyes avoided mine. At last he said, 'If it sets your mind at rest –'

'Mathew,' my mother said warningly.

He shook his head. 'I don't undertake to answer every question. Very well, what do you want to know?'

I thought rapidly. 'What class of persons are they lodged with?'

'With a gentlewoman. They form part of her private household.'

'How did you persuade her to take them on?'

He laughed at this. 'How do you think? I pay her.'

'That can't be much, Father. They're used to living on so little.'

He rolled his eyes. 'Nothing at all, just a doctor for Joan, bedding, linen, food . . . They have a blazing fire day and night, and there Joan sits, hugging it.'

He paused and sat watching me.

'She must think she's in paradise,' I remarked.

He waited a little longer. Then: 'Ask after Tamar.'

'Can I ask anything?'

'Anything I think fit to answer.'

'How do they treat her?'

'Their hostess believes her guests to be gentlewomen like herself, but disinherited and degraded by the war. Tamar was presented to her as a girl of good family, raised like a peasant and forced to marry beneath her station; the lady takes it upon herself as a Christian duty to raise her from the mire.'

'Raise her, how?'

'By instructing her in breeding and manners. A schoolmaster is employed for the rest and he finds her an apt scholar.'

'She would be.' I wondered what Tamar was teaching the schoolmaster. 'And the child? What of that?'

'Tamar's a widow.' He put his hand on mine as if to comfort me. 'That makes her safe, son. While she stays where she is, none can expose her.'

'So I'm dead,' I said, more to myself than to him. 'You've put an end to me.'

'To your folly; not to you.'

Sometimes reason is less bearable than rage. 'Is she happy?' I burst out. 'Does she cry, does she ever ask after me?'

'Of course not,' Father said. He was in command of himself now, sure of his ground. 'She has everything she needs. You would be happier, Jon, if you followed her example.'

Mother gave way over the damson trees, so Father set me to mark out a plot for them. I hammered in the stakes, feeling as if I were nailing down my coffin lid. This was to be my life, then: making marks wherever my father pointed out the place, marrying where he wanted me to marry. I had rebelled once, and it had cost me dear.

Both he and Mother talked more frequently now of the desirability of my taking a wife. The woman they had set their hearts on was Poll Parfitt.

❧

It was not until the beginning of March that Master Blackett came to the house with news. He had also brought the miniature left me by Uncle Robin, so while Mother went off to fetch some wine, Father and I unwrapped my legacy. For the first time I was face to face with the lad the village girls called Absalom. There was no hint of the coarse, ruddy uncle I had found so distasteful. As a young man Robin had a neck like a tower of ivory, as the Bible says, and carried his head proudly atop of it. He had crinkled blond hair, a broad jaw, a full mouth. As far as the hair and the mouth went, I could have sat for the picture. I thought how Aunt Harriet must have hated me for that.

'I suppose it's like?' I asked.

Father nodded. I wondered what it was that Robin had, and I did not, that so drew women to him.

Mother returned and served the three of us with wine and cake before returning to the kitchen.

Wiping his eyes, which were wet from looking on his brother's picture, Father now said huskily to the lawyer, 'How did you get this? Not from my sister-in-law?'

'It was left with Ousby,' Blackett answered. 'The only bequest that your brother chose to leave in his keeping. Finding *that* was nothing, compared with finding Abel Canning.' He set down his goblet and I noticed that my mother had poured me a much smaller measure.

Father frowned. 'Is he dishonest, this Canning?'

'Oh, no. After Master Ousby's decease he couldn't find another place; he went to live with some cousins in Gloucester. He's seen the will now, and your Seatons are lucky: he remembers witnessing it.'

'I don't see that, myself,' said Father. 'Why would he?'

'Because Mr Dymond seemed so fearful.'

I said, 'Mrs Dymond is a passionate woman.'

'Hmm.' Blackett took another sip of wine. 'On that subject, I must ask something of you. You may wish to consider it before agreeing.'

Father and I pulled up our chairs as one man.

Blackett said, 'I wish you to accompany me when I go to break the news to her.'

'To Harriet!' Father looked as if he didn't know whether to laugh or cry. 'What do you say, Jon? Shall we go?'

'I'll wait in the stable, most likely,' I said. 'I doubt she'll let me into the house.'

I tied the miniature around my neck, under my shirt. I wished to have it about me, but not in any way that might pain my mother and father, or suggest I had rather be Robin's child than theirs. Still, he sired me. There can only be one man who does that. The fear I once associated with him was gone entirely: the will was come to light and Robin was sunk back into his grave. I knew, now, why he had singled me out from all the rest, and like Aunt Harriet I could even find a part of me that would have clung to his ghost. Had he come to me one last night, and stood by the road in the old way, I might have called him Father – it was the only gift I could still bestow – but he never appeared again.

Was his spirit bound for Heaven or Hell? For Heaven, I hope. I would have him rest in peace; he was a sinner, but I know a worse one. Still, even should she sneak into Heaven, he will be safe from her. According to Scripture, there is no marrying there.

No, marriage is a thing of Earth, where my aunt's good fame shines bright throughout Tetton. What took place within the Guild Hall is never spoken of. The soldiers, like sparks carried on wind, went off to lay waste to other lives; if any of them remembers, I would like to think he trembles, looking on his own daughters, when he calls to mind what was done here. A frail hope! More likely he recalls a willing whore; he smiles to think he came through the wars, after all, and sighs for his youthful time, and thinks he will take his wife early to bed. As for the village men, that despicable crew, their hands have been clean and their memories blank ever since that night. My poor lustful, cowardly father, you were weak, not merciless; compared with their sins yours were as nothing; and yet your wickedness opened the way to theirs and went on deepening the wound afterwards. Even so, I do not hate you. I am too like you for that.

&

When the time came to visit my aunt, Master Blackett took us in his own cart. The land was starting to show green and the trees thickening up, but the roads were still boggy; in places we were all obliged to get out and push, even the learned lawyer himself, so that it was dusk before we arrived.

'Are you quite ready, Jon?' my father asked as we came out from the wood into Tetton Green. I said I was, but when I saw the dark shape of End House backed up against the trees I felt myself grow cold. Father must have noticed, for he said, 'You're with us, now.'

'And we're armed,' Blackett said.

I stared. 'Armed?'

He waved the satchel that contained the paper. I could barely smile in reply; the chill was spreading through my limbs and my teeth chattered in my head. It came to me that this was how I had felt after my near-drowning: my body remembered.

'You've left a copy with your clerk?' Father said for the third time. The lawyer smiled and clapped him on the shoulder.

Three men armed with law, about to ambush a solitary woman. One would say that woman had little chance, even though she was my aunt. The blood stung its way back into my cheeks and hands; the qualm had passed.

As we went by the Guild Hall with its altered windows, I found myself compelled to look inside, as if by so doing I might glimpse the riot and brutality once enacted there. The interior of the Hall was dark, so that I could barely make it out. Yet it seemed to me that the building must retain some trace, some distant echo too faint for human hearing, some tenth part of a tenth part of a fleck of dust from a soldier's coat. The world is full of these gossamer threads, like Robin's signature on the will, tying the present to the past; once perceived, they breed and multiply in the mind.

No matter where they lead us, we have need of them. That what once existed is lost utterly, that time's river can never return to its source, is a thought more terrible than any act recorded here. So I choose to believe in such traces, of which I am one – the record of a certain act committed upon a certain day – and every man and woman on earth another.

I could wish that Robin had written to me, as well as to my father. Then I might trace back the trail of ink to his first mark upon the paper and see it as a thread stretching between his breathing, blooming time, long gone, and mine, which is now.

And now.

20

How I Lost Part of My Hair

She was not expecting us – of course not. I say this because fear had made me as superstitious as an old trot whenever I thought of Aunt Harriet: I almost thought nobody could deceive her, and would not have been surprised to observe her stationed at an upstairs window, holding a musket. In the event, we passed through the gate in the usual way and a boy (not Billy; I wondered what had become of him) took charge of the cart while we knocked at the door. We were admitted by Geoffrey Barnes, whose face was tight with suppressed curiosity. That he knew of my connection with Tamar was obvious; Aunt Harriet had most likely covered it up for as long as some shred of polite pretence remained between us, but not a moment longer.

The lady of the house was upstairs with her maid. We were shown to some seats near the fire and requested to wait while she was informed of our arrival. After some twenty minutes or so Aunt Harriet, splendid in a mourning costume trimmed with black pearls, came swishing down the stairs and walked right up to my father.

'Mathew,' she said as we rose to greet her. There was nothing gentle in her demeanour; she was brusque, even mannish.

My father nodded. 'Harriet.'

Me, she looked straight through. Returning the compliment, I wondered if she had been wearing that rich dress when we were announced, or had donned it specially for our benefit.

My father now presented Blackett, but without mentioning his profession. Aunt Harriet looked the man over with quiet insolence and did not ask us to sit. We stood awkwardly, the fire popping and hissing behind us, waiting for that courtesy.

'You will be aware, Harriet, that after what Jon has told me I would not come here without good cause,' Father began. 'You may not wish the servants to hear our business. Is there a room where we can be private?'

My aunt said stonily, 'Here will do.'

He shrugged. 'Then have a table fetched for documents.'

She glanced at him, then, and at Blackett, before going to the bell-pull. Rose entered, looking every bit as strained as her husband.

'Tell Geoffrey to come in here and move the walnut table over to the fire. And we want light.'

'Yes, Mistress.'

Barnes arrived, making a show of strength as he single-handedly carried the heavy table to the fireside.

'Not so close, you fool, it'll scorch,' my aunt snapped. Meekly he moved it to her directions. Rose entered with candles in silver candlesticks and set them down on its polished surface.

'And Geoffrey, remain outside the door until I call you,' my aunt said, as if we were ruffians who might do her some injury. My father retorted that she might bring in the entire household and seat them round the table with us, if such were her wish; it was nothing to him. My aunt did not deign to answer, and Barnes withdrew.

At last we were seated. Aunt Harriet chose the chair directly opposite mine and skewered me with that blue glare of hers. I will not deny she could still frighten me. I thought everyone in the room could hear my heart; perhaps it could be heard as far off as the stables.

'Master Blackett's a lawyer,' Father said. Her eyes flicked away from me then, towards the stranger. He went on, 'Another will has come to light – Robin's will. It's drawn up by the same man as –'

'Ousby?'

'Yes, Ousby. But it's of a later date.'

'My husband never mentioned any will.'

'It was found among Master Ousby's papers,' Father said, giving the truth but not the whole truth. 'Master Blackett here has checked the will and spoken with the witness. Everything appears to be correct.'

What self-mastery my aunt could exert, when she chose to. She sat upright, folding her hands on the edge of the table, and waited.

Blackett now brought out the paper from his satchel. 'This, Madam, is a copy of the original, which I believe to be the only legitimate will of the late Mr Dymond. As you will see, there are significant alterations to the bequests.'

My aunt pushed the candles towards him. 'Read.'

The lawyer inclined his head and in a soft, deadly voice, like poisoned honey, began to read Robin's will, explaining each foreign term as he came to it just as he had done with us. Sometimes she anticipated him with a brusque 'Yes, yes, go on,' but mostly she was silent. She was not, however, at peace: the rise and fall of her bosom were visible even in candlelight. I would have laid any money that her skin, seen by day, would have shown pink.

'You have a life interest . . .' Blackett began to explain the provision made for her. She closed her eyes – so that we could not read them, I am sure – and listened without the slightest flicker of her features. Her body she also held rigid and motionless, always excepting the throbbing within her stays. *That*, she could not master.

'. . . and after your death to Joan and Tamar Seaton,' Blackett finished.

The room grew so quiet that I could hear the wax being sucked up the wick of the candle nearest me. Still my aunt did not open her eyes. Father, Blackett and I glanced at one another.

'You have a life interest,' Blackett said a little more loudly. 'Do you understand what that means?'

My aunt swallowed and opened her eyes. Despite the darkness her pupils showed as pinpricks. 'And if I wish to sell the property?'

My father said, astonished, 'You don't, do you?'

'What if I remarry?' She leapt up, smacking her hand on the table. 'Your will's a forgery. Robin would never have tied me like this, never!'

'I assure you –' Father began.

'Those women had it made by one of their acquaintance! Some hedge-lawyer!' She stopped, her eyes moving from Blackett to Father and from Father to me, and I saw ugly thoughts take shape in her mind.

'Your surprise is natural,' said Blackett, whose calm manner betokened many years' experience. 'However, Master Ousby's widow attests that the will was stored –'

'You're all in it together! Your creature, here,' my aunt spluttered, 'he drew it up.'

The lawyer's smile had the faintest tinge of pity. 'I repeat, all is correct and duly witnessed. The clerk who witnessed it remembers Mr Dymond.'

'Does he, indeed. How much did you pay him?'

'Pray, Harriet, be reasonable!' my father exclaimed. 'What have you lost? You've everything you need for as long as you live –'

'Aye. As long as.' She resumed her rapid walk. 'And how long'll that be, eh, with those creatures waiting on my death?'

'I believe she served here and did you no harm,' Blackett pointed out.

'She soon finished off Robin, though!' my aunt spat, striding back and forth with her fists clenched in her skirts. 'Yet you dare pretend this house belongs to a pack of beggars –'

'They're not beggars, not these days,' said Father.

'Thanks to you. What are they giving you in return, a share in an inheritance? Robin would *never* have put me in such a position. If he were here, to see this . . . !' My aunt's voice had tears in it now; her eyes glittered and her bosom heaved so violently that I wondered she could breathe. She turned towards the door, screaming, 'Geoffrey! Geoffrey!'

He came in at a run, then slowed to see us sitting harmless at the table while my aunt rampaged about the room.

'Fetch Dr Green!' she flung at him, stamping her foot. 'And tell Rose to come here. Now, now!'

Barnes disappeared.

'Are you saying Tamar Seaton did some injury to your husband?' asked Blackett.

She glared at him and did not answer.

'Calm yourself, Harriet,' Father urged. 'There's nothing to be done.'

'Hold your tongue – you and your bastard!' She turned and resumed her pacing, her arms wrapped round her now as if to keep off rain.

'You mean my adopted son,' Father said sharply. My aunt looked loathing at both of us and opened her mouth to make some retort. What it was to be I will never know, since at this moment Rose entered and performed a quivering curtsey.

'Mistress?'

'Come and stand by me,' her mistress ordered. 'Now, listen, Rose! Remember what I say. These people say all my property is forfeit.'

'Do we have to leave here?' Rose exclaimed, forgetting her place.

'When I die, fool! This house goes to Joan Seaton.' Rose looked helplessly from my aunt to us. 'And then Jonathan there marries her daughter and the vermin eat their way through my estate.'

My father said, 'You know full well they won't marry.'

'Oh, they might; they'll keep mum –'

'*Harriet!*'

'– but they needn't think I will. We'll put a stop to you, Mathew – a stop – !'

'Madam, this is madness,' Blackett said, voicing my own thoughts, for she seemed to have taken leave of her senses. 'Pray consider: supposing we had forged this will, why would we give away the property to Joan Seaton, when we could've made it over directly to Master Jonathan?'

She hesitated, but then said, 'Perhaps you're subtler than that. If you ask *me*, my life's not worth a candle. Stay, Rose. Don't go away.'

It was as Master Blackett said: fear and hatred had clouded my aunt's reason. To comfort Rose, who had begun to weep, Father said, 'Don't be afraid, Rose, we make no threats. All the threats have come from your mistress. Stay by all means, and welcome.' He waited while Rose struggled to suppress her sobs. When she was quieter, he went on. 'We have found Mr Dymond's last will and testament – later than the one you know of. It gives Mrs Dymond only a life interest in the property. Nothing alters, for you,' he patiently repeated to Aunt Harriet. 'You continue here, just as you would have done.'

Aunt Harriet snorted with rage.

'Father,' I whispered. 'Perhaps she *was* going to sell.'

He shook his head.

'This is all because of you,' my aunt said, coming closer. 'You disgusting little spy, you worm! Coming here to help with the cider!' She was panting. 'What *you* wanted was to see the house, see what was coming to you –'

She rushed at me. I half rose to defend myself but her hands were in my hair, twisting, before I could get out of the chair, and her body, tall and heavy, pinned me down. I struggled to move my legs, swaddled as they were in the folds of her skirts.

I heard Father cry, 'Harriet! Govern yourself!' as he tried to drag her off. She kicked at him and the chair fell sideways with both of us on it. I fell underneath, and took the impact all down my left arm and my chest; I lay stunned, my head pressed against the table leg. My aunt's features, horribly distorted, loomed over me and I thought she was going to scratch at my eyes.

'Let go, you mad bitch!' I shouted.

She gave a fearful cry and screwed up her mouth, then dropped motionless onto the floor by my side, her hands still knuckling my scalp and her eyes staring into mine.

'What in God's name – !' exclaimed Blackett in horror.

'She's in a fit,' my father said, bending down and shining a candle in my aunt's face so that a streak of saliva glistened on her chin. 'Quick, Rose, unlace her.'

Rose hurried forward and knelt down beside him, her hands trembling as she endeavoured to loosen Aunt Harriet's bodice. My aunt gave a stifled groan like one who has been crushed and then – nothing. I disentangled her now limp fingers from my hair and got up from the floor as best I could, dazed from the fall and unable to make sense of what was happening before my eyes. My aunt's face was an unsightly purplish red. A pale tress, bloody at the roots, fell from my head onto her sleeve.

Having unlaced the bodice, Rose laid her ear just beneath my aunt's left breast and listened. I could hear all the breathing in the room: my own, ragged, loud and unreal; Father's, steady and purposeful; Blackett's, expelled in what sounded like prayer; and the sobbing exhalations of Rose. Only my aunt was silent.

'Is she gone?' Blackett whispered. Rose clapped her hands to her own mouth in disbelief, and then – curiously, abruptly – my aunt made a snoring sound, after which we observed her bosom rising and falling in the usual way. Four people sighed as one. It was at this moment that Dr Green entered the room.

I hate to think how the affair might have gone for us, had Rose not been present and witnessed these things for herself. As it was, Dr Green entered at a run, as if to catch us in the act of pillaging the dead. When he saw my aunt, he dropped to his knees, bent towards her, and seemed as if he would raise her; then he glanced fearfully at us, as if he thought we might seize our chance and attack him while he was off guard.

'Pray let me help you,' Father said, understanding. He crouched to put himself at a disadvantage and also gestured to Blackett and me. The two of us moved away to the far end of the room, while Dr Green and Father lifted Aunt Harriet, not without difficulty, and laid her lengthwise upon the table.

Blackett and I then approached again and stood with the others in a silence broken only by the quickened breathing of Father and Dr Green. My aunt's face, draining of its high colour, was almost pale again. She might have been asleep but for the persistent grimace that tightened her lips. Father smoothed them with his hand, an action that reminded me, and perhaps others, of the forcible closure of a corpse's eyes. Though well meant, it was not the most politic of gestures.

'A doctor. A doctor.' The parson seized hold of Rose, who had commenced whimpering, and propelled her bodily across to the door. 'Send your man to Hibbertson! Bid him drop anything he has on hand, I'll make it worth his while. But hurry!' He shut the door after her as if to speed her on her way.

'Should we take her upstairs – put her to bed?' Father asked. It was a delicate question: we men could hardly undress her, and she might not wish Rose near her either. Somebody must fetch Hannah Reele. I went upstairs to find her but my aunt's chamber, with its little alcove where Hannah slept to keep her company, was empty, and though I called along all the corridors I failed to flush Hannah out. Possibly she was gone into the village. I returned to my aunt's room and fetched a quilt.

Coming back, I found my father and Blackett with their chairs pulled back from the table, as if to emphasise that they would not meddle with anything belonging to the sick woman. On Dr Green, however, she worked like fire on a cold day. He could not get near enough; he kept rubbing her hands and her face. I laid the quilt over her, and Dr Green elbowed me aside so that he could arrange it snugly round her body. His own complexion was a dull greenish-white, like a fish's belly, so that he looked near fainting.

I said, 'She has cordial and cups in the sideboard,' and made to fetch some, but Blackett rose and laid a hand on my shoulder, saying quietly, 'If anyone is to administer medicines, Jon, it must be Dr Green. And since a sick lady is delicate, and can take only what's wholesome, I shall be the first to drink.'

I said, 'My aunt wouldn't keep bad cordial.' But Dr Green understood the lawyer better than I did, and having fetched the cordial he first presented a cupful to Master Blackett, who downed it in one go. Only after this did Dr Green pour a measure between my aunt's lips.

'She swallows, at any rate,' he said, taking the chair that had been hers and settling himself where he could dab her lips with his handkerchief. 'Now, how did this come about?'

Father said gently, 'We brought unwelcome news and Harriet flew into a rage. I begged her to govern herself but it only made her more passionate.'

The parson gazed at the now colourless face before him. 'She is known to me as a most decorous lady.'

'I'm sure,' Father said. 'But home and abroad are different things.'

'What can you mean?' The man frowned. 'Her household was well ordered and godly, like everything about her.'

'Well ordered, certainly,' my father agreed. 'My meaning was that family quarrels provoke more anger than any other kind. A pastor of your experience will have found this out.'

Dr Green's face showed that he had. Father went on, 'Our news concerns Mr Robin Dymond's will – a most painful subject with Harriet. You remarked her features before I smoothed them?'

'What else would you expect after an apoplexy?' the parson retorted. By now he was losing his greenish tinge, but he was still almost as pale as Aunt Harriet herself. I suggested that we should all benefit from a dose of cordial, and went to the sideboard to fetch more cups.

Dr Green reproved me – 'You make free with another's goods' – but I was not inclined to obey him: I gave my father a cupful, and even offered one to Dr Green himself, but he only shook his head and every so often let out a tiny dry sob like a hiccup. I wondered what he made of us, tearless and relentless as we were. Seeing my aunt still and waxen on the table, how should he imagine her spitting and screaming at me, trying to pull the hair from my head? I put my hand up to my temple, which was stinging, and found a raw bloody place where she had torn the skin away.

Dr Green, who had been watching me, turned towards Father. 'You spoke of her late husband's will.'

'My brother had made certain changes, but said nothing of them to Harriet – to Mrs Dymond,' Father explained. 'We came to explain the arrangements.'

'You're saying he left less to her . . . more to you?'

'No,' Father firmly corrected him. 'Not more to me.'

'You don't wish to discuss it,' the man said, as if he had expected nothing else.

Here Blackett coughed. 'Perhaps, if I may . . . ?'

'That might be best. This is Master Blackett; I apologise for not presenting him earlier – it was not the moment, as you will appreciate. Master Blackett's a lawyer, but the will we speak of was not drawn up by him. It was made by Master Ousby, who dealt with all my brother's business.'

'The later will grants Mrs Dymond a life interest in the property,' explained Blackett, 'after which it passes to Joan and Tamar Seaton, illegitimate connections but acknowledged by Mr Dymond at the end of his life. This is what Mrs Dymond found so offensive.'

'Cruel,' Dr Green murmured.

'With all due respect, I would disagree. While Mrs Dymond cannot be expected to welcome the changes, the provision made for her is liberal.'

'I don't doubt it, but she planned to leave this house.'

Here I looked at Father as if to say, *I told you so*, but he was staring at Dr Green.

'Leave? Did Harriet tell you that herself?'

'She and I intend to marry.'

I think all of us gasped. Dr Green wiped his eyes. 'My elder brother has a liking for this part of the world. We had agreed to an exchange: he was to take End House and in return he would make over to us a handsome house in Devonshire. You see now what a blow this is . . .' – he remembered himself in time – 'this will be, *if* it stands in law.'

'It will stand,' Blackett assured him.

My father was still incredulous. 'This house was Harriet's childhood home.'

'To her,' said the parson, 'it has been a Vale of Tears.'

A Vale of Tears. As if, from Guild Hall to cave, Harriet had been the sufferer throughout! No doubt it had tried her sorely, having beggared her sister and one of her sister's children, to fail in drowning the other. Up to this point I had begun to experience a creeping pity for the parson, whose regard for my aunt, however deluded, appeared sincere. That pity was now washed away in a flood of disgust. It must have shown in my face since Father, coming out of his amazement, looked a warning at me – one that I ignored.

I said, 'You know this Joan Seaton, I think, and what she is to Mrs Dymond.'

'An affliction.' He said this as if delivering a sermon; it was one of the most provoking things I ever heard in my life. 'Mrs Dymond has borne her sorrows with fortitude, and never ceased to hope that her sister might be reclaimed.'

So he did know. Not for the first time in my life, I stood amazed at the monstrous prodigy that is love. It is not so rare a sight, after all: a mean-souled man worshipping a mean-souled woman. That he *did* worship her was plain; yet they had not a grain of compassion between them. Who knows? It was perhaps this stony-heartedness that bound them together. More than anything else, I wondered if my aunt could have confessed her crime to the man before me. There is said to be honour among thieves; might there also be, between liars, a species of truth?

⚬

We returned home sobered by what we had witnessed. Even the lawyer, familiar with wickedness and folly, kept repeating that although the reading of wills was often attended by ugly scenes, never in his life had he seen anything like my aunt's fit of passion.

As for me, I was wondering how I might now be feeling had she fallen dead beside me, her hands still in my hair which was also Robin's. There had been a moment when I thought … again I saw that blond lock drop onto her sleeve, and I shuddered.

Nor was this all. Within a week someone from the house sent a letter, confused, unsigned and in a halting, stumbling character. I seemed to remember that Rose could not write, and I wondered if our informant might be Geoffrey, or perhaps even Hannah Reele. The news was that Aunt Harriet, though conscious, remained enfeebled and Dr Green was questioning all the servants, trying to find us out in some criminal action.

We were naturally worried at this. However, nothing came of it, and we concluded that without actually putting the servants on the rack Dr Green had not been able to make them say what he wanted, and had been obliged to let the matter rest.

I have no doubt that, could Aunt Harriet and Dr Green have strung us up on gibbets, they would have done so without a twinge of conscience. We were opposed to the wishes of a rich lady, which for many in this world is crime enough.

I omit here the lengthy business of the proving of the will. Be it sufficient to note that despite everything my aunt could do, it was upheld, and – contrary to the thunderings of Dr Green – the outcome did not kill her.

21

Settling Accounts

My father was grown busier than ever, and shut himself away with papers he kept carefully from my sight. I knew, as well as if he had told me, that he was preparing to settle accounts with Tamar and Joan. Under the terms of the will they were provided with a maintenance until they were able to inherit, which meant they had no further need of us; our dealings with them were coming to an end.

An end! The finality of such partings was something I was only just starting to learn. In getting by heart this first of all lessons, that each of us owes God a death, most children were far more advanced than I, since I knew it only in a bookish and unfeeling way. My grandparents were all dead before I came into the world, so I had never missed them. My parents still lived, and as their only child (as I thought) I had lost no brothers or sisters when young. Even my natural father had never been a favourite of mine, shameful though it is to admit, and besides, no sooner was he laid in the ground than he climbed out of his grave and into my dreams.

Now, however, he was sunk down again. More, I had seen my aunt, that close-pent furnace of a woman, go in a trice from screams of rage to a mute, constricted helplessness. A little more passion, or a little less bodily strength, and she would have entered upon the life eternal.

Learning the meaning of 'coming to an end' was a bitter business. Stupidly, painfully, I got it by heart that any talk, any quarrel or kindness I had shared with Tamar would never be taken up, never finished, not if I lived to be ninety. The thread between us had been snapped. *An end. Never.* These words, that had been mere sounds before, now grew teeth and gnawed at me.

I cannot tell how I got through the next few weeks. As March moved into April and the birds carried out their shameless courtships in trees and on house-tops I struggled through each day as if imprisoned in a long dark tunnel. In April came warmth and sweetness: the earth opened up, breathing that nameless, stirring odour that rises from the abundant body of Nature waking from her long sleep.

During that time I was tormented by the desire to speak with Tamar. Was it lust – wanting to take up again something I knew was foul and forbidden? It might be so. I could not say what I wanted, not exactly; I could not think like other men. What I yearned for was an abomination, and that knowledge taught me to find excuses even in the privacy of my own thoughts. And yet, even in the midst of all this confusion, there was one thing clear in my mind: I had a question I must put to her, one only she could answer.

I think I may say, in all modesty, that I had gained a little wisdom, though not much, from the events of the last few months. I endeavoured not to yield to melancholy without a struggle; I strove to be content. I was constantly in company with my parents, I returned to my old friendly fellowship with our neighbours, I dug until my limbs trembled, I even read sermons. Starved, my desire grew thin and keen as a blade and dug into my heart until I thought that organ would be sliced in two. I told myself that Tamar and Joan must think themselves in heaven; that God and my earthly father (I mean Mathew) had brought goodness out of my evil, and the least I could do was refrain from meddling, and leave their work to bear fruit.

Spring came on apace. By May the bushes were clotted with blooms and young girls carried armfuls of white blossom into the houses. A maypole was set up on the green; lovers ran laughing into the woods to seek flowers there, and no doubt found a few sweet blossoms not mentioned in the herbal. May filled me with longing so that I was weak as the new lambs staggering in the fields.

It was in May that I received a letter from my aunt, summoning me once more to End House.

'You're not going,' Mother said, beating up the pillows more roughly than was necessary. 'You've suffered enough at her hands.'

'I don't think she would be violent, not now,' I said.

'Mind yourself – out of my way.' She bustled round the bed, tweaking at the covers.

'Father could go with me.'

Mother straightened, pushed back her hair and stared at me. 'You said you'd never have any more dealings with her! And now, you *want* to go. Don't you?'

'I suppose I do,' I said, laughing.

Aunt Harriet's letter informed me that she was confined to bed. I was frankly curious as to how the virago bore up under her suffering, and whether she still terrorised all around her. Besides, it was plain that she had summoned me for *something*.

What might that something be? I allowed myself to indulge a senseless hope that Tamar might be there, or near there, or might have taken possession of some part of the house – even that she might be installed once more in the cave. Any man who has been crossed in love (I will no longer shrink from the word) knows how these fancies rise up like steam and waft themselves about the brain.

Naturally, I spoke only of Aunt Harriet.

'Mother, how can she hurt me? She's bedridden.'

'She's Harriet,' Mother answered. 'I can't say worse of her than that.'

*

My father also opposed my going when we discussed the letter at supper-time. I gathered that Mother had talked with him beforehand, prompting him to accompany me to End House, but he was unmoving: he would not.

'Haven't you had enough of running back and forth over half the county?' he demanded. 'I thought our troubles might have taught you something.'

I pointed out that this was no mad freak like my taking Tamar to the inn. Hateful as my aunt might be, there was no wickedness in paying her a visit.

'There's folly; and sometimes there's not a hair between the two.'

I said I was not proposing to sneak away by deceit.

'But you're defying me.'

'I'll be back in no time,' I promised.

'What, on foot!'

My heart sank as I remembered that both horses, ours and Simon's, were on loan to Samuel Beast, but I looked Father in the eye and said, 'Two days.'

'I can say no more,' he exclaimed, throwing up his hands. 'Whatever she gets you into, you must get out of by yourself.'

Harsh words, had I not known them to be prompted by love and fear. 'I'll come back in one piece,' I said. 'I promise.'

⁂

When I did leave for Tetton Green I rose in darkness, long before anyone else was stirring. This was not a deception – my parents would naturally guess where I was gone, and I had left them a note to dispel any doubt – but I wished to avoid last-minute pleadings from Mother. It did cross my mind, as I placed the note on the table, that Father might repent of his sternness, reclaim the horse and come after me; but this was not likely. Both my parents had maintained a more distant

304

demeanour towards me during the past few days, as if accepting that though stubborn, I was still of age, and could no longer be guarded and guided like a boy.

In a calm frame of mind, then, if not precisely a cheerful one, I filled up my pockets in the pantry and set out to walk to End House.

Between Spadboro and the next village lies a stretch of lane that cuts through a long, thin wood. The wood sprawls for some two miles and the lane is bordered, on either side, by shallow ditches whose purpose is long forgotten. Folk walking on moonless nights had been known to fall into these ditches, but the moon, though on the wane, gave sufficient light for me to pass safely between them. I walked briskly, not for fear (ours is a quiet stretch of country) but to keep myself warm.

The sky was clear as fine old cider and the Plough hung sparkling in the sky directly before me. I have seldom time or inclination to gaze at the stars but on this occasion, deprived of company, I amused myself with a fancy that it had cut open this passage through the wood, expressly for me. Its brilliance and that of the other lights sprinkled over the heavens told me that once the sun was risen, we were set for a warm day. I marched along admiring the beauty of God's creation until, happening to glance to my right, I saw something large and white move in the ditch and at once sink down again.

Of the scalding terror of that moment, the best I can say is that I felt it, and hope never to feel it again. I strained to see the white thing, whatever it might be, with such intensity that dots swarmed before my eyes and I was good as blind – so the flesh betrays us at our time of need – and when my sight cleared, everything was as it had been. The movement did not come again, though I could perceive a small white edge that convinced me I was not mistaken. As I began to fear less, and think more, it came to me that the mysterious object might be a sheep fallen in and injured. But no: a sheep would have cried out by now, and this presence, whatever it was, made not a sound.

I was long past any dread of Robin. My fear was that I had glimpsed a living soul crouching in the ditch, a man who would do away with me for my coat (just then a precious shield against the chill breeze) and my shoes. If, on the other hand, he had not noticed me, the chances were that he was drunk, and I might creep away if I allowed time for him to fall asleep.

Standing stock-still, fearing that at any moment the white shape might rise again, was agony. At last, persuaded that any man intending to harm me would have done so by now, I crept forward to the ditch.

It was indeed a man – and a woman, too – lying wrapped round in white cloth. This, then, was the source of my terror: a bed-sheet stolen from some line and spread over the pair while they slept. It was not hard to understand the rest. A tramping couple, weary and finding the ditch dry, had crawled into it out of the wind. What I had witnessed was some attempt to ease their limbs as they lay huddled together; that they were now sunk into sleep again, I was assured by a faint, buzzing snore. The woman's face, upturned in the moonlight, was pinched and degraded. She wore no cap, and I thought how her hair must be full of dust and leaves and vermin. Of the man I could see only the swell of his back, and a part of his jaw and ear.

It came to me that this might well stand for some episode from Joan's story, or Tamar's, and the thought filled me with sorrow. Was the woman the child of godly parents, ruined by the love of a masterless man? Or was she a Delilah who had brought low some village Samson once respected by his neighbours? Perhaps they had neither of them known a better life. My heart contracted with pity. I was not such a fool, however, as to fancy myself safe in their company, and I delicately moved off until there was a good distance between them and me. As I walked on, I carried with me the melancholy gleam of moonlight on that sheet of theirs, such a wretched shelter as to be scarcely worth the stealing. I wondered was it a bridal bed of sorts, and whether, one cold night, it would be their shroud.

And now the sky was streaked with light: cocks on distant farms began to greet the sun. The wood and the ground beneath me turned grey, then green. I was strolling over banks of grass and flowers that a few weeks before had been bare and slimy with mud, spring's sweet carpet spread for me. The world, that had treated harshly those two in the ditch, seemed for once to be on my side and of my mind.

I kept my spirits up by telling myself no evil could come of this visit. It had angered my father, but he could not forbid me to go and once I returned home unhurt, we would quickly make things up. Nor could anything I did harm Tamar and her mother, who would never lie cold again as long as they lived. They had, of course, ceased to draw an allowance from my father; they no longer needed his help. I am as selfish as most men, but not entirely so, and in this instance I can honestly say I was free of grudging jealousy; nay, I even took pleasure in the knowledge that the Seatons were heirs to End House. I pictured Tamar dozing by the fire and eating comfits, instead of washing foul linen, and Joan (if she lived that long) sleeping once more in her old bed. Or would she prefer to gaze up each morning at Harriet's richly embroidered hangings? I wondered what the servants would make of them, and if they would go elsewhere or stay on under their new mistresses. Geoffrey, for instance: surely he must go? He had sent Joan on her way too harshly, too many times – unless she retained him for the pleasure of giving him orders. With such fancies as these I shortened the way to Tetton Green.

&

Rose opened the door and stared in disbelief. Manners prompted her to a hasty curtsey, after which she remained, speechless, planted in the doorway.

'Well, Rose, aren't you going to let me in?' I hinted. 'I'm invited, after all.'

This Rose seemed unable to comprehend. I supposed that after the scenes she had witnessed her slowness was quite natural, so I produced my aunt's letter.

'Who took this for her?' Rose murmured. 'Not Geoffrey! Not I!'

'Hannah, then.' Smiling, I watched her puzzle over it. Her eyes went straight to the signature, which was evidently all she could recognise, then looked back into mine. She handed me the letter, saying with more frankness than flattery, 'Is it really an invitation, Sir? I never thought you'd show your face.'

'Of course it is.' I hemmed to indicate that I meant business, and made to enter the house. Rose stumbled to one side.

'Oh, pardon me – pray enter, Sir, enter –'

She was scarlet. Could this really be the same Rose who used to gossip with me in the kitchen? I wondered what had been said of me in my absence, if here was a servant shaken to pieces merely at finding me on the doorstep.

'If you'll wait here, Master Jon,' said Rose, leading me to the chairs Father and I had occupied on our last memorable visit. As then, a splendid fire burned in the grate – End House was never very warm, even in May – and as I sat by the crackling logs, stretching my legs towards them, I recalled how I had helped Tamar to pilfer from the woodpile. Though only a few months past, it seemed distant as a childhood prank.

My intention on the road had been to maintain a kind of chill dignity towards Aunt Harriet, neither shouting nor wrangling but making my disdain quite clear. I had even rehearsed some shrewd and telling speeches, if I could but find a way to introduce them into our talk. Now I was arrived, however, and soon to confront her, those marvels of eloquence I had composed on the road went flying up the chimney with the sparks.

'If you please, Master Jon,' said a soft voice, making me jump. Hannah Reele stood next to me. 'Mrs Dymond is abed. She'll receive you in her chamber.'

We climbed the stairs in silence apart from the squeak of Hannah's shoes on the polished wood. They continued to squeak and creak all the way along the corridor where I had searched for her on my last day in this house. Hannah knocked at the chamber door, opened it without waiting for a reply and led me to the bed, where the hangings were already pulled aside. I was in the presence of my aunt.

I saw at once that her health was decayed. She was leaning back, propped upon cushions as if too weak to sit up without them. Though the blue eyes were as bead-like as ever, the cheeks they glared from were sunken in, and her skin, that had been tight and youthful, hung slack from her jaw. The finger of Disease had traced a line from each corner of her mouth down to her chin, and when I looked at those creases in the flesh I perceived, for the first time, a sisterly resemblance to Joan.

The covers lay almost flat across the bed. It was hard to believe that they concealed a human body, let alone the imposing frame of Aunt Harriet. She had wasted, and wasted, until she was the ashes of the woman I had known; I felt that if Hannah lifted her up in the bed, she would break and crumble into dust.

She had told me of this in her letter. I was no saint; I was come there partly hoping to witness her pain, an ugly hope but excusable in one she had so nearly murdered. I had expected to exult and go on my way cruelly rejoicing that she was, at last, hamstrung and hobbled. In the event, I was quite unable to exult. What I felt was not glee, but unease: it was impossible to look on her and not feel Death gaining on *me*.

All this passed through my mind while my aunt was still working her jaws and trying to pronounce my name. She managed 'Jon', but with difficulty, and I saw that her mouth moved only on one side.

'You asked to see me,' I said, in the tone of one who discharges an unpleasant duty.

Aunt Harriet glanced towards Hannah Reele. 'Your aunt wished for your company earlier,' the maid explained, 'but she wasn't able to make herself understood until a fortnight ago.'

Wished for my company!

Aunt's jaws, again labouring, brought forth the word, 'Mathew.'

'She thinks I'm my father,' I whispered. Hannah shook her head, which I took to mean that Aunt Harriet was enquiring after him.

'Father's very well. He knows I'm here.' Aunt seemed disappointed at that; doubtless she would have preferred to sow lies and deception between us. 'Mother knows, too,' I added for good measure.

'They – pleased? Eh?'

I supposed she meant, did they approve of my being there.

'They wish my happiness, as always. Pray be brief in stating your business.'

Hannah murmured, 'To that end – brevity – and because it tires her, I'm to speak for Mrs Dymond. Should she wish to speak for herself, she'll cough.'

This my aunt confirmed with a jerky nod.

Hannah then asked, 'When are you to be married, Master Jon?'

This was not at all what I had expected. Something in Aunt Harriet's eager eyes warned me not to mention Poll Parfitt.

'My parents wish to see me married but there are no plans as yet.'

Hannah cleared her throat. 'Your aunt means, when are you to marry Tamar Seaton?'

Despite my resolve to remain dignified, I fired up at once. Was there no end to her insults? I said, 'My aunt knows it to be impossible,' and added, 'This is the sort of talk that brought on the apoplexy.'

Hannah glanced at Aunt Harriet, who nodded for her to go on.

'You write to her, do you not? At her lodgings?'

'I'd lose my time if I did,' I said, speaking directly to Aunt Harriet. 'Have you forgotten she can't read?'

'*Couldn't* read,' Hannah corrected me. 'We hear she's learning her letters.'

I very much disliked her tone and said, 'Lord! To see how people can rise in this world!' to which Hannah, unabashed, replied, 'I speak for my mistress. Do you know where Tamar Seaton is lodged?'

'No.'

Aunt's stiff jaws ground out, 'Mathew knows.'

'Father may know, I don't.' I saw the ghost of a laugh form on her lips at my use of the word *father* and I hated her for it. 'He wishes us to remain apart.'

My aunt looked as if she had just turned up a guinea in the bedclothes. I understood it to mean that she took pleasure in my sufferings, and that spurred me to a revenge.

'When are *you* to be married?' I asked. 'To Dr Green?' My aunt breathed in sharply, her eyes a blue blaze, so that I felt all the satisfaction of a man who throws a stone and brings down a goose. 'I can't tell you where Tamar is,' I said. 'If you've no more to say, I'll be on my way home.'

My aunt coughed and beckoned me close. I approached warily; there was an aroused, predatory cast to her features and for an instant I wondered if she was strong enough, after all, to do me some hurt, but the sight of her poor wasted neck put paid to that notion. She was muttering now, repeating something over and over. I strained to understand and was finally able to make out the words: 'Here – whisper.'

Not without misgivings, I bent down to the bed. She gave off a sickly, dirty odour unlike anything I had smelt on her before. When her breath rustled in my ear I imagined miasmas, infections, plagues; it was as much as I could do not to shrink from her.

'Chitton,' she whispered. 'Say it.'

'Chitton.' Was that the word? There was a place called Chitton, did she mean that?

'Mrs Eliot. Say.'

'Mrs Eliot?'

Again that look, as if I had just presented her with a diamond ring. Perhaps her wits were going; if so, it was not my concern. I rose, ready to depart.

'Is that all, Aunt Harriet?'

My aunt's mouth stretched in a noiseless laugh until her face seemed about to split open. She said, distinctly this time as if putting all her strength into the utterance: 'Tamar. There.'

'There – !'

Too late, I saw it all: since our last visit here, she had understood her mistake. Once she had grasped that – far from being his darling scheme – my connection with Tamar caused my father pain, she had made it her business to hunt out where my sister was hidden. She had lands in more than one parish, connections, money to fee intelligencers; she had at length found out a place where two women were being sheltered and her choice revenge on 'Mathew' was to break the secret to me, the last person who should be told.

She could not forgive my father. For what? For upholding the will, to be sure; but also for being ten times the man Robin was, and yet loving his erring brother despite all. Mathew

Dymond's natural goodness was a standing reproach to her, an open sore.

'You needn't think I'll go,' I said, though the words *Mrs Eliot, Chitton* were already branded on my memory. She had even thought to make me repeat them. There was no doubt about the look that was on her face now: it was a hot, stinging triumph. I bent down to her again and said softly, 'One of these nights, while you're lying here so snug and warm behind the bed hangings, a door will slide open to the other world. You'll see, then, who's waiting for you.'

She managed to say, 'My Robin.'

'Oh, no! Your *true* love: the Gentleman.'

'For shame,' Hannah said in a curious flat voice that seemed secretly to agree with me.

'He may come for you tonight. Sleep well,' I added, going out of the room.

22

Advice to Live Happy

You needn't think I'll go.

Every rational argument was against my going: it was playing Harriet's game, my father would be distraught if he found me out, and there was an excellent chance of my coming home still more beaten and wretched than before. I do not know how long I stood in the lane, torn between reason and desire, before I was obliged to jump aside to let pass a cart – the boy at the reins must have been calling to me for some time if I may judge by the perfect shriek he gave just before it rattled by, which finally alerted me to my danger. In the end, what decided me was no kind of reason at all, but something I felt in my bones: that if I hung back now I was no man and never would be, only Mathew Dymond's boy.

Though I had heard of Chitton, I had never been there and had not the faintest notion how I might reach it from End House. I must find out, and quickly, for with luck I might find Tamar and hurry back home in one day, and my parents be never the wiser.

It was not yet noon. After a moment's thought I made my way to the inn and asked if anyone could tell me how to get to Chitton, for I was called there on urgent business. I was proud of my quick-wittedness, and prouder still when a gentleman finishing up a plate of cold meat said the village lay in his way, and he would take me in his coach if anyone could vouch for my respectability. That was easy enough, since several of the men in there could attest that I was Mrs Dymond's nephew and (so they believed) her heir. It was scarcely the moment to disabuse them.

'Can't she spare him a horse?' someone murmured behind my back, but fortunately the stranger did not hear. Despite everything Aunt Harriet could do, the world was still on my side and of my mind.

I got into the coach with this benefactor, who seemed a generous, Christian man: the sort of man, indeed, whose company acted as a restorative after the hellish atmosphere of my aunt's house. When I pulled some bread and beef from my pocket (I had not eaten since raiding Mother's pantry early that morning) he produced a bottle of wine and offered me a pull at it to help the meat down. I took only one swig, but as I was already drunk with my good fortune, and the food, and being free of my aunt, and going to see Tamar, I grew so excited and flushed and repeated my gratitude so often that he must have thought me overcome by a single mouthful of drink; I suspect that by the end of the journey the poor man heartily repented of his kindness.

'I'm forever in your debt, Sir,' I cried, leaping at last from the coach onto the grass. 'May God reward you.'

'And also protect you, young man,' was his wary reply from the window as the coach rattled off again.

I was standing on a low bank or bailey surrounding the church, the village sloping away below. Those houses I could see were large and handsome, much in the style of Tetton Green, but of a lighter-coloured stone. However, they were laid out differently; whereas Tetton Green stretched itself out in a line, the buildings here huddled in a flock. A fresh, clean scent came to my nostrils: somebody was cutting up wood. I stood breathing its perfume for a moment, clearing my mind and allowing my cheeks to cool, for I was still a little flushed. Then I crossed the road to where a maidservant was spreading washed shifts on bushes. Watching me approach, the girl giggled as if she liked me, but she could tell me nothing of the lady I sought. Nor could a man hoeing in another garden across the

315

way. I began to wonder if my aunt had made a fool of me; had she perhaps, in one last act of spite, sent me on a wild goose chase?

At the third place where I asked, a woman came to the door and said she knew of a Mrs Eliot, yes, and I would find her at the house round the corner. 'A big one with a big gate. There's a mulberry leaning out into the street,' she said. As I went away she did not close the door. When I looked back she was still there, staring after me as if at some freak of nature. I suppose I *was* a strange object, my chest working like a bellows from the fear that I might find myself unwelcome and come away from the house more wretched than before.

I rounded the corner and at once observed the mulberry in the distance. As I approached, I saw it was intended to form one of a pair stationed on either side of the front gate, but this tree was diseased; that was why it drooped through the fence and into the way. When I came up to the house I was struck by how much more fitting a healthy tree, a flourishing emblem of prosperity, would have been, for the house *was* prosperous. It stood back from the road, imposing beyond anything I had imagined, with a fine staircase sweeping up to the door. Between it and me stretched a garden laid out for show, its beds in formal knots and a yew avenue trimmed into fantastical shapes. I have never seen the point of such extravagances. I am not even fond of espaliers: the best shapes for plants are the ones God makes them in. Mrs Eliot evidently had other ideas and employed gardeners to keep her trees fashionably deformed.

The tall gate in front of me looked so discouraging that I was surprised to find it open. Passing through, I made my way along a gravelled alleyway between the beds, intended for carts and coaches but also catering admirably for gentlemen and ladies who might wish to stroll and admire the garden.

The front doorknocker was a great coiling, toiling knot in

brass, difficult to lift: it seemed that in this house nothing was undertaken lightly or unadvisedly. For a brief eternity, I weighed it in my hand – there was still time to go away – then let it drop.

A manservant answered and would have sent me round the back of the house, but I said I was not there as a tradesman; I was come to visit Mrs Eliot; upon which he made an insulting show of looking round for my horse and servant. I was in no mood to bear with this and said, 'Pray do as you are bid.' At last he took my name and went off to enquire, leaving me in a small damp-smelling room where the warmth of the spring day was yet to penetrate. Against one wall stood a musical instrument, the lid painted to show scenes of gay life: cavaliers drinking and a gentleman and lady playing lutes together. I admired it from a distance, not liking to touch.

After a few minutes the manservant came back and showed me into a long, thin, chilly apartment that left the musical instrument in the dust, as it were, since its entire ceiling was painted. At the same time as I observed this, I became aware of a lady seated at the far end of the room. It would not do to approach her with my eyes rolling in my head, so I ignored the marvels above me in order to appear before Mrs Eliot as a sane, though horseless, man.

She was arranged in a gilt chair by the fire, her feet propped up on a little stool. As I neared her, I put my hand to my hat, in preparation. I had my story ready: I was come from Mathew Dymond of Spadboro to enquire after the health of Joan Seaton, and to ask if I might have a few words with her. No mention of the younger woman; that must come later. If Mrs Eliot believed Tamar to be a widow there was no reason why she should think ill of me; I was resolved to be careful nonetheless.

The manservant went on ahead and murmured something to his mistress. He then stepped aside and indicated that I might approach. I had the hat off my head, and was sweeping it before me in the approved style, in the same instant that I realised the woman in the chair was Tamar.

'Jon! Welcome!' was the first thing she said, while my heart whirred like a beetle under a glass. The second was, 'Fetch refreshments,' to the manservant, and the third, 'Is there bad news?'

'Bad?' I stammered. The man left the room with a suspicious backward glance at this nobody from nowhere. 'No, I mean, not that I know of.'

I would have given anything not to speak in that ridiculous, squeaking fashion but her eyes showed only delight.

'Doubly welcome, then,' she said, indicating a chair. 'Pray sit – rest. You look bone-weary.'

I could not have said the same of her. Gone was the tough, mannish frame of the drudge I used to know. Health glowed in her cheeks, in the thickness of her red-gold hair, in the creamy softness of her bosom. This was a woman who ate well and slept well, a woman who knew what it was to be warm. My eyes crept lower: yes, she was plumper in the belly than elsewhere.

As I sat down Tamar took a small pot, dug a finger into it and began rubbing ointment into her hands, pausing from time to time to observe the effect. A scent of roses and beeswax wafted across to me; either the perfume, or the heavy ring she wore (*not* my keepsake, by the by) reminded me of Aunt Harriet.

'See that, Jon?'

'What?'

She held her hands out towards me.

'White as snow,' I said.

'Liar!' She grinned. 'But they're growing whiter. I've no work to do – nothing at all.'

I pictured her poor blue feet in the lock-up and wondered if she put beeswax ointment on those, too, and if the flesh of her entire body was now creamy and perfumed. As soon as this thought took root in my mind, I plucked it up: it was a poisonous weed.

'What must I say to Mrs Eliot?' I asked.

'Shhh!' She giggled. '*I* am Mrs Eliot. The mistress of the house is Mrs Godolphin.'

'Is that why you wear a ring?'

'Mr Eliot died of the plague. He was a coarse, common sort; I'm the daughter of gentlefolks.'

'And Mrs Godolphin believes all that?'

'She says she does, and that's the same. Besides,' she gave me a hard look, 'they *were* gentlefolks.'

I supposed so, if gentry compensated for bastardy. What else gave me the right to look down on Hannah Reele?

'Did my father pay for you to be lodged like this?'

She laughed. 'Of course not! Not that he pinched us, mind; I don't complain of him, only we pay more now. Mrs Godolphin allows us the run of the house.'

'Do you dine with her?'

'She's all the company we have but Mathew – and now you. But never you mind her! She's not here to see us.' In those words I heard the old Tamar, not yet polished away.

'And Joan? How is she?'

'She cried when Hob flew off –'

'Oh, did –'

'– but she's better than she was. Her bad teeth have been pulled. She's the widow Seaton, now.'

I said, compelled by politeness, 'Would she wish to see me, do you think?'

Tamar put her head on one side as if considering. 'She's asleep.'

The sullen manservant knocked and entered with a tray. She signalled to him to set it down on a nearby table.

'Will you take something, Jon? Some wine? Gingerbread?'

'Thank you, I'll wait,' I said and then, yielding to impulse, 'No, I'll have the wine if you please.'

The man's nostrils flared as if he had expected nothing more from such a boorish visitor. I flushed as he poured a glassful and brought it over to me.

'Go now.' Tamar spoke sharply; perhaps she, too, had suffered his contempt. When he was gone she rose and waited on me herself. Standing, she was heavier round the middle than I had first perceived.

'The best wine I've ever tasted,' I said. 'Better even than my aunt's.'

'And the gingerbread? Can't I tempt you?' Dangerous words, between us two. I smiled in answer, she returned my smile, and for an instant, despite the delicate sweetmeat laid so neatly upon the salver, there was a whiff of the wood and the cave.

As if to restore us to our civilised selves, Tamar went back to her seat and began to prattle like any pampered miss. 'How did you know I was here? Come, you *shall* tell me.'

'Aunt Harriet found you out. She must have a spy.'

Tamar at once grew serious. 'Here, in this house?'

'No, no. She only wished to know where you lodged.' Even as I said this, I knew it was a lie. 'I can't say,' I admitted at last. 'Perhaps she has a spy here; I don't know.'

'The servants dislike me,' she said thoughtfully.

'She did it to spite my father.' And she had succeeded, thanks to me and my dishonest, promise-breaking ways. 'He mustn't know of this visit. You won't tell him, will you?'

'Never.' She was protecting Father, not me. 'Why *are* you come, then? To find out how we live?'

'I can see you're thriving – both of you.'

Another woman might have blushed, but she gazed on me in such a frank and friendly manner that I could not care about the blush. She said, 'Joan hopes the little one'll favour

Robin. She thinks *I* favour Robin, now I've got some flesh on me; *you're your father's child*, she says.'

'Your hair curls like his.' And like mine. Yes, I thought drily: all considered, the child had every chance of favouring Robin. But then Tamar's hair was reddish, and she had those tawny eyes. Could it be, after all, that she was not his daughter? Not that it made any difference: full sister, half sister! I took another sip of wine to give me courage and said, watching her face for signs of jealousy, 'Father wishes me to marry.'

She nodded. 'Aye, you should! Who is she?'

'Nobody you know. Poll Parfitt.'

'Poll Parfitt. Poll Dymond.' She tried out the name. 'Does she love you?'

'She's foolish enough.'

Tamar smiled.

'You don't care,' I accused her. 'Did you never think *we* might marry? I mean if . . . I could marry you.'

'I shan't marry anyone,' Tamar retorted. 'I haven't lived poor so long, and got a bit of money at last, only to give it away to a husband!' She laughed at the very idea.

'Well,' I said, striving to appear cheerful, 'When I'm wed, my father may perhaps allow me to visit you – at End House, I mean.'

'Oh, no, Jon! Mathew says we must rent it out.'

I stared. 'In God's name, why?'

'We're known. I can't be Mrs Eliot, not in Tetton.'

'No,' I said dully. Had anyone told me how much I would suffer on hearing that news, I would have called him a liar. I tried another way. 'Tamar, when I said you don't care, what I meant was –'

'Don't, Jon! You've surely not come for that, to ask if I would've married you, things being different? Things are as they are!'

'Tamar,' I said, trembling because it was agony to speak, and worse to remain silent, 'I swear to God, if I could marry you, I would. There's nobody I love more.' She turned her face away from me, towards the fire. I said, 'Things *being* as they are, then, I repent of it all – all the harm I did you.'

'You took me out of the lock-up,' she replied, still looking away. 'Got us blankets – food. You did more good than bad.'

'Not enough,' I said. 'It can never be enough, not now.'

'I bear you no grudge. I want for nothing.'

'That's the worst part. There's nothing I can give you, and I, I –'

'You love me best.' Tamar nodded to herself, as if she was only now coming to understand. Then she added, more mockingly, 'Hark at me. I sound like Joan.'

I thought: And I, like Robin.

The room was growing dark. We sat side by side listening to the spit and crackle of the flames, she smiling on me from time to time, I swallowing down a lump of sadness that kept rising in my throat and would not let me speak.

At last I took her hand. 'Tamar, there's one thing I must ask.'

She glanced around the fire-lit room. 'Here we are, all peaceful. Don't spoil it.'

'I must. Please, Tamar, don't look away.'

She obeyed; yet her fox-eyes, as she gazed into mine, held a reproach.

I asked, 'Do you know why I can't marry you? What we are to one another?'

'*Why will you – !*' she exclaimed with the quick anger born of fear.

A thread snapped in my heart. I had scarcely strength to go on, but go on I must, or live the rest of my life in ignorance. I said, 'Be patient, I beg of you. The day we went to the inn . . . did you know then?'

'So that's your Great Question?' She pulled her hand out of my grasp. 'No, I did *not*!'

I was like one stunned. 'But surely Joan, did Joan never – ?'

'It was Mathew told me.'

I stared.

'When he brought me here. He told me why I mustn't see you.'

'You had no notion of it?'

She shook her head violently. 'None. I cried myself to sleep, nights and nights. But then I got to thinking there was nothing to be done, and if I kept up my crying the child might be born blind. So each time I started, I would say to myself, Nothing to be done, and in time I came to feel a little better.'

I thought how like Tamar this was. She might be a mere scrap thrown onto raging seas, but she was a scrap of cork. Even as she was speaking, however, a troubling recollection came to mind. I said, 'But, Tamar, you asked me to touch the wilding. You knew it was my tree.'

Again she shook her head. 'Joan's tree.'

'So why . . . ?'

'Oh, to see what you'd do.' She shrugged. 'Don't think you were the only one. Lots of folk touched it.' I was wondering whether I believed this when she added, 'Why d'you ask? The wilding's nothing, only a tree; it makes no difference, does it?'

'I want to think well of *you*,' I burst out. 'Not to believe you capable . . . Tamar, don't laugh, I beg of you – don't laugh –'

My voice thickened and I broke off, humiliated. What a ridiculous creature I was; I was afraid to look at her. When at last I forced myself to do so, I saw her eyes were wide and glistening and very beautiful.

'Nobody ever spoke to me like that,' she said soberly.

I muttered, 'I won't again.'

'To want to think well of me. Not even Mathew wanted to think well of me.' Her mouth trembled. 'Nobody. Ever.'

Her tears and sobs were fierce. I was witness to a rare transformation: Tamar moved. For years she had been driven with stones and blows, like an animal, from one place to another. An animal can only be punished; a human soul can be shamed and implored. I wanted to think well of her. I had spoken to her as to a human soul.

&

We sat in the darkness, holding hands. I would prefer to write, *Not like lovers, like brother and sister*, but it was not quite that; I cannot tell exactly how it was. A maid came in and went out from time to time, fetching and carrying. I am sure she came in more than was needful – she was perhaps that spy of my aunt's – but we cared nothing for her as we sat in quiet talk, weaving together our two-sided tapestry. These were perhaps the sweetest hours of my life, passed not in lust but in mutual forgiveness, than which there is nothing more tender. I was at once a man who had at last come home, and a man who must go away forever; after that night we could be nothing to one another, and I must content myself with picturing her happiness. So that I should have some knowledge of her in the barren times to come, I asked how she was progressing in her studies.

'Reading's well enough,' she said. 'And writing.'

'And embroidery?' I had seen some coloured stitching, clumsy as a child's first attempt, flung down on a nearby chair.

'Oh,' she exclaimed crossly, 'Mrs Godolphin says a woman must embroider, to show off the hands and arms.'

'To catch you a husband.'

She gave a wry smile. 'I'm all scars up to the elbows, I don't know who'd be caught by that.'

I knew one man at least. I said, 'You can always wear your sleeves long.'

'That's what *she* says. She had me laughing, Jon, asking did Mr Eliot use to beat me. It's only marks from work!'

She had a supper brought to us and served up on little tables, near the fire. Tamar's manners were so improved, when I recalled her attempts to eat fried eggs at the inn, that I thought a day might come when she would indeed pass as a gentlewoman. Alas, the meal also reminded me of Father and Mother, who must now be waiting for me. To leave Tamar was a wound, but there was nothing to be gained by spinning out our parting. It would hurt just as much when the moment came, and in the meantime my mother would be greatly distressed . . . yet I could not leave just yet.

After supper we still sat on in the firelight, no longer talking but perfectly harmonious.

'I shall have to go,' I said at last.

Tamar would not permit me to depart on foot. She explained that Mrs Godolphin would be brought home in a neighbour's carriage.

'You shall have hers,' she said.

'How will you explain to her tomorrow?'

'Oh – my cousin required it.'

'Will she believe that?'

Tamar shrugged.

So I was spared another cold walk under the stars. Tamar came outside, bareheaded, to wave me off. At the door of the coach we embraced.

'Well,' I said. 'Sister!'

'Marry Poll.' She kissed my cheek. 'Live happy.'

One minute we were there, a torch casting its fitful light over us and the coachman, poor wretch, yawning at the reins. Tamar held out her hands and I clasped them. I gazed on her, on my darling, upright and fruitful as a young tree and with as little need of me. The next minute gravel rasped under the wheels, and Tamar went out of my life.

1674

23

Writings and Writings

She has been true to her word. My father has no notion that I was ever at Chitton; so on that occasion I got the better of him, if on no other.

Since then I have been occupied in keeping a memorandum, to the best of my ability, of everything that passed during those few months. My account of myself is now almost complete and I shall not be sorry to make an end of it. For one thing, I have been obliged to keep the writing a secret, which is no small task in a house like ours. For another, I have been perplexed over whether I should omit certain passages. In the end I chose to keep everything in its place, and in this way much has been preserved that would otherwise have been lost and forgotten. Whether I now tear it out is another matter.

Our family, that was forever changing, is changed again: a child is come into the world, and an old woman departed. Mrs Harriet died a month ago. Her death had been expected a good year earlier; as Master Blackett said, she doubtless argued the case with the Destroying Angel but was forced to yield at last.

My aunt's second marriage never took place and Robin's will made ample, not to say lavish, provision for his widow's funeral. We all thought it strange, therefore, when Dr Green paid for a brass plaque to be fixed above her grave; but nobody, least of all the Seatons, cared to interfere. The plaque is the largest on that side of the church, and deeply engraved. It represents a woman struck down by three skeletons, one of them clutching a scroll. Any man who sees it may judge for himself whether Dr Green forgave Father, Blackett and me for depriving him of a house in Devonshire.

So much for the old. What of the young?

Tamar is now able to write, after a fashion and with my father's permission. The child appears to be a likely boy. With a father's pride, and a father's pangs, I gaze on a little painting she sent me. My son has hair like lamb's wool; in him I see my youth again.

These days I often think of Robin, for whom the lad is named. Indeed, I have never stopped thinking of him, shamed yet returning like the dog to his vomit, as my father once said of me; and I am forced to bow to Father's wisdom in keeping Tamar and me apart.

For all Robin's wickedness, I pity him. Who would choose to die with such secrets weighing on his breast? Not I; nor would I wish to haunt any man's dreams. After such painful thoughts as these, my way seems to lie clear before me: on my son's coming of age he should be sent my private account and read every last word of it; in this mood, I would not withhold the dot of an 'i'. Better he should feel anger or disgust towards me, than be taken in by a sham, told his father was an angel, &c., &c., and all the time be deceived as to how he came into the world. And if I can forgive *my* natural father, then he may bring himself, in time, to forgive me.

But then I come always to the same stumbling block: the boy's mother. Were I to scratch out the worst of my meetings with her – as indeed I would – still, *brother* and *sister* are not easy words to soften down.

What, then, shall I tell him? Truth is a purge, best given full strength. Wrap it up in sugar pills and it fails of half its effect. Purge too much, however . . . I am in sore need of advice, and perhaps not my father's.

How many people became lost to me, almost without my noticing, while I fancied myself the offspring of Mathew

Dymond! I lost my natural parents from the start, and also my sister, and my son. Now that I come to reckon it up, I am like an orphaned child.

❧

Joshua Parfitt has been here talking with my parents about the money Poll brings with her. I cannot say I care much for that. If I may say so without pride, I gave away more than her entire portion comes to when I handed over Robin's will. Besides, we have land enough and everything we need. Father, though, says things must be done in the proper way, as is fitting. Put more bluntly, he is resolved that we should not appear desperate to ally ourselves with the Parfitts. I cannot help but be amused at this, since it strikes me that *he* is indeed not far off desperation, not so much for their money as to get me off his hands at last. I am sure nobody could think it of *me*, whom the families have dragged to the altar as if to sacrifice.

Still, Father is in the right. Parfitt rents part of his land whereas we own all of ours; it is Poll, not me, who marries into the warmer nest, and her father should give her what he can.

We thought it best to say nothing of Tamar or the child. Wives grow curious and knowing a little, as Mother said, quickly turns to knowing a lot. It is a pity. I would have as few lies in my life as possible, and yet they go on breeding.

I wonder if Poll and I will have children – if there will be more Dymonds at last? If so, they will not cut out my boy. There is so much I would wish to say to him, were he old enough to understand. At nights I dream not of Poll, but of little Robin, a grown man and in conversation with me. I have written two or three letters that he might read upon coming of age, and torn them up again. I found part of one the other day, in the pocket of my coat:

331

To Mr Robin Eliot

Sir,

You are now of age, and it is fit that I explain my intentions towards you. This letter, which supplements the provisions of my will (should that have been read) is for your private information.

You will be aware of the allowance I have made you since your birth . . .

That letter I destroyed. What could be less like a father's embrace? And then, he would naturally wish to write back and ask why I had kept away so long. What could I reply?

Let me try again, and send the letter to Tamar to see how she likes it. If we can once agree on what the boy is to know, I shall go to my wedding as cheerfully as a drunken man to his hanging. Indeed, I shall go one better and put my head in the noose sober.

To Mr R. E.

My Dear Son,

Pray prepare yourself for some unexpected news. You have been told that this is a letter from your father, and so it is; you naturally expect a letter from Mr Roger Eliot, but what you hold in your hand comes from your most loving father, Jonathan Dymond. You may remember a Mathew Dymond who has sometimes visited your mother; that is my father, and your grandfather.

I beg of you, do not start away, but hear me out. To know yourself, it is necessary that you know something of me.

Mine is a sorry tale of youthful ignorance, an ignorance born of mistaken kindness but with results no less painful for that. Like all young men I had moments of folly, and like some others I fathered a child. Had I been able to, I would certainly have married your mother, but my situation ren-

332

*dered this impossible. That is the exact word: I was forced to
come away, for both our sakes, and never to see her again.
The loss, dear son, has been a heavy one. I treasure up every
scrap of intelligence that reaches me concerning her doings,
and also yours.*

*Perhaps you think these mere empty excuses. You should
know that I have stood your friend in more than words: it is
by my help that you are become the heir to End House.
Should you doubt it, ask your mother. You are also heir
(under the name of Robin Eliot) to my estate along with any
other children I may have, and though I may not see you, yet
I swear you shall never be loved the less. I have your miniature, limned when you were just six months old. I keep it by
me and look at it every day.*

*By the time you read this I shall be married – perhaps
many years married, if God spare my bride and me – yet
your allowance shall go on just the same. It may be that in
time I will find a way to tell my wife where it goes, and why.
Nothing, I repeat, nothing, can dislodge you or your mother
from my heart.*

*You may wonder why I choose to write to you now. In a
sense I do not choose now, for my now is not yours: this letter
has long been written, to be given you when you come of age,
or when your mother believes you capable of understanding.
As a young man I walked blindfold and tumbled into a pit; I
wish you to walk with your eyes open. My own natural father
(for here I am in the same case as you) died with a conscience
so burdened that his spirit could scarcely find rest after death.
I would lie quiet in my grave, and so I give up my secret
before my day of reckoning.*

*There is also another whose secret this is. Never blame
your mother; think of her rather with admiration. As a
young woman she endured hardships painful even to speak
of; it is for her to tell you more, if she will. I will say here*

only that she has performed marvels; were all known, most folk would appear mere dust beneath her feet. This letter is given to you with her full knowledge and agreement. That is a mother's sacrifice requiring no little courage, and a mighty act of love towards a child. Though it may humble you to learn what she used to be, be sure to weigh her by what she is, and by the pilgrimage she has made, for that is what God sees.

And now, my son, I take my leave of you, praying that you may forgive us all. Should you be inclined to be harsh upon me, consider that every crime I committed has been paid for; I lost the title of father, that would have been so dear to me, along with many other precious joys.

Your most loving father (for I may, at last, use this word to you)

Jonathan Dymond

Post Scriptum:

Should this paper reach you on the occasion of my death, there is one last thing; a small matter, but dear to my heart. During my happiest time I owned and worked a marvellous device for pressing apples, but ever since a certain accident I had, the labour brings on shaking fits and I am forced to give it up. The villagers in these parts say I took against my press at last, and burnt it.

The device is not burnt. It was an invention of my adopted father, the child of his fruitful mind. There is no other machine like it, and for love of him, as well as the cider-making, I have looked to it and kept it in repair. You have been raised to gentler pursuits and will not wish to press cider. Nevertheless, when my will comes at last to be read, you will find yourself in possession of the thing I have loved best in the world. Should you dispose of the press, pray do not break it up or sell it. Give it freely to a man who will preserve

it and preserve his family by its use, since such was my
father's wish, and for that purpose was it made.

Is this enough? Still I am unsure. I will sleep on it, and perhaps send it tomorrow.

Acknowledgements

Thanks are due to my agent Annette Green for her insightful advice, to the Rabses for their never-failing generosity and to all at Faber, especially Sarah Savitt for her energy and enthusiasm and Michael Downes for his patient attention to detail.